It's obvious this author knows nothing about the south, or about ginetics [sic] or cultural biology[what?]. This book is full of hate for whites and our way of life, and any white girl who thinks like this should maybe keep her mouth shut.

— *D. Lariet, KKK Loyalist (a rant from one of our advance copy readers)*

Allen displays the plotting chops of someone with five thrillers under her belt. A masterly indictment of America's failed racial politics that remembers to entertain.

— *Kirkus Reviews*

Wow, this one was devised to light the fuse, by a twisted young lady. Extraordinary contemporary drama of life in the south with all the trimmings. Racism, hate, hope, humor, love— all the good stuff we need to keep turning pages until the end. And then the gut-wrenching disappointment of knowing there are no more pages left to turn. What a gripping tale by a terrific new talent.

— *Weekly Review*

Magnetic and provocative story, with characters you'll love, and a master villain you'll love to hate. What begins as a murder mystery then shifts gears for a ride through a volatile land where all societal rules come to die.

— *The Novel Reader*

Gripping, imaginative, and frighteningly prophetic.

— *Christine Abbot, Author*

Megan Allen's debut novel is a chilling modern-day tale of racism in the Deep South. Replete with everything unexpected, including its shockingly controversial premise. Bound to be a new favorite for all fiction buffs.

— *Publishers Daily Review*

An honest, unique and fictionally relevant look at racial tension in our modern age—one of the toughest hot button topics of our time. This smartly-written novel will give you pause, make you think and stick with you long after you savor the final words. 5 Stars!

— *Que Sara Sera*

The SLAVE PLAYERS

MEGAN ALLEN

This is a work of fiction. Names, characters, businesses, places, events and incidents are either the products of the author's imagination or used in a fictitious manner. Any resemblance to actual persons, living or dead, or actual events is purely coincidental.

Published in the United States by

1050 Crown Pointe Parkway, Atlanta, Ga. 30338
www.burnhousepublishing.com

Jacket and book design by Chelsea Jewell

Names: Allen, Megan, author.
Title: The Slave Players/ by Megan Allen
Description: First hardcover edition. | Georgia : Burn House Publishing, 2017.
Identifiers: ISBN-13: 978-0-9990548-0-2 | ISBN-10: 0-9990548-0-5 LCCN: 2017945317
Subjects: BISAC: FICTION / Action & Adventure. | FICTION / Thrillers / Political. | FICTION / Historical.

If you'd like to contact the author with comments, or find out about her life or future projects, she'd love to hear from you.
Meganallen012@yahoo.com.

MANUFACTURED IN THE UNITED STATES OF AMERICA

First Edition

Dedicated to my dad, who said, "The odds of you making it as a writer are extremely slim. But baby, you go for it, because your chances of making it at anything else are even more limited."

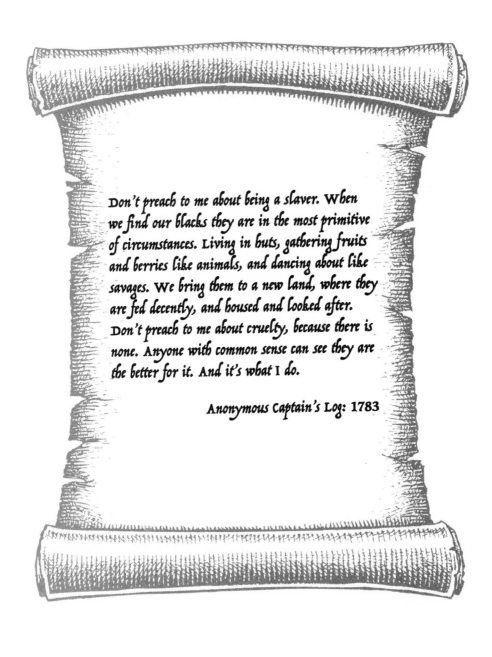

Don't preach to me about being a slaver. When we find our blacks they are in the most primitive of circumstances. Living in huts, gathering fruits and berries like animals, and dancing about like savages. We bring them to a new land, where they are fed decently, and housed and looked after. Don't preach to me about cruelty, because there is none. Anyone with common sense can see they are the better for it. And it's what I do.

Anonymous Captain's Log: 1783

PART ONE

Chapter One

THE INCIDENT

The yellow bus wound its way for an hour or so along the Chattahoochee River, on the Georgia side of the Georgia-Alabama border. The writing on the side of the bus proclaimed in bold, black script, *Freedom Church*, and somewhat less boldly, *Blue Ash, Ohio*. It was a hot day, hot like it gets in July in the south, with that clingy, damp heat that really isn't damp at all, but life-sucking and desperate. A young girl seated near the back tried to slide open a window, hoping the rush of air from outside would offer at least some degree of relief from the heat.

"Tiffney." A large woman, with teeth that flashed bright-white against the black of her skin, spoke sharply. "Enough with the windows. It's ten times hotter out there than it is in here. Everyone just sit back and relax." She smiled then, an old, patient smile, and where her cheeks cracked into deep age lines, sweat flowed down her face, with one or two drops managing to make it onto the collar of her blouse. "Just another few hours and we'll be at camp. There's a pool there with water so cold you'll wish you were back on this bus."

"That's right girls." The man who drove the bus turned his shoulders slightly, and allowed his head to swing even further. He was a young man, with soft, kind features. "Miss Marcy speaks the

Lord's truth. I been there before when I was a boy. I seen it. That water pours straight outta the mountain. It's so cold it's gonna hit your skin and you'll be screamin' like babies. You just wait." Aside from the lady and the driver a dozen young girls sat or lay in scattered heaps all around the bus.

"Ezekiel five-twelve," one of the girls hollered out. "The Lord brought the cooling rains and Satan brought the fire. Choose one but not both to provide for your soul. And choose the one that most pleaseth the Lord." Several of the girls scrambled for their bibles.

"Ezekiel what-what?" they cried out. "That's not Ezekiel. That's not anything. You just totally made that up."

"Did not," called out the girl defensively. "Look it up. Just 'cause you don't know about it doesn't mean it isn't there."

One of the other girls thumbed furiously through the pages of her bible. "As usual, you're just nuts. There's nuthin' like that in here." She paused and raised one of her hands. "Or anywhere else, for that matter."

"Oh, sure, like you'd know," the scripture quoter shouted. "Well it's right here in mine. Maybe you just have a dumber version," she laughed. "Or maybe you're just dumb."

"Miss Marcy?" Several voices rang out as the old lady lifted herself and turned to face the girls.

"Enough," she said. "You girls settle down." She stared sternly at one of them. "And you, Elizabeth. You keep making up scripture and the Lord's going to send you a very special message. The Book is the Book. It says all that needs to be said without any help from you."

"Yes, ma'am." The girl called Elizabeth smiled obediently and waited until Miss Marcy had reseated herself and her eyes moved away from the girls. Then she lifted both hands high over her head, her middle fingers extended straight up.

"Miss Marcy!" cried out eleven voices.

An hour or so later the bus swung hard right, and moved out onto a bridge spanning the river. They had now crossed into Alabama. Evening came, and with it twilight, then darkness, and the bus rolled on. There were no lights turned on inside the bus, and so it grew as dark as the night outside. The girls slept. Sometime later, around midnight, the bus slowed.

"I think we're here." The driver spoke as Miss Marcy lifted her head and looked through the blackness.

"What do you mean, *think*, Tommy? We're either here or we're not. And *here* is not subjective. It's an absolute."

"What?" Tommy looked out through the windshield and then through the front side windows. "I dunno. I mean, I haven't been here in twenty years. I just saw a sign that said *Camp*, and I'm pretty sure this is it."

"Then why isn't it lit up? And where is everybody? They're supposed to be waiting for us."

"I dunno. But I'm pretty sure this is it. You want me to turn in?"

Miss Marcy continued to stare off to the right side. The headlights illuminating the highway ahead allowed little residual light to escape to the sides, and all either of them could make out was a patch of dirt roadway leading through an open gate and into the woods. "Well, I guess this could be it. But there's supposed to be lights." She paused. "I suppose everyone could have gotten tired of waiting and gone off to bed. Maybe they think we're coming in the morning."

Tommy clicked on his phone, which flashed *No Signal*, as it had for the past several hours. They were deep in the Alabama countryside. He turned the bus then, without waiting for further instruction or resolution, and they moved away from the main highway into the thickness of a forest. The road was narrow and winding, and seemed to go on and on. Only a moment or two passed before he spoke. "Well this sure as hell isn't it."

"Tommy!"

"Sorry, ma'am. I mean this can't be it. The camp house should be just off the highway. I remember it was right next to the highway."

The bus inched forward as they searched for a place to turn around. Finally a light shined through the blackness and they drove into a sort of yard, a small, open field with a single lamp at one end. The lamp was as confusing as the dark, as it cast its light directly at them and everything beyond was blocked out by the brightness. Tommy eased his foot down on the brake, and with a slight squeal the bus stopped. "Well I sure as heck don't know where this is," he said. A light spray of dust from the braking wheels swirled up around them.

Miss Marcy turned her face away from the glaring light, trying to reason out what sort of place they had encountered. "I think we should just turn around," she said in a whisper. "This place gives me the creeps." Tommy looked over at her.

"I hear that." He revved the engine slightly as he turned to drive. Then he screamed, "Shit!" Miss Marcy's admonishment froze in her throat as her eyes swung toward Tommy, but they never made it past the windshield. Her mouth flapped open and stayed that way. For there in front of the bus, and so close they could almost touch him, stood a man with a rifle. A grinning man. He stepped forward slightly, rapping on the hood with the barrel of his gun. His lips moved as though he spoke, but they could hear no sound. Suddenly the glass on the door just to their right shattered. Tommy screamed again. Another man stood there, and this one they could hear.

"Open the goddam door," he said.

One of the girls stirred awake. "What's going on?" Other girls were also stirring.

"Quiet girls. Not a sound." Miss Marcy turned her attention to the man standing just outside the shattered door. "There's been a mistake," she said, her voice shaking. "We're going to go now."

The man punched hard at the remaining glass. It exploded in a shower of shards. His hand gripped at the frame of the door and yanked on it. It refused to yield. The hand dripped blood but he appeared not to notice. "I said open the goddam door." His other hand came up and pointed a massive pistol at Tommy. "Now, Nigger!"

Tommy's eyes widened. His hand went to a lever at his side. He pulled on it and the remains of the door flapped open. "We don't want no trouble," he stammered. "We was just lookin' for our camp, that's all." The man stepped up the two steps to the platform of the bus. Reaching over he gently plucked a shard of glass from Tommy's hair.

"You gotta be careful," he said, wiping his bloody hand on the front of Tommy's shirt. "That shit will cut the crap outta you." Smiling, he patted Tommy on the head. "You got lights in here? It's darker than hell."

"Yes, sir." Tommy flicked a switch on the dash and lights flooded down the aisle of the bus, showing a dozen very awake and very frightened young girls.

"Toby. Get your ass in here. You gotta see this." The man slowly worked his way between the rows of seats, inspecting each of the girls as he passed. The man called Toby came from his position outside, climbing up to where he could press the barrel of his rifle hard against Tommy's chest.

Miss Marcy cleared her throat to speak. "Listen, we're very sorry if we have inconvenienced you. We'd really just like to be on our way. Please."

"Inconvenienced?" The man inspecting the girls turned and moved back to the front of the bus. He stopped only when his crotch moved right up against Miss Marcy's head. "What kinda shit talk is that? You be one of those trained up intellectualized darkies." He stuck his still bleeding hand in her face, wiping it against her cheek. "You see this? Your bus did this to me." He turned to address the girls. "Let's put it to a vote. How many of you all think I should be paid for my injuries here?" He held up the hand. "You can't just come onto a man's property and bloody him up like this without payin'." He grinned wickedly. "How many think I should be paid?" No one spoke and no one moved. But a dozen pairs of wide eyes were trained on his. The man's grin lessened somewhat. "Well I'll be goddammed."

Tommy spoke. "We'll pay you." Toby lowered the butt of the

rifle and the barrel swung upward slightly until it just nudged into the flesh of Tommy's neck.

"You goddam right you'll pay."

The man with the bloody hand began to move again down the aisle among the girls. Mostly he found them much the same. Dark, plain, and too young to have developed much in the way of womanly features. But one was different. With long legs and long, raven hair. A lighter complexion than the others, and certainly the beginnings of curves in all the right places. "What's your name, darlin'?" he asked her.

The girl looked up at him defiantly. "Elizabeth," she said. "Why don't you just take what you want and go?" The man laughed, deep and guttural.

"That's exactly what I intend to do, baby." He grabbed Elizabeth by the hair suddenly and yanked her upwards, nearly ripping her off her feet. She screamed as he dragged her to the front of the bus. Miss Marcy came up out of her seat and tried to yell something, but the man shook a hand free from the girl and smashed a fist hard against the front of her face. There was an audible crunching sound as the bones in her nose exploded and she was flung back into the space between the front seat and the railing. She lay there moaning for a moment, half on the seat and half on the floor, and then went still. Tommy tried to move, but the rifle barrel pressed deeply into his neck. "You stay here, Toby," said the man, dragging the still screaming girl. "Keep an eye on things till I get back. Me and the missy here got business."

———◆———

A few hours later, just after dawn, a young couple driving down from Montgomery to visit friends in Jacksonville came across the twisted wreck of an old yellow bus. It seemed as though the driver had failed to navigate a turn and the bus had crashed through a

barrier, careening into a couple of black oaks before winding up on its side in a patch of marshy grass just off the roadway. There were a few bodies scattered outside the bus, young girls mostly, with even more inside. By the time authorities arrived spectators were already gathering up and down the road.

Chapter Two

THE RESPONSE

Colby County is about as far down south and east as you can go and still be in Alabama. In fact, it almost wound up as part of Florida when the lines were drawn, but the Colby clan, rich in numbers acquired by a massive breeding program, put up such a squawk that the lines were drawn a bit more to the south. Patriarch Nathan Colby was often heard to say, "There is nuthin' close to Redskin about this family and we ain't gonna be part of any damn Seneca nation." The statement was as close to racism as it got in those early days, and only pertained to Indians. As far as blacks went, you either owned them or you didn't. And Colby owned a few. So the county lines were drawn just south of the main hub at Dolan City, and continued south another thirty miles to the border, with two minor highways running through, one running a trade route into Georgia, and the other slashing downward into Indian Territory.

Onto this southward highway, some two hundred years later, a sheriff's car moved methodically toward a call. The radio inside the car crackled to life. "Sheriff, you coming?"

A uniformed man inside the car responded. "I'm comin', Larry. About ten minutes out. You have the place secured?"

"Yes, sir," came the response. "Folks are out here already,

but I've got 'em pretty well backed off. You're not gonna believe this shit."

"I heard." The sheriff smacked his lips. "It's bad, huh?"

"Bad." Larry's voice was shaking. "Man, I've never seen anything like it. There's gotta be a dozen or more. Laying out all over the place. And everyone's dead. Deader than hell."

John Parrish had been sheriff of Colby County for over twenty-five years. He'd run and won the first time on a platform of firm and fair justice, citing the completely fabricated fact that a distant step-cousin was a man of color who'd married a white woman, which seemed to make him a bit more palatable to half the county's inhabitants about whom he and his cronies would whisper were racially impaired. And he'd stayed in office through four more elections by being a most intimidating man with a cunning ability to discourage possible opponents. Now he lowered his voice. "All darkies, right?"

"Yes, sir," came the quick response. "More than a dozen, I think. And all dead."

When Parrish arrived a few minutes later, the first thing he did was walk along the roadway above the crash site. He bellowed at the onlookers to move along, and out of respect or fear everyone complied. Cars scattered up and down the highway, and as they departed an ambulance and a couple of tow trucks arrived. The ambulance driver looked at him hopefully, but the sheriff shook his head. "Bodies only," he said. "A bunch of them." He pointed at the driver. "You wait here till I call. Gonna be a while." He then moved down a sort of pathway cut into a slope marking where the bus had slid along on its side. He studied the bus first, then motioned to one of the truck drivers. "You guys might as well go back into town. Come back this afternoon and you can haul this baby outta here." The drivers looked like they wanted to stick around, out of morbid curiosity, but a look from the sheriff and they started up their trucks and drove away. A deputy emerged from behind the bus.

"Hey, Chief. Told you it wasn't pretty. I spent the first ten minutes puking my guts out." They walked together over to a body.

A young girl, around fourteen. One arm had a deep gash and her neck was slashed so deeply that her head tilted back, away from her body, like a hand puppet with no hand inside.

"You see anythin' wrong with this, Larry?" The sheriff prodded at the girl with his foot, turning her slightly.

"No. What do you mean? She's dead."

"I mean there's no blood. At least not here there isn't." Looking up, the sheriff paused until his eyes rested upon another body. "Don't you think with a cut like that there oughta be a little blood?"

Larry tipped a visor back on his head and scratched at his ear. "Well, yeah, I guess. But maybe the blood is in the bus."

Sheriff Parrish spoke even as he began to move to the next body. "So she bled to death in the bus and then threw herself out here as an afterthought?"

"What are you saying?"

"Nuthin'," said the sheriff. "Just thinkin'."

They moved to the bus then, and had to crawl up onto one of the wheel wells before climbing down through the shattered door and into the bus's interior. And here they found the blood. Lots of it. Together with lots of torn bodies and caved-in heads, and the driver, whose face was smashed beyond recognition, lay in a near fetal position with one arm still locked around the steering wheel. A slight smile played at the sheriff's lips. "You know, we could have just walked in through the windshield," he said.

Sometime later a coroner's van arrived and the bodies were stuffed into the van and the ambulance. All together there appeared to be one large male, one equally large adult female and eleven young girls. While the bodies were being loaded the tow trucks reappeared. With the two drivers jockeying a hoist and a pair of winches they soon righted the bus. And what at first had seemed a horrific crash brought something of a surprise. The bus had suffered very little. The front windshield and door had been shattered, and some of the side windows had broken out, but there didn't seem to be much major damage. It was as if the bus had merely slid off the incline, impacted a couple of minor trees and tipped. The sheriff mumbled

something to himself and then joined the coroner in a caravan back to town.

The town was Harbor Springs, Alabama, about twenty miles southeast of Dolan City, though strangely there was no harbor and no springs. The town's name might have originated as a sort of joke. No one ever really knew. But it was a tidy place, with clean streets, lazy dogs and a kind of southern charm if one didn't probe too deeply. Shawn Briggs served as coroner here, coroner for the whole county, in fact. He had come down from St. Louis a year earlier with his daughter, Olivia, to start a new life. In St. Louis he had been accused of tampering with evidence in a poisoning case involving one of the richest families in the state. He hadn't tampered, of course. He hadn't done anything but reveal evidence that would have put a very important man into a most unpleasant circumstance. And so he had fallen, from the big city to the most remote of places.

A couple of older black men who were always about town seeking odd jobs had heard about the crash and stopped by as the van and ambulance pulled in. "You need some help, Mister Briggs?" one asked. The back door of the van swung open just then. "Jeezus," gasped both men. "There's a whole bloody pile of 'em. Jeezus." Sheriff Parrish walked over to the van and the coroner signaled him.

"Look, I don't have room for all this. I've got six lockers and some table space. And it's going to be hotter than heck today." Briggs raised his hands helplessly.

The sheriff nodded. "We can take some of them down to the butcher shop. George has a big ice room. That should do it." He smiled sheepishly. "His customers are gonna love the hell outta seein' all these little darkies hangin' up there with the beef. But it's the best we can do." The two black men looked sharply at the sheriff, but then quickly lowered their eyes as he looked back. "You know I don't mean nuthin' by that boys. Hell, it coulda happened to anyone, white or black. And we'd still have to ice them down. That's just the way it is." He clapped one of the men on the back, then turned dismissively back to Briggs. The coroner caught the downcast eyes of the men, and his own eyes dimmed in shame.

"Look, Sheriff. It will take a few days to get the autopsies done. And we'll have to bring the bodies back and forth." He raised his hands. "Is that going to work?"

"Autopsies?" Parrish reached out, placing a firm hand on the coroner's shoulder. "Look, man. This is a bad situation for everyone. We're gonna go to work identifyin' everybody and gettin' the next of kin down here to claim the bodies. From what we found I think they're all down from Ohio. It was an accident, for god's sake. We all saw that. Let's get them the hell outta here and save ourselves a whole kettle full of grief. The last thing we need is a bunch of autopsies slowin' things down."

By the time the sheriff returned to his office in the middle of the township of Harbor Springs, throngs of people were waiting. Most were from the church camp a few miles outside of town. He patiently stood there on the steps with them, listened to them wail and cry and scream out in despair even as he wondered what in the hell he was having for dinner and why in the hell he couldn't have been out fishing when this whole thing occurred. Maybe with a little luck it would all just blow over.

That night, to his own personal consternation, nearly every television station, local or national, led with the story:

Thirteen African Americans Lose Lives in Fiery Bus Crash
Most Are Teenage Girls.

"Fiery, my ass," he thought to himself. "A little wax on, wax off and that bus would look like new."

The next morning crept in with ominous signs. A thunderstorm struck as a deluge of rain pounded down over much of the county. People poured in from all over, soaked from the rains and drained of spirit. There was a meeting hall set up at the Baptist church on the outskirts of town. Families were arriving all the way from Ohio, having driven through a long night of agony. And sometime before noon it was discovered that a girl, on the original roster of bus passengers and presumed present with the others, had

not been found. Sheriff Parrish returned to the crash site with a group of townsmen, but a thorough search of the site turned up nothing of substance. The missing girl was just that. Missing. Her name was Elizabeth Courtier, and the one thing the sheriff noted when comparing her photo to that of the other girls was her beauty. It was remarkable. She would stand out in any crowd.

"Strange," he said to his deputy. "She's gorgeous."

"Yeah, she is. But what's strange about it?"

"I don't know." He pursed his lips together, making a smacking sound. "But if someone was to pop in and pluck one of these girls away, she'd be the one."

The phone rang then. It was the coroner, and he needed to see Parrish right away. When the sheriff arrived at the mortuary, Shawn Briggs met him even before he could exit his car.

"I have something to show you," he said. He led the way into a small alcove, and then down a flight of steps beneath the mortuary wherein the coroner had his office and laboratory. "I've been working all night on the bodies." He turned and looked directly into the sheriff's eyes. "This was no accident." He pointed to one of the tables. A large black man lay there, cut deeply open in a variety of places.

"What the hell." The sheriff spoke sharply. "I told you no autopsies. Just let this thing go so we can get these people outta here. We're gonna have a goddam circus on our hands."

"I didn't cut the man. I just laid him out there." Briggs spoke softly, but a firmness gripped his voice. "I didn't like it yesterday and I like it even less today. You know as well as I do that crash couldn't have done all this damage. These people were cut to bits, and not by a damn bus tipping over on its side."

The sheriff's face reddened. He stepped towards the coroner. "Listen to me, you dumb sunovabitch. This was an accident. Just an accident. Do you know what could happen if folks, especially black folks, got wind that this was anythin' else? We'll have a goddam riot down here. A goddam riot. Is that what you want? No matter how it happened, it was a goddam accident. You come down here

from St. Lou thinkin' you're all kinds of big shit. I've seen the report on you. You were a dumb sunovabitch up there and you're a dumb sunovabitch down here." He moved even closer to Briggs, until they almost touched. Turning his head the sheriff looked around the room. Several battered bodies lay about on the tables in varying degrees of undress and mutilation. "Now what's to say you didn't do all this crap yourself? You're a cutter, right?" He moved away to one of the tables, allowing a very intimidated Briggs to draw a breath. Reaching onto a tray he picked up a long, narrow scalpel. Bits of cloth and tissue still stuck to the blade. "So we say you did this. During your autopsy. Hell, man..." Parrish brought his hand down hard, implanting the blade deeply into the belly of a young girl. Briggs gasped, mouth open wide, as the sheriff continued. "Anybody asks and we just say you're a lousy cutter. Or that you're overly enthusiastic. And we say nuthin' else."

The coroner gathered himself and slipped a hand into the pocket of his waistcoat. "And what about this?" he said. He opened his hand, palm upward to display a small, shiny chunk of metal. Stepping over to the table where the body of Tommy, the driver, lay, Briggs slipped a hand gently under the man's head, tilting it to one side. And there, just above an ear, matted with a mass of dried blood and hair, was a hole. A small, precise, penetrating hole. Sheriff Parrish stared hard at the hole for a long time, speechless. Finally, he reached out a hand in a silent request for the lump of metal. "A rifle, I think," said the coroner softly. "Fired at very close range." He pointed across the room to where Miss Marcy lay, her face badly bludgeoned and her body rife with bruises. "She has one, too. In her back."

Chapter Three

THE COVERUP

The sheriff looked deeply into the eyes of Shawn Briggs, probing at the depths of this man. There were several ways he could handle the coroner, and his mind raced through a variety of scenarios trying to figure out which one suited him best. That the man feared him he had little doubt. He had seen the fear cloud Briggs' face during their confrontation. But fear as a binding tool is usually only temporary, and with time and circumstance can be overcome. In his mind the sheriff sought out a more permanent solution. Finally he spoke. "Listen, we need to be very careful about this." His face softened. "I've seen what can happen when folks get the wrong idea about somethin'. When they see hate instead of tragedy. If we lead people to believe this was anythin' more than an accident all hell is gonna break loose. And if you haven't seen hell in the south, then you don't know hell. I've lived it. Seen it. Down here everythin' boils down to race. It's a sad fact but it's a fact." The sheriff held out his hand, exposing the torn bullet between his fingers. "And it doesn't matter who the hell did this. If it's blacks that are killed it's gonna be blamed on whites. It's always been that way. Hell, for all we know it was their own kind done this, but that's not the way it's gonna come out if we're not smart. I remember way

back to the eighties, when I was a boy. Every black man down here was screamin' about his new-found rights. Seems every other day my daddy would come home and tell us about some darkie who'd been strung up or beaten and there would always be this rush to judgement. Hell, feds would pour down from the north, pointin' fingers and blamin' all the whites. You'd be hard-pressed to find a case of a nigger killin' another nigger, even if the nigger done it." The sheriff reached out —not aggressively, but purposefully— and tapped at the coroner's chest with the bullet. "We gotta be careful, is all."

Shawn Briggs tried to meet the sheriff's eyes, but the eyes held too much strength and he was forced to look away. He stood there, about as frail as a man could stand, still shaking slightly as his glasses slipped down his nose, stopping abruptly at its very tip. He tried to refocus on the sheriff without being too obvious about it. Sheriff Parish was undeniably a big man. A big man with a strong face and a strong jaw that appeared unbreakable. Adding to this look of invincibility, a long, jagged scar slashed downward from beneath one ear, running its way down the neck until it disappeared into the collar of the man's shirt. Briggs considered for a moment whether it might be the one who handed out the scar who was the invincible, but quickly realized it didn't matter. The sheriff was there, standing over him, and the scar-giver was not. So he continued to tremble, his eyes finally moving away to focus on one of the bodies lying nearby. He lifted a weak hand and pointed. "What are you saying? These folks are dead. And it wasn't the bus that killed them. What are we supposed to do about that?"

The sheriff's voice lowered and became friendlier, and pointedly conspiratorial. "Look, all I'm sayin' is we don't wanna start somethin' that'll be bad for everybody." His mouth twitched as an idea came to him. "I saw your daughter the other day. Down to the market. Sweet young thing. Her momma musta been somethin'. This is a good place you've brought her to. A fine place to raise a youngster. But we've gotta be smart and keep it that way. And this ain't St. Lou. Things are different here. Folks down here don't reason as much as

they do up north. Everybody's a goddam reactionary. They're not like you and me. You know, sensible. And sometimes the best of us or the ones we love wind up hurt for no other reason than we weren't smart enough to keep our mouths shut and do what's best."

The coroner looked up, trying to read the meaning in the sheriff's words. "Are you telling me not to report this? To just let it go?"

Parrish nodded, smiling warmly. "Hell, boy. I'm just sayin' let's wait a bit, that's all. I've got somethin' to do this afternoon that can't wait. But later on I'll be back and we can work it out. We can work out what's best for all of us." The sheriff extended his hand as a bond, and waited a long moment before Briggs reached out to take it.

The sheriff had a problem. A big one. The bullet that now resided in his pocket was familiar to him. The lower most portion of the metal, the part last to enter a body and the least likely to be damaged, had a system of rings molded into its sides. Three of them. They were unusual and easily recognizable to even a casual eye. In addition, the caliber was also familiar, and quite rare. A Thirty-Forty Krag. First cast for the early army Springfields, the round had not been particularly popular and over the succeeding hundred or so years had just about died out. Few people owned a Krag, and fewer still used one in any regular fashion. But the most amazing thing about this particular bullet was its composition. It shined more than a normal casting would, and upon impact had cracked apart a bit instead of just mushrooming out in the way one would expect of lead. This bullet was made from pewter, a sort of lead-base with a portion of tin melded in. He recognized it immediately for a very special reason. He had cast it. Together with his son Toby, to whom he had presented an old vintage Krag, they had broken down and

melted an old mining stanchion, feeling the pride of a pioneer using the resources at hand. It had been a bonding moment for both of them, as Parrish knew the road he had presented to his son had not always been a pleasant one. There had been years of firm discipline and punishment and beatings, not cruelly undertaken, but in the same way his father had raised him. Still the boy seemed to persevere, and even prosper. So when his son finally arrived at manhood, a great change came over their relationship. Parish had begun to treat the boy as an equal, for they had both survived a trial by fire, and from this pride emerged the exchange of the rifle as a sort of rite of passage, with a touch of penance.

The sheriff drove now, east on the highway to Georgia. He passed by the church, and rolled on into the countryside. Soon he passed the sign for the Freedom Camp, and a few miles further along came to the crash site. He slowed to survey the trees and the meadow, and then drove even slower for a few hundred yards as his eyes probed the roadside and every clump of brush that might have helped camouflage the body of a girl. He suspected there would be nothing to see and he was right. Finally, after a time, he came upon a narrow drive, cutting off to his left. A broken sign near an open gate read, *Camp*, and propped up against a post on the ground nearby was another portion of the sign, mostly covered by weeds, which read simply, *Dixie*. Turning left he drove down a winding country road. It was not well tended, and clumps of swamp sage growing from its center where tires were seldom felt brushed roughly against the bottom of the car. Finally he emerged into an open field. Off to one side, and mixed into the brush, were several old cars, and parts of cars. On the opposite side were a series of pens built up close to the trees. In better days they might have held goats or sheep or hogs, but not anymore. Torn boards and busted wire would have had a hard time holding back anything that wanted to escape. Straight ahead, and tucked back in a cluster of oaks, stood a house, or shack, dismal and worn from many years of harsh southern weather. He drove further across the field, pulling up close to the shack. A man moved out from the trees and approached as the sheriff stepped from the vehicle.

"Hey, John," said the man. He was tall and rangy, with unkempt clothes and a hand bandaged by a bit of white cloth.

"Vern." Parrish moved to one side, ignoring the man, while his eyes inspected the house. "I guess you heard about the crash."

"Yeah. Heard about it this mornin'. From the trash boys. Terrible thing." The sheriff turned to face the man, who began to fidget uncomfortably. "All darkies though, right?"

The sheriff nodded. "What did you do to your hand?"

Vern looked down at the bandage. "Ah, shit. You know me. Bustin' up some wood for a fire. Hit the shit out of it."

The sheriff smiled. "A fire? In July? What the hell you got goin' on, Vern? A still?"

Vern laughed, but nervously. "Hell no. You know me better than that, John. I'm long done with that shit. Hell, last time you put me away for six months."

Parrish began to move around to one side of the house. "My son around?" he asked.

"He's out back, I think. I'll get him for you."

"I can do it." The sheriff continued alongside the house until he came to the backyard. An attempt at growing a lawn had taken place there, a long time ago, and a few yards further back was a pen and an old shed. Suddenly Vern hollered out loudly from behind.

"Toby. Your dad's here. Toby!" John Parrish turned his head and stared hard.

"Some reason you're announcin' my presence, Vern?"

"No, sir." Vern looked down. "Just wantin' to let him know you're here."

As the sheriff turned back, his son Toby climbed out and over a wide board bracing the bottom of the shed. "Hey, Dad. What's up?" The boy walked quickly away from the shed, distancing himself, and approached his father. At the same time, Vern turned and retreated just as quickly back around to the front of the house and disappeared from sight.

The sheriff's eyes seemed to lose some of their brightness as he looked at his son. His voice was almost sad. "You still got the Krag?"

Toby looked at his father curiously. "Yeah, I think so. Up to the house. Why?"

"Use it lately?"

"Nope." The boy paused, scratching his head. "I mean, I shot a pig a while back." He tried to smile. "Big sunovabitch. He about took my foot off. Had to stick the barrel in his ear to get him off me." The sheriff pawed at the ground with the toe of his boot. His eyes now bore deeply into the eyes of his son.

"I'm lookin' for a girl. I'm thinkin' she's there in the shed." He continued to stare at his son. "What do you think?"

Toby began to visibly shake. His hands grabbed at his pockets and the color flushed from his face. "I don't know, Dad," he stammered. "I don't know."

"You don't know what?" Anger began to rise in the sheriff's voice. It danced there like a living thing. "You don't know if there's a girl in the shed? Or you don't know about a girl?" He moved menacingly toward his son. Reaching out a hand he grabbed a fistful of hair, twisting it as he forced Toby to his knees. The boy cried out.

"We found her, Dad. I swear we found her. We didn't do nuthin'." A foot swung up and crashed into the boy's stomach. He retched and rolled onto the ground as his father released his grip. For a long moment Parrish stood there, looking down.

"You damn, miserable fool," he said. Then he turned and walked to the shed.

The door to the shed swung inward, which was not usual, as it was more likely to allow wind and weather access that way. But it had been broken and mended and broken again until the door just didn't care anymore which way it swung. As the sheriff's eyes grew accustomed to the dim light filtering in, he noticed an old, worn mattress lay off to one side. Just beyond the mattress, where the light was even dimmer, sat the huddled mass of a young girl. She sat in a corner with her head bowed, pressed right up against a wall, with a length of burlap pulled up loosely around her. Her face came up as the sheriff spoke. "It's alright darlin'. Everythin's gonna be alright."

For a moment her eyes nearly closed as they struggled with the light to make sense of his shape. Then she saw the uniform and the badge, and the broad, smiling face, and she rose swiftly and ran to him. "There, there, little one," cooed the sheriff. "It's over now. It's all over." The girl sobbed openly and uncontrollably as she clasped her arms tightly around his waist, with great tremors of anguish racking her body. He bent down, stroking her hair gently with both hands. "I know," he whispered softly. "I know." His hands moved down from her hair, stroking her face, then moved even further down until they found her neck. They stroked there gently for a moment, and then her eyes told the story. They went efficiently through phases of relief, then confusion, then terror as his fingers began to squeeze away at her throat. She clawed at him then, but not much. Mostly, she just yielded herself up to him. As if even she knew this was the best possible conclusion.

When Parrish came from the shed a bit later he looked blankly at his son, still lying there in the grass. "You clean this shit up," is all he said. Then he walked back alongside the house to his car, and drove back to town.

Chapter Four

THE COVERUP: PART TWO

On the morning of the second day following the crash Shawn Briggs was returning in the county van back to the mortuary. He had just delivered the last of the young girls to the church, where they would be prayed over before their next of kin journeyed with them back to the north. He tried to reason with his guilt. The fact that they were dead was undeniable. And regardless of circumstances, dead they would stay. He placated himself somewhat with the thought that the accident provided a much easier venue for the families to deal with, and knowing their loved ones had in fact been brutally murdered would only intensify their agony. Therefore, it could be argued that his actions were more of a charitable nature, and not deceitful. He smiled briefly at this line of reasoning, but the smile did not last long. The mortuary, as he arrived, stretched a fair distance along a short block. Built mostly of concrete and stone, it held a large parlor in the front, facing the street, and had a simple two-bedroom living quarters attached at its rear. Underneath, and built right into the side of a large mound, were a series of long, segmented chambers, the ones closest the front having been converted many years ago from ice storage into a fairly modern laboratory with extra rooms for refrigeration and examination.

The upper portions —the mortuary and the home, and a small crematorium out back— were leased out to him privately, while the lower, coroner level was paid for by the county. He parked on the upper level, grabbed a pair of body covers from the back of the van, and made his way down an outside stairway and into the lab. His daughter Olivia waited there, just inside the door.

"Dang it, Ollie," he said. "You know I don't like you coming down here."

Olivia sat on a stool, munching away on a sandwich, her face innocent and sweet, and covered by a constellation of freckles, the color of which perfectly matched the loose tangles of hair curling across her forehead. An open jar of peanut butter with a scalpel sticking out of it was on the counter close by. "Nice to see you too, Dad," she said with a laugh. She waved the sandwich in front of her face. "I just wanted to see if they were all gone yet."

"Yes, they're gone." He reached over to extract the blade from the jar. "Did you at least make sure this was sanitized?"

She laughed again. "No, Daddy. First I went all around the room to find out what sort of yummy contagions I could wipe it on."

Briggs had raised his daughter alone since her mom died a little over three years before. And she had been all the daughter he could handle. Many times he had caught her roaming about his lab, or inserting herself in some way into his work. In fact, one time well before her seventh birthday, and when her mother was still alive, they had discovered her sitting up in the middle of a dissection table with broken Barbie bits scattered all around. "Bad accident," she had said. "I think we're going to need some backup." Her mom had smiled and speculated that she would probably grow up to be a great forensic scientist, while Briggs, sweeping up a panful of tiny plastic limbs, speculated silently on the closest related occupation, *serial killer*. Now, she was just about to turn sixteen. Even worse, she owned him, and she knew it.

"Well I need you to go. Now," he said without much conviction.

She sat there, swinging her legs while her tongue stuck out in mock defiance. "I've been reading your notes."

"You should mind your own business."

"What's this?" She held out her open palm. In it was the second bullet he'd discovered. The one dug from Miss Marcy's back. His chin rose abruptly and his eyes widened. His voice though, was surprisingly nonchalant.

"Nothing. Just a hunk of metal from the crash." He took it from her hand. "You shouldn't be playing with my stuff." Olivia stared at her father. "What? I told you, it's from the crash. Probably a piece of a nut or bolt from the engine or something, and it got torn off. As you can see, it's beat to heck."

"And it came from someone's body?"

"I guess," he replied, growing irritated. "Look, when you have a crash like this all kinds of things are flying around. Why don't you go find yourself a frog to dissect?"

Olivia reached out and took her father's hand. She swung it playfully as they looked at each other. "It's a bullet."

Briggs felt a sudden anger building up inside. Pulling his hand away, he turned his head to one side, trying to find something else to focus on. But in a quick moment he turned again to find his daughter's searching eyes. She was smiling, and in an instant, he was broken. "Yes, it is," he said simply.

She reached again for his hand. "What are you going to do about it?"

Briggs sighed deeply. "Look, baby. Sometimes things are not the way we wish them to be. There are a whole lot of people involved here. People who could be really hurt. And sometimes the truth can be the very thing that hurts them. There's lots of times when the kinder thing is to just let something go." He released her hand and pulled up a stool, swinging himself down on it so they were eye to eye. "Remember when I taught you that a lie doesn't always have to be a bad thing? If it comes with good intentions?"

Olivia leaned back on her stool, distancing herself from her father. "Are you talking about white lies? And you're comparing this

to that? We're not talking about telling someone their dress is pretty when we know it looks like hell." She moved her face back in close, until they almost touched. "Someone got shot here. Murdered. Am I right? And that means someone out there did this. And no one cares. That's what you think you taught me? And it's okay with you?" Kicking her feet against the floor she pushed her stool away. Rising, she placed a gentle hand on her father's arm. "I never thought I'd be sorry for you," she said.

That's all it took. Six hours later the coroner's van rolled into the *Staff Only* parking area of the governor's mansion in Montgomery. Shawn Briggs and his daughter stepped out and asked to speak with the governor.

"Sir, I don't wish to be rude." The aide who spoke was a tiny, bespectacled man, whose tone indicated he didn't mind his rudeness in the least. "You don't just waltz in to see the governor. It's simply not done." He looked at Olivia and smiled. "It's not like having a tea party, you know?"

"We're aware." The young girl stepped up close to the man, already hating him. "And we're not here for tea. My dad's the coroner for Colby County and he has discovered something the governor needs to know about. It's extremely important."

"Indeed. A coroner. And this couldn't have been relayed by phone because?"

Briggs spoke. "I've been calling for the past six hours. All the way here. And you know as well as I that all the recorded mumbo-jumbo you guys throw at us doesn't get you anywhere." He paused, glancing at his daughter, then back at the man. "We know we're not getting in to see the governor himself. We'd just like to get as far up the food chain as we can, and go from there. Okay?"

Olivia smiled sweetly, adding, "And it's obvious we haven't started in the direction *up* yet."

The aide scowled as Briggs continued. "Look, some information has come to me in my capacity as coroner that is vital to the state's interest. It's about the bus crash that killed all those little girls down

in my county. I have no doubt the governor is going to want to hear about it."

"Indeed," said the man again, showing genuine interest for the first time. The crash had been major news just a few days prior, splashing its way all across the nation. The governor, as well as the president, had both offered public prayer and eulogy upon hearing of the tragedy. So this news brought in by the actual coroner in the case had potential. He ushered them into a hallway which could in no way have been contrived as a waiting area and asked them to wait. Portraits lined the hall, one much larger than the rest.

"Governor Perry," observed Olivia, pointing. "Larger than life."

Governor Bruce Perry was a politician's politician. As had been his father before him and his grandfather as well. And his great-grandfather had grown up on and inherited one of the largest plantations in all of Alabama. Until the Great War and the repatriations which accompanied it had torn the family and its land apart. The governor still owned a sizeable chunk of property not far from the capitol, and had considerable wealth, but it was a far cry from what he often lamented was his true birthright. It's strange to think that bitterness and contempt can reign in the heart of a family through multiple generations, especially a family that has never known a day of hunger or want, but reign here it did, and he longed for a return to the glory which was the south, even though he himself had never actually lived it.

After a long wait, the aide returned. Some of the haughtiness had left him. "You're very fortunate," he said. "The governor is holding public hour and would like to see you personally. To thank you for your service." He waved a hand impatiently. "It will only be for a moment though. He is a very busy man."

The one word that most adequately described the appearance of the governor was rotund. He rose from behind a great desk of polished wood, moving toward them more like a living mass than a man. Olivia had an instant vision of him eating a pig, a whole pig, and she quickly decided to hate him also. He reached out both hands in a grasp and shake suggestive of a person seeking attention,

clasping first her father's hand, and then more delicately taking both of hers in his. "Charming," he said. "Simply charming." He pointed to a couple of plush chairs set up to address the desk. "Please, have a seat, have a seat." The governor wasted no time. Even before he had returned to his own chair he spoke, "So, I hear you have brought me news of the tragedy." He plopped down heavily. "Terrible, simply terrible to think of all those sweet young ladies. All twisted up. It must have been a horrible thing to see." He then clenched his hands together, laying them out solidly on the desk before him. "Now," he said abruptly. "Why are you here?"

Briggs cleared his throat. "I have some news. News about the crash. It's not very pleasant." He looked at the governor as calmly as he could. "It appears there's a lot more to it than just an accident. In fact, it might not have been an accident at all."

"Indeed." The governor mimicked the aide's favorite response. "Indeed."

Olivia looked at her father. "Might not?" she asked sternly.

Governor Perry looked at Olivia. "Should she be here for this?"

Briggs glanced at his daughter and noticed she was staring back at him. "Well, yes, she's sort of my assistant."

The governor raised his hands from the desk to his chin, but still maintained his elbows on the desk. He tapped at his chin with both hands still clasped. "Then go on. What exactly are you trying to say? The bus crashed. The girls died. You're telling me there's more?"

"Yes, sir. There's a lot more. During my autopsies I noticed lots of bruising, abrasions and lacerations that were not necessarily compatible with the amount of damage suffered by the bus itself."

"Is that it?" The governor smiled condescendingly. "You think they were beat up too much? Is that what you're saying?" He separated his hands and brought them both down on the desk, making a solid thump. "Exactly how many bus crashes have you investigated in your tenure as a coroner?"

Briggs squirmed uncomfortably. "Well, I've never had anything like this actually occur on my watch before, but I am trained forensically in accident evaluation. And the damage done to those

passengers goes way beyond anything the bus could have done to them."

"Dad." Olivia poked at her father. "For god's sake." She shoved her hand into his breast pocket, extracting the bullet which she plopped down hard on the desk. "They were murdered, okay. Shot like dogs. Or at least one was." The governor's eyes widened.

"Actually, two," added Briggs. "There was another one." Olivia sent a puzzled glance at her father, who shrugged back at her. "I dug bullets from two of the bodies. Both of the adults. One of the wounds, the one to the driver, was immediately fatal, and the second, to a lady who was acting as chaperone I think, appears to have been less than fatal, but certainly debilitating."

There was an extraordinarily long silence. Finally the governor reached over, picked up the bullet and fingered it thoughtfully. "Who knows about this? You know, aside from the two of you?"

"The sheriff. John Parrish. I told him about it. Discussed it with him, in fact."

"When?"

"Yesterday. As soon as I found out."

"And what did he say? What was his response?"

Briggs hesitated. He did not wish to anger the sheriff further by betrayal. But when he answered it was honest. "He said we should keep quiet about it. That this was a powder keg, and if we went public it could become a major incident, possibly with racial implications."

Just then the door opened and a different aide stuck in his head. "Sir, we're backing up out here. Your four o'clock, four-o-eight and four-sixteen are all waiting. And then there's the commerce meeting at four-thirty." The governor raised a hand.

"Put them off. The appointments, I mean. Reschedule. And tell commerce to hold onto their pants. I'll get there when I get there."

"But, sir…" The governor scowled, pointing his finger in pistol fashion at the aide, who said simply, "Yes, sir," and was gone.

"Now," said the governor. "So the sheriff advises you to keep quiet and yet you decide instead to bring it here to me. Commendable.

Really quite commendable." He nodded pleasantly at the coroner. "We need more men like you, stand up men. Men who know right from wrong." He turned his attention upon Olivia. "And you, my pretty lady. I have no doubt you're one of the reasons your father is here today. Do the right thing and teach the right thing. That's a grand way of doing business. A very civilized way. That's how a country gets to where it needs to go. And you should be very proud of your dad, and even more proud of yourself." He turned his attention back to Briggs. "I wonder if I might speak with you privately. You know, man to man. There are things, government things that are probably best kept between the two of us."

Olivia, seeing that she was about to be dismissed, said, "I have to pee." The governor smiled, pointing to a chamber off to one side.

"We'll just be a moment, my dear," said the governor. He paused while the girl left the room, waiting patiently until the door to the chamber clicked shut, then he turned to squarely face the coroner. "So, let's sum this up, shall we? You have a number of dead bodies, at least two of which appear to have been shot. Right?" Briggs nodded. "And a horrific crash which seems to have caused a lot of the other deaths, yes?"

"I wouldn't say the crash was all that horrific. That's what I've been trying to say."

"But it was a crash. And people inside and around the bus are dead. Am I right?" The governor stood then, still speaking as he rounded the desk. "Doesn't it make more sense that the crash actually did cause the deaths, and anything else may just be incidental?"

"Incidental?" For the first time the sense of nervousness flowed away from Shawn Briggs and a rising irritation replaced it. "Incidental? I'm digging bullets out of these folks, and the bus, by the way, was barely damaged. I don't think any reasonable forensic would conclude that even one of those people died from a crash."

"I'm not suggesting they did." The governor sat heavily in the chair abandoned by Olivia. "What I'm suggesting is we continue to say they did, because it's the better way to handle this. Hell man,

think of all those families. Think of their anguish. Let's make it as easy as possible on them. On all of us. Your sheriff is right, you know. Things like this have a way of turning nasty. And to be honest, it appears we have already reached a point of resolution."

Briggs looked at the governor somewhat incredulously. His last job had ended because of a refusal to record facts not indicative with his findings. And here he was being asked to do the same thing. "I'm not sure I can do that," he said.

The governor scowled for a moment, but then his face brightened. "Look, I have an idea. Let's just not be hasty about this. If questions need to be answered, then of course we should answer them. But let's do so carefully. How about if you go back down to Harbor Springs, get back to doing the great job I know you're doing, and I'll have some of my people look into this. You know, sort of investigate quietly. Let's get to the bottom of it, find out what really happened, but do so in such a way as to put no more pain on the table. Hell, man, those families have been through enough. What they need now, what we all need, is a conclusion that serves everyone's interest."

Briggs wriggled uncomfortably in his chair. He looked at Governor Perry, whose face glowed back at him expectantly. "I don't know, sir. And I don't mean to be disrespectful, but we've got these facts that have maybe moved beyond a quiet investigation. I mean, we're talking bullet wounds on the bodies of people who reportedly died in a crash. It's beyond the realm of believability to suppose there is another reasonable explanation that comes without violence. It's incredibly obvious what happened. How much more do we need?"

The governor chewed on his lower lip for a moment. He nodded agreeably, but as he did so his face reddened. "I see," he said, "I see." Then, without warning he reached out, grabbed ahold of Briggs' arm and twisted it away from the chair. "Now listen here, you goddam fool. You have no idea what you're talking about. You don't just rush into shit like this. We have a system, a way of doing things. I'm not going to let some little shit like you come along and mess things up." The governor had a thought. "And what proof do

you have? Do you still have the other bullet?" The coroner quickly lost his feeling of irritation. The hand clamping down on him felt like a vise and his mind moved immediately into a state of fear.

"No," he stammered without thinking. "The sheriff has it."

"Does he now? So the sheriff has one and I have the other. That doesn't leave you with much, does it? Just a couple of wounds that may have been caused by anything. Possibly even by an incompetent coroner poking holes where they don't belong." The governor smiled amusedly at that last thought, and his hand tightened its grip. He rose from the chair, pulling Briggs with him. "You get the hell out of my face and get your ass back down to Colby where you belong, or there will be severe consequences. I said I will look into this and I will. In the meantime, if I hear even a breath of your crap theory you will regret the day you ever stepped foot in the great state of Alabama." He released his grip, moving his hands up to brush and adjust Briggs' shirt. "I will ruin you, man." The side door clicked open and Olivia stood there.

"Hello, my dear." The governor smiled warmly. "Your daddy and I were just finishing up." As he opened the corridor door a moment later to let them out, he whispered to Briggs, "There's a good fellow."

Chapter Five

Somewhere in the woods, east of Harbor Springs and north of the highway, and at a place where solid ground gave way to sponge grass, bog and swamp, Toby Parrish dragged a game bag filled with the remains of Elizabeth Courtier, the missing girl. He'd driven his four-wheeler as far into the wild as he could, until the wheels began to sink, the tires spitting up great gushers of mud and grass. Then he had hoisted the bag over his shoulder and stumbled his way along through the muck, until finally, after only a hundred paces or so he reached the point of exhaustion. He let the bag slip down into the bog, and because there was no solid resting place nearby, he sat down heavily on the remains. At first the topmost portion of the bag stayed dry and he sat there in relative comfort, but after a time his weight and the soft, muddy bottom began to suck away at the bag, until it submerged and he found himself sitting there, chest deep in slime. A burning hate began to tear at his insides. Not, as one might suppose, at his father or the circumstances of his life, but a hatred of the girl who lay beneath him. She had caused him humiliation and the contempt of his father. He doubted things would ever be the same between them again. Rising to his feet, he

stomped on the bag, driving it even deeper into the mud. "Bitch," he said aloud. Then he sloshed his way back to the truck.

The Courtier girl had been missing for four days. State and federal investigators were about to swarm down on Harbor Springs when an interesting thing occurred. Word came from Blue Ash, Ohio, the girl's home town, that it was believed she might not have even been on the bus. No bags or clothing or anything else identified as hers had been found among the wreckage, although it was admitted that bystanders arrived at the crash site well before any officials and might have picked up the girl's belongings. It seemed that other packs and phones from several of the riders were also not recovered, or at least not reported. And then it was discovered that Elizabeth had been a very troubled child. Local police in Blue Ash advised authorities they had received multiple runaway reports on her over the past couple of years, she was usually found hanging with a bad crowd, and it was only recently her parents had signed her up with the church group as a means of offering a healthier environment. Her father did report receiving a phone call from his daughter on the afternoon before the crash, and she claimed to be aboard the bus, but there was no way to authenticate this pending a search of cell tower records, and even then, if it was shown the bus was still in the vicinity of Blue Ash when the call was placed, they probably wouldn't learn much. Almost all of the other girls, as well as the two adults, had also made calls, and not one had mentioned the fact that Elizabeth was on board. In addition, at least a half dozen reports flooded in about Elizabeth sightings up in Ohio soon after her photograph was spread across the local news. So interest in the case waned almost immediately, at least in southern Alabama, and although talk about the crash continued, the Courtier girl was soon a forgotten topic.

Olivia Briggs spent the afternoon of the fourth day after the crash cleaning up for her father in the laboratory. They hadn't spoken much in the last two days, the coroner telling her that some things were beyond their control and it would be best if the crash and the deaths and the mystery surrounding them were forgotten.

"So you're going to do nothing?" she asked him.

"There's nothing we can do," the coroner responded. "We've gone all the way to the governor with this. He said he'll look into it, and I am just a lowly employee. Who am I to question the word of the governor? And we've done the best we can. It's really not up to us anymore."

"But we haven't done enough. Not nearly."

"Look, what else are we supposed to do? I can lose my job. My career. We can lose everything."

"Even your self-respect?" Olivia had a way of barbing him in just the right places. She picked up the folder with photos of the girls paper-clipped to the cover. She glanced down at them before looking up at her father with glistening eyes. "Don't you want to know what happened to them? Don't you want to give them some sort of justice?" She slapped the folder down on a table. "And what about Elizabeth Courtier? Do you really think she's not still part of this? Did you see her photo? Someone took her. I can feel it."

Briggs spoke. "We don't know that, and that's not fair. The point is, nothing I can say is going to make a difference." He paused, weighing his words. "And it could cause us a lot of personal difficulty."

"Then you're scared."

"Maybe. Yes, I suppose, a little. But I'm also old enough and wise enough to know that nothing good is going to come from this, regardless of what we do."

"Well I guess that's that then." She put the folder down and headed for the door. "I've got something to do." Olivia went up the stairs, through the mortuary and into their residence. She sat on her bed for a time, staring at a poster of little ants grappling with a giant pineapple above a caption which read, *Together We Can*. Her father had bought it for her at a trade fair soon after her mother died and it was very special to her. Pouting her lips she kicked at a giant stuffed bear laying at her feet. "Alone I can," she thought to herself. She rose then, packed a bag of essentials, checked to see that her phone was fully charged and walked outside into the street.

Thirty minutes later Briggs went to check on her and found her gone. Also gone were her backpack, her wallet and her phone. He opened the top drawer of her dresser, moving aside a jumbled pile of underwear. The credit card they kept there for emergencies, and a small amount of cash he knew she'd been saving for a new microscope, were also missing.

As Briggs pulled out of the driveway to go and search for his daughter the sheriff's car pulled in, blocking the way. John Parrish swung his large frame out and approached. "Mornin', Briggs," he said cheerfully. As a matter of courtesy, the coroner also stepped from his vehicle.

"Sheriff," he said. "I'm just on my way into town."

"Oh, I only need a minute." Smiling, the sheriff stopped, his hand reaching out to tug on a piece of weather stripping loosened above the rear window of the coroner's van. "You oughta have this looked at. Storm hits and you'll be swimmin' in there."

Briggs sensed that there was more to the man's visit than just weather talk. "What can I do for you? I'm sort of in a hurry."

"I'll only take a minute." The sheriff studied the coroner for a moment. "You're a big load of shit, you know that?" Briggs stiffened, but said nothing. "Got a call from the governor last night. The goddam governor calls me. Think about it. Thanks me for doin' such a wonderful job down here. And I'm feelin' all warm and fuzzy and then he says he got a little visit from you. Seems you don't like the way I handle my office."

The coroner shuffled nervously. "I'm sorry about that. I assure you I said nothing about the quality of your work. I just thought he needed to be told about the incident, that's all."

"Incident? You mean accident, right?" Briggs silently measured the distance between himself and the sheriff. Not liking his calculation he took a half step backward.

"Well, whatever it was, I guess that's open to interpretation. But I didn't say anything bad about you. I just laid out the facts. I felt it was my duty as coroner."

The sheriff nodded. "Well in that case I guess things are just dandy then. As long as you was just doin' your duty."

"I'm sorry if it cast you in a bad light. That was not my intention."

"Of course not. You're a stand up kinda guy, Briggs. I like that. A guy who tells it like it is. Hell, man, the governor invited me over for cognac sometime. Imagine that. Me and the governor sippin' cognac." Parrish extended his hand. "So it looks like you done me a favor. No hard feelin's?"

Briggs looked at the outstretched hand, sensing a trap. But he also knew there was no way he could avoid shaking the sheriff's hand. He reached his own out meekly. "No hard feelings, Sheriff." Two things, or maybe three, then happened simultaneously. The coroner's hand was crushed as he was flung around and slammed hard into the side of the van. His shoulder made impact first, followed quickly by his head. His eyes closed, and before he could open them a force crashed into the side of his face, causing him to lose all sensation for a moment as he slumped to the ground onto one knee. The crushing force released his hand and his eyes slowly regained focus.

The sheriff spoke. "You say another goddam word and you're gonna be doin' an autopsy on yourself, you hear me, boy?"

They say a man's character is often exposed during times of great pain or great stress. Briggs looked up at the sheriff. With considerable effort he pushed himself up until he stood erect on wobbly legs. He then said something so stupid he would remember it as a defining point in his life for many years. "Now just how in the world do you suppose I could be doing an autopsy on myself?" That was the last thing he remembered for a long while. Sometime later he picked himself up again, and staggered into the van.

He found Olivia at the Harbor Springs bus depot, sitting on a bench, her ankles crossed and looking quite forlorn. A bus was just pulling out as he arrived but she made no move to board it. His window down, he reached a hand out and slapped it against the door of the van. "Baby," he called out to her. Olivia looked up, recognizing her father's voice and prepared to do battle. Then she

saw his face. Or at least the mask of caked blood which covered a good portion of it. Jumping up she ran to him.

"Dad, for God's sake. What happened?"

Briggs laughed a little. "Nothing much. Had a little visit from the sheriff, is all. He's a very robust man."

"Shit," said Olivia, feeling it entirely appropriate to swear. "This is because of me." Her face leaned in as she reached to touch his hair, gently combing it into place with her fingers.

Briggs laughed a little more. "Well that's great. I just needed my hair brushed back a little. I'm feeling much better now."

Olivia was crying, a big, sobbing cry, with tears running down the sides of her cheeks. "I'm so sorry, Dad. I didn't think."

Briggs reached out his hand and began brushing back her hair as well. "Sweetie," he said. "This has nothing to do with you. You're the only one in this whole mess who has any sanity about them. And bravery, and honor." Their eyes met. "I'm so proud of you." He pushed playfully at her forehead. "Where the heck were you going anyway? Back to see the governor?"

"No. The president."

"The president!" Briggs grinned widely, then grimaced as his face contorted in pain. "Oh, baby, lord I love you. You can't just hop on a bus and go visit the president."

"I know." She touched his face, then walked around and got in the passenger side of the van. "I just figured if there was one person who could do something about this it would be him. I know it was dumb."

"It's not dumb. In fact you're probably right. But there is no way I know of to get to him." Briggs had an idea. "We can drive back up to Montgomery. Take it to the papers. They could blow the lid right off this thing. But we'd have to pack up all our stuff first. We can't be coming back here. My friend the sheriff will probably take issue with me again."

"I hate him."

"It's a growing club."

"I'm serious. He needs to be locked up. Why did he do it?"

"Got a call from our other friend, the governor. Seems they chatted and both decided I'm unworthy."

Olivia pouted her lips, deep in thought. "What if the newspapers turn out to be friends with the governor too? What if they call him instead of printing our story? I think we need to get away from here."

"We have an even bigger problem."

"What?"

"I had two great pieces of evidence. The bullets I dug out of those people. They're gone, both of them. All I've got now are some photos which basically just show a couple holes and a whole lot of body damage. We won't have a lot of credibility. Especially since the governor of the great state of Alabama is standing squarely in the other corner."

Olivia smiled, her tears now forgotten. "I've got your back, Dad."

"What?"

"I have your back. Did you think I would just run off without any way of proving what we're saying?" She pulled her backpack up from the floor, opening a side pocket.

"Ollie, what the heck are you talking about?"

"My cell," she said, extracting her phone from the pack. Holding it up and pointing it at her father, she clicked a button and the governor's voice resonated throughout the van. *"I'm not going to let some little shit like you come along and mess things up. And what proof do you have? Do you still have the other bullet?"*

"You little freak. God, I love you right now. But how…"

"I didn't really have to pee. And my phone slipped right under the door." She patted his arm. "I thought you were very nice by the way. Letting him shake you like that without retaliating."

"Retaliating? I was peeing my pants." He took the phone from her hand, his voice trembling with excitement. "This is going to do it. And you're a genius."

"I know, right?"

"But why didn't you tell me before? You don't trust me all of a sudden?"

"Don't be a baby. I just wanted to hold onto it for a while. For safekeeping. I knew eventually you'd come to your senses. So I was just waiting until you got your head on right."

"Oh, so all of a sudden I'm not safe?" Briggs scowled. "For sixteen years I've wiped the snot off your nose, my little princess. You've put me through more hell than any father we're likely to run into, and now I'm the one who has to get his head right? Really?"

"Dad," she poked at him. "You lost both pieces of some very critical evidence, by your own admission you peed on the governor, and then let the sheriff use your face as a punching bag. I think we need to reassess exactly who the rock is here."

"Okay," Briggs said meekly. "You can be the rock. But only till my face heals."

Chapter Six

THE WHITE HOUSE

Four men met in the oval office. One, Chester Benton, chief advisor and best friend of the president, sat behind an ornate cherry-wood desk, the president's desk, a Superman action figure prancing on the desktop before him in tune to his dancing fingers. Two others, Daniel Rumstaadt, Chief of Homeland Security, and Thomas Banks, the Secretary of State, sat at opposite ends on a leather couch, while the fourth man, Errol Clarkson, the president, paced the perimeter of the room like a lost soul. The president spoke. "I am not stupid, gentlemen. I am aware the numbers are both mounting and disturbing, but certainly not unprecedented. As far back as I can remember, and that covers a significant amount of time, there have been periods of unrest." He paused, disconnected from his thoughts as he watched his friend swoosh the superman overhead like a jet fighter, before landing him proudly upright in the middle of the desk. "Really, Charlie. That's all you've got?"

Chester Benton, nicknamed Charlie by his friends, lowered his head to the level of the desk, hiding his mouth directly behind the figurine. "Superman has heard all of this before, Mister President. Over and over and over. America is going through another period of unrest. Another black church is bombed, another race related

riot sweeps across a campus. And we're going to do what, exactly?"
He pushed a hand out aggressively, causing the plastic Superman to
crash hard onto its face. "There's nowhere to go with this. There
never is. You can't change the attitude of a people without bribing
them notoriously or beating the hell out of them. There's not much
else folks understand. So unless you've got one helluva lot of cash
stashed away or one helluva big club I say we all just go get drunk."

Tom Banks, the secretary, pushed himself upright on the couch.
"Do you always have to be so damned glib? This is far worse than
we've seen in decades. All hell is about to break loose out there.
We're having a bombing a week. A riot a week. And there's no sign
it's going to let up. And the flag pole incident in Georgia a few days
ago. They knocked a lady off a pole with a fire hose for chrissake. A
goddam fire hose. For dragging down a confederate flag."

Benton grinned defiantly at the secretary. "And as I recall she
didn't actually get the flag, now did she?"

"Hell no she didn't get it. I just told you, they knocked the hell
out of her with a hose."

"That's First Amendment shit." Benton's grin grew wider. "Or
at least water abuse or something. You can't just knock folks around
with one of our precious natural resources. What were they thinking?"

The secretary stood, turning his body to fully face the desk. His
head swung to the side, to face the president. "Are you listening to
this guy? We've been taking his crap for a year now, and he's never
made a bit of sense. I understand friendship and all, but how in the
hell he became your chief advisor is beyond me."

"Charlie," the president nodded at his friend, "I don't want to
listen to the two of you bicker. Do you have anything substantive
to add?"

Chester Benton flicked out a finger, sending the action figure
twirling off the desk and onto the floor. It spun there madly for a
moment as all four men turned their eyes downward to watch it spin.
Benton then also stood, placing both palms firmly on the top of
the desk. "You think I'm glib? You think I sit here and joke because
I can't feel? In case you haven't noticed I'm the black guy in the

room, like the elephant, only smaller and darker. You think I don't
get it? You think I can't feel the goddam hose ripping into that lady?
Can't hear her scream as her fingers are torn loose and she falls?" All
eyes riveted on Benton as he spoke. "I remember my father telling
me about marching on Selma, thinking they stood for something
and could somehow get folks to change their hearts and their minds.
And how, one week later, his best friend was found hanging from a
tree just outside town." Benton moved around the front of the desk
and approached Tom Banks. "My father used to cry when he'd tell
that story. He'd sit on the old rocker in his living room, his head
would sort of fall into his hands and he would cry. And I'd sit there
with him and say, 'It's alright, Papa.' And I'd watch my daddy cry.
Well, Tommy, they're not hanging us much anymore. Now they're
just bombing the shit out of us when we go to church to give thanks
for all the blessings of this wonderful country. The truth is, the real
truth is, a lot of folks would like us to just disappear somehow, like
Rosewood all over again." Stepping up so close to the secretary that
they nearly touched, Chester Benton's face softened. He reached
out to tap the secretary on the shoulder. "So don't you tell me I'm
glib. Enlightened maybe, with a good dose of reality thrown in, but
never glib."

Tom Banks eased back a step and sat back down on the couch.
He looked up at Benton and nodded contritely. Then the president
asked, "What's Rosewald?"

Daniel Rumstaadt, who had not spoken till now, leaned heavily
on the armrest to his right. "Rosewood, Mister President. Back in
the twenties, I think, depression times." He looked up at Chester
Benton who nodded back. "It was a small black town down in
Florida. Mostly sharecroppers and subservient household help for
a nearby white community. There was a married white woman there
who had apparently taken up with a black man. When her husband
found out, he threatened to beat her and she screamed that she'd
been raped and not a willing participant. The whites rose up when
no one bothered to point out that the lady had been visiting the
black man's house for a number of weeks and must have been raped

a lot. At any rate, they hung a bunch of blacks, shot a few more, and burned the town of Rosewood to the ground." Rumstaadt raised an arm, slashing his hand across his throat. "In one night, gone. The whole damn place."

President Clarkson pursed his lips, nodded solemnly and looked at his friend. "Without seeming disrespectful Charlie, I'm not sure I see the relevance of an incident which occurred a hundred years ago. Those were different times, and different circumstances. Hell, *civil rights* weren't even known words at the time. Even with our current situation, things are a lot better now."

"You don't get it, Errol." Benton's eyes swept the room, acknowledging each man before coming to rest on the president. "Rosewood didn't disappear. It just changed places, and bred itself, like a virus into a thousand replicates. There are Rosewoods all over America, and especially in the south. You think all those folks down there who wave that goddam flag around have any respect? For anything? They just want us gone." He grinned again, but this time his face grew cunning, as if it held a secret. "They look at black folks with contempt. Always have and always will. It's so sad it's stupid. You take a bunch of black kids and throw them in with a bunch of white kids with no outside interference and they'd all be friends in about ten minutes. But you let a granddaddy get ahold of a daddy who gets ahold of a kid and fans the flames of a dozen generations of hate, and it never ends. It can't. There's no way to put out the fire."

Tom Banks spoke. "You could cut out the middleman. You know, kill the daddy." Benton looked sharply at the secretary, probing to measure the intent of his comment. Finding nothing offensive there he nodded, and Banks nodded back. Then Benton continued.

"I hear that. What an intriguing way to solve the country's daddy issues. But what I'm trying to say, what America is failing to grasp, and perhaps what we in this room are failing to grasp, is that the fire is burning on both sides. We just haven't seen it yet. Blacks are just now beginning to sharpen up their swords and they're not going to be content with flag pole climbing for long. Or marching

across town or across a campus in a wasted effort to enact change. You can only bomb so many churches before the folks inside stop praying for salvation and start praying for bombs of their own."

"What are you saying exactly?" It was Daniel Rumstaadt, the homeland chief, who spoke. "You talking about an insurrection or something? You think African Americans are going to rise up and start something significant? I can't see that happening. Not in any meaningful way, I can't. First of all they don't have enough of a population base. And all the cases we've seen are isolated. Mostly in the south or inner cities, but always isolated. And they always extinguish themselves in a matter of days." He shook his head almost savagely. "No, never going to happen."

"I don't know." President Clarkson moved around the side of the desk and plopped down in the now vacated chair. "It's not without precedent. I remember many years ago at Quantico we studied tactics in warfare. You've all heard of Spartacus? A warrior slave, a gladiator, beaten down so badly by years of abuse he inspired his fellow slaves to rise up in open revolt. It took just a few thousand of his fellows who decided they would rather face death in battle than a life without freedom to very nearly topple the Roman Empire."

"Yes," said Rumstaadt, "but that was in the days of sticks and stones. That would hardly be possible using the weapons of modern warfare. Any insurrection, no matter how well intentioned, would be easy to decapitate."

"Listen to yourselves," Tom Banks scolded. "Mister President, with all due respect sir, this entire conversation is ludicrous. It's true we have seen more racially sensitive occurrences than usual. As you yourself pointed out, we've always had them, always will. But to think there is the potential for some sort of conflict to erupt of any major significance is simply not feasible. All we can do is continue to educate unilaterally and hope at some point it takes. And if it doesn't, then it simply becomes the status quo, and must be accepted as a social norm, nothing more, nothing less. America is certainly not going to fail because a small minority number of our citizens are color sensitive and fail to get along."

"Color sensitive?" Benton spoke. "Did you really just say that? What the hell is that anyway? Sounds like a commercial for bleach alternative, not a human condition." He reached down and picked up the Superman toy, displaying it in front of his chest with both hands. "And we don't have a superhero who's going to come along and save our world for us. People under duress always reach a boiling point. A point where the mind wills the body into action."

The secretary waved an idle hand. "That's just it. That's what I'm saying. They reach a boiling point, and we all know what happens when water boils. It lets off a little steam. That's all there is to it. Reality check, okay? I know problems exist out there. Hell, I'm the one who got us all in here today because of the potential explosiveness of the situation. But all I'm saying is we need to take precautions. Maybe drop more of this on the individual states where it belongs. So if it does explode, it doesn't do so on us. If trouble is brewing, we need to be the innocents in all this. Put a little distance between us."

"Oh my god." Benton swung around and fired the action figure intentionally over the head of Tom Banks. It very nearly toppled a vase before smacking into a wall. "Do you hear yourself?" He turned impassioned eyes on the president. "For god's sake, I thought at least this once he cared about the people who are out there suffering. I thought that's what this meeting was all about. In reality, he just wants us to make sure we have plenty of shit paper available to be certain we all come out of this with clean assholes." Benton turned again to face the secretary. "You make me sick. We're sitting on a powder keg and all you can suggest is we watch our backs, our political futures and throw the blame on whoever's handy." Spinning around in a circle he glared at those in the room, including his best friend. "I wish to hell I wasn't black right now. So you could both see the idiocy in his way of thinking, and not find my words tainted by my color. They're not, you know. There's simply a right and a wrong way of handling things, and becoming politically evasive when the country needs us to stand up and shout is more than just wrong. It's contemptible. I'm telling all of you that at some point in the

very near future we will face an incident so heinous it will send this country into its darkest hours. Perhaps even anarchy. And we need to be prepared to face whatever the hell comes at us, not crawl under the damn covers and hide."

"Bravo," said the secretary, clapping his hands together, his voice dripping with sarcasm. "That would take a hell of an incident, my friend. If and when it happens I intend to be on mission in China." He looked over at Rumstaadt. "You coming with me, Daniel?"

Chapter Seven

It was late July, two weeks before alligator season was scheduled to open. Two wardens patrolling the swamplands east of Harbor Springs set up a small observation post at the edge of a popular hunting bog. At a place where poachers might be tempted to sneak in ahead of the opening to seek out the giant gators that lurked deep in the swamp. The morning air was still and a thick fog lay there, coating everything with a pleasant, cool dampness that would soon be replaced by intense sunlight and a hot bath of heat and humidity. For now though, the fog prevailed, broken only occasionally by a few flecks of light that managed to twist their way through tiny pockets of thinning air. As the two men hunched there waiting, a flight of geese moved in, brushing its way across the tops of a small grove of cedars which grew right up against one end of the swamp. The sound of wings whistled around them as the birds dipped low, seeking a place to land. The lead goose, an old female, cried out suddenly, sensing movement from the direction of the wardens. She banked hard to the right, and with her flock following, soon disappeared behind the trees. The men looked at each other and smiled. This wasn't work, they thought. This was paradise.

A short time later they heard the distinct sound of a mud truck

approaching from the west, across the dense fields of marsh grass. The engine sounds of the truck grew louder and more labored as the grass gave way to muck, and they could hear the tires spinning as they fought their way closer. One of the wardens shifted position slightly, until he could view the vehicle churning its way to within a few yards of their position.

"Toby Parrish," he said.

"The sheriff's kid?"

"Yeah, and up to no good, I'm bettin'." Both men crouched low, behind a clump of scrub oak, and sat very still. They watched as Toby exited the truck, dragging from its bed a large canvas sack which he slung heavily over his shoulder. The wardens had encountered the Parrish boy before, on several occasions, always in the act of violating one game law or another. They had found him in possession of pig parts, bear parts, and more than once with an untagged gator tucked away under blankets in the bed of this same truck. Each encounter had led to a sort of informal arrest, a trip to the sheriff's office and a courtesy release of the boy into the custody of his father. "He's got a sack of bait." The men crouched there watching, grins spreading across their faces like school boys out on a prank. Oftentimes poachers would spread large amounts of meat or carcass remains near a likely site, returning a day or two later to slaughter any alligators that may have closed in for a feast.

One of the men whispered. "Hell, that looks like a body."

"Boar, probably," said the other. "Which I'm sure he also obtained illegally." The warden shook his head. "The kid's a walkin' violation."

They continued to watch as Toby sloshed his way into the swamp, finally depositing the sack and pushing it deeply into the mud. This puzzled both of them. It would be difficult if not impossible for a gator to smell from a distance a submerged rotting carcass. It made no sense. Ordinarily, a poacher would tie the meat to a tree or at least stake it down on a stump where the winds would carry the scent great distances. But the Parrish boy seemed to take great lengths to see that this particular bait bag lay deep beneath the surface. He even

stomped on it several times, encouraging it to stay down. He then collapsed upon the disposal site, sitting there like a muddy sailor in a foundering boat as he sank lower and lower into the muck. Finally they heard him call out "Bitch," as he rose and sloshed his way back to the truck.

"Should we take him?" one asked.

"No," said the other. "We know where to find him, and his dad's not gonna do anything about it anyway. Let's just sit here a bit and then go check out that sack."

"What?" The first man grimaced. "I'm not diggin' up that shit. Hell, I just got this shirt."

The second warden laughed. "We're both diggin' it up. There's somethin' funny goin' on here. I've never seen anyone bury a bait bag before. Kind of defeats the whole purpose of the hunt, if you ask me. I've got a hunch that ain't a boar, my friend."

The law in Alabama ran itself loosely, using the principles of a *good ole boy* philosophy. In the suburbs, and most certainly in rural areas with limited populations, officers quickly learned which citizens worked within the framework of the legal system, and which did not. Most violators, especially hunters who abused the game laws, became well known and were often arrested time and time again for the same infractions. Toby Parrish was one of these. In fact, the previous warden, a man who had worked in Colby County for more than thirty years, had apprehended the Parrish boy so many times that officials in neighboring jurisdictions began to call the boy the warden's *bitch*, a term that did not sit well with the sheriff. So one day the sheriff invited that particular warden over for a private chat, and when the chat ended the warden spent a week or two recuperating and then it was said he retired to live out the remainder of his days in another state. It was a simple case of the law handling the law,

practically a southern tradition, and it did not take long for Sheriff John Parrish to earn the sort of reputation that made men walk softly in his presence. Jim Smith and Landon Cox were the latest wardens to join the Colby County force, and they had already brought the Parrish boy to his father on a number of occasions, always timidly, and always with a quiet apology attached to their arrival. So they now drove into Harbor Springs with a certain amount of trepidation.

"This isn't good," said Jim Smith to his partner. His face had grown pale. "We need to take her somewhere else. Like up to Dolan City, or somewhere way the hell out of here."

"That's crazy," said Landon Cox. "We're not goin' behind the sheriff's back on this. I'm not messin' with the man. And this is his county. It's what the law says we're supposed to do and it's exactly what we're goin' to do."

"Then how about the state police? Maybe the station over in Madrid. Hell, this isn't even a county issue. This is way too big for us."

"Look. There was a grocer in Harbor Springs a couple of summers back. Just before you came on. Every mornin' he'd block the alley behind his place with a produce truck. Folks was complainin' but he just didn't give a shit. One day the sheriff shows up and tells him to move the truck. The guy says in a while. I'll do it in a while. Sheriff says do it now, and the guy tells him to go screw himself. A week later the guy's truck is hauled out of Cabe's Canal, south of here. Guy's still sittin' in the front seat under about eight feet of water. I heard the look on his face wasn't all that pleasant."

"You're not sayin'..."

"I'm not sayin' anything. I'm just tellin' you what happened. And I'm sayin' we're gonna let the sheriff deal with this. It's his jurisdiction and we're just followin' the law. No one can fault us for that. And right now followin' the law seems to be about the safest thing we can do."

A few minutes later the warden's car pulled up at the sheriff's station. John Parrish stood outside on the top of three steps, talking into his phone. As the two men exited their car and approached, the

sheriff clicked off the caller and waved a hand. "Damn," he said, and then whistled. "You boys look a little ripe." He then held up both hands in a blocking motion. "Don't even think I'm invitin' you in. Hell, you need a bath. Bad."

Landon Cox tried to smile as he spoke. "Been out diggin' in the swamp east of here. We kind of fell in."

"It shows. You all need to go over to shanty town." The sheriff laughed. "Maybe they've got some duds down there you can borrow. Even those folks don't stink this bad."

Cox smiled weakly. "We need to show you somethin'." Both wardens turned a bit to the side, motioning the sheriff toward their car. "In the car."

The sheriff continued to smile. "What you got? A skunk? Sure as hell smell like it." Neither man responded, and their attempts to match the sheriff's smile failed.

An awkward silence followed, and then Cox said, "In the trunk. We've got somethin' in the trunk." He turned fully and headed to the rear of the patrol car, popping the trunk and standing aside for the sheriff.

Stepping up to the car, Parrish bent down to inspect the contents of the trunk. A large, long canvas bag lay there, wedged in and folded around an assortment of tools and emergency gear. The bag was covered in a thick layer of mud, one end tied loosely with a drawstring. "Bait bag," he said. "What the hell you got? A gator?" He glanced at Jim Smith, standing to his right, and noticed the man's face had grown white and cold. "What the hell," he said again. He reached out both hands to loosen the cord, spreading it wide and pulling back on the flap covering that end of the sack. Then he jumped up and back, slamming his head into the lid of the trunk. "Holy shit," he yelled out. "Holy shit."

Landon Cox reached out a hand to steady the sheriff. "We think it's the missin' girl."

"Hell no," answered the sheriff. His face had also grown white and he shook uncontrollably. This puzzled both of the wardens. Parrish must have seen more than his share of carnage during his

years as sheriff, and his reputation as a hard man made his reaction all the more puzzling. "This ain't her. Hell, she's back up in Ohio. She's been seen up there all over the place."

"No, sir," explained Cox. "She's still missin'. There's a fresh bulletin out on her every day. I've seen her picture. She's not so pretty now, but I'm sure this is her. Elizabeth Courtier."

"That's crazy." The sheriff forced himself to lean in for a more thorough examination. He reached in to brush a clump of hair that covered a good portion of the girl's face. "That's crazy," he repeated. "I don't think it's her." He turned to face Cox. "Where did you find her?"

"In the swamp, east of town." Landon Cox drew in a deep breath. "Back of your son's place. About a mile in from the highway."

"What? My son's place. What the hell does that have to do with it?" John Parrish stepped away from the car and turned to fully face Warden Cox. "How the hell did you find her anyway? I mean, what happened? She's just lyin' out in the swamp and you guys come along and find her?"

"No, sir." Cox took a few tentative steps towards his fellow warden, feeling a sudden urge for solidarity. "We were on a stakeout. Gator season opens next week and we were lookin' for early birds." He paused, lowering his eyes and concentrated hard on the body in the trunk. "We saw Toby. He drove up in his truck and carried a bag into the swamp. We just happened to be there." Cox paused, raising his eyes to meet those of the sheriff. His voice, when it came, was trembling. "It was just dumb luck. We just happened on it."

The sheriff raised both hands then, brushing them roughly through his hair. "Dammit," he said, his voice now surprisingly calm. "How do you know this is the bag? How do you know? Did you just see him with a bag, or did you actually watch him dispose of it? And how do you know this is the same bag?" The sheriff's eyes flashed. "Hell, man, these bags are a dime a dozen. I can show you thirty guys who've got one in their truck right now."

"No, sir." Jim Smith spoke for the first time. "We watched him. We watched Toby carry this bag into the swamp. Watched him bury

it in the muck. And as soon as he left we retrieved it. We walked right over to the place he'd been, dug around a bit and this is the bag we came up with. I'm sorry, sir. There's no mistake."

"And that's your report?" The sheriff looked at each man in turn. There was no challenge in his eyes, no anger in his voice. He was a man at the end of a road with nowhere else to go.

"Yes, sir. It has to be."

"Okay." Parrish's tone became firm, and resolute. "Then let me take care of it. Let me bring him in. There has to be more to this than we know. There has be a reason he was out there. A reasonable explanation. There has to be." The sheriff glanced at his watch. "It's a bit after three. I'll have him in here by five, and we'll figure this out."

Landon Cox spoke. "Sheriff, I don't think that's wise. I mean, this is your son. There's a conflict here. I think it's best if we call in the state police. They can pick him up and keep you out of it. We just came in here out of courtesy."

The sheriff's voice rose. "I said I'll do it. And you're damn right he's my son. That's why it's my responsibility to handle this." He stared hard at both wardens. "I need to figure this out, and I'll have him in here at five. Now you get the hell out of my face."

John Parrish's mind raced as he drove to the outskirts of the county where his son lived. Both his life and the life of his boy depended upon his actions in the next couple of hours. The problem was he had never been a great thinker. When trouble arose in his jurisdiction or his life he dealt with it swiftly, eliminating obstacles before they had the chance to fester into something beyond his control. His son had kidnapped and raped a girl, and most certainly had a hand in butchering her companions as well. And he had come along to dispatch the girl as a sort of collateral containment. So they were both heavily involved. He swore out loud at the dead girl, much as his son had done earlier, understanding that without her participation it was unlikely a crime would have even occurred. "Goddam bitch," he said. Then his thoughts turned to Vern Evans, his son's companion. "Goddam Vern," he said. A smile crossed his

lips then. Not a happy smile, but one that conveyed open contempt and perhaps vindication for himself and his boy.

When the sheriff arrived at Dixie Camp, he drove slowly through the entrance, stopping just a few yards onto the property. He got out and swung shut the old wood gate, tying it to a post with a bit of worn rope lying atop the fence nearby. He then drove into the woods, curving along on the road until he arrived at the opening of the field in front of the house. He parked there, before entering the field, and well back into a grove of oaks. He checked his pistol, jacking a round into the chamber before reholstering it. Skirting the edges of the woods he approached the house from the side, using the skills acquired from a lifetime of hunting game and tracking men. Pressing himself up against a wall he listened. Somewhere inside a woman laughed, and his eyes closed somewhat as he tried to decipher other sounds. He heard applause and cheering, puzzling sounds, until a male voice started up, in rhythmic song, and he realized the sounds came from a radio or television. Suddenly a door opened, loudly creaking and then slamming shut as the springs caught hold. Peering around a corner to the front of the house he watched as Vern Evans moved out onto the porch, then down the steps heading in the direction of Toby's truck, which was parked in the field a short distance away. He called out, drawing his pistol as Vern swung around at the sound of his voice. Vern's eyes grew wide.

"Sheriff," he stammered.

"Hello, Vern," said the sheriff as he moved away from the house and towards the startled man. "Headed out somewhere?"

"No, sir." Vern stared at the gun, held waist high in the sheriff's hand. "Just gettin' somethin' from the truck. Toby's inside." He waved a friendly hand. "You want me to get him for you?"

"You rape that girl, Vern? You kill all her friends and bring her up here to rape her, and then make my son drag her into the swamp when you were finished with her?"

Vern looked surprised. "No, John. You know me. I never done nuthin' like that. I never done nuthin'." Vern raised both his hands then, taking a tentative step towards the sheriff. His face showed

confusion. "I don't understand, John. I mean, you were here. You're the one told Toby to get rid of her. I seen what you done."

"You saw what, exactly?"

"You know. You were coverin' for us. Takin' care of us. I seen you go in with the girl. That's all."

"What did you see?" The sheriff smiled wickedly. "What did you see, Vern?"

As Vern started to speak, stuttering out, "I don't know, John," John Parrish shot him in the stomach. As the bullet struck, Vern Evans spun sideways, screaming out as he fell to the ground. He rolled his body into a tight ball, both hands clutching at his middle. Raising his head, his eyes searched out the black, soulless eyes of the sheriff. "John," he called out, as the sheriff shot him in the mouth. The porch door slammed again, and Toby stood there at the top of the steps.

"Dad," he screamed.

Parrish turned to face his son. He slipped the gun back into its holster and reached for a set of cuffs dangling from his belt. "Vern here just tried to kill me." He tossed the cuffs toward the boy. "Put these on," he said. "We've got a lot of talkin' to do before we get back to town."

Chapter Eight

It was late afternoon as Willie Scarlett drove out of the bog and up onto the levee. It was the same road he had driven almost daily for the past fifty years, and the one his father had driven for fifty years before that. Willie owned a small truck farm deep in the delta. The land there was rich enough but usually flooded by rains or the periodic release of water along Cedar Creek, the system designed to irrigate the several large plantations in the area with little regard for the poorer farms in lower lying places which suffered under an overabundance of water for much of the year. Still, Willie and others like him were able to eke out a subsistence living growing lettuce, melons and, where the water lay deepest, small crops of cranberries and aquatic plants. He looked across the creek and across the road, where the Cedar Creek Plantation rambled for several miles, first along the creek and then the roadway into Harbor Springs. The fences showing off the borders of the plantation were always impressively white, with massive, locked gates every mile or so just to remind Willie and others without proper business where they were not allowed to enter. The Claytons ran the plantation, and were among the wealthiest families in the county. Tom Clayton, the eldest, who was the same age as Willie, and his brother Cole,

owned the place. Willie had known them since childhood. In fact, he remembered a time one summer when he and the Clayton boys had played together along the creek, splashing and running and embracing their youth. Then one day the boy's father caught them there. He stood atop the levee, hollering down to his boys to step away from the nigger. Willie remembered the looks on their faces, especially Tom's, as their eyes lowered and they crawled to the top of the levee. That was the last time there had been a friendly word between them. A year or so later the two caught Willie fishing in a small pond, not on the plantation, but on the same side of the highway, and where the Claytons figured they owned everything. He had tried to wave and smile at them, but before he knew it they were chasing and pinning him down, pressing his face deep into the mud along the edge of the pond.

"Look what we have here," Tom had said to his brother. "A nigger. You want to buy him?"

"Buy him?" said Cole. "What does that mean, exactly?"

"You know, purchase him as a slave. To do whatever the hell you want." Willie had tried to squirm free, and when he couldn't he twisted his head enough so his eyes could look straight up into Tom's. Tom brought a boot down hard then, forcing Willie's face to twist back into the mud. Willie made no sound. "Don't look at me, boy." Then Tom said to his brother. "So, you wanna buy him or what?"

"You can do that?" asked Cole, somewhat amazed. "You can just buy a guy and put him to work?"

"Hell yeah. And he has to do whatever you say. No matter what, he has to do it."

"Wait. What? He has to do it?" Cole scratched his head. "What if he don't wanna do it? What if he just says no? And after I spent good money on him."

"No?" Tom straddled Willie's back, pressing down as hard as he could. "Willie ain't gonna say no, are you Willie? Willie's a good nigger. And if he does, why you just beat him. You beat him real good until he learns to do exactly as you say."

"Wow," said Cole, crossing his arms and looking as though he'd just discovered a great secret. "I didn't know you could do that. Sounds pretty good."

"That's what I'm sayin'."

"But what about when people say you just can't go around ownin' folks?"

"Well that's the beauty of it," said Tom as he raised himself up and kicked roughly at Willie's leg. "We've found a way around that. We just call him a nigger, and that's all he is, and we can treat him like any other farm animal."

"You mean you have your cows, your pigs, your horses and your niggers?"

"Yup. Just like the good Lord intended. Haven't you been listenin' to Pa?"

"Okay," said Cole, the younger. "I'm in. From now on I own your ass, Willie. You hear?" Both boys laughed and warned Willie he'd better stay on his own side of the roadway. Then they kicked at him once or twice more and left him lying there.

Willie never forgot a single word of that encounter. Nor did he ever speak of it. Not to his mother. Not to his father. Not to anyone. Ever. But he never forgot. And through the years he always gave the Clayton boys a wide berth. They would run into each other occasionally, as people in small towns will, but Willie would always lower his head as they passed, and go about his business. Somewhere along the way he began to call himself *Nigger Willie*. Openly, and with no outward resentment, he embraced the term, reasoning that if that's what he was, then that's what he was, and that's just the way things were. And if white folks were going to call him nigger behind his back, he may as well just say it out in front as well. He did notice how uncomfortable it made the folks hearing it, black and white alike, and he found a strange empowerment from that. A residual grew from it that left him somewhat isolated. His acquaintances were few and friends fewer and that's usually the way he liked it.

Now as he drove the old road up to the main highway he noticed a large hay wagon parked ahead, blocking the way. There

was no truck or tractor attached to the wagon. It just sat there, apparently abandoned and making passage impossible. He stopped and stepped down from his pickup, walking alongside the wagon and then onto the highway, where he looked at some length in both directions. Finally a farm truck appeared, its green and white paint stripes slashing through the sunlight as it neared him. A Cedar Creek truck. The driver swerved suddenly toward Willie, and as he jumped back instinctively the brakes squealed, the truck rumbling to a halt. Tom Clayton leaned out the driver's side window. "What the hell, Willie? You lookin' to get yourself killed?" Clayton looked around, at the wagon, the road and then back at Willie. "What the hell are you doin' in the middle of the highway?"

"I'm sorry Mister Tom," Willie's voice dropped submissively in tone, his eyes lowering as he remembered the lessons of his father. "I was just wonderin' if you knew anythin' about this hay wagon in my drive here." He pointed to the wagon. "I gotta get into town and it's blockin' the way."

Tom Clayton seemed to study the wagon for a long moment. Then he said, "Well it's sure as hell mine. One of the boys must have dropped it off this mornin'." He nodded pleasantly. "I'm headin' into town, but I'll be back in an hour or two and I'll have someone come and fetch it."

"Yes, sir," said Willie, still without looking up. "But I really need to get into town myself. I've got some produce that's about to spoil back here." He pointed to his truck, shuffling his feet uncomfortably. "Could you maybe have it tended to a little sooner?"

Tom Clayton's mouth opened just a bit. He leaned his head out further and spat. The wad of spittle hit inches from Willie's feet. Willie looked up then and their eyes met for the first time. "I told you, Willie. I'll have it tended to when I get back." His eyes narrowed to slits and turned hot. "Now I suggest you get the hell off this highway before the next truck maybe don't miss. We don't wanna have no nigger pie spread all over the road, now do we?"

"No, sir, Mister Tom," said Willie, a weak smile playing at his lips, his face once again cast downward. "We sure don't." Tom Clayton

gunned the engine and without saying another word lumbered off in the truck. "Yes, sir, Mister Tom. I'll just sit my ass right here and wait till you decide to move your damn hay," said Willie as he turned, moving back to the wagon. He studied it for a time, finally reaching up and pulling down firmly on a long red-painted handle. "Hmmm," he said softly. Pushing forward against the side of the wagon he moved it a foot or so with little resistance. "Hmmm," he said again. Returning to his own truck, Willie drove slowly forward until his bumper contacted the rear of the wagon. He pushed on it until he had enough of it out onto the highway to allow his truck to pass. Then he stopped and just sat there. For a time he raised his hands, covered his face and made small indecipherable sounds. Finally, for no particular reason he could think of he smiled, long and wide, let the clutch slip out as he accelerated, and shoved the wagon across the road at a great enough speed that it crashed through a small barrier fence, turned somewhat sideways and rolled over and down and into the creek. "Yes, sir, Mister Tom," he called out loudly. "I'll just waits myself right here."

As Willie drove into Harbor Springs a few minutes later he still carried a smile on his face. For the first time in his life he embraced his age. As a young man he never would have acted so rashly, but as an aging one he considered the situation and the worst that could happen. And that, he concluded, wasn't all that bad. He noticed the game warden's car pulled up in the driveway of the mortuary. On the street just below, the sheriff's car also sat, and sitting in the front passenger seat was Toby, the sheriff's son. He'd had an encounter or two over the years with the boy poaching pigs or gators on his farm, as had everyone else in the valley, and considered the boy as what he liked to call *white trash quality*. Pulling over just in front of the sheriff's car, he got out, nodded to Toby and walked up the drive to where two wardens, the sheriff and Shawn Briggs, the coroner, were engaged in chatter.

"I'm tellin' you," he heard the sheriff say as he approached, "I've looked at all the facts and listened to my boy. I've no reason to doubt him. Vern Evans found the girl dead on the road just after the

accident. He brought her back to the house to hold onto her, figurin' a reward would be posted for the body and he could collect on it. It was a dumb thing to do, but you all know Vern ain't bright. And then later, he got scared thinkin' folks might not believe his story, so he asked my boy to take her out and dump her in the swamp." The sheriff shook his head. "Again, I'm not sayin' it was bright, but certainly Toby meant no harm to anyone. He just figured he was helpin' out a friend. He knows he's gotta pay for what he done. And that goddam Evans? He run off before I got out there, but we'll find him."

Willie cleared his throat as the four men turned to look at him. "What's up, Willie?" asked the sheriff.

"Hello, Sheriff," said Willie, lowering his gaze respectfully. He then looked up briefly and nodded to Shawn Briggs and the wardens. "Good to see you, Mister Briggs."

"Hi, Willie," said Briggs. He and Olivia often bought greens or cranberry preserves off Willie's truck when he would pass by, and the two of them felt a lonely connection to the old man. "Good to see you."

Willie turned to the sheriff. "I got a bit of bad news, Mister Parrish. My road was blocked this mornin' by a hay wagon from Cedar Creek. I was in a hurry to get to town so I sorta pushed it out onto the highway to give myself a little room. Well, the darndest thing, I musta pushed too hard 'cause the wagon kept right on goin', across the road and right on down into the crick." Swirling his hands around, he continued. "It sorta got all twisted and wound up upside down and pretty messed up. I figured I'd better tell you."

"Damn, Willie," said the sheriff. "That's one of Clayton's wagons." He laughed aloud. "He's gonna be a real bitch about this." The sheriff looked back at the wardens, neither of whom showed the slightest interest in smiling. "Look, Willie," he said. "I got business here. Come down later and we'll talk about it and I'll see what I can do to keep your ass from gettin' busted up." As Willie nodded gratefully and turned to leave, Briggs called out to him.

"Wait, Willie." He motioned with his hand, pointing to the

warden's car. "I wonder if you'd help me with something." The two of them walked away then, leaving the sheriff to continue his explanation to the wardens. When they arrived at the car, Briggs moved to the back and swung open the lid to the trunk. Both men peered in to where a large, muddy sack lay bent and twisted. "Elizabeth Courtier," said the coroner. "Or so they tell me. Found her out in the swamp this morning."

"No way." Willie stepped back a bit, then moved in closer. "The missin' girl? She was thrown from the bus?"

"No. She was found miles from the bus. In this bag." Briggs reached down, tugging at one corner of the sack. "Help me carry her inside so we can figure out just what in the heck happened to her."

Willie's eyes grew wide. "Sunovabitch," he said under his breath. Then he grabbed the other end of the sack and the two men lifted it gently, carrying it down the steps alongside the street and into the lab. Olivia met them at the door.

"Is it really her?"

Briggs looked at his daughter with a certain amount of contempt. "Must you snoop and listen in on everything?"

"Absolutely. So is it? Is it her?" She ran ahead of the men, pulling a gurney from one of the lockers and wheeling it into the center of the room.

"We don't know yet. I haven't seen her. But that's what they're saying." The men swung the sack onto the gurney. They could feel through the cloth that whatever was inside remained stiff and hardened, almost like a chunk of wood. "Rigor mortis is still strong," said Briggs matter-of-factly. "If it's her, she hasn't been dead more than a day or two."

Willie scratched at an ear. "The accident was four days ago. Don't a body get stiff and stay stiff?"

"No," answered Olivia, before her dad could respond. "Rigor sets in a few hours after death, but after a day or so, when the tissues start to decompose, everything softens up again." She poked at the sack, but gently and not irreverently. Her eyes misted over as she looked up at both men. "They kept her."

"Olivia." Shawn Briggs reached out, physically moving his daughter back and to the side. "We don't know anything yet. We don't even know if it's really her." He motioned aggressively towards the door leading up to the residence. "Now you take Willie upstairs and get the heck out of my way." He nodded, smiling slightly. "Thanks for the help, Willie."

Just then the outside door, the one they had just come through, opened and Sheriff Parrish stepped into the lab. All three of them turned to stare at the man. Willie's eyes stayed high. "So," said the sheriff, his voice surprisingly gentle, "I guess this about wraps up the mystery." He pointed at the gurney. "We need to get her ready to ship back up to her folks. Let's put this whole mess behind us."

Briggs moved a step toward the sheriff. His arms spread a bit as he brushed his way past the other two, pushing them back slightly, as if shielding them from harm. "That's a good idea," he said. He could feel Olivia staring hard into his back. "No sense in dragging this out. I'm just glad it's finally over." He smiled slightly, attempting to laugh. "This has been the darndest thing I've ever been involved in."

Parrish looked at him for a long moment, gauging. "So we're okay here?" he asked.

"Yes, of course." Briggs glanced back at Olivia, his eyes begging her to keep quiet. Willie also noticed the look. Then he turned back to the sheriff. "I'm just going to clean her up a bit. How do you want to handle it?"

The sheriff pawed at the floor with a shoe. He pursed his lips thoughtfully. "I guess I'll pick her up. I wanna drive her up to Blue Ash myself. Outta courtesy. It's the least we can do. Then we can put this whole thing behind us and get back to life." He pointed at the gurney. "So, say an hour. You'll have her ready for me?"

"Of course. An hour is just fine." Briggs looked down at his watch. "I'll straighten her up a bit, make her as presentable as I can and you can be on your way."

"Good," said the sheriff. "I'm gonna go fill out a report, and I'm gonna need you to sign it. We've gotta dot all our *i*'s on this. Make sure everyone is happy. Isn't that right, Briggs?" He looked

deeply into the coroner's eyes, still wondering. "And we don't need no autopsy here, right?" Without waiting for an answer he looked past Briggs, at Olivia and Willie, nodding politely to them. "And you two stay out of the coroner's hair so he can get this done." Reaching out, he tapped Briggs on the arm. "We gotta stick together on this," he said, as he turned to leave. As the door swung closed behind the sheriff, Olivia leapt up beside her father.

"Oh, my god," she said. "That man's a monster." She looked at her dad in an appeal. "You're examining her, right?"

Briggs walked over to the door, clicking shut the dead-bolt. "Yes," was all he said.

A full examination of a corpse, especially one where foul play is suspected, could take the better part of a day. Briggs knew he had just minutes to compile whatever information he could find. He looked first at his daughter, then Willie, and said simply, "Both of you go." Neither of them moved. Ignoring them he stepped over to the gurney, untied a drawstring and pulled on a wide strip of canvas until it loosened, exposing a matting of long, black hair and the side portion of a girl's face. The face, although noticeably black, appeared pale almost to the point of whiteness. The one visible eye distended somewhat from its socket. As the coroner brushed the hair back to expose the rest of the face the head moved slightly, the eye oozing further out until it seemed to stare horribly at the three in the room.

Willie clasped his heart. "Oh, lordy," he cried out, stumbling backward into a counter. Olivia reached to steady him.

Briggs spoke loudly. "Ollie. Get him out of here." This time the girl responded, grabbing Willie by the arm and pulling him to the stairs.

"Oh, lordy," he called out again.

As the coroner cut away the sack to expose the rest of the body he noticed the girl was naked, except for a torn shirt, a man's shirt, unbuttoned and flapped open to about her waist. He repositioned the body, aggressively massaging tissue to make it more compliant, and turned the corpse until it lay flat, belly up, with the face now pointing to the ceiling. There was no time to inject formalin or anything else

to soften the limbs, so Briggs simply bent the extremities into workable positions and began his examination. His eyes swept the body, stopping quickly as he noticed redness and tissue bulging from the middle of the neck. "Asphyxia," he said aloud. His fingers gently probed into the engorged muscles surrounding the throat. There were dozens of tiny red spots there, and several full lines of redness extending part way along the sides of the neck, signs of hemorrhaging due to the bursting of blood vessels put under tremendous pressure. The marks were lower on the neck than one might expect in a case of ligature strangulation or hanging, where a rope or cord of some kind would generally be pulled high and tight, and much nearer the chin. In this case it was likely the victim was throttled manually by someone with very strong hands. Picking up a scalpel Briggs made a slight incision high up on the throat to confirm his suspicions. He ran his fingers into the hole he had created, running them along the hyoid, a tiny, wishbone-like bone used as a support between the head and the neck. As he suspected it was still intact. The conclusion was an obvious one. Hands constricting and thumbs digging deeply into the middle of this girl's throat, and well below the telltale bone, had ultimately caused her death. This was most definitely a murder.

Next, Briggs scanned the body, his eyes moving downward past the breasts, the stomach and into the vaginal region. The right breast of the girl had been bruised badly, with possible bite marks or other indentations present. He noted them but decided to concentrate on the reproductive tract, as it was more important with his limited time frame. The outer vaginal walls were damaged, but not badly, showing a certain amount of bruising but not necessarily violence. He wondered at that. Then he noticed the hymen had been recently ruptured, the inner flap just now beginning to mend and withdraw into the body. So she had been a virgin only days earlier. Using a forceps, he opened the vagina further, reaching for a scope and a magnifier. He didn't have to look hard to find the violence he suspected. The interior vaginal walls were badly torn, mutilated actually, as if someone had inserted something abrasive.

Under light and magnification it became apparent there were tiny splinters of wood or a wood-like substance protruding from myriad places. He extracted one with a tweezer and visually inspected it. A branch or limb of a tree, he thought. Or maybe the worn handle of a tool. This girl had been through hell, with death probably coming as a relief to her. He began swabbing then, mopping up anything near or inside the vaginal region with a liquid or mucous feel to it, and when finished he began a series of minute dissections, retrieving bits of tissue that appeared to have been damaged or compromised by an outside source. He did this for a long time, meticulously. The examination had taken almost an hour. It had seemed like minutes. And though it had been less clinical than he would have chosen, Briggs felt confident that if asked to, he could present a strong case as to exactly what fate had befallen Elizabeth Courtier. He grabbed his camera from a nearby shelf to further document his findings, and began to take photos of the entire torso. That's when Olivia opened the upper door and came racing down the steps to inform him that the sheriff was just pulling up the drive. Quickly the two of them went to work. Olivia raced to a closet at the back of the lab, returning with a clean, white body bag, while Briggs dampened some towels, scrubbing the body from head to toe. He sprayed it with a strong antiseptic aerosol, and roughly combed with his fingers the long tresses of hair into place. Then he and Olivia lifted the body, slipping a gown similar to the ones used by hospitals over its shoulders, where it draped loosely down to around the knees. The coroner glanced at his daughter and marveled at her. She hadn't said a word or made a sound. She looked at him and smiled. "Looks good," is all she said.

"You're amazing," he replied. "A little twisted, but amazing." They heard someone turning the handle on the outside door. And then came a loud knocking. "Shhh," Briggs whispered. He pointed at the body bag, lifting the Courtier girl with a sweeping motion while Olivia slipped the bag down around her feet, and then up the torso as the coroner adjusted his grip to accommodate the bag. In seconds it lay out flat, its contents secure and sanitary. He pulled the

flap up over Courtier's face, securing it tightly with the drawstring. Olivia, meanwhile, went to answer the door as Briggs followed her with the gurney, putting as much distance between himself and the examination area as he could.

As the door opened Briggs looked up and smiled. "All ready, Sheriff. Washed her up and made her a bit more presentable." He looked down and tapped at the body almost fondly. "I didn't inject her with anything and she's getting a little ripe. You're going to have to get her up there pretty quickly."

The sheriff looked sharply at Briggs. "You just cleaned her up. That's it?"

"Yes, sir. Just like you asked."

"You didn't notice anythin' unusual? Nuthin'?"

"No." Briggs cleared his throat, glancing at his daughter. "She was kind of beat up like she'd been in an accident." He looked back at the sheriff. "Just like you said."

John Parrish stepped inside the doorway of the lab. He looked around. Briggs held his breath, hoping the sheriff would not notice the mild carnage strewn about on one of the far counters. The sheriff seemed not to care. His eyes wandered idly about, coming to rest on Olivia. "There's been a change of plans," he said as he turned to look at Briggs. "I want to cremate her. Now."

"What?" One of the coroner's hands went around his daughter's shoulders, the other rose and rubbed away on his chin. "We can't do that. You can't just cremate somebody without authorization. I mean, it's the law."

Parrish reached out a hand and brushed it against Olivia's hair. "I've got authorization. Spoke to the family a few minutes ago. This is what they want. I told 'em we have a crematorium right here, all ready to go. Want to spare 'em the agony of seein' their baby girl all torn up."

"They said that?" Briggs pulled his daughter backward, turning her with both hands. "Ollie, go upstairs." He looked at her with imploring eyes. "Please." The girl looked at her father, then at the sheriff.

"Okay, Dad," she said. She moved off then, across the lab and toward the stairs that led to the residence. As she passed by one of the counters she casually picked up a length of white linen, draping it out like a sheet until it covered the surface of the counter. Then she went up the steps and was gone.

"I don't like it," the coroner continued. "I'm not saying they didn't tell you that. I'm just saying you can't burn up a body without a heck of a lot of paperwork. There's a protocol that must be followed."

The sheriff put a friendly hand on Briggs' shoulder. His eyes, however, held a spark that was all too familiar. "Look, you're the coroner, right? And you're the only man who can authorize a body released for cremation. That's the beauty of it. We have all the authorization we need, right here." He smiled benignly. "This has been tough on all of us. 'Specially you. Let's just end this thing right here and right now. And I'm promisin' you I've spoke to the family. We're only carryin' out their wishes."

"I guess," said Briggs. "I should talk to them though. If not as a coroner, then as their mortician. I mean, I can't do anything without assurance they won't change their minds. I can be held very accountable here."

The hand tightened on his shoulder and Briggs felt himself flinch. "I told you, you have my word, Briggs. This is on me." The sheriff pointed to the body bag. "Now we're gonna cook that little lady up. And then this will all be over. No more questions. No more trouble. It's just over." Inwardly, the sheriff was already calculating how he would explain that the dumb-ass coroner had accidentally cremated the Courtier girl without any authorization whatsoever. Outwardly he smiled, extending a warm hand. "Then you and me can go back to bein' friends," he said in a voice that implied they already were.

Chapter Nine

By the evening of the next day, the fifth day after the crash, news media throughout the south had picked up the story about the discovery of the remains of Elizabeth Courtier. An official statement had been released earlier in the afternoon from the governor's mansion concerning the circumstances of the find, and the state's great sadness at finally putting an end to a horrific tragedy. The report stated that two officials from Alabama Fish and Game had come upon a local hunter who had recovered parts of human remains deep in a swamp a mile or so from the crash site. It was speculated that perhaps a gator or other swamp creature had dragged the girl there, and it was an amazing stroke of luck she had been discovered at all. The hunter, the son of a local sheriff, received the warm thanks of the governor, and the two officials, game wardens who had gone to great lengths to return the remains, received official commendations and high honors from both the governor and their department. There was no comment on the disposition of the remains, and members of the Courtier family up in Ohio were sequestered and not yet ready to make any public statement.

Olivia and her father spent much of the day lying on the couch, listening to new reports filtering in, each one more incredulous than

the last. "They think it's over." She looked at her father with fire in her eyes. "And what about Toby Parrish? He's some kind of hero now?"

"I guess you really don't know the power of the government until it comes in and sits on your face." Briggs shook his head, his voice trembling. "We have to get out of here. Pretty soon someone will want to talk to me and I'm not sure what I say will be in our best interests. I'm still ashamed of myself for last night."

"What are you talking about? What were you supposed to do?" Olivia touched her dad tenderly. "First of all, the sheriff's a maniac. There's no telling what he's capable of. And we didn't hurt anything. She may have been cremated, but we still have enough evidence to fry whoever the bastard is who killed her. Like you said, let's just get out of here and find someone who wants to listen. Find a lab you can trust. Find people we can trust. Let's just go."

Briggs leaned over, collapsing his body until his head rested on Olivia's lap. He looked up at her. "I really wish you wouldn't swear so much. It kind of points to a bad upbringing."

"What? Bastard? That's not a swear word. Not if it's an accurate representation. And if you think about it I come up with some really good shit." She tugged at his hair. "You want me to go all Stepford on you? Yes, Daddy, no Daddy, anything you say, Daddy."

"God, I would love that."

As they talked a horn honked out on the drive. Olivia pushed her father's head aside and rose to look out the window. "Dad. There's someone coming. I think it's a coroner's van." Briggs rose and together they stared for a moment as the van rolled right up behind their own van and a man got out, heading for the house. They both walked over to the door to meet him.

"You Briggs?" he asked.

"I am," said the coroner, somewhat surprised.

"Then this is for you." He handed Briggs a set of keys. "Enjoy," he added. Then he turned without another word and walked down the drive to the street below. A red pickup pulled up just then and the man stepped inside and rode away.

Briggs and Olivia looked at each other. "What the hell," they said at exactly the same time. They exited the door, moving outside and down a couple of steps to where the new van waited. And it looked entirely new. Glistening chrome, with bright white paint, gold stripes and a fresh gold seal, which proclaimed, *Coroner, Colby County*. Briggs opened the driver's door. There on the seat was a large envelope typewritten with his name and address. Olivia muscled past him, grabbing at the envelope, tearing it open even as she stepped away. "Shit me now," she exclaimed as she looked at the contents.

"Shit me now? Ollie, really?" She turned the envelope towards him, her hand reaching in to display more hundred dollar bills than either of them had ever seen in one place at one time. "Wow," said Briggs.

"Told ya."

A few minutes later they sat at the nook-table adjoining the kitchen, money scattered all across its surface. "Twenty-five thousand dollars," Briggs whistled. "I guess that buys a lot of silence."

Olivia looked at her dad. She cocked her head to one side. "But not ours, right?"

Briggs reached out and ruffled her hair. "Of course not. But I'm betting there are a couple of wardens right now who are jumping up and down in the beds of their new pickups."

"So do we send it back?"

The coroner thought for a moment. "No, baby, I'm thinking not. We'll consider this pain and suffering money, and maybe a little stake for us to get the heck out of here. Let's gather up what's really important and maybe drive it out to Willie's for safekeeping. I think we can trust the man, and I don't know if we'll be coming back here or not." Briggs pulled his daughter close. "Are you okay with that?"

"Dad," she replied, reaching up to kiss his cheek. "I hate this shithole."

An hour later they were on the road, not in one of the vans, but in an old Ford wagon that Briggs had owned since before Olivia had even been born. The wagon was filled with as much as it could hold, with the coroner's private lab equipment, small pieces of furniture,

a flat screen, and all of Olivia's clothes and stuffed animals. She also brought the poster her father had given her a long time ago, the one with the ants and the pineapple. She held it up high in her hands before tucking it safely behind the front seat. "Together we can, Dad," she said. They drove south on the highway, then swung east through the delta. It was already past seven in the evening, but being July in Alabama they still had a couple hours of daylight to journey in. On their right they began to see the long strips of white fence marking the boundaries of the Cedar Creek Plantation. Willie had told them briefly of his encounter with Tom Clayton, the owner, and the demise of the hay wagon. They relived the story now, chuckling as they drove along. Soon, on the left, they began to see a grouping of smaller farms, some, the luckier ones, elevated at the same level as the levee that bordered Cedar Creek, but others were tucked way down in the bottomland, in small valleys inundated by marsh and mud. Briggs slowed as a sign drew near. *Produce, Preserves and Perishables*, it read. *Willie Scarlett, Proprietor.* "He must like the letter *P* a lot," Olivia observed with a grin. They turned in at the gate, driving for some distance along the top of a levee before banking sharply left, down an embankment and into the marshlands. The wagon struck mud several times. Not the sticky kind that claws away at you like the tar pits, but just wet, squishy mud erupting in geysers of brown as they sloshed past. Rounding a bend and passing through a dense thicket of cedar, the farm and the house came into view. And the view taught them a lot about Willie. Everything, from the fencing to the barn, to a number of small pens and sheds, and the main house itself, was immaculately kept. That's not to say it was modern and new and shining in the afternoon sun. Quite the contrary. Willie's farm lay there, weathered, with great age showing on almost everything made from wood. And that was almost everything. But there was not a thing out of place. Not a thing unkempt. Fence rows, though old, were perfectly aligned, with not a board missing. Barrels, running alongside one wall of the house and across a courtyard to the barn, were spaced in exact formation, inches apart, each one a mirror image of its neighbor. And the house itself. It is hard to

describe how a house can appear loved. But this one most certainly was. The steps up to the porch were smooth, whitewashed and swept clean. Long rows of planters adorned with bright orange geraniums hung all along the porch, separated only by the steps, which led to a pair of massive, hand-carved doors at the front of the house. Even the yard, where they pulled in and parked, had been freshly raked, with parallel rake lines running across the earth in military precision. Briggs felt a tremor of guilt as he realized the tires on the wagon were conducting open warfare on the lines, but then he noticed other tires had beaten him there, tread marks sweeping in and out of the yard in a broad circle. It made him feel less guilty.

"Wow," said Olivia as they exited the wagon and moved toward the porch steps. "Willie is rather...neat." Briggs reached out to grab her hand as they ascended the stairs and approached the great doorway. One of the doors was closed, lock-bolted in place at top and bottom. The other door, the one on the right, hung partway open, just a few inches, but enough to appear strange, especially considering the afternoon heat which still struggled to push its way inside. Briggs pushed on the door, opening it enough so his head could squeeze through.

"Willie," he hollered out. "Willie, you here?" There was no response, so Olivia moved away from Briggs, sliding along the porch where she could peer through a nearby window. "Willie," Briggs called out again. Suddenly Olivia's hands flew to her face and she screamed.

"Oh my god." She ran at her father, brushing him aside, and swinging the door open so harshly that it crashed loudly into an interior wall. Then she was inside, with a startled Briggs following her as fast as he could. The inside of the house was the antithesis of the outside. Furniture was strewn about, a chair, a table upended, lamps lying broken on the floor. A large wall mirror had been torn from its place over a mantel, with glass and pieces of the frame scattered about. Willie lay on his side in a far corner of the room. His head lifted as they raced at him, fear in his eyes, but then he recognized Olivia and he smiled through a badly beaten face. Olivia

sank to her knees and nearly slid into him. "Willie," she cried out, as she reached to cradle his head. "It's okay." Briggs arrived then, and Willie looked up through a mist of sweat and blood.

"Oh, lord," he said. He tried to smile. "It's the coroner. This can't be good." Briggs swung down beside his daughter, landing on his knees.

"My god, what happened?"

"Funny thing," said Willie, his voice low and stumbling. "I'm thinkin' I shoulda showed a little more respect for that hay wagon."

"Tom Clayton?" asked Briggs.

"Nah," said the old man. "He'd never dirty himself with sumthin' like this. A long time ago he would have, but not now. A couple of his boys came by. Said I owed 'em for the wagon. They said it real convincin' like. I told 'em I'd pay. I'd go into town and get the money right then, but they just laughed and started in on me." He paused as his mouth twisted into a grimace, and he appeared shamed. "I'd like to say I gave 'em what-for, but the truth is I just sorta curled up in a ball and let 'em beat me down." Olivia lowered her head and kissed the old man on the forehead. Briggs watched his daughter and was again amazed by her. They barely knew this man, and yet, because he hurt, and because he felt shame, she loved him. He smiled as he considered that he might have misdiagnosed her. She might not grow up to be a serial killer after all.

"You see my face, Willie?" Briggs tilted his head back, exposing his face to the light. "I've still got the bruises. It only took one to do this to me. We're all beatable."

"I seen your face yesterday. I wondered." He shifted his gaze to Olivia. "You do realize you just kissed a black man, right?"

They all sat there on the floor for a good piece of time, until Willie felt maybe he could stand, at least well enough to make it up onto the couch. Olivia helped him while Briggs went off to find the kitchen to make some tea. They spent the night there, napping and talking and napping some more, occasionally forcing the old man to eat some stew they found in the freezer, hoping he could regain some of his strength. By morning Olivia had him cleaned up and

sitting up. Briggs examined him as best he could, and found nothing he considered terribly serious. "How in the hell do you know what serious is?" Willie challenged him. "You ever fix up one of them dead folks to where they went off dancin'?"

"Yeah, Dad," sang Olivia. "From what I've seen your results have not been all that positive."

By late morning the three had come to some compatible conclusions. Willie decided he did not wish to risk another visit by the Cedar Creek boys and asked if he might be allowed to accompany Briggs and Olivia on their mission. They unloaded the wagon, making room for necessities, and a bag or two of the old man's belongings. The coroner had decided Atlanta would be their destination. It was only a few hours away, was home to *The Daily Herald*, one of the most respected newspapers in the country, and sat far enough away from Alabama on the map to give them a little breathing room. Willie still had his concerns though. He sat out on the porch steps with Briggs.

"Do you really think folks are gonna care what happened to a bunch of little black girls?" he said to the coroner, but close enough to Olivia that she also heard. "No one's gonna do anythin' about this. The only one who cares about a nigger is his mama."

"Willie," she said, in a caustic voice usually reserved for teachers. "I don't like it when you say that. I don't like it at all."

"Come on, missy, I don't mean no harm." The old man shook his head sadly. "We is what we is. And you is what you is."

Briggs spoke up. "Not everybody feels like that, Willie. In fact, if you could get yourself out of the south you would find there's a whole lot of people in the world who couldn't care less about the color of someone's skin. We came down from St. Louis last year. It's better up there but we still have our problems. The truth is, though, you don't have to play the game. You find enough people who feel the same way you do, surround yourself with them, and pretty soon life doesn't look so bad."

"Well, Mister Briggs, I don't wanna sound disrespectful, but down here there's niggers and there's not niggers. It's always been that way." He grinned then, one side of his mouth swollen and

distorted, but still a grin, nonetheless. "And I jus' happens to be on the nigger side of the road. And you seen last night what happens when one of us tries to cross over that road, say pushin' a hay wagon. It jus' reminds you who you are."

Olivia spoke. "Look, I have no way to know what you feel. But I remember after my mom died and everyone came up and said how sorry they were and they understood what I was going through. I wanted to smash their faces. How in the world could they possibly know how I felt? And I resented the crap out of them. All of them. But later I realized a lot of them were really good people who were just trying to offer me a little comfort. I was wrong."

The old man frowned, then growled out. "I have no idea what that means. I'm not talkin' about my mama dyin'. I'm talkin' about bein' a black man who everybody knows is jus' a nigger."

"Stop it." Olivia, who had been standing by the wagon a few steps away, moved to the porch and sat down a couple of steps below the two men. She turned to face Willie directly. "If you want me to be your friend you need to stop saying that. I know very well you know it's a word that carries a lot of hate." She placed a hand on the old man's knee. "You need to understand that you're not in that world now. You're in my world. You're in my dad's world. I'm glad you're here with us. But if you use the n-word again I swear I'll resort to violence." She swung at him suddenly, her hand just missing his nose.

Willie laughed, a genuine laugh, with a certain joy attached to it. "You can't even say it."

"I can say it. I just choose not to."

"No you can't. Go ahead, say it."

"I told you. I don't want to say it. That's my whole point. I want to get rid of it. Forever."

"Just say it then. Just say it once and I won't say it anymore."

Olivia jumped at the proposition. "You promise?"

"I'll do'er," the old man said without much conviction. "But I've got some other words I'm gonna pull out from time to time."

Olivia stood, turning to fully face the two men. She looked first

at her father, who had an amused smile tugging at his lips. "Bite me," she said to him. Then she turned to Willie. She leaned over, placing a hand on each of his shoulders. Her face closed in on his. "Nigger," she said, with shocking authority.

Willie laughed again, even louder. He leaned over and poked at Briggs. "You're the one who has to live with her. I'm just gonna be her friend."

Chapter Ten

THE WHITE HOUSE

E rrol Clarkson sprawled loosely in one of the side chairs located just to the left of the president's desk in the oval office. He sat in the side chair because Chester Benton —Charlie— his advisor and friend of many years, would be arriving soon and would undoubtedly trick him or bully him into surrendering the Big Chair if he was found to be in possession of it. The president sat there, his long legs hanging some distance into the room, his head, cupped by his hands, tilted back until his eyes stared straight up at the ceiling. This had been one hell of a week. Perhaps the most arduous of his entire presidency. Major bombings in Istanbul and Johannesburg had claimed the lives of three hundred people, including eleven Americans. A hate crime out in San Diego, where three Muslim men were found beheaded, Isis style, in a canyon, and just yesterday a major riot had broken out on a campus in Virginia when it was discovered that a white police officer had raped or molested more than a dozen students, most of whom were black. The university was closed down now, its administration building besieged by protestors, and the governor of Virginia was calling out for the National Guard. The president thought how much easier life would be if white officers only raped white women and

left the black women for officers of their own color. As he felt a brief moment of shame, the door opened and in walked Charlie.

"Chief," he said, as he strolled over to his customary position behind the great desk. "There's something going on you need to know about."

"More?" asked the president. "I'm sitting here right now thinking about driving myself off a cliff somewhere." Raising his head, he tucked his legs in beneath his body. "I guess you heard they're requesting a troop presence down the road."

"I heard." Benton picked up his Superman toy. "We can't do it. We can offer some support from the sidelines, but sending in troops would be a big mistake. It always is, and we're apt to create a bigger incident than the one we're responding to. Let's get some mediators in there and see if they can find some middle ground. Then you go on the air publicly and face this thing." He tossed the action figure through the air where the president reached out a hand and deftly caught it. "And how many of these riots have we gone through anyway? Seven? Eight? Three days tops, maybe four, and it'll be over. Just let the people know we stand with them."

Clarkson toyed with the figure for a moment, then looked up at his friend. "I don't know," he said almost wistfully. "It just goes on and on with no end in sight. Sometimes I wish to hell we were back in Kuwait. At least we felt we had a purpose then. Right or wrong, at the time we knew exactly what we were doing."

"Probability and outcome. That's what you were always saying." Benton laughed, pushing out his hand in a request for the toy. The president threw it back to him. "Like the time I had to carry your sorry ass across an oil field, with you screaming like a baby the whole way. We got our probabilities handed to us that day."

"You saved me."

"You're a crazy sunovabitch. I only picked you up because I figured your body would protect me from all those bullets whipping by."

"My ass," said the president. "You saved me."

Charlie glanced around the room, bobbing his head, pretending to look for listeners. He leaned across the desk towards the president. "Well, if I did, it was only because I knew you had potential and might possibly amount to something someday." He waved his hands over his head. "And look where you've gotten me. Here I am today, commander-in-chief of the whole damn nation."

"You're in the wrong chair."

Opening a top drawer on the desk Charlie plopped the Superman toy into it, slamming it shut. "You've just ruined a beautiful moment for me."

"So," asked the president, "what's this new piece of news you're bringing me? Good stuff for a change, I hope."

"Banks has been on the phone for the past two hours. Seems he got a call from an old friend of his down in Atlanta. An editor or something. It's about that bus crash with all the little girls. He didn't tell me much because he was on the phone, but he did say 'tell the president to brace himself'."

"Oh, god. I thought they wrapped that up the other day when they found that last girl. The one from Blue Ash. Elizabeth something."

"I don't know," said Charlie. "But he used the word *brace*, so that can't be good."

A few minutes later there was a knock at the door and Thomas Banks, the secretary of state, entered the room. He nodded to the president, then focused his attention on Chester Benton, still sitting behind the desk. "Do you know how offensive it is to see that man sitting there every time I come in?"

"Hi, Tommy. Good to see you," Benton smiled. "What can I do for you?"

Banks ignored the question, turning to face the president directly. He made no attempt to sit down. "I'm not sure how to approach you on this, so I'm just going to say it." His eyes intensified, his manner stiffened, and seeing this, Errol Clarkson immediately sat upright at a position of attention. "The bus crash. The twelve little girls down in Alabama." Banks took in a great gulp of air. "They were murdered.

All of them. There appears to be a cover-up that reaches all the way to the governor."

"What?" The president rose quickly to his feet, and Benton, who had been sitting there somewhat at ease, slumped further back until he seemed to sink into the chair. "What in the hell do you mean? Talk, man."

Tom Banks sat then, on the long leather couch, his eyes first concentrating on the floor, then back up to meet the president's. "I have an old friend, Sheryl Fenn, who works as one of the chief editors for *The Herald* down in Atlanta. Earlier today, right out of the blue, in walks the coroner of Colby County, where the crash took place. He tells her he's been assaulted and intimidated, and drove all the way to Atlanta to get the story out. He claims the bus crash wasn't a crash at all, just a staged accident scene to cover a massive murder, possibly committed by the son of the sheriff down there."

Chester Benton interrupted. "What do you mean possibly? What does any of this mean? Is this just a disgruntled lunatic?"

Ignoring Benton, Tom Banks continued. "It started out the minute the coroner arrived on the scene. He says he found a whole lot of carnage and very little accident. And then, get this, when he gets the bodies back to his lab, he starts plucking bullets out of them. A couple of them anyway. Most of the girls were either hacked to death or strangled, and the Courtier girl, the one they just found... wait till you hear this. He says she was murdered at least a day or two later, after an intense period of rape and torture."

"This is crazy." Errol Clarkson shook his head, moving to the front of the desk, where he sat down on its polished surface. "What...I mean, is there anything to back up what he says?"

Benton then leaned forward, placing his elbows on the surface of the desk. "Wait. Before you go any further, please tell me the sheriff and his kid are black."

"Nope. White as snow."

"Shit, where's a brother when you need one?"

The president spoke. "You've said nothing about proof. I mean, is this coroner nuts? What the hell is going on here?"

Tom Banks smiled then, but a sad smile, not a happy one. "This is going to hurt," he said. "But there's forensic evidence all over the place. It appears that two bullets were found, but then confiscated, one by the sheriff and one by the governor, but this guy has photos and semen samples and dissected tissue and, oh yeah, this is the best part. He has a crystal clear recording of Governor Perry threatening his ass if he opens his mouth. I mean threatening him good."

The president moved back to the chair opposite the secretary. He sat so they were eye to eye. "Is *The Herald* going to press with this? I mean, there has to be time to check out this guy's facts. If they just throw it out there it's beyond irresponsible, don't you think?"

"I don't know what they're going to do. She just gave me a courtesy call out of respect. How do you hold back the press once they get ahold of something?"

Charlie Benton rose for the first time. He stood behind the great desk, looking very presidential. Then he spoke. "I'm going to tell you both something right now. And this time I'm speaking as a black man. If you think all those campus riots we go through every month or so are, how do I say this… distasteful, you just wait till the minority community gets ahold of the fact that a couple of good 'ole white boys, and from Alabama, no less, and one of them possibly a goddam sheriff, are out there raping and hacking up little black girls. Gentlemen, you're in for a real treat. This is going to make campus rioting look like a day at the beach."

The president then asked succinctly, "How do we contain it?"

"Contain it?" Benton continued, "Mister President. If what we've just heard is true, even partly so, there will be no containment. There will be Hell unleashed such as we have never before seen, not in our lifetimes anyway. There are over thirty million blacks out there, about eighty percent of whom have attained very little of our hypothetical American Dream. Right now they are extremely localized. If there's an incident in Chicago, Chicago blacks respond. Minority abuse on a campus in Albany, and the New Yorkers come running out to play. This time it runs much deeper. This isn't just Alabama. If this turns out to be true, it's every little black girl in America who

just got raped. And every young black man with a pocket full of nothing is coming out for this one. They've been fed nothing but shit for a hundred and fifty years. Dog shit yellow, shit. And they're just looking for a reason." Benton raised his arm, turning his hand into a pistol which he pointed at the president's chest. "If this goes public, they've just found it. Bam!" he said loudly.

———◆———

Not far from the Oval Office exists a long hallway, at the end of which is a plain white door opening into a smallish, nondescript room very few have ever entered. It is used only by the president, and rarely so, and only for occasions where the utmost privacy is required. The room is quite Spartan, with two chairs pushed right up against the left wall and a large computer-generated screen located at eye level directly across from them, on the right wall. The president and his aide sat in those chairs now, chatting as they waited for the screen to come to life. Within minutes the screen flashed on, then off, then on again, this time staying on. And they were looking at a meticulously dressed middle-aged woman, a slender man of about forty, and an impish teenage girl who had just blown a face-sized bubble-gum bubble. The man admonished the teenager, who popped the bubble, some of the gum residue sticking to her nose.

"Hello," said the president. "Can you hear me? See me?"

"Oops," said the girl. "Is that him? Oh, yeah, that's him."

The woman spoke. "Hello, Mister President. We can see you fine, sir. Usually when we turn on *Falcon* with the big screen all we get is fuzz. I miss the days of Skype."

President Clarkson laughed lightly, relaxing everyone. "We're not using Falcon," he said. "We're coming to you on *Starr*, a new satellite technology which does away with those crazy cell towers and the need for signal strength. This signal is coming in straight from the sky."

"Well I love it," said the woman. "Please send me some for Christmas." She leaned somewhat forward in her chair. "I'm Sheryl Fenn. I suppose Tom Banks has already told you, and this is Shawn Briggs, the coroner of Colby County, and his daughter, Olivia." Olivia raised a hand to wave while the woman continued. "I've spent the better part of the day with Mister Briggs, as has our legal department. I'm fairly certain we've got something big here, sir. We thought it would be ethical to give you a heads-up in case you need to prepare a response."

"I appreciate that. Thank you very much. I wonder if I might speak with Mister Briggs for a few moments and maybe get a better handle on this. We're all pretty shocked." Clarkson turned to his friend. "This is my top aide, Chester Benton, by the way. Talking to him is the same as talking to me." He paused, biting his lower lip. "Are you sure you want the young lady in for this?"

Shawn Briggs spoke. "Hello, Mister President. It's a great honor, sir. And yes, unfortunately talking to my daughter is also the same as talking to me." Olivia poked at her dad while everyone chuckled.

"Okay then. Let me start by saying how grateful I am that you are bringing this to me first. As you must be aware, the volatility of this incident has the potential to create some real problems, not just down there by you, but possibly all across America." The president fidgeted, trying to find just the right thing to say. "If I appear nervous, I assure you it's because I am. We've never had anything quite like this happen before. I wonder if you, Mister Briggs, can give us a rundown of exactly what we're up against. Not so much the circumstances, but maybe some of the forensics you've done and the conclusions you've drawn from them. That would be very helpful."

Briggs cleared his throat to speak, and Olivia retrieved from her pocket a cell phone. The president broke back in. "Excuse me, is that the phone that holds the recording of the governor we heard about?"

"Yes," said Olivia, "But Miss Fenn has already rerecorded it from here, so she has it too."

Sheryl Fenn spoke. "Would you like to hear it? We've already

had some of the best voice recognition and sound techs in the business look it over. Fortunately we have an unlimited number of test samples to run it against. He is a governor after all, and it's his voice. Our boys guarantee it to a mathematical certainty. It's not DNA, but it's darn close."

"I would enjoy hearing it if that's alright," said Clarkson. It was played then, at a conversational level, and the president, who was already well acquainted with Governor Perry's voice, could do nothing but sit there shaking his head. "Okay," he said, when the tape had been played twice over for him. He looked up, directly at the screen, focusing in on the coroner. "Now, Mister Briggs, if you will, please."

For the next few minutes Shawn Briggs spoke. He began by pointing out that little blood appeared at the scene of the crash, yet each of the passengers was mutilated horribly. The only conclusion was that they had bled out elsewhere, were piled back on the bus and driven to the staged location. He produced photographs, excellent and extremely clear photos, of the bullet wound to Miss Marcy's back, slash wounds on many of the girls which appeared to have been inflicted by large knives or machetes, and then the grisly autopsy photos of Elizabeth Courtier. Briggs had also bagged over forty bits of evidence from Courtier's examination alone, ranging from as-yet unidentified semen samples to small snippets of neck tissue which possibly contained some of the killer's DNA, transferred while he throttled her. Briggs also had a mountain of skin cells, hair and the tiny splinters of wood removed from her vaginal region. His assessment, as he spoke to the president, was of courtroom quality, and left little doubt as to his conclusions. He finished by mentioning the two wardens and the sheriff, who each had intimate knowledge of both the disposal and retrieval of Courtier's body from the swamp. When he was done, he sort of bowed his head apologetically, while his daughter reached behind him to rub his back.

Charlie Benton spoke then. "That was impressive, Mister Briggs. Really. I'd hate to be in court and have you testifying against me, I'll tell you that. I guess what I'm wondering..." He glanced at the

president and then back at the screen. "I guess what we're wondering, is exactly who all this DNA is going to belong to. It would be tragic if we jumped the gun here and raced to any conclusions."

The president nodded in agreement and Sheryl Fenn spoke. "We're aware, gentlemen. We're also aware we have an obligation to get this right." She smiled, "We're not the *Washington Press*." The president smiled back as she continued. "The sheriff's son, Toby Parrish, has a roommate, so to speak, name of Vern Evans. His DNA is already on record in Georgia, from some previous criminal activity, so we'll have accelerated tests run against him by tomorrow. As for Toby Parrish, we are in the process of obtaining his even as we speak." Her smile broadened. "Please don't ask how, but we're confident we will soon have it. We're also attempting to get ahold of the sheriff's in case this turns out to be a *like father, like son* situation. He also assaulted Mister Briggs here, so we have an interest."

Clarkson asked, "So, are you saying you're not going to run with this in tomorrow's edition? You're going to wait for test results?" The president stood then, but found he had to bend over a bit to fit back into the screen. "I guess what I'm asking is for a little more time. To please not run anything until we have a few more facts."

Charlie Benton also stood, coming to his friend's aid. "We're certainly not desensitized. But I think what we're concerned about most, because the victims were largely young black girls, is real potential for a massive racial outcry. Please understand we hold the freedom of the press just as sacred as you do. And the truth is the truth. But could you just hold off on this till we have a bit more evidentiary support?"

Sheryl Fenn also rose to her feet then, sensing the end of the meeting was at hand. Being not a tall woman, she still fit nicely into the screen. "We're extremely excited about this. If this got out and somebody beat us to the story, heads would roll. Mine in particular."

President Clarkson smiled at her reassuringly. "I give you my word. There will be no leaks at this end under any circumstances. And if you'll grant us a couple of days here, you will have complete access to my office for anything you need. That's a promise."

"Two days then."

"Thank you," said the president. "Very much. And Mister Briggs, it's been an honor sir." His eyes then found Olivia's. "And you, young lady. I'm quite sure that you've had a certain impact here today. I thank you." The five then exchanged goodbyes and the screen went dead as a voice came on over an intercom.

"All clear, sir."

The two men stood there for a good long moment. Then President Clarkson motioned to the chairs as both men sat. They didn't look at each other, but rather continued to stare straight ahead, at the blank screen on the opposing wall. "So," said the president finally. "Where do we go from here? That was powerful stuff."

Still focused on the screen, Charlie Benton responded. "Well, I think we can safely assume this guy is no crackpot. In fact, I'm thinking he is beyond credible. We have no way to know that for certain, but I'd lay down some serious money right now that Mister Briggs is one honest hombre caught up in the middle of one helluva circumstance. In my head, I guess, I'm trying to gauge the impact this incident is going to have when it's released to the public." Charlie paused for a moment, pondering, before he continued. "And there's another thing that bothers me. According to Miss Fenn, it's possible that there's a sheriff right smack-dab in the middle of this. Or his son. We've just gone through a decade of cops shooting blacks and blacks shooting cops. If she's right, and law enforcement winds up in the middle of this in any way, we're in for a real treat."

"There's no way we can stop it, right? Nothing that doesn't include the two of us suicide bombing *The Herald*."

"No. This is one of the few times I'm glad you're the commander-in-chief, and not me. I will say, though I'm repeating myself, that this has the potential to go nuclear on us. We've always had our problems, but right now America is a tinder box. We both know that. And I think the match is about to be struck."

"Well, at least we've got a day or two to come up with a response. I'm wondering if this is going to stay localized, you know, be an

Alabama problem. Or do you think this has the potential to move off grid, maybe way off?"

Charlie Benton turned his head to face the president, who still looked forward. "Way off," he said.

The two men sat there in silence for a long period of time. Benton knew what was happening. The president's mind was calculating the degree of volatility, the odds of containment, and the most tenable form of response. Of the two, Charlie was the reactionary, making him the perfect juxtaposition to the president, who believed that with deep thought came deep revelation. So he sat there in quiet contemplation with his best friend, knowing whatever the president came up with would be their answer.

Finally Errol Clarkson spoke. "I want you to go down there. As me, as my eyes. Get this coroner back on the job if you can, be his protector and take care of him and his daughter. Make everything as normal as possible." He turned to face his friend, placing a hand on Benton's leg. "It's always fusion, never fission. If it starts it will start right there, in Colby County. Possibly also up in Ohio, where the girls are from, but most likely at the scene where all the hell was unleashed. That's the way people think. They will sanctify it, memorialize it, gain strength from it and then, if it can't be contained, it will explode outward from there." The president rose, walking the few paces to the screen. He reached out an open palm, pressing it against the glass and leaving a distinct imprint as he pulled his hand away. Raising his index finger he traced a circle pattern in the middle of the hand-print, the middle of the palm. "Right here," he said. "It will start right here." He then traced outward, along the lines formed by the imprint of his fingers. "And if we can't stop it..."

"I'm on my way," said Benton as he rose and headed to the door.

Chapter Eleven

Perhaps as many as half a million people drive near the Georgia Capitol Building every day. It is located in Atlanta, just blocks away from at least one artery to every major highway in the state, and very close to all major commerce. It wasn't always located so conveniently however. There was a time, a long time ago, when the capitol was in Tom's Ferry, a small plantation-based township to the east. The town itself is nondescript and it would be hard to believe something as important as the royal chambers of an entire state would ever be constructed there. But things were different then. Commerce was cotton, and cotton was king, deserving of a palace situated in the heart of plantation lands, and with no way of knowing that one day the lands would burn in hate and a new destiny lay west in Atlanta. One impressive feature still stands at Tom's Ferry: the old capitol building which rose in splendor well before the Civil War. It was burned down a time or two before rising once again in the glory days of the great land barons and the slavery ships which poured into nearby ports with thousands of dark-skinned men of lesser pedigree who were consigned like oxen to work the fields. Then the Civil War came pounding in and the

life of a southern gentleman was forever changed, with a new order dictating where the capitol should stand.

The old building still sits there, an hour's ride from its heir, and has found for itself a new glory, housing the offices and meeting halls for the Southern Military Academy. It is run mostly by retired military men, a major general at its helm and, beneath him, a mixture of aging colonels, majors and captains who do most of the actual teaching there. Now, at the same time the president was meeting with Chester Benton, his chief advisor, another meeting was taking place in Tom's Ferry. Deep in the bowels of the old capitol, in a chamber which once held hordes of screaming members of the legislature who cried out for secession from the union.

A colonel sat there, in full army uniform, twenty-three ribbons arranged in perfect rows adorning his chest. He sat not stiffly, but laid back in a rich leather chair, hands tucked behind his head, and a cap, with polished visor, lying at attention on the desk in front of him. "I'm not sure you're hearing me," said the colonel. He spoke to another man, a less distinguished one, and well past his prime, who stood on the opposite side of the desk in a dark grey suit, with a wide, blue tie tucked loosely into his waistband.

"I hear you, Sedge," said the man. "I'm just not as willing as you are to get all fired up about this until we know for certain. We've had a lot of… disappointments over the years."

The colonel shifted his hands to the front, massaging his temples. "This is a very reliable source. One who's come to me many times in the past, always with something useful. She says the story is going to break within twenty-four hours. And she says there is no doubt. It was no accident. It's brimming over with racism. And it was as violent as hell." The colonel lifted himself to a more attentive position as the other man leaned in with voice lowered.

"If it's true. If it's really true, then Alabama is going to explode, no doubt about that. But it may be more than we can handle. We're not that strong. Not yet, we're not."

The colonel then also leaned forward, striking at the desk with a fist. "Shit man, do you hear yourself? We've been waiting for fifteen

years. Fifteen goddam years. And we've had incident after incident pass us by. Always too small, or too distant, or too unimportant. A lynching over there, a shooting over here, a bombing over there. Are you living in a goddam vacuum? And it's a miniscule place in the south we're after. Surely you must get that. Let Birmingham and Montgomery go up in flames. We'll have no say up there. The fucking mobs can tear them apart. Don't you get it? What the hell will the response be if a million brothers all go crazy at the same time? And all up in northern Alabama. Do you think the government is going to care about a small swath of land to the south? Hell man, their hands are going to be so goddam full they won't give us a thought. Not for a long time they won't. Months maybe." The colonel's eyes brightened. "That's all we need. More than we need."

The man moved to one side of the desk, plopping himself down in a chair. "We have what? Two hundred men? Ready to strike? That's peanuts, man. Alabama has a hundred times that many, just in state troopers. And then there's another twenty thousand cops and sheriffs and god knows what else they could throw at us. I don't like the numbers."

The colonel now attacked the desk with both fists. "You're not getting this. Not at all. It will be the governor they're after. Every sunovabitch in the state with a gun will be called on to defend the capital to the north. Who gives a shit about the woodshed when the goddam house is on fire? There will be no resistance. None. We can roll into this Harbor Springs place and create our own personal wailing wall. It will look like a grand memorial to all those little girls. I'm even willing to bet there will be a hell of a lot of sympathy for our cause, if we do this right. There are four major plantations tucked down there in the southeast corner of the state, and we will cut through them like a knife through the belly of a pig."

The man stood again, stepping up close to the desk. "And then what? I don't get it. We just take it over and impose our own agenda?"

"Exactly." The colonel stood so the two men were eye to eye. "We free our people, exactly as we've always planned. It's been over a hundred and fifty years since the war and it's just about time they

finally get to feel freedom. Real freedom. We'll put the crackers to
work picking the cotton and slopping the hogs. And every black man
will have his own whip. It'll be like a goddam Afro-Disney World,
only with the greatest role reversal of all time. Hell, man, we'll go
down in history as two of America's greatest martyrs."

"You mean, after they hang our asses, right? That's the only
ending here, you know?"

The colonel smiled. A patient, almost kindly smile. "That's the
plan. We've known this day would come for a long time. I've been
a nigger long enough. I've spent forty years watching the stupidest
white boys you've ever seen promoted past me time and time again.
'Oh, you're not ready yet,' they'd tell me. Or, 'I'm sure you'll be on
the next list.' When they finally promoted me to colonel they made
this big ass deal out of it. Like, 'Look at the black man. A colonel,
no less. Isn't that wonderful.' And look at you." The colonel pointed
at his friend. "A goddam United States senator, elected five times
only because you've got so many black folks out here in Georgia
you couldn't possibly lose. And they've given you every shit job
Washington could come up with. While all your white-skinned *equals*
are deciding the fate of the free world, you're down here with me,
deciding how much funding to give a little hick military school so we
can train more killers to go forth and prosper." The colonel lowered
his hand. "You're the saddest nigger of all."

The senator's lips curved upwards, into just the slightest of
smiles. "Well I'm glad they didn't promote you to general. We'd
probably be attacking Washington D.C. instead of Shithole, Alabama."

The colonel smiled wickedly. "You see, you do get me."

Chapter Twelve

There is a saying among members of a notorious prison gang known as the Del Nortes. "If it moves, kill it." It's a simple saying created by men who, by all accounts, are not the deepest of thinkers or the most compassionate of human souls. But by its very briefness, its simplicity, it offers a conclusion that removes all question. Some members of the gang carry the saying around in their minds, others adorn their bodies with the very words. So it is more than just a saying to them. It's a statement of life, and the end of it.

Two men headed east, out of San Diego, across the low plains of California and into the Arizona desert. One was Manuel Ortiz, a son of Mexican immigrants, freshly released from a nine year prison term up in Folsom. The other was Trayon Palmer, a young black man of twenty, who had a much less impressive criminal past, limited to minor infractions like burglary or petty theft. So Trayon idolized Manuel from the moment they met. The two had come together by chance one night at a bar on the outskirts of San Clemente, on California's southern coast. Three men had just caught Trayon in the parking lot, trying to burglarize their car. They had him pinned down and laid out on the hood, two of them holding him, while the third

kicked away savagely at his groin. That's when Manuel happened by. He stopped for a moment, amused, and then observed that the three men appeared middle-eastern, Arabic perhaps, and he hollered out to them. "Hey, you guys fuckin' Muslims?"

The man who had been doing all the kicking paused, and turned. "What the hell, man. Who the hell are you? Some kind of fucking cop?" The next minute or two were a blur to Trayon, who was suddenly released and slumped off the hood and onto the ground.

The next thing he remembered, a man knelt down beside him. He grabbed Trayon by the hair, ripping his face up into the light. "Oh, shit," the man said. "I thought you was a Mexican. I saved me a fuckin' nigger." The man sat for a moment, thinking. Finally he reached down, picked up Trayon and carried him to an old pickup parked in the dark, at the very edge of the lot. He threw him then, over the rail and into the bed. Landing on something soft, Trayon lay moaning for a moment, and then passed out once again.

When he woke, a hot sun blazed down. Raising his hand, he grabbed hold of a metal rail, pulling himself into an upright sitting position. The railing was hot, so he quickly snatched his hand away. He was in the bed of a truck, a pickup, and he was in the middle of nowhere. As his mind cleared he looked around. A large barrel cactus sat a few yards away, and there, right in the middle of it, impaled on its four-inch spines, was a man. Trayon jumped up, feeling himself shake violently. "Holy shit," he cried out.

A laugh came from somewhere behind him, at the front of the truck. He wheeled around and saw a large Mexican man standing there. "Thought maybe you was dead," said the man. "You remember me?"

Rubbing his head and his eyes, Trayon fought to clear his mind. "Last night. I was getting the crap beat outta me, and then you came."

The Mexican grinned widely, walking alongside the truck until he reached the end of its bed, where Trayon stood, just above him. "You wanna kill some Muslims?" he asked, in much the same way as

one might ask if you'd like fries with your burger. Trayon just stood there, his mouth open and his head shaking slightly.

"What?" he said, finally.

"I asked if you wanna kill some Muslims." The Mexican pointed off to one side, a short distance from the man who rode the cactus. Two other men sat there, backs to a large mesquite. They were heavily bound, with rags stuffed into their mouths. Even so, Trayon could hear them whimpering and could see the fear in their eyes. "You know, the sunovabitches who beat on you last night. You want them?"

Trayon looked at the men in surprise. "How the hell did you get them? I mean, there are three of them."

The Mexican laughed. "I am not a meek man." He reached down near the rear wheel-well of the pickup. When his hand came up it held a machete, its blade flashing in the sun. "I won't hurt you," he said. "I figure you're kind of my personal property now." He tapped the machete against the side wall of the bed, before pointing its tip down the road. "You can go or you can stay." The Mexican flipped the machete in his hand, catching the blade and offering out the handle. "But if you stay, you have work to do."

An hour later the two drove along a dusty country road and picked up Highway 10, heading east. Trayon sat slumped back in the passenger seat, his shirt front covered in blood and vomit, his vomit, but not his blood. "It'll get easier," Manuel promised him.

A day later, on the news, they heard of three men found beheaded in the desert. Both of them cheered wildly. By this time they were well bonded, and heading fast through the heartland of America. While they drove, Manuel, the thinker of the two, created for them a sort of manifesto. He and Trayon would be the start of a new movement. A savage one. The goal, to extinguish as much of the establishment as they could. They had no idea yet how to accomplish this, but they were willing to work hard at it. Manuel laughed at the folly of shooters who occasionally rampaged into workplaces where they would be recognized or onto campuses where they would be shot down like dogs before any possible escape.

"We will learn how to kill," he said. "We will blow in like the wind, slaughter what we can, and drift away before anyone can respond."

One night, at a roadside stop, Manuel brought out a hunting knife, its blade honed to razor sharpness. Without giving it a thought he carved the letters *KKKR* deeply into his arm. He handed the knife to Trayon, now completely devoted to him. *KKKR*, Trayon carved, just as deeply.

As the blood ran rich and thick down their arms, Trayon asked, "What does it mean?"

"It's the Resurrection," answered the Mexican. "Only we play no favorites this time. We kill blacks, whites, Jews, Muslims, Christians, anyone we can find, anywhere we find them."

"What about Mexicans?"

Manuel laughed heartily. "You smart fuck. You find me a Mexican and I'll kill it."

Trayon expressed a bit of skepticism, but respectfully so. He mopped blood from his arm, handing the towel to Manuel. "Can it really be that easy? To kill someone, I mean. And then get away with it?"

"You some kind of dumbass? You just cut the heads off three mutherfuckers. You have any trouble gettin' away?"

"No. But, I mean we already had them isolated. No one could see us or stop us. But if we're on a college campus there will be people everywhere."

They were parked out behind a Burger King while they spoke, just off the highway, and as Trayon expressed his concerns a young white man came out from the back door, wheeling a canister of garbage. He pushed it across the driveway in front of them until he arrived at a large green dumpster. The two men watched him for a time, and then Manuel, without even glancing at Trayon, opened the driver's side door, moving out into the drive and towards the same dumpster. When he arrived there he turned, waved in the direction of the truck and said something to the young man. They both laughed. A moment later the two disappeared behind a far wall of the container. Trayon sat up nervously, but only for a few seconds,

and then Manuel walked quickly out in the open, heading back to the truck. Stepping up into his seat he reached over, wiping the bloody blade of a six-inch cutter across the front of Trayon's shirt. He smiled at his companion.

"It ain't hard to isolate," he said.

They moved north, up onto Highway 70, and east from there, headed towards Virginia, where news reports said there was rioting and unrest at a university. Manuel wanted to see what it would be like to blend into a college community, especially one in the throes of unrest. There should be plenty of work for them there.

If one were to look it would not be hard to find the reason for Manuel's hate. Born to immigrants who drifted up through the Central Valley each summer, Manuel began working the fields by the age of four. His father would issue him a quota each day, not an unattainable one, but one that perhaps required a bit too much labor for a child so young. If the quota was not met Manuel would receive no supper, or would be beaten, or both, and was sent to sleep alone in the back of the family's old Dodge. Sometimes his mama would sneak out to bring him treats, but this was very dangerous for her. On the one occasion that would never escape his mind, she had been beaten so badly that for three days she had to crawl about. Still, whenever she failed to arrive with treats he was saddened. Eventually he became hardened, and too hard for his father to handle. At fourteen, he was turned over to an uncle who lived on a farm up in Sacramento. "He's a very rough thing," his father had said of him. "He needs to be taught." His uncle was a fine teacher, wielding discipline like a weapon. Punishment came in the form of perversion, as he would be stripped down, laid out flat on a table and a broad paddle would work its way up and down his bare legs and buttocks. When sated, the uncle would begin to massage away at the damaged tissue, sinking his fingers deeply into Manuel's flesh. The pain was unbearable, but he never cried out. Finally, just a few days before his sixteenth birthday, he broke. His uncle had accused him of tampering with a radio, a radio Manuel knew he had never touched. So he grabbed the radio from his uncle and began to beat him with

it. It wasn't a weapon one would ordinarily choose for a beating, but in Manuel's hands it became a thing of beauty. The beating went on for a long time. In fact, so long that there was not much left to beat, and the authorities decided he should be sent away to an adult prison for nine years. Now he was out, reformed, and back into the embrace of a society he was promised would welcome him. He had no doubts about that.

Night came as they drove along, and traffic thinned. They turned on the radio, and listened to the soft sounds of jazz. For a long time neither man spoke. The news came on and Manuel listened intently for a time, then pulled to the right, onto the shoulder of the highway where he stopped. "Did you hear that? Did you hear it?"

Trayon sat up. "Hear what?" The inside of his head was still playing music.

"A riot, down in Montgomery." He grinned through the darkness. "A bunch of little black girls just got raped and butchered by some white guys. It's all over the news, baby. They said the governor's mansion is bein' overrun by protesters for shitsake. All hell is about to break loose down there."

Trayon, who had heard none of this, shook his head. "What does that mean?"

"It means hate, my brother. Black on white, my favorite colors. We need to check this shit out."

"Hell yes," said Trayon, catching up to his friend's enthusiasm. "KKKR, Mutherfuckers," he hollered, holding high his still bloody arm.

"KKKR," shouted Manuel. They both began to chant the letters in unison, building in intensity as they waved their arms madly about the cab. Then while they were still screaming, Manuel gunned the truck back up onto the road. After a few miles they saw the signs for Highway 65, which turned them due south, like a dagger, headed straight into the heart of Alabama.

Chapter Thirteen

One day earlier, just hours after his talk with the president, Charlie Benton landed at a private airfield outside Atlanta. It was sometime after midnight, and a car was waiting. Climbing into the back seat he asked the driver, "You know where I'm going?"

"Yes, sir, Riverdale. I should have you there in about forty-five minutes."

Benton leaned back then and relaxed. As was his nature he tried not to think too hard about the task ahead. Since the situation would not be waiting for him, and was instead expected to develop around him, he would simply have to anticipate and adapt. And he was very good at adapting. This was exactly his kind of operation. No deep thinking, no long-term solutions. Just observe, assess, react and report. The military aspects of it were quite appealing. Especially the *react* part. That brought out the part of his personality that made him such a good fit for the president and assignments like this. And they both knew Charlie would do anything for his friend. In his new life, the life he'd led since coming to Washington six years ago to live among the tailored elite, he was struck by the amount of wasted time and wasted motion. Everything required compromise now. And understanding. He longed to be back in the

days of military glory, when you knew exactly what the objective was and where it was to be found. He'd come up with a slogan during his time of war in the desert. He would often shout it out just before entering a combat situation. The president, his squad leader in the marines at the time, would grimace whenever Charlie was about to scream it, but then he would raise his own rifle, and the two would rush to meet whatever fate awaited them. "If it moves, kill it," Charlie would scream. He had no idea the thought was anything but his alone.

Soon the car, a plain, black Ford, pulled off the highway and into the parking lot of a brightly lit Day's Inn. It was almost exactly one a.m. "We're here, sir," said the driver. "It's room 207. Second floor, up those stairs in front of us and three doors to the right." Something about the driver's quick and efficient manner attracted Charlie's attention. He opened the rear door, but before stepping out leaned forward in the seat. "Marine, right?" he asked, already knowing the answer.

"Yes, sir," came the curt response. "I'll be waiting right here."

Room 207 had no *seven*, just the *two*, and a *zero*, and a few scratchy abrasions where the missing numeral should have been. Charlie's mind was alert now, and always at work. It was a nine-to-one shot that mathematically it would be any of the other numbers. But it was a *seven*. The lucky number. The most coveted one. Someone had plucked it from its home as a wall hanger, a token, a lucky charm. At least, those were the odds.

Knocking at the door, he waited, hearing the noise of someone stirring inside. Soon the door opened, just a crack, and the face of an older black man appeared. It was Willie. Charlie stepped back, bowing his head slightly. "I'm sorry," he said, "I'm looking for a Mister Briggs."

Willie studied the man for a brief moment, assessing him. He wasn't as good at doing the math as perhaps Charlie was, but he could find no fault with the man's appearance or demeanor, so he opened the door wider and said, "Please come in." Willie moved to a

side door, inside the room, knocking on it lightly. "You know it's like three in the mornin', right?"

"One, actually," said Charlie, "but, yes, I know it's late and I apologize."

"You're with the government." It was not a question.

"'I am." Charlie smiled sheepishly. "Hopefully that doesn't present a problem for you."

"Not yet," said Willie.

A few minutes later Chester Benton had three rumpled but very attentive people sitting along one side of a double bed. He recognized Olivia and Briggs from their live chat a few hours earlier. The black man he did not know. Sensing he was being scrutinized, Willie pointed to his own chest. "I'm the muscle," he said quite seriously.

Olivia laughed. "Funny stuff." She looked up at Charlie, liking him immediately. She had strong instincts about these things. "I recognize you, from today. You know, it's quite rude busting in on people this way."

"I'm sorry ma'am, but time is of the essence and we really need to talk." Charlie turned slightly, his attention on Briggs. "Mister Briggs, we have very little time to avert what could turn into a major problem for us."

Willie spoke. "By us, you mean you and me?"

Charlie smiled, then grew serious. "We all know what happened is going to have serious racial implications. If it turns out to be whites who did this terrible thing there will be hell to pay. We're very much afraid that when your story hits the news, people, especially those of color, are apt to react aggressively, maybe even violently." He looked at the three warmly. "I know you don't want that to happen. Not if you can help us avoid it."

"Color?" Willie spoke out aggressively. "Mister, you haven't spent a whole helluva lot of time in the south, now have you? Down here people of color are just plain nig..." The old man caught himself, glancing at Olivia. Instead of scolding him, she touched his arm, smiling proudly.

"They're made to feel like niggers," she said. She looked at Charlie. "Have you ever been a nigger, sir?" she asked. Willie stared at her in amazement, but she ignored him.

"No, ma'am," Charlie answered. He liked this girl. "At least not for a long, long time."

There was fire in Olivia's eyes. "Well down here…" She pointed up at him, "That's what you are. You get pushed around for it, you get laughed at for it…" She turned to Willie. "You even get beat for it. Maybe it's time for a little unrest."

Charlie shuffled uncomfortably. He was not, by any means, a diplomat. He tried now to put his mind into the mind of his best friend, the president, and channel or feel what it would take to communicate here. Pulling up a side chair, he sat, eye level with the three others. "I get it, I really do." He had an idea. "Listen, when things go bad in situations like this they can get way, way out of hand. I'm talking about Mister Briggs here potentially having more bodies slapped down on his table than he could ever possibly examine. And we're talking color-blind. Death doesn't really care who it grabs onto, and we could have more dead bodies, both black and white, than we've ever seen."

"Shock and awe," said Willie. Everyone looked at him, but he had nothing to add.

"I'm not sure you're being entirely fair." It was Briggs who spoke. "All I really did was get the hell kicked out of me for trying to do my job." He pointed at his daughter. "We've been threatened by the governor, threatened by the sheriff, I've had evidence stolen right out of my hand. I don't know what you're going to ask, but my life, my daughter's life and the life of our friend here have pretty much been turned upside down lately. And your racial implications seem to be slapping us in the face every time we turn around." Briggs' face saddened. "We're not even sure we have a life anymore."

Charlie adjusted his chair, pulling it in closer. "Look," he said. "Think for a minute. I'm the chief advisor for the President of the United States. I am without question one of the most trusted people in his life. That's not bragging, it's just a fact. And with the whole

world blowing up out there, he sends me here, to you." Leaning back, he folded his hands onto his lap. "He thinks, the president thinks, this could be our own personal Armageddon. He hasn't said it to me, but I know he's thinking it. Every country in history has its moment of downfall. Its moment of demise. And it almost always starts from within, with a spark, a moment of hate. And this might be the biggest moment of hate we've ever seen." Charlie rose then, pulling his chair back into its original place. He stood tall, turning again to address the three. "I don't want to go all apocalyptic on you, but if you remember, just a year ago one little black boy in the Bronx was hung from a lamppost outside his school. They still haven't found out who was responsible. But that didn't matter to the almost one million blacks in Harlem and the Bronx who nearly torched the damn city to the ground. They still haven't recovered from it. And that was one little black boy with unknown assailants. And now, right here in the south, with a minority population base that rivals the whites, we've got twelve beautiful little black Christian girls who have had heinous atrocities committed against them. Twelve of them. You throw a couple of white men into the pit and we're in for hell on earth."

No one spoke for a long minute. Then Briggs said, "What is it you want?"

"We need to go back there, all of us." He looked at Briggs. "You need to conduct business as usual. Soon everyone will know that you are the one who exposed this whole affair. In a day or two it will be splashed all across America. People will expect you to run, to hide, but you won't. You'll be at the exact site of the incident, a white man with no agenda who stood up against the entire white proletariat. No black man, woman or child will want harm to come your way. In fact, we think you will have a mass of black defenders at your disposal. You will be as the golden child, at the epicenter, and if we can keep the violence away from there, we can quite possibly contain it altogether."

Briggs shook his head. "Are you saying because they won't wish me harm they'll just go away? I don't get it."

"If they won't harm you, they almost certainly won't harm your town. Not if that's what you ask of them. And if we can keep the peace in Harbor Springs, we may be able to remove the eye from the hurricane altogether."

"I get it." It was Olivia who spoke. "Dad, if Mister Benton is right they'll give us a free pass. Like lamb's blood over the door."

Willie spoke next. "What about the whites? They ain't gonna be so happy."

Chester Benton smiled. He walked the two steps to where the three sat on the bed. Dropping to his knees in front of them, he much resembled a man at prayer. "That's what I'm here for. I'll protect you. Whatever they bring, I'll protect you."

"Protect us?" said Willie. "Man, you haven't seen hate. And they don't send just one."

Olivia stood then, and being the tallest person in the room she smiled smugly. "He'll do it." She tapped Charlie on the shoulder, as if knighting him. "I believe him," she said. "He'll do it."

Chapter Fourteen

A little after five that same morning, Chester Benton, Willie Scarlett, Shawn Briggs and Olivia arrived by helicopter back near Harbor Springs, Alabama, setting down in the open yard adjoining Willie Scarlett's home. It was the safest, most private and closest to town location they could think of, and ten minutes later they piled into Willie's pickup and headed for the mortuary. Willie drove, with Olivia and Briggs beside him, while Benton, at his own insistence, bundled himself up on some old burlap and rode into town in the bed of the truck. It was still dark when they arrived. Briggs had been away from the mortuary for two full days, so they hoped the coroner's absence had not yet sent off an alarm. A large manila envelope was taped to the door when they arrived.

"More money," said Olivia, not unhappily. She grabbed the envelope before anyone else could, but then sighed in disappointment at its contents. "It's from Merton, Dad, the ambulance guy. He says there's one in the cooler, an eighty-three year old man from over in Jack's Town. Says *died in sleep* on the ticket, and he wants you to call him when you get a chance." All emergency personnel in the county had keys to the lower lockers,

or knew where Briggs kept a hidden copy, so it was not unusual for bodies to be dropped off if Briggs was away.

"Good," he said, looking at Charlie. "Looks like I wasn't missed. I wonder if our friend the sheriff paid us a visit in the last day or so. It's been a week since his imaginary bus crash. Maybe he's calmed himself down by now."

They rested then, the four of them, Willie and Charlie taking over Olivia's room, with Olivia moving into the small, spare room just off the kitchen. It was decided, for health reasons, the old man would move temporarily from the farm to the Briggs' house in town. Sometime later, around noon, Willie announced that he was driving home to gather up a few things, do some watering and check up on his chickens.

"I'll go," said Charlie. "Maybe you can show me around a bit. I'd like to see how things work down here, where everything is."

"I'll go," said Olivia. The three looked at Briggs, who shook his head.

"I've got work to do." He looked at Olivia, then Charlie. "You'll be careful."

"We'll be careful." As they began the drive out to the farm, Willie detoured slightly, taking a right bend instead of a left one, to show Charlie the town. Harbor Springs, like most small towns in the south, consisted of one street, Main Street, lined on both sides by a number of shops, stores and restaurants. There was a bank at one end of town, a drug store at the other, and then, as they swung around to meet the highway again, they passed a series of school yards and buildings, an elementary school and a high school tucked in closely together.

"Is this where you go to school?" Charlie asked Olivia.

"No." Olivia paused, and bit down on her lip. "I don't really get along all that well with other kids. I'm kind of different. I'm home-schooled."

"Who teaches you then, your dad?"

"Mostly. Or I just teach myself."

"Yourself? How can you teach yourself?"

Olivia thought for a moment. "I just do. Ask me something."

"What, like a school question?"

"Any question."

Charlie smiled. He liked games. "Okay, what's the capital of South Dakota?"

"Please," said Olivia condescendingly. "Pierre. Named after a fur trader, Pierre Cadet Chouteau, who, interestingly enough, didn't even live there. He lived at a fort on the other side of the Missouri River. He dealt in beaver pelts until there were no more beavers, then switched to buffalo hides, until, you guessed it, there were no more buffalo. It's great to be flexible."

"I did not know that," said Charlie, impressed and amused. "That's very impressive."

"Got anything else? Push me a little."

"Okay, okay." He thought for a moment, then brightened. "What are the four forces?"

"Really, that's all you've got? Do you know them? I mean really know them, and how they function in the universe?" Charlie bit down on his lip, not quite understanding how the question had been thrown back at him and not sure he could function in a world that required more than just simple memorization.

Olivia saved him. "Did you know there's also a fifth force, anti-gravity, which may be the antithesis of the other four? It may even be more powerful than all the others combined. In fact, if string theory can be proven…"

"Wait, wait, I surrender. Maybe the school system is not all it's cracked up to be."

"Anyone got a question about cranberries?" Willie stammered out and the three laughed together. Soon they arrived at the levee, Willie swinging off the highway and onto his own road. As they approached the farmhouse they noticed a truck in the driveway, green with white stripes. "The Cedar Creek boys," Willie's voice lowered to a whisper. "We should go."

"Are those the guys you were telling me about? The ones who beat you?"

Willie looked down. "That's two of them. Let's just go."

"No, it's okay," said Charlie. "Just pull over for a minute." Willie brought the pickup to a stop at the entrance to the drive, some distance from the main house. "Please wait here," said Charlie as he swung open his door and stepped out. As he walked across the yard Charlie began an assessment. He might not have the best working knowledge of the universe, or the forces that ruled it, but the one thing he understood above all others was men. He could sense weakness in a movement, see it in the eyes. Subtle changes that showed themselves, like tells to a poker player, always came over an adversary just before confrontation. There were two men standing near the truck, one large, larger even than Charlie, who was not small, and the other of medium build, but who stood more upright, more confidently than his companion.

Charlie raised his hand and smiled warmly. "Hi," he said. "Can I help you boys?"

The smaller of the two, the confident one, stepped forward. "Boys? Just who in the hell are you?"

Charlie moved up quite close before pausing, perhaps six or seven feet from the two. "I'm Willie's nephew, down from Saint Louis. I'm wondering what you're doing here."

The bigger man moved up alongside his companion. "It's really none of your business, now is it?"

"Oh," said Charlie, still not unfriendly. "I'm sorry. I thought maybe because he's my uncle and this is his place that it was my business. I mean, he's sitting right there in the truck."

Charlie turned, waving at Willie and Olivia who sat nervously in the pickup. "Hi, Uncle Willie," he called out. Then he turned back. "See, told you he's my uncle. I call him uncle and everything. You just saw me. Now I need you to tell me what you want."

"What?" said the smaller man. "Are you nuts? We don't have to tell you a damn thing." He stepped aggressively forward. Suddenly and without warning he reached out and slapped Charlie hard across the face. Charlie didn't need a warning. He knew the slap was coming before the slapper did, and he just stood there and let it happen.

"Wow," said Charlie, as the hand stung its way across his cheek. "You guys must be part of the Triple-K Gang. We hear lots of good stuff about you up north. I'm told you just love to beat up on black folks who get in your way." He studied the two men intently. "Yeah, I can see it now. I can definitely see the similarities. Low foreheads, limited brain space. All that inbreeding has made you both a little stupid."

"What the hell?" The smaller man swung then, this time with a closed fist. That's what Charlie was waiting for. An open hand is harder to grab hold of, having less compacted mass. Plus, it's generally coming in from the side. It's easier to block, but not to grab. But a closed fist comes at you all giftwrapped, like a tennis ball or a gearshift knob. And you can just reach right out and grab it, which is exactly what Charlie did. In less than the time of a breath he snapped the hand backwards and up, like shifting from second into third. He both felt and heard the wrist bone crack. The man screamed, falling to his knees, completely restrained. Charlie calmly walked him over to the green pickup, maintaining his grip, escorting the now sobbing man who scrambled along beside him, still on his knees. The big man jumped back when Charlie thought he might jump forward. He ran to the rear of the truck, reaching into the bed and extracting a three foot chunk of two-by-four. Charlie swung open the passenger door of the truck and, reaching down his free hand, grabbed the back of the smaller man's jeans, lifted him and threw him into the cab. Then he closed the door, brushed his hands against his pants and turned to face the big man.

"Excuse me," he said, eying the board. "Is that for me?"

The big man swung the two-by-four then, aiming at Charlie's head. If Charlie moved at all it was very little. He'd learned a long time ago not to waste any energy he might soon need. The board swished past his head, slamming into the window of the door he had just closed. The glass exploded inward into thousands of crystal pieces, coating the man lying inside in a shower of broken glass. "Uh, oh," said Charlie. "Your boss is so not gonna like that." He moved in then, while the man was still off balance, swinging his

foot up hard into the man's groin. There was a distinct *thump* as the foot sunk in, almost the same sound a football makes when booted. The man gasped, stood there for a moment and silently sunk to the ground. Charlie walked up to the man and knelt beside him. He placed a friendly hand on his shoulder. "Look," he said, "when you leave could you please drive out slowly? My uncle doesn't like a lot of dust."

Throughout the entire incident Olivia and Willie, sitting attentively in the pickup, had not said a word. They both sat, eyes wide and growing wider, staring out the window as if they were watching a movie of a lion on the hunt. Finally they both turned to look at each other.

"That's what I'm talkin' about," said Willie.

"Shit, yeah," said Olivia.

Chapter Fifteen

Early on the morning of the next day President Clarkson received a pre-dawn call from Sheryl Fenn of *The Herald* in Atlanta, informing him that preliminary tests had just come in on their accelerated DNA request. The suspect, Vern Evans, friend of Toby Parrish, had come up as a positive match to semen samples found on the Courtier girl. The president tried to stall then, asking them to wait until results on Parrish could also be obtained, but *The Herald* felt they had all they needed. At six o'clock eastern time, the Atlanta area would know the whole shocking truth, or at least *The Herald's* interpretation of it, and by seven the entire country would know. One of the first people Clarkson contacted was his friend, Chester Benton.

Charlie was sitting out on the couch, chatting with Olivia — who never seemed to sleep— as the first rays of dawn moved in over the eastern sky. He rose as the phone began to beep, signaled an apology to Olivia and walked out onto the screened privacy porch adjoining the residence.

"It's starting," said the president, his voice bland and distant.

"Now?" was all Charlie asked.

"Yes. Right now. Turn on CBN. In about five minutes you'll know exactly what I know."

"You're the man," said Charlie.

"You're the man," said the president.

Within a few moments Charlie had gathered up Briggs and Willie, both a bit scruffy and half asleep, and joined Olivia on the couch. The four bundled up there together, while Olivia turned on the news. The screen flashed to life, and there was Brad Norton of the morning show, sitting at a desk, a blood-red map of Alabama at his back.

"So," said the newsman, shuffling a stack of papers but not looking at them. "I've just been informed we'll be hearing from the president momentarily. Right now, though, let's recap what we've learned so far. The *Atlanta Daily Herald* claims to have irrefutable evidence that the tragic bus accident which killed fourteen, including twelve young African American girls down in Alabama ten days ago, was no accident at all, but rather a scene staged to cover up a horrific murder. Samantha King has more." The camera then focused in on the giant map and a much too pretty female reporter with a pointer in her hand.

"Thanks, Brad," she said. "This is one of, if not the most horrific of stories we've ever had to report on. In fact, in about an hour this reporter will be on a plane to Montgomery to join our crew already in place there. At the capital. According to reliable sources at *The Herald*, DNA analysis indicates that at least one of the girls on that bus, Elizabeth Courtier, the girl not immediately found at the scene, in fact spent several agonizing days being raped and tortured before she, too, was killed and dumped in a swamp a few miles from the crash site. At least two of the other victims were shot to death as a cover-up began which appears to reach all the way to the governor's mansion. No comment has been made available to us at this time, but we're working hard to get a definitive response from Governor Perry or members of his staff." The reporter then turned to the map, using her pointer. "This is Harbor Springs, a little township in Colby County, way down in southern Alabama. You may remember

this was a church bus, filled with young teenage girls on their way to prayer camp. It was first assumed the driver may have fallen asleep at the wheel, causing the crash, but that now appears not to be the case. In fact, the DNA analysis I spoke of has already been linked to a suspect out of Harbor Springs who is believed to have taken the Courtier girl hostage at some point prior to the murders. We're not sure exactly how the governor is linked to this, but we will let our viewers know as soon as we find out something more substantive."

Charlie Benton, still holding on tightly to his phone, put it down on a side table, rose and turned to face the others. "Let's talk," he said, as Olivia muted the television. "There's still a bit of time." He looked down intently, first at Willie and the girl, before finally locking eyes with Shawn Briggs. "Normally, a thing like this takes a day or two before we can gauge its impact." His voice rose in intensity as he spoke, the words gaining momentum. "But I want to make it very clear. There will be a response. A strong one. Right now, it's as if we're all sitting on a beach in California and the radio has just informed us of an earthquake in the Hawaiian Islands. We know a tidal wave is coming. We just don't yet know its size or intensity. But we know it is coming. Under ordinary circumstances the wise thing to do would simply be evacuate the beach. Well, that doesn't work for us. We're like damage control, and we're all there is." Charlie paused thoughtfully, and continued to stare at Briggs. "But I've been thinking about something, ever since we met. Mister Briggs, we need you. Badly. There's a possibility you may be the only voice of reason in a world that's about to go insane." He then shifted his gaze to Willie and Olivia. "But you two don't have to be here. Shouldn't be here, in fact. I can have a copter here in an hour and have you whisked away to wherever you'd like to go. And I'll arrange everything. Please."

Olivia, ignoring Charlie, looked instead to her father. "No way. We're a team. We've always been a team. Always. No way."

At the same time, Willie shuddered slightly, and asked Charlie, "What's the worst that can happen? You've seen it. You've been there

before. What's the god awfullest thing that can happen to us? Say it straight."

"Okay." Charlie moved to a window some distance away. Pulling back a curtain, he gazed out onto the street. "I think there will be massive protests, probably some of the biggest this country has ever seen. Because we're so isolated from any large population base down here we may get lucky. The brunt of the problem will probably take place up in Montgomery, the capital. Especially since the governor is involved. People don't like it when their own government conspires against them. It really pisses them off. So most of what's going to happen may erupt somewhat to the north. But trust me on this. The scene of any incident always becomes very important. Like a rallying point, around which hatred can grow like a life force, rolling over everything in its path."

Scratching his head, Willie waved a hand through the air. "I don't have even the damndest idea what you just said. Except the rollin' over part. What I'm askin' is if there's some kind of chance I can die here. Or come to great bodily harm. I wouldn't like that much."

Olivia moved closer to Willie, putting both her arms around him. She hugged him mightily. "No, Willie. We won't let that happen." She looked at her father, daring him to speak. "And Mister Benton is going to take good care of us. He promised." She stared up at Charlie, whose face hardened.

"And I will," he said. "But it would make my job a whole lot easier if you weren't here for me to protect."

Willie spoke again, his voice brightening somewhat. "But if there is trouble down here, it's gonna be brothers who brings it, right? I mean, isn't that what this is all about?"

"Yes, Willie," Charlie smiled weakly. "It will be brothers. The problem is there might be more of them than we can handle. And they may not be in the best of moods."

"Well, hell," Willie said. "If it's just brothers, like you're sayin', that might not be so bad. I figure I'll be fittin' right in. And maybe I can talk 'em into havin' a picnic out at Cedar Creek. Tom Clayton

would probably love the shit outta me showin' up at supper time with a hundred more like me." He smiled at Olivia, nodding his head, as if seeking her approval. She kissed him on the cheek.

"That's right," she said. "It will be lovely."

Chapter Sixteen

Samantha King sat uncomfortably in the plush armchair in her boss's office. "You've been wanting something like this," said her boss, Carl Lyons. "Ever since you came to this network you've been grousing about getting yourself out from under the green screen and hitting the field where you can make a real contribution." Grinning callously, he leaned forward onto his desk. "This could be a very promising opportunity. You know, if you play your cards right."

"I'm not sleeping with you, Carl." Samantha also leaned forward, a challenge in her eyes. "Get over yourself. I deserve this. I've been sweating under the lights downstairs for three years now. I've accomplished about all I can with a stick and a screen. And you've been promising me and promising me. Let me do this."

"I've never asked you to sleep with me," said Carl, pouting. "That would be... unprofessional. I've just suggested we get to know each other on a more social level. What the hell's wrong with that?"

Samantha's eyes flashed. "What's wrong is what you consider *social* goes way beyond the boundaries. You know damn well I do a good job here. A great job. And I've put up with your bullshit

because, frankly, you do a damn good job too, when you're not hitting on me. Now let's make this happen. Give me a chance."

Carl rose from his desk. He moved around to where Samantha sat, putting a hand on her shoulder. "Oh, god," she said.

"Alright," he replied, letting his fingers dig in slightly. "Do it. Go down to the stock room and grab Eddie. He's a little green, but his camera work isn't bad. And he's big enough to provide a little brawn if you guys get into trouble."

"Really?" Samantha reached up, removing the hand. Then she stood. "I'll do a good job on this."

"It'll be your ass if you don't." Carl studied her for a moment as they stood face to face. "We've got a shitload of equipment and eight of our people down in Montgomery now, and I'm thinking just about every news organization in the country will be well represented, so it's liable to be a madhouse. Just choose an angle and focus on it. I trust your judgement. But watch your back. A lot of people will get hurt if things get out of hand. Usually the media is exempt, but not always."

Biting her lip, she asked him, "So we both know there will be a thousand other news reps on site, including ours. Why don't we consider sending me south, you know, to Harbor Springs, where this all originated? That could be the story. The real story."

"Not yet. If Governor Perry is involved as they say, the head-hunters will be coming for him. And that's at the capital. We don't want to be caught down in the sticks if all hell breaks loose up north." He scolded her. "Just do your job, King."

"Yes, sir."

He reached for her. "So do I at least get a hug?"

"Yeah," she said with a grin as she dodged her way out the door. "I'll send Eddie up."

Less than ninety minutes later a driver pulled up in front of her flat on East Seventy-Ninth street in New York's Upper East Side, and, with a small valise clutched tightly in her hand, Samantha piled in beside Eddie Hatten, her cameraman. The driver sped off then, headed for Kennedy airport.

"This is gonna be great, Miss King," he said to her. He was a young man, and something of a giant. He reminded her of a huge teddy bear. A soft one. "I watch you all the time. I'm a big fan."

"That's nice," she said as she looked him over. "Are you any good with that stuff?" She pointed at several large camera bags, clustered on his lap.

"Yes, ma'am. I can make these babies sing. Oh, and our tickets are waiting for us at the Eastern desk. We fly out in about an hour."

"There's been a change about that, Eddie." She looked earnestly over at him. "Sort of a last minute thing. We're not going to Montgomery. Mister Lyons felt we've got plenty of help down there already. We're headed to Tallahassee. We'll rent a car there and drive over to Harbor Springs, the site of the crash. He felt there might be a better story waiting for us there."

"Yes ma'am," said Eddie. "You find the story, and I'll get you the best film you've ever seen."

Chapter Seventeen

Manuel Ortiz and Trayon Palmer entered Alabama from the north, less than twelve hours after news of the cover-up splashed out over the radio. For Palmer, the journey was more an adventure than anything else. In Manuel Ortiz he had found someone he could idolize, emulate, a protector unlike anyone he had ever known. The fact that Ortiz appeared bent on the destruction of the human race seemed to him not all that unusual, and while Trayon had no particular desire to kill, neither did the thought bother him much. Willingly, he would do whatever the Mexican asked of him. He was the perfect worshiper, Ortiz the perfect oracle.

For Manuel, the reasons for his quest were much darker. And it had very little to do with the abuses by his father, or the eventual bludgeoning to death of his uncle. Those were wounds, to be sure, leaving his mind raw and jagged, but there were other, even darker denizens hiding deep inside. Folsom Prison had not been the best of experiences for a boy of sixteen. In fact, it was extremely rare to send one as young as he to such a place. But because of his crime, and what they deemed his incorrigible nature, send him they did. His second day there became his indoctrination day. The prison system in general, and Folsom in particular, is a seething ground of groups

and gangs who lean heavily upon their members for survival. And Manuel, being a Mexican, and being alone, was immediately sought out by the Del Nortes, one of the most feared gangs in the prison. Actually, it was not the entire gang who sought him, but rather their leader, a man known as El Lobo, *the wolf.* He found the young man intriguing, and quite attractive. Unscarred and unblemished, a flower to be plucked for his own personal use. So he had the young man brought to him, first on the yard for an introduction, and then later to his cell for a more meaningful meeting.

"You're my bitch," he told Manuel. "You'll serve me and do everything I say." El Lobo had laughed then, rich and deep. "If you do, your time here will be pleasant and you will learn many things. If you don't..." he pointed to a group of his followers leering through the cell door. "You will serve them." He had reached out, stroking the boy's hair.

Manuel had cried then, sobbing just a little, pressing himself up against one wall of the cell. He said nothing. Then El Lobo motioned the others to leave and Manuel's membership in the Del Nortes began. For the first year or so he belonged exclusively to El Lobo, whose appetites ran deeply into perversion. He also served as an errand boy to his *patron*, fetching cigarettes or money or drugs, or delivering messages among the various factions of the gang. Eventually El Lobo tired of him, passing him along to his second in command, who, after a few months, passed him along further. At some point his sexuality became a dormant thing. He knew he was not a homosexual, as each attack left him with a sick feeling of discomfort and disgust. But he also felt no desire toward members of the opposite sex, seeing the naked bodies of women, whose photos were smuggled in, as unattractive paramours of human flesh. That's when he began to hate, sensing there would be no place in the world for him, and nowhere he could turn for acceptance, or safe haven. By the age of nineteen his body began to develop, from long hours in the yard, whenever he could find time to himself, pumping iron and fanning the flames of his hate.

Since all inmates are required to work, he was appointed a job in

the prison's woodworking shop. There he found a certain amount of solace, even taking pride in the fine pieces of furniture he would turn out. He developed a love of tools, which came alive in his hands, saws and chisels and fine planes. For the first time in his life he found something over which he had control. Whatever he asked of the tools they would do for him, and his skill grew. One day his chisel required sharpening, so he checked out a rasp, a rat-tailed one, which appeared much like a well-muscled icepick, with a long pointed end and a steel shaft that grew conically larger, like a lance, as it neared the handle. The rasp had a series of teeth imbedded into its sides, like tiny shark's teeth. And being forged from a carbon steel that is much harder than regular tool grade steel, the instrument could whittle away at a dulled chisel or saw until it shined like new. As he sat there, grating the rasp back and forth against the sides of the chisel, a heavily tattooed white inmate came into the shop. He looked around as Manuel watched him curiously.

"You all by yourself, Mex?" he sneered. Manuel tensed. This was a big man, who seemed to be on a mission.

"I am. What do you want?" Manuel, by this time, was no little man himself, but a lifetime of subservience and abuse had dealt him a hand of very little courage.

"You're El Lobo's boy," the man said.

"I am nobody's boy," answered Manuel, looking past the big man to the door, hoping someone would be passing by.

"Your daddy owes me money. Owes us money. Lots of it." Ortiz recognized the man as a member of Aryan Nation, another of the most feared gangs in Folsom. Ordinarily the Aryans and the Del Nortes would have little to do with one another, but there were times when one acquired something the other wanted, and a trade for money or goods could be worked out.

"I know nothing of that," said Manuel, now shaking badly. "Why don't you go talk to El Lobo?"

"Fuck you," said the man. "I'm talkin' to you." The man lunged at him suddenly, but tripped over a strip of wood lying on the floor. As he stumbled past, Manuel, more from reflex than anything else,

swung up hard with the rasp. He spun around, catching the man from behind, the tool striking at the base of his head. The thrust had been an upward one, and by good fortune or bad, the rasp bit into the man's upper neck, slid into the soft cavity of flesh there and sliced its way through the brain stem and into the lower portion of the brain. Manuel had found perhaps the most vulnerable place on the human body, a place where, with minimal effort —if one could entice an enemy to turn his back— havoc could be wrought directly on the nervous system. The man stumbled to his knees, his hand reaching to the back of his head where he felt the tool, still imbedded there. He mumbled something incoherent, then slumped to the floor, quite dead.

Manuel had been suspected in the death, but it was never proven, and a few years later, upon his release, one of the first things he did was burglarize a hardware store, cleaning off a whole rack of the long, pointed rasps. Now as they drove, he considered the possibilities and the questions brought about by them. How could he come into close enough quarters to employ his deadly arsenal? How could he entice someone to turn his back, exposing the rear of the head and opening up a pathway to the brain? And if there were others about, how could he slip away, escape without detection?

They arrived in Birmingham, a city north of the capital, driving slowly down one of the main streets off the highway. Already the unrest had begun there. Hundreds of people pushed their way along, marching like an army of ants to an uncertain destination. It became obvious the destination was uncertain when they ran into another group, coming in the opposite direction. The two groups merged, chanting and screaming, some of them holding aloft signs proclaiming the importance of black lives and their hatred of the government. Almost all of the marchers were black, but here and there stood a smattering of whites or Mexicans or others with a sympathetic view. At this point they seemed to get along well together, the different races, and Manuel smiled cruelly. Incite them, he thought. Incite them and they will be at each other's throats. His mind began to formulate a plan. Kill anything with black on it and

whites would be blamed. If he did it skillfully enough there would rise a thousand like him, compliant assassins who would continue the carnage, and a black-white war would ensue.

He turned to Trayon. "I'm gonna stop here for a while. There are lessons to be learned."

"What will we do?"

"We?" Ortiz waved his hand idly. "*We* will do nothing. You will sit and wait while I explore. I need to find a weakness, and I need to do it alone. I won't be long."

Parking on a side street, Manuel exited the car and casually moved away, leaving Trayon to wonder. Tucked in behind his belt was an eight inch rasp, honed to razor sharpness. He found the bulk of the crowd a few blocks away, and worked his way into the midst of it. Bodies pressed against bodies, swaying in undulating rhythm. He moved when they moved, swayed when they swayed, blending in like a mantis, mimicking its surroundings as it waited for prey. As he studied, watching the mass swirl around him, the answer came. Carefully drawing the rasp from his belt he began to move up close against the backs of those nearest him. Their necks were completely exposed. A group of protestors pressed in close and he found himself sandwiched tightly in between two men. Bringing the rasp up carefully, he glanced around. Frenzied eyes were everywhere, but not one focused on him. He touched the tip of the lance to the neck of the man in front of him. He could feel the blade slip into the fleshy cavity. The man flinched, turning his head slightly as if an irritant was at his back. Manuel smiled. One quick thrust and the man would fall, flopping to the ground while the crowd milled right over the top of him. And Ortiz could slip off to the side, lose himself in the mob and strike again, and again. He eased his hand down then, withdrawing the tool and tucking it back into his waistband. There weren't enough people here, he thought. It was a good crowd, but not nearly enough to offer the security he needed. A few kills and he might be found out. He needed a raging, maddening mob of thousands. He needed the capital, Montgomery, where it had been reported the governor was under siege and hordes of protestors could be found. There he could kill to his heart's content.

Chapter Eighteen

A grey sedan pulled up and parked on the street just below the mortuary. It stopped in front of the door to the coroner's office, directly in the middle of a red zone reserved for ambulance or emergency personnel. Olivia watched from the screen porch above as a very attractive lady with long, slender legs, and a skirt cut short enough to reveal them, exited the driver's side. A large man sat in the passenger seat, but stayed seated there while the lady made her way up the walk to the side door. "Dad," she hollered out. "Check the door. I think someone just sent you a present from *Hookers Anonymous.*"

"What?" Briggs walked from the kitchen, wiping his hands on a towel. "Olivia, what?"

She replied, "Get the door," at exactly the same time the doorbell rang.

When Briggs opened the door, his mouth silently formed the word, "*Wow*," and the lady smiled.

"I'm Samantha King from CBN." She extended her hand. "Are you Shawn Briggs?"

Olivia arrived then, standing alongside her partially paralyzed father. "He is," she said. Then she brightened. "I recognize you. I

saw your report last week, proclaiming that all Americans, in a spirit of enlightenment, I guess, should arm themselves with guns in case terrorists come crashing into their homes. Smart choice. It's nice to know you can shoot someone anytime you need to. Great lesson for the kids."

"Ollie," Briggs stammered, glaring at his daughter. "I'm sorry for that," he said, recovering enough of himself to speak. "My daughter is rather opinionated, and seems to have misplaced her Prozac. I am Shawn Briggs. What can I do for you?"

Samantha King smiled then, first at Briggs, then at Olivia. "It's okay. They pay me to stand there and report the news. That doesn't always mean it's what I think." She turned back to Briggs. "I'm here to do a story. You sent out a very positive message to the American people when you stood up against the establishment like you did. It was quite brave. And it can't have been easy, flying in the face of some very powerful people who wanted to hush you up." She paused. "We've been sort of reading between the lines and wondering how you're holding up. And if there's been any backlash from the governor or anyone else. Especially with you being an employee of the state. My understanding is he's very close to being indicted."

"Oh," said Briggs. "I did not know that."

"He's a pig," said Olivia. They invited her inside then, Briggs and Samantha moving to a couch in the living room, Olivia going over to the window overlooking the street. "You know, there's a guy sitting in your car in the heat," she said.

"That's Eddie, my cameraman. He'll be okay."

Olivia moved across the room to the door. "I'm going to get him," she said.

Samantha King had been picking away at an idea. It had been brewing since she landed in Tallahassee. One she hoped would make her a household name. Turn Shawn Briggs into a national hero. Her hero, her creation. Let Montgomery to the north explode in a shower of racial sparks. That's what everyone expected would happen, and what those in the media desperately wanted. They circled the capital

like mad wolves waiting for a wounded deer to die so they could feast. She would wait right here and if Harbor Springs also exploded she would be in the perfect position to exploit whatever conflict arose. In the meantime she would work on her hero, dressing him up for public display. She looked at Briggs, studied him. He was not a big man. He was fortyish, bookish, rather drab looking, about as average as a man could be. But that could work to her advantage. Just a simple everyman who, due to circumstances, was able to rise up in defiance of wrong and defend the principles of right. She trembled at the thought of introducing him to her world, already hearing herself in primetime, "Samantha King reporting."

"I wonder, Mister Briggs," she asked, "if you could tell me what it feels like? I mean, according to *The Herald* you faced down a sheriff, and then the governor. You've been threatened and beaten. I've read the reports and listened many times to the recording of Governor Perry. It must have been harrowing. What could have possibly made you want to go through all that?"

Briggs smiled. "My daughter. You haven't seen her in a very good light so far, but she has a better grasp on right and wrong than anyone I've ever known."

"You must be proud. It also reflects quite highly on you, don't you think?"

"No," he laughed aloud. "I have no idea where she gets it from. Maybe her mom. She was also a very strong woman. All I know is if Olivia says something is wrong and we need to do something about it, well, there aren't really a lot of alternatives. I'd love to take credit, but the fact is I just about begged her to allow me to keep my mouth shut on this. She can be a most persuasive young lady."

"You mention her mother. In the past tense. Is she gone, or deceased?"

"She died a few years back. It was hard on Olivia, on both of us. But she is filled with an inner strength you wouldn't believe. She also has the mental capabilities to cope with just about anything. Sometimes I just lean on her."

Samantha cleared her throat. "But ultimately it's been your

decision making that put you here. For all of this. I think a lot of people out there are going to relate to that."

Just then the inside door leading down to the coroner's lab and the ice lockers opened, with Willie and Charlie stepping into the room. "That's some sick shit," said Willie. "A body shouldn't be all cut up like that."

"Oh, hello," said Charlie, seeing the two on the couch. "We were just out exploring."

Briggs stood. "This is Miss King..."

"From CBN," said Charlie, not using his friendliest tone. Briggs looked first at Samantha, then at Charlie.

"You two know each other?"

"We've met. And I've had the pleasure of being torn to bits by Miss King over the years. Both myself and the president. She takes great pride in referring to me as his sidekick, and referring to us as a comedy team. She has the sharpest talons in the business."

Samantha King's eyes closed slightly, and her voice, when she spoke, was melodic. "Hello Mister Benton, so good to see you again. You know it's never been personal. I have a job to do, just like you. Doesn't mean I believe everything I say."

"That's just about exactly what she said to me." Olivia walked into the room, followed by a large man. "This is Eddie," she said, nodding to the man and pointing at the couch. "She left him outside to fry."

Charlie laughed quietly. "I know the feeling."

Samantha King rose then. "Look, I've come in the spirit of good will. I have no agenda other than to report the news and maybe make a difference in the way people see things down here, but I can see I'm not going to get much accomplished in the present atmosphere. Animosity, by the way, only works if it's growing from a reliable resource." She looked warmly at Olivia. "We're okay, yes?" she asked.

"I'll get back to you on that."

"Mister Briggs." Miss King turned to the coroner. "I'm staying at the Harbor Glen, just down the street. I'd like very much to continue

our discussion if you would be so kind as to make some time for me."
Placing a hand on his arm, she looked deeply into his eyes. "Maybe
we could chat privately. I think we have a great story to tell here. An
important story that might just fill America with new hope. I'd love
us to tell it together. We could be a great team." Smiling at each of
the others in the room, she signaled to Eddie, who followed her out
the door.

"Oh, my god. Bitch city," Olivia scowled. Briggs looked at his
daughter, again not too happily, but Charlie raised his hand and high-
fived the girl as he walked to the window to watch the reporter's car
drive away.

He watched intently for several moments, and then said, "You
all better come see this."

Puzzled, the three moved over to join him at the window. Down
the street, and coming towards them very slowly, drove a work bus. A
converted school bus used mostly to transport farm workers among
the various plantations. Every window along its visible side had at
least one pair of arms waving madly about. It added up to a lot
of arms. Behind the bus came a truck, its bed loaded with young
black men, also waving their arms about. Behind that was one more
truck, then a long caravan of cars, each tucked in close to the one
in front of it, as if they were connected and being pulled along by
an invisible chain. The sedan driven by Samantha King was stopped
at an intersection a block or so away, waiting for the caravan to pass.
The third truck in line stopped suddenly, right in front of it. Three
black men jumped from its bed, racing over to the sedan. One leapt
up on the hood of the car and began pounding on the windshield
with closed fists. The other two ran crazily around the car in a tight
circle. The horn on the truck sounded, then sounded again. The men
appeared to be laughing as they ran back, hopping up onto the truck
as it moved off to follow the others.

"It's starting," said Charlie.

Willie responded. "Hell, that's just some guys lettin' off a little
steam. Probably from one of the plantations to the south."

"You recognize any of them? Or the trucks?"

"Well, no. But I seen trucks full of guys before. Lots of times."

"You notice the plates? Georgia. Kind of strange that a shitload of guys from Georgia would drive all the way over here just to let off a little steam. No, it's starting. They're going to come like locusts now. And they're not even from here. If out-of-staters start pouring in it will cause problems even beyond what we're already expecting from the locals. Way beyond."

Briggs spoke. "Well, maybe they're just passing through. I mean, we don't even know what they want or where they're going. They could be headed for Montgomery, where all the trouble is."

"Nobody on their way from Georgia to the capital is going to choose this highway to get them there. There are several superior alternatives, all to the north." Charlie shook his head, "No, they're here for us, you can bet on it. Our little town is about to start jumping."

"But what makes you think they won't be peaceful? Not everybody's on a mission to beat somebody up."

Charlie looked at Briggs incredulously. "Were you not just watching? You think what you just saw was a onetime thing, just some good ole' boys having fun? It wasn't. Those boys are looking for a place to play. And I think they've just found it."

Over the next several hours the four sat out on the screen porch observing the roadway below. Dozens of trucks, buses and cars continued to stream into town. Some carried banners, one proclaiming, *Justice Should be Color Blind.* Another read, *Harbor Springs is Hell, and Hell is on Fire.* That one caused Charlie to poke Briggs on the arm. While they watched with wary eyes the procession pounding its way into town from the east, they also kept close eyes on the news, with special emphasis on reports from the north. The capital of Montgomery was besieged by protestors, the governor responding by surrounding his mansion with hundreds of state troopers. So far the demonstrations, though massive, were peaceful. But many waving signs called for the governor's resignation or impeachment, and a few called for worse than that. The mansion was under lockdown. No one in, no one out, and because of fears it would be

burned to the ground, a call had been put into Washington for federal assistance, requesting a call up of the National Guard. News people on the ground reported no sign of federal intervention anywhere, but troopers protecting the grounds wore heavy faces, maintaining their positions grimly, like the last men standing at the Alamo.

"It's just going to take a spark, you know?" said Charlie. "Some crazy sunovabitch is going to shoot somebody or gut somebody and it will start. It always does." He made eye contact with each of them. "Same thing here. And down here you've already got the fuse ready to light. They get ahold of the Parrish kid they will skin the poor bastard alive. His daddy too, if he tries to intervene."

Briggs' eyes narrowed. "Hey, we haven't seen my friend the sheriff since we've been back. I'm surprised he's not over here bashing away on my face." Olivia reached over to her father, putting a hand on his shoulder.

She looked at Charlie. "That's off the table now, Dad. We're going to be fine."

Charlie smiled weakly. "Keep the faith, baby. And let's hope you don't see me running off to a bar somewhere."

Suddenly Willie, who had been looking out through the screened windows of the porch, shouted out. "Smoke. There's a helluva lot of smoke comin' from down the street." The other three joined him on the porch.

"Damn," said Olivia and Charlie at the same time.

Briggs looked on curiously for a moment, then his eyes widened. "The lodge. It's coming from the lodge. That's where Miss King is staying." Without further thought he ran for the door, but quick as he was Charlie beat him there. The two dashed down the steps to the van parked nearest the street, piling in while Briggs fumbled through his pockets for the keys. "Dammit," he yelled. He jumped from the van, racing down the embankment and onto the sidewalk. Charlie caught him within a few seconds. "There," pointed Briggs, thrusting out his hand. "Right at the sign and about a quarter of a mile." By the time Briggs reached the corner some fifty yards away, Charlie was already half-way to the lodge. Another great cloud of smoke

also began to billow up in the distance, from somewhere across the highway. "Damn," Briggs said to himself, taking in great gulps of air. "They're burning the town." A horn honked behind him, and Briggs jumped, almost falling down. The coroner's van pulled up, brakes screeching, with Olivia swinging wide the passenger side door. He could see beyond her, to where Willie sat behind the wheel, his mouth wide open, his eyes large and white. Briggs leapt in and Willie hit the accelerator.

As they approached the lodge a group of black men moved out onto the street, heading right at them. Most were armed with rifles and one carried a short, tubed weapon which may have been a rocket launcher. "Oh, lord," called out Willie. "We're gonna die. We're all gonna die." Charlie Benton was nowhere in sight. The men drew near and one, who seemed to be their leader, pointed at the side of the van. They moved away then, several dozen of them marching down the street in the direction of the town. Willie pulled the van into the parking lot. Smoke poured from the office area of the lodge and from another spot behind several of the cabins, but there was no visible fire. As they looked around, Charlie appeared from a cabin near the rear of the property. He had a very frightened looking Samantha King at his side. As they drove up to the couple, Briggs jumped out to help Miss King into the front of the van. He and Charlie Benton clamored into the back.

"What the hell happened?" Briggs asked, his voice cracking.

Samantha responded, her voice shaking just as badly. "It's just smoke. The bastards have these smoke bombs and they're running around terrorizing everyone. They had me trapped in my cabin, locked in." She looked at Charlie almost adoringly. "I thought they were going to burn it down, until Mister Benton kicked in the door."

"Like you said, it's just smoke," said Charlie. "It's not terror yet." He thought for a moment. "But I'll tell you something. If they're all running around setting off smoke bombs there is almost certainly some sort of organizational thing going on. No crazy rioters are going to just blow smoke. It makes no sense. Someone's sending them out, and sending the townspeople a message. I'm certain of it."

"Why would they do that?" Briggs, still breathing heavily, spoke. "What does it mean?" While they sat there, a disheveled white couple stumbled from the lodge office. They looked cautiously around before running down the steps to a nearby car. In a brief moment they screeched out of the lot and onto the highway, headed east, out of town.

"Those are the Duncans," said Briggs, whispering for no apparent reason. "They own the place." He thought for a moment, then tapped at Samantha's shoulder. "Hey, where's your partner?"

"The bastard left me. A bunch of men came up as we were getting out of the car. I ran inside, and he took off." She laughed sardonically. "He was supposed to be my great protector, and he ran like a scared rabbit."

"Well, that might explain more than you think." Charlie leaned forward from his place on the small bench that served as a rear seat in the coroner's van. He placed his elbows on top of the front seat as he leaned in. "I remember a time back in Kuwait, just before the Iraqis snuck out for their homeland, they lit hundreds of oil wells on fire. Everyone thought it was retaliation for having their asses handed to them, and we had a thousand men running around trying to figure out what to do. I always had a different idea. I don't think we gave them time to even think about retaliation. And the way it was planned, with more and more fires being set as they ran, it seemed like more of a diversion, trying to get us off their backs long enough to pull off an escape. And it wasn't a bad idea. It took us the better part of a day to figure out that most of them had slunk off into the desert under a dense cloud of smoke and fire."

"The Highway of Death." Samantha King turned to face Charlie. "As I remember they didn't get very far."

"No." Charlie shook his head. "They didn't. But they had no way to know what was waiting for them. And like I said, it took a while to figure out they were gone, or the death toll would have been even greater."

Briggs leaned forward and inward until he pressed right up against Charlie's side. "So you think this smoke is just a diversion

of some kind?" His brow furrowed and his lips tightened as he struggled with a thought. "What could possibly be the point?"

Charlie smiled almost mischievously. "Provocateurs have only one agenda. They provoke. I think they're trying to create fear. To a subject observer, the perception of fire will produce exactly the same results as a real one, without all the mess to clean up. And the intended targets will enter into one of two plausible scenarios. Fight or flight." His smile broadened. "And as we've seen from our friend Eddie and the Duncans there, confrontation does not seem to be the popular choice."

Sirens began blaring then, first in the distance, then closer, as a fire truck raced down the street in their direction, but turned left at the last second, away from the lodge and toward a large warehouse which had great plumes of white smoke billowing out through several vents in its roof. Charlie looked at Samantha King, whose eyes questioned him. "If that turns out to be just smoke, and I'm guessing it will, you're about to have one hell of a story, lady. Somebody wants to own this town. And they don't want to knock any peaches off the shelves on their way in."

Driving home a few minutes later they noticed new clouds of smoke now came from dozens of locations. Cars and trucks filled with white families or white couples or white individuals raced past them, headed east, for the state line. There were blacks present everywhere, even a large gathering directly across the street from the mortuary. A black man crossed the street and approached as they exited the car and headed for the safety of the house. "Mister Briggs," the man called out.

Briggs turned to face him, Charlie at his side. The other three walked quickly to the top of the steps before turning. Briggs nodded as the man moved to a small lawn area between the sidewalk and the slope. He pulled a bit of cloth from a pocket, wrapping it tightly around a small metal rod he held in his hand. Plunging his hand downward he drove the rod deeply into the soil, where it stuck. The cloth unfurled. It was black, with a large white eye painted at

its center. The man returned the nod, adding a slight smile, before walking back across the street to join his companions.

"What the hell is that?" said Briggs.

From behind him, at the top of the stairs, he heard Olivia. "Lamb's blood," she said.

Chapter Nineteen

All that afternoon and well into the evening more vehicles poured into Harbor Springs, almost all coming in from the east, from Georgia. The town's population, steady for many years at around two thousand, burgeoned to three, then edged its way back down to two again, to accommodate the fleeing whites. It had always been a fairly even mix, about half white and half black, with maybe a few Hispanics or other ethnicities mixed in, but now with nearly half the community's citizens fleeing the township, there was, for the first time, an overwhelming majority of black inhabitants. As darkness fell, gunfire broke out, sporadic at first, with just an occasional blast or two echoing through the night, but as the night deepened, the staccato sound of rapid fire came on with more and more frequency. Some residents of the town had apparently decided not to run. Fight or flight, Charlie had said. And not all were fleeing.

The five now at the mortuary sat out on the screen porch in the dark and watched. Occasionally the night sky would burst forth in flame, as real fires began to replace the smoke that had ruled much of the day. There weren't many fires though, as if a deliberate attempt was being made to flush out reluctant residents while doing as little actual damage to the town's infrastructure as

possible. The five had repeatedly tried to relay cell messages of the town's predicament to anyone who would listen, but right around dusk when the first rounds were fired, the phones all went uniformly dead, their screens reading *Searching*.

"The towers are down," said Charlie. "That's the first thing they thought of. Remove the towers, cut off all the land lines and isolate the whole damned place, maybe even most of the state. We have no idea how widespread this is. But I have a pretty good idea somebody is at the top of this heap, shouting out instructions. And he's very good at it."

"How can you take down all the towers? There are hundreds of them. And where the hell are the state troopers, the authorities?" Real concern spread across Samantha King's face.

Everyone looked at Charlie, as if seeking guidance. A grim smile crossed his lips. "There won't be any authority. At least not ours. Not for a while anyway. I remember hearing about the Watts riots in Los Angeles, many years ago. In the sixties, I think. Cops refused to even go near the place for the better part of a week. It was complete anarchy. And right in the middle of California, for chrissakes. It would be suicide for anyone to attempt to come in here now. Like I said earlier, whatever is going on here is very organized, very structured. I would daresay by dawn you three…" he nodded at Briggs and Olivia, then at Samantha. "You may be the only whites left in town. We were right about them giving you free passage here, but I don't know how long that will last. Right now you are heroes to them. Voices of reason against the establishment. Let's hope it stays that way."

Olivia spoke. "We're going to be okay. They have a plan, and we're part of it."

"What do you mean?" asked Briggs.

"Well, Charlie thinks they're engaged in some sort of psychological warfare. Am I right? That has to have a purpose."

Charlie nodded at her, and said, "Go on."

"Well, it seems to me if you send a large enough group into anywhere without a firm command structure, chaos will erupt

almost instantly. You can't even have a sale at K-Mart without ladies rampaging over one another once the doors open. And that's supposed to have at least some level of civility. And here we're seeing hundreds of combatants pour into our town in an obvious attempt to take it over, and yet they seem to have it planned out like an army would. We've all seen mobs. We've all seen rioters. Here we're seeing none of that. They're just marching around removing obstacles and doing as little damage as they can. If it was me, and I had a real grudge against a place, I'd burn it to the ground." Briggs grimaced, but reluctantly nodded in agreement.

"Makes perfect sense."

"Where did that come from?" Samantha looked with new eyes at Olivia.

"You'll get used to it," Charlie said with an amused chuckle. "She knows stuff."

Willie wrapped a proud arm around Olivia's shoulder. "That's exactly what I was thinkin'," he said. "Let's go make an icee."

Tucked away in a small pouch in a case that seldom left Charlie's side was a small, intelligent looking device. Samantha King's immediate observation upon seeing it was that it looked rather like a cellphone on steroids. Olivia became excited enough that she grabbed at it, insisting she be allowed to perform a dissection in an attempt to see what made it tick. Charlie laughed, "Whoa, girl. It's called a _Quasar_. Half phone, half computer, and doesn't rely on wires or towers to function. It transmits off a new form of satellite technology."

"I like it," said Samantha. "Can I use it to contact my boss at CBN?"

"I wanna talk to the space station," said Olivia, still entranced.

"Sorry, ladies. This is strictly zoned for the president. Other than that it's just about useless."

"You can call the president on that?"

"Yup. That's what it's for." Charlie pressed a button on the side of the device, and a small red light began to flash. In a few seconds a tiny screen lit up, and Errol Clarkson's face, bearing fresh scars of frustration, looked out at them.

"Hello, Charlie. Been worried as hell about you guys. I don't know what kind of crap technology this is, but it appears I can't use it to call out, and I've been waiting for you to call in. We're receiving very little communication from Alabama. Mostly just satellite stuff. Lines are down. Towers are down. I don't know what the hell is going on, but it's big, I can tell you that. It's making the march on Selma look like a Sunday School picnic." The president paused, concern spreading over his face. "Are you in danger?"

"I think we're safe for now, but Harbor Springs has been pretty well overrun and is under some kind of lockdown. It would certainly be nice to see a few of our boys heading down this way."

Clarkson shook his head. "We're doing all we can. Montgomery and Birmingham have also been overrun and thousands of blacks are pouring in by the minute. As of a few minutes ago, our intelligence is estimating more than one hundred thousand have already found their way in, and about half that many whites have crossed the border to get out. And they're coming from everywhere. Mississippi, Missouri, Louisiana. Hell, we just got news of a convoy of thousands of blacks heading over from the Carolinas. It's big. When the word on something like this gets out there's no containing it." The president smiled wearily. "The most amazing thing is it seems to be fairly peaceful. Unorganized but peaceful. At least up until now. But Governor Perry over in the capital has a busload of trouble in his lap. He's screaming for help."

Charlie whistled lightly. "You may think it's unorganized, but that's not what we're seeing down here in the south. Someone has their hand in the pie, bigtime. It seems like everyone has an assignment. For now, they're leaving us alone. As we suspected, Mister Briggs is being given a free pass. So are the rest of us, but I don't know how long that will hold. How about you send in a little help and maybe get us the hell out of here. I'm not so sure this was the great idea we thought it was."

"We can't." The president shook his head sadly. "If you were here you'd be the first one to say it. If we send in troops we'll be inviting our own personal Armageddon, pure and simple. Can you

imagine the consequences of having thousands of troops march in there? One thing goes wrong —and we both know it will— one thing sets off a spark, and we'll have more blood on our hands than the Civil Fucking War." Seeing Olivia standing behind Charlie on his screen, Clarkson stammered uncomfortably. "Sorry," he said. "Miss Briggs, right? That was no way for me to speak. I guess I'm a bit on edge and not completely in control of my faculties. Please forgive me."

Olivia smiled innocently. "Hey, I'm sixteen. I've heard the word before. And I think you're right. It would be a fucking catastrophe. Do what you gotta do, Mister President."

Clarkson sat there, mouth open, in awkward silence. Charlie spoke. "I'm tired of saying this, but once you get to know her you'll love her." He then grew serious. "So, what are you saying? We sit here and fry maybe?"

"No, of course not. But if you're right, and someone is down there with a purpose, we need to find out what that purpose is. Find out what they want. I need you there, Charlie. And Mister Briggs too. I've had the warmongers on my ass all day. And of course they want to march into Montgomery and smash face. But right now we don't have a realistic plan. I could send a copter for you, but if they happen to shoot the damn thing down on the way in we could start a real war. And if they shoot it down on the way out, well, I'm thinking the results will not be all that pleasant for you. We just don't know their capabilities yet, and we need to figure out what's really going on. Until we figure that out we need to tread very lightly. And I'm concerned about your assessment. Nothing has come across my desk to indicate any sort of organization at work down there. Just chaos and mob rule. That's the way these things usually work. I can't even imagine how anyone would go about setting something up, something structured, I mean. When a people have had enough of a thing they just react. They're not in any sort of mood to interact obediently. At least I've never heard of it."

"Nonetheless," Charlie nodded, but not agreeably. "There is a force at work here. They even planted a flag on Mister Briggs' lawn

a while ago. A sort of peace flag, I think. Or immunity of some kind. A mob without leadership doesn't usually stop along the way to offer exemptions."

"I'll put someone on it right away. We'll figure this out. You hang tight, and if it gets out of hand call in immediately and we'll pull off an extraction." The president smiled warmly into the screen. "I trust you, Charlie. You know that. And I trust your judgement implicitly. Keep me apprised." With a polite nod he reached out to tap a switch on top of his desk. The screen went blank, and the president was gone.

Chapter Twenty

The crowd gathering around the governor's mansion grew stronger by the hour. Troopers guarding the place still stood fast, but there were rumblings among them, their obedience beginning to waver. The crowd began to edge its way in even closer, taking on more of a mob mentality. A man moved among them, like a shadow, dark and mysterious. He squeezed and pressed his way along, learning how to move among the undulating mass. In his right hand he held a rasp, but his left hand also held an interesting accessory. He had picked up a small cardboard sign with the word *Justice* printed boldly on both sides. The sign was stapled to a stick, and he waved the sign in front of his face, appearing as any of hundreds of others in the crowd. Holding the sign at about chest level, he found he could raise his right hand, the one with the rasp, and comfortably keep it there, between the cardboard and the back of whomever was unfortunate enough to be located in front of him. The tool was completely invisible. He rubbed the sharpened tip gently across back after back, even tapping it at the shoulders of those around him. No one noticed. Laughter erupted from deep in his chest, and he felt the pure joy a wolf must feel when it has worked its way into the center of a flock. El Lobo would be proud,

he thought. A large, black woman loomed in front of him, her shoulders wide, the fattened folds of her neck offering a most enticing target. Raising her hands to the sky she screamed out, "Justice," exactly as his sign proclaimed. It was prophetic, he thought to himself, and as a kind of honor he chose her as his first.

As the lance found its mark, nestling in high up on the back of her neck, he thrust forward and upward. The tip sliced its way into her flesh, but did not penetrate as deeply as he thought it would. It slid in to about half its length, then rammed into some form of hardened tissue. He quickly withdrew the rasp, and as he did so the woman spun around, her bright black eyes beginning to glaze over. She stared blankly into the distance, then stumbled, almost falling against him. As she slumped to the ground her body went limp, and Ortiz felt himself convulse mightily as a great fear exploded from within. Then, at almost the same instant a rush of adrenaline washed over him, and he slipped away, deeper into the crowd. He attacked again, this time a tall, slender, very dark man, and this time his thrust became a powerful, driving force. That was the key. Power the tool deeply into the flesh, then ease it out, and slip away to the side as the body swayed for an instant before the call of death brought it to the ground. It became a dance to him. Slide to the right, thrust and withdraw. Slide to the right, thrust and withdraw. He tried to count his victims, but found counting an impossible task. His mind pounded with a pulsing, throbbing bloodlust. The very feeling he had so desperately longed for now became everything he had hoped it would be. And the crush of the crowd became as a womb, embracing him in a warm cushioning fog. At some point he had an awareness that the mood of the crowd was changing. He was jostled, nearly losing his footing. Then the screams began. Voices were shouting, hundreds of them shouting in a sort of macabre terror. He tried to focus on it but the crowd continued to sweep him away. Finally, as he fought his way to the edge of the horde, he was able to stumble free, slipping behind a long row of vans parked up close against one wall of the mansion. The crowd swirling nearby had fallen into a complete panic, now moving in a great tangle away from the building

instead of towards it. After a time the mob was broken, retreating into the night. A number of bodies lay about, in the wake of the mass, but as Ortiz counted them he was disappointed. His mind had tallied dozens of kills, maybe even as many as a hundred. The actual number was closer to twelve, or fourteen.

As he wound his way back to Trayon in the waiting car, a lonely misery swept over him. He had failed. His plan had been to incite the crowd. Let the ripple of death slowly catch on until the mob realized it was being attacked from within. Then they were supposed to rise up like harbingers and become his agents, destroying everything in their path. Instead they had run like cowards, fear replacing anger. There was no sense to it. Where was the pure animal hatred in them that poured so generously from his own spirit? Did others not possess it? Were they that afraid?

Trayon was waiting, eyes and mouth wide for the story. "What happened? Did you kill? Did they riot?"

"Dumb bastards," moaned Ortiz. "I butchered the shit out of them. And then they realized what was happening. They all panicked and ran away like little children. The whole fucking mob. They were supposed to attack, not run. Goddammit!"

"Maybe we need a new plan. Something that doesn't make them run, and just makes them mad instead." Trayon looked over at Ortiz, his face full of pride at this line of reasoning. "That would work."

Ortiz looked back, a sneer forming at the corners of his mouth. "You dumb fuck," he yelled out. He pulled the rasp from his belt, slashing it savagely at Trayon. The tip of the tool drove deeply into the man's arm, high up near the shoulder. Trayon screamed, which only incensed Ortiz more. He thrust the rasp again and again, driving it deeply into the side of his companion. "How the fuck do you like that?" His voice became as much a weapon as the rasp. "Is it making you mad?" In desperation Trayon grabbed at the handle to the door, clawing it open as he crumbled to the sidewalk outside. He lay there sobbing, and bleeding badly. Ortiz started the engine then, gunning it into gear. He crushed his foot down hard on the gas pedal, the passenger door smashing Trayon on the head as it slammed shut

from the quick acceleration. "You sunovabitch," he cried out as he drove away.

He headed south, drawn there by the prospect of fresh blood. The site of the incident, he thought. Mourners would gather there, probably by the thousands. It would be a good place to start over. A good place to hunt. His head hurt terribly. After a time the pain lessened and he grew drowsy, pulling the pickup to the side of the road so he could rest. When he awoke the sun shone down brightly, a new day with new prospects. Turning on the radio he fumbled with the dial for a news station. He did not have to fumble for long. Every station was broadcasting the same thing. A sniper had attacked the crowd assembled around the governor's mansion the night before. The administration adamantly denied it, but there was clear evidence. Seventeen bodies had been found in the courtyard of the mansion. Each with a precise bullet hole drilled into the back of its head. Only a skilled marksman could have accomplished such a feat, one most assuredly trained by the government, probably at the behest of the governor himself. A coroner tried to explain they were not entry wounds created by gunfire, and no bullets had been extracted, but no one believed the report. "Another cover-up," the masses began chanting. "They murder little girls, and now they're murdering us."

By mid-morning, tens of thousands had already gathered once again in the courtyard of the mansion, swarming the grounds. And this time the mood was anything but peaceful. As the guards surrounding the veranda began to seek safety inside, the crowd began calling out for the governor to show himself. Sometime around noon a helicopter swung in low, hovered there for a few moments, then landed on the rooftop of the grand house. The king was abandoning his castle. Seeing the copter and sensing the escape, the crowd surged forward. Torches were lit as the swarm moved up the steps and into the residence. Gunfire erupted then, but this time the mob refused to flee. Smoke billowed from the windows, and soon long streams of flame could be seen licking their way up the outside walls. Within an hour the mansion was engulfed in fire. News crews retreated, screaming out that this was it. War had just

been declared. And as the building gasped mightily before imploding in upon itself, much of the mob emerged. You could feel its energy, its hate, as it began to move away in the direction of the city.

Ortiz sat there in the truck for a long time, feasting on the reports. His misery vanished as quickly as it had arrived. He lounged there like a glutton, laying his head back on the padded rest, filled up to bursting, and overcome by the sheer joy of his circumstance. "I'm the best goddam sniper the world has ever seen," he said. Then he began to laugh.

Chapter Twenty-One

By noon on the following day bodies began to show up at the mortuary. Not a mass of them, but trucks would arrive every so often, driven by young, sedate black men with one or two corpses, mostly of white men, laid out in their beds. Few words were spoken by the men delivering them. Charlie, Willie and Briggs moved downstairs, setting up chairs on the sidewalk near the entrance to the coroner's lab. Willie, helping with the unloading, recognized one of the first bodies to come in. "Cole Clayton," he said as he grabbed the legs of a deceased man.

"Yeah," said Briggs. "From Cedar Creek."

"You know this one?" asked Charlie, grabbing at the corpse's shoulders.

"Yes," said Briggs. "He and his brother Tom run one of the biggest plantations in the south. Just south of here. Across from Willie's. That means they're working over the countryside as well, and not just the town."

"I know Tom," said Willie plainly. "I guess he's still out there."

"Those were his boys I met out at your place, yes?" asked Charlie. Willie nodded.

Charlie asked the driver, who stepped down to lend a hand, "I

don't suppose you'd care to tell us what's going on?" He glanced down at the dead Clayton man. "I mean other than the fact that there appears to be a fatal disease smacking down certain members of the community."

"I don't know, sir," said the man.

"Well, can you tell me anything about your command structure? Like who's in charge, maybe? Anything?"

The man looked at Charlie directly. He was young and strong, with a firm, proud face. There was no evasiveness in his voice. Just training and discipline. "I don't know, sir. Just doing what I'm told."

As the man climbed back into his pickup to drive away he turned to face the three. "I'm sorry," he said softly. Then he wheeled the truck around and headed back out of town.

The body count totaled eleven: eight white men all cleanly shot through, one old white woman who appeared to have died of natural causes, and two black men who also appeared to have been shot. Briggs, having only six cold lockers, doubled them up, saying, "Any more and we're going to need ice. Or a hell of a lot of disinfectant."

Well into the afternoon they sat there. Finally around four, when they were just about to pack up their chairs and head inside, a long, black limousine wheeled its way down the street. The vehicle pulled up close to the three men. So close, in fact, that its tires scraped in tightly against the curb, causing blurred, black scars to scuff along the bright white of the rubber sidewalls. As a forensic, Briggs noticed it right away and found it disturbing.

"Well this should tell us something," said Charlie, as he whistled sharply. "Either that or your pizza delivery system is very upscale." A door opened on the far side of the limo, the street side, and a uniformed man —tall, black, and showing more age than one would expect from a man in the military— extracted himself, leaning his elbows across the top of the car as he studied Briggs and Charlie carefully. Willie had already gone inside.

"Good afternoon, gentlemen," he said crisply. The visor on his cap shined brightly in the late afternoon sunlight, between patches of golden brocade swirling across much of the visor's surface. They

could see just the topmost portion of what appeared to be a massive ribbon bar adorning his chest, while four silver stars aligned neatly atop each of his shoulders shouted out at his importance. His eyes focused in on Briggs. "You must be the famous Mister Briggs," he said. "It's an honor to meet you, sir."

Charlie stepped forward. "I recognize you," he said, still trying to place the man.

The military man's eyes shifted. "And I you. And I apologize, but I can't recall the name. You're the president's bodyguard though, right? Ex-marine, as I recall." His right hand held a riding crop, a sort of stiff, shortened whip. He lashed it against the black top of the limo. "And does this mean I've struck gold and the old man is here?"

"No." Charlie laughed, not nervously, but pointedly. "I'm on vacation. Just down here visiting friends. Having a wonderful time counting bodies. The president is still back up in Washington wondering just what in the hell is going on down here. And I'm Chester Benton. Advisor, not bodyguard." He pointed loosely at the man. "Seems to me the last time I saw you, you were a colonel. Now you've got four stars. Nice promotion."

The man smiled, and the smile held a warning. "Battlefield promotion," he said. "Sometimes in life what's not given must be taken. So it's general now. General Anthony R. Sedgewick."

A light went on in Charlie's mind. "I remember now. It's funny, I always remember rank before name and location. You're from the academy near Atlanta. We met you a few years ago on a tour of your facility. Tight ship."

"Still is. A good portion of the men you've been seeing lately are from there. You might say they're my disciples."

"Well," said Charlie. "How holy of you." Just then Willie poked his head out the door. The general motioned to him.

"Come out, man. And who might you be?"

Willie shuffled out onto the sidewalk nervously. "Me? I'm nobody. Just Willie. I'm their friend."

The general smiled again, but this time benignly. "Nobody is nobody, Willie. We all have our story."

"Yeah," said Charlie. "And some of us just make it up as we go along."

"I'd be careful, Mister Benton. I came here out of courtesy. And I'm completely prepared to like you, all of you. If given the chance you'll find I'm quite amenable, even peaceful. I'm not here to make enemies."

Charlie walked the few steps to the limo, leaning his arms out comfortably on the top of the car in a manner mimicking the general's. His face warmed. "Come on," he said. "As one black man to another. What the hell are you thinking?"

The three were invited inside the limo then, with the driver instructed to drive them about. They drove a mile or so, past the Harbor Glen Lodge, turning left soon thereafter and heading back into town. Along the way they noticed clusters of men, all young, black, strong looking men. And occasionally a number of whites could be seen, usually just one or two, but sometimes more, and mostly out on the street where they were being herded, also in the direction of the town.

"Where are you taking them?" asked Briggs.

"You'll see," said the general evasively. "They're not being harmed."

Soon they arrived at the grounds of the two schools, the ones Olivia refused to attend, driving up onto an athletics field before pulling up and parking next to the largest building on the campus. There were many black men waiting outside, young men mostly, dressed like soldiers. They were part of what the general liked to call his *army*, and he had gathered them carefully. He had developed a most effective way of ferreting out followers. Early on in his tenure at the academy he learned that the vulnerabilities in a recruit's character could usually be found in the records of their youth. So he had volunteered for long hours in the personnel office where he could study each of his prospects on paper before confronting them out on the drill field or in the barracks. He looked particularly for the very youngest ones, still soft in the mold of human experience. Ones who had been raised with a firm hand, or a forgotten

one—orphans, foster children, those from broken homes, or ones who had gone through long periods of neglect or abuse. They were easy to find and heavy in numbers at institutions such as this. They were societal throwaways, and the general preyed heavily upon them. When the Black Lives Matter movement swept America it was easy to radicalize blacks, who sensed salvation lay through immersing themselves among those who were racially similar, and disavowing anyone else. This became the general's favorite tool. Wielding a handy ideology to remind his young men that it was the white world that had cast down upon them the nets of tyranny. This worked well for a long time, and when the *BLM* movement was swept away, even stronger movements rolled in as America moved deeper into the throes of unrest. Soon there were over two hundred cadets tucked safely into his flock. They would train covertly, nights and weekends, with the understanding that a time would come when they would be called upon for the good of their people, to make a statement before God and humanity of tremendous importance. Having no idea what that meant, they still reveled in the fact that they were united in a cause much greater than themselves. That's all young patriots need. And patriots they became. Occasionally, as they matured, graduated and moved on, they would join other communities or other causes and be drawn away from the general. But even then they would come to him first —treating him like a godfather— to ask his permission to move onto a different life path. The general would always greet these deserters with a smile, his hand firmly gripping down on their shoulders. He would tell them life asks many things. It was a calling, he would say, and it was only natural they should respond to it. This moment of warmth and farewell ended with a handshake, wherein the general would press a small placard into the palm of the defector. As the general turned away the card would be read, and printed there were the words:

There is a secrecy worth more than life, a bond which must be respected. If a man should break with this pact, all that he holds dear will be taken. Swiftly and surely, taken.

The men who waited for them now on the field formed twin

ranks in a gauntlet newly arriving whites were forced to walk. The lines led directly into the building, which, when they entered, they could see was a large gymnasium. The floor was polished wood and brightly painted lines, and a painting of an eagle whose wings spanned a good portion of the center circle. The walls were crisp and white, another eagle or two winging its way across them, and down low, rimming three sides of the gym, were long rows of bleachers. And the bleachers were full, almost brimming over with silent, anxious white faces. It was so quiet, in fact, that they could hear their own footsteps as they crossed the floor, finally reaching the head of the eagle directly in the middle of the gym. Briggs and Willie locked arms, their discomfort at standing there an obvious one. Even the never ruffled Charlie seemed a bit taken aback, moving over closely to the other two. The general spun himself around, giving all in the room ample time to view his magnificence.

"I am General Sedgewick," he said, in a loud, clear voice, "And it is an honor to be here with all of you today. I'm sure you're wondering just exactly what is happening to your quaint little village, and exactly why we're here." The general stepped away, separating himself from the others. "First I would like to apologize for the disruption. I know a number of you have suffered hardship at the hands of my men, and I want to assure each and every one of you that whatever steps were taken were important and necessary ones. And there have been a number of fatalities, no sense in denying that. Each of those saddens me greatly, but again, because of certain pockets of resistance, we found lethal force to be occasionally necessary to obtain our objectives." The general continued to spin slowly as he spoke, like an entertainer wishing to give each member of his audience an equal view. "I am sure you have all noticed the color of my skin is different from the majority of you in the room. But not unusually so. In fact, many of you are probably uttering the word *nigger* even as I speak. And that's okay. It's perfectly understandable. Two hundred years of programming by your ancestors is not an easy thing to overcome in a short span of time. My point here today is to show you all how insignificant that term is in its reality. As whites, especially

here in the south, you have been brought up to believe your race is simply superior, in all ways." The general pointed across the gym to a number of his men, who lined the few wall spaces where there were no bleachers. Most of them were armed, some with sidearms, some with automatic weapons. He waved his hand aloft and two broke off, walking along the floor where they intently scanned the audience. They selected a man finally, a large, burly man who looked to be in incredible physical shape. The two entered the bleacher, each grabbing one of the man's arms. He was escorted then, with little resistance, to the middle of the floor where the general stood. The two men departed and the man stood there, awkwardly. The general turned to Charlie.

"Chester," he spoke softly. "I need your help. I want you to beat this man until he can no longer stand. Have fun with it. Beat him up really well."

"Screw yourself," said Charlie. "I'm not your boy. You want to beat him, you beat him. But you leave me out of it."

General Sedgewick smiled warmly. He walked the few steps to his three guests, stepping up very close to Chester Benton. "I knew I was going to like you." He patted Charlie's arm. "And I do. It will be fun watching you do my bidding. Whenever I ask. Now I want you to beat the hell out of this man. And you have just one minute to accomplish it. If you refuse, or god help you, if he beats you, I will kill... her." The general paused, pointing to a young lady in the nearest bleacher. She sat there, squeezed in among a group of several men, fear haunting her eyes. "I will have her shot like a dog right here in front of everybody. Right now." The smile broadened. "Please, Chester," he said. "Please." The general pulled lightly on Charlie's arm, and Charlie allowed himself to be led over to the burly man. "Now," said the general, addressing the man. "I have an interesting proposition. If you can best my friend here I shall grant you complete and absolute freedom. You can leave, take your family and friends with you and never look back. You have my word."

The man stared hard at the general, gauging his circumstance

and the worth of the general's words. Then he turned without warning and swung mightily at Charlie's face. The general had awarded Charlie one minute to fulfill his responsibility. It took less than half that. When the fist arrived Charlie's face wasn't there. He moved swiftly closer, targeting the man's groin and the softer tissues of his belly. As his fists struck home the man doubled over where his own face was met by a knee. His head snapped backwards with his body following. In seconds he was laid out, barely conscious on the floor. The crowd gasped, but just for an instant. Then a gripping silence fell over the entire audience. The general stepped up, raising Charlie's hand high over his head. "Advisor, my ass," he hissed. Then he stepped away to address the crowd.

"Friends," he said. "What we have here is a failure to communicate." Laughing aloud he continued. "God, I love that." He spun around joyously, pointing at Charlie, then turned to the crowd. "And this nigger didn't even want to fight. The point I'm trying to make is you're really no better than anyone else. At least not physically. But you already knew that. Anyone who watches football, or basketball or baseball already knows that. Anything but tennis. God, the niggers hate tennis. So you just sit there making your racial slurs and passing the beer. And the truth is you're not even equals here. You're inferiors." He winced as he spoke. "That's gotta hurt, huh? And intellectually? What the hell. You're sitting out there like a bunch of goddam sheep, while I stand here at the lectern giving out the daily lesson. Now about half of you don't even know what a lectern is while the other half is looking for one. That's how stupid you people really are." The general brought his hands together, tapping the tips of his fingers against one another. "So to sum this up, it should become obvious at some point that you're generally weaker as a species, and you're not intelligent enough to realize it, so that just makes you a bunch of really dumb mutherfuckers. And I apologize to the younger members of the audience. Mutherfucker is not really appropriate language for some of you. Unfortunately I can get away with it because your daddies and your mommies are too fucking weak and too fucking dumb to do anything about it."

"Fuck you," a man's voice called out from one of the bleachers. "Who said that?" the general spun around. One of his aides, one of the ones lining a near wall, ran to the middle of the court, pointing into the crowd. Several others ran in from the side, and following the aide's directions, soon had another burly looking white man dragged out onto the floor. He was pinned there, sprawled out with arms and legs stretched wide. "Sweet," said the general as he walked over and placed a foot against the man's head. "Another lesson in progress. Who doesn't like a lesson?" Pulling his crop from a side strap attached to his hip he handed it to an aide. An exceptionally strong looking one. "Strip him," he said. The man's shirt was torn from his body and he lay there on his back, staring contemptuously up at the general, who then addressed everyone in the room. "If you are obedient, and if you cause me no problems, no harm will befall you. And you're even welcome to vomit out your petty slurs behind my back. Hell, I would think less of you if you didn't. But to my face I consider it somewhat insulting." He turned to look at Charlie, then Willie. "We've been listening to it for hundreds of years now, and I'm thinking it's about time for it to stop. At least to our faces. That's the greatest sign of contempt." Waving his hands in a broad circle over his head, he continued. "From now on you shall be entirely subordinate. And you'll stay that way until you learn a level of civility, a level of compassion for those different from yourselves. We will be here among you until we are forced out, or killed, and you are liberated. Inevitably that will happen, so you can take solace from that. Your freedom is assured. It's just the time frame that is in question. But until that moment you belong to me, to us. You will be treated like negroes, in exactly the same fashion as you have treated all of us for centuries. Respond well, do the work asked of you and we will get along famously. The black members of the community will be coming forward soon. They will identify those among you who have treated them fairly, perhaps even with kindness. If that's you, you will be rewarded by being allowed to go about your daily tasks without any interference whatsoever. And you will be treated with respect. Respect you have earned. For others, most

of you, I suspect, the future will be rather bleak. If you have wasted your life cloaked in a blanket of hate and racism you will become the new glory of the south. The new slaves. You will work the mills, the plantations, and the deepest, darkest cesspools we can find for you to clean. It will not be pleasant. Obey your new masters and your treatment will be, at the very least, fair. Disobedience, however, is not advised. As you're about to see." The general motioned the aide with the crop. "Until I tell you to stop," was all he said.

A beating commenced then, a beating unlike anyone there had ever before witnessed. Even Charlie, who had seen more than his share of torture and barbarity, found the spectacle hard to watch. The aide dropped to his knees, to be closer to his target and gain better leverage with the short whip. By the third or fourth lash blood began to flow, and by the tenth, large strips of flesh began to hang from the man's chest in loose threads. The man screamed for a while, at least at first. But after a time the screaming stopped, and was replaced by a wailing cry, then a quieter moaning until, somewhere around the thirtieth blow, there was no further sound. Members of the audience gasped audibly, some women crying out hysterically. But when the general raised his hand for silence they all immediately obeyed. Finally the general moved in, reaching down to feel the man's pulse. "Good," he said, dropping the man's limp hand. "He'll be just fine. And I think we all have a better understanding of what we need from each other now." He moved over to where Charlie, Briggs and Willie stood, their mouths and eyes wide in shock. Placing his arms around the men almost affectionately, he ushered them towards the doors. Once there, he turned briefly, offering some parting words to the crowd. "I enjoyed meeting you all," he said, in a voice that spoke of fellowship. "Tomorrow we'll meet again and lay out some ground rules I hope we'll all agree are fair and just. And we can learn a little more about each of you. You will be fed now, and bedded down for the evening. Rest well, my friends."

Chapter Twenty-Two

Samantha King and Olivia Briggs sat out on the screen porch. They watched throughout much of the afternoon as trucks pulled up at the coroner's lab in the street below. When bodies were unloaded, Samantha would stand briefly, using her phone to snap photos, while Olivia pressed her face tightly up against the screen as she attempted to identify the few corpses who came in with faces uncovered. Occasionally Briggs would glance up at her, nodding solemnly as he went about the grim task of carrying or escorting the bodies into the lab. When a limo arrived, both women felt a rush of excitement. And when a high ranking military officer stepped out to confer with Charlie, their enthusiasm became obvious.

"This might be it," said Olivia, her voice filled with anticipation. "Our salvation."

A moment later confusion weighed in as Willie and Charlie climbed into the car, followed by Briggs, who waved up at Olivia as he mouthed the words, "It's okay."

"Where do you think they're going?" asked Samantha, her eyes staying with the limo as it swung around and headed down the street.

"I don't know." Olivia also watched them drive away. "But they're okay. And Charlie's there."

"He's not Superman, you know."

Olivia studied Samantha for a time. "He's close, and he made me a promise. I'm thinking he's a man of his word. Not everyone is."

Samantha studied back. "You don't like me much, do you?"

"I haven't completed my assessment of you yet. I do know you lack empathy and Charlie, by the way, thinks you're a bitch. So there are one or two points against."

"Look, I'm a reporter. I report. It's not always glowing, but if you think about it, I'm just doing my job. Essentially someone tells me what to do and I do it. I don't have all that much control."

Olivia smiled coyly. "Wow, that's really close to what a prostitute says."

Samantha's eyes flashed. "You know, not everyone gets to be exactly what they want, say exactly what they want. You don't seem to have many restraints, but there are a lot of us out in the real world who just do what we're told. It's how we survive. For such a smart kid, I'd think you would get that."

"I'm not a kid."

"And I'm not a prostitute."

For a few moments the two sat there in silence, measuring each other. Then Olivia rose. "Come on," she said. "Let's go downstairs and see what they've brought us. It's just the beginning, you know."

"The bodies? You want to look at them?"

"I always do. Sometimes death gives you a different perspective. It points out the path we're all on. It's a very sobering experience." The two moved across the porch then, entering the house and the stairwell leading down to the lab. As they flicked the lights on at the bottom of the stairs, Samantha was immediately struck by the cleanliness of the place. Everything was either sparkling white or shining metal. The cold lockers lined a far wall, six square metal frames, perfectly aligned like picture frames, and to their right stood a highly scrubbed counter with several trays of instruments laid out in neat rows. The floor was also polished, a satiny gunmetal grey, but near the street side door an anomaly lay. A square bit of paper, splattered with dried blood, was pushed up against a baseboard.

Olivia crossed the room and reached down to pick it up. She could see the imprint of just the tip of a shoe imbedded there, wavy marks creating a pattern in red. As she turned the small square of paper over, Samantha joined her. It was a photograph. One of a boy standing proudly beside an older man, while a dog looked up lovingly at them both. "I told you," said Olivia solemnly. "One day this is the path you're on…" She held up the photo, "and you have no idea where it's going to take you." She nodded in the direction of the lockers. "Let's see if we can find him." Slipping the photo into the pocket of her blouse she walked back across the room, to where the lockers waited. Samantha followed her.

As Olivia pulled the first door open, Samantha gasped aloud. "My god," she said.

"You'll get used to it. You'll never like it, but you'll get used to it." Two men lay there, one black, one white, frozen in time. They had been thrown together hastily, face to face, the two colors combining in sharp contrast. The face of the black man appeared winsome, almost sedate. Like time had called for him during a moment of calm. There was no outward cause of death, so Olivia pulled back a section of the man's shirt covering his chest. A small, clean hole was present there, charting a course directly into the heart. Olivia explained that sometimes, but rarely, an object could pierce the heart in such a way that a flap of tissue would slam shut behind it, like a trap door at the entrance of the wound, as pressure from a ruptured artery shot outward. In such cases little external bleeding would occur, as massive amounts of blood spilled into the inner cavities of the body. The white face showed a less fortunate circumstance. The man's mouth lay partially open, exposing his upper jaw, while the lips curled upwards in an eternal growl. One eye was closed, the other wide open, but no eyeball was present. Only a gaping hole where a bullet had ripped through from the back of the head, exiting directly through the socket of the eye. Each man had probably died instantly, and equally, even though their appearance said otherwise.

Samantha looked down at them for a long time. "It's so awful," she said finally. "And they're so young." Her face had turned pale, but

Olivia could read the early signs of compassion in her eyes.

"Maybe they killed each other. That would be fitting."

Samantha looked up, her eyes beginning to mist over. "That's a little harsh, don't you think?"

"No. As I said, it would be fitting. As if some divine being wanted them to kiss and make up. How do you get more fitting than that?"

"You just seem so flippant about it. I think maybe you've seen way too much death. I'm wondering why your father doesn't restrict you."

Olivia laughed. "Believe me, he's tried. Once, when I was a kid, I took a hand to school. Just a hand. Snuck in and got it while he was making me breakfast. God, the other kids loved me for it, at least to my face, but school officials found it to be a bit much. My dad was reprimanded and fined, so he wasn't terribly happy with me at the time. We kind of home-schooled me after that. That was up in Saint Louis. I remember the neighbors began referring to me as *The Dead Girl*. I think they thought I was a vampire or something."

As they pushed the locker closed, Olivia observed that Samantha whispered something. "What are you doing, praying?" she said almost sarcastically.

"Just wishing them well."

"Well? They're dead. There's not much a wish will do for them now."

"You don't believe in much do you?"

"You mean like God?" Olivia smiled condescendingly. "You going to preach to me now? Listen, every day all over this planet shit happens. Bad shit. To some very good people. So I'm thinking this god of yours, if he exists, doesn't possess a whole lot of compassion. Girls are raped, people are bullied or burned or bombed. The three *B*'s. Like I said, shit happens, and apparently he doesn't do a damn thing about it. Maybe he's got his head buried up there in some celestial sand and doesn't know what's going on. If he does know, he needs to be confronted, and if he doesn't, he needs to be informed. Either way he doesn't strike me as my kind of guy.

Not somebody I'd be interested in praying to." Olivia headed for the stairs. "So," she said, "to be a little more succinct and just answer your question. I don't."

"Wow." Samantha frowned, biting down on her lower lip. "You have it all worked out. How lucky for you. I was smart at sixteen too. Not creepy-smart like you, but I was pretty sure I had all the answers."

"Did you?"

"Of course not. Like you said, stuff happens. And you have to learn from it."

"I said shit, not stuff. There's a fundamental difference. They belong to the same phylum, but shit is much more odiferous and specific."

"God you're weird." Samantha couldn't help herself. She looked at the young girl and began to laugh.

Olivia tried to be offended, but it wasn't working for her. She also began to laugh, and soon the two collapsed together at the foot of the stairs. "I guess I can start thinking of you as less of a bitch," she said after a time. "It won't be easy, but I'll try."

<hr/>

An hour later the men returned. Briggs was surprised to find his daughter and the reporter sitting together in the living room, apparently amicably. Both women sat up. "What happened?"

Charlie and Willie followed Briggs into the room and the three sat, Willie joining Olivia on the couch, where she hugged him warmly. The other two pulled chairs up close. Briggs began, "It's been one crazy afternoon. The man you saw, he's a general or something. I think he's gone nuts. He took us to the high school, into the gym, where he's holding most of the townspeople. The white ones, anyway. There were probably seven or eight hundred in there. All frightened to death. He also had a lot of men with him,

men with guns, and they've taken complete control." Briggs paused, seemingly confused by his own words. "I think he wants to turn things around, turn back the clock a couple hundred years and create a black utopia where it's the whites who are enslaved. Something like that."

"He's not nuts," Charlie spoke then. "Fanatical maybe, but not insane about it. He's a man who's been pushed around most of his life, and it's been burning inside of him like white-hot coals. But he's very dangerous. In his mind he's conjured up a way to right what he considers to be a great wrong. He won't let anything stand in his way."

"He's nuts," said Briggs again. "Sorry, Charlie, but by any definition the man we met today is not in complete charge of his faculties. And that, my friend, is nuts. We saw him beat a man very nearly to death. And he made Charlie beat another man, just to make a point."

Olivia spoke, eyes on Charlie. "You beat someone? Because he told you to?"

"There weren't a lot of options." Charlie swung his head around, addressing everyone in the room. "Listen, he wants to play a game. And we're all going to be part of it. I don't think he wishes any of us harm. In fact, I don't think he wishes anyone harm. My read on the man is he desperately needs to make a point, and not just for us. We're isolated right now, but soon he'll want the whole world to know what's going on here. To feed his ego. So he needs us. If he has to beat someone along the way he'll do it, but I don't think he derives pleasure from it. At any rate, for now he owns us, and it would be unwise to think otherwise."

Samantha King spoke out. "What do you mean? We're all prisoners here. Permanently?"

"It's not permanent. I'm certain even he understands that. He's buying time right now, and with all the hell unleashed up north it will be awhile before anyone thinks about coming down here to resolve this. So for now, yes, we're prisoners. How long it will last is anybody's guess."

"What about your friend, the president?" Samantha said. "Surely he's not going to stand for this? It's like a grand mutiny or something."

Charlie smiled. "That would require a ship. This is more like an insurrection, and a hostage situation. The biggest one this country has faced since the Civil War. The president's job at the moment is to keep it localized here in Alabama, and not allow it to spread like plague to other states. Our particular situation will require a lot of thought and a lot of preparation. It won't be easy storming in here, and it won't happen soon. Things need to play themselves out first. So let's not rush the man."

Briggs spoke. "But what's the general's point? There has to be a theme here larger than hate or mental instability. Some grand scheme. What is he after, exactly?"

"I get it." It was Willie who spoke next. "The man's tired of bein' treated like dirt. I wouldn't mind beatin' on a few folks around here myself." A fire came into his eyes, surprising everyone in the room except Olivia, whose arms tightened around her friend.

"I hear you, Willie," Charlie continued. "I've had my moments."

"Me too." It was Olivia who spoke then. Everyone stared at her. "I have."

Charlie looked at her and their eyes bonded. "What this all boils down to is the fact that we're in this together. That's just the way it is. And the president is no fool. If someone tried to come in here right now, a bloodbath would ensue. I'm not sure anyone would survive it. So we need to show patience, and resolve. This guy wants to play some kind of slave game, and he wants us to be his players." Charlie stood, folding his arms across his chest. "Let's give him what he wants," he said. "Let's play."

PART TWO
THE SLAVE PLAYERS

Chapter Twenty-Three

Later that same night, as Briggs and Willie slept, Charlie and Olivia once again brought out the Quasar, opening up communications with the White House. They told the president of their situation, and as Charlie had surmised, no help would be forthcoming. The president informed them that civil war had broken out up in Montgomery and, for the first time in over a hundred and fifty years, America was being attacked from within. The governor's mansion had fallen first, razed to the ground by a massive uprising, which then turned on the Capitol. That too had been destroyed, but not as easily. Over two hundred state troopers and an equal number of state and federal employees inside and around the building had been killed in a vain attempt to protect it, and it was estimated another thousand or so of the rioters had also fallen and lay scattered across the grounds. Now, much of the city was either burning or had already been destroyed by fire. Within hours, the president told them, the National Guard and localized units of the army would begin to deploy, forming a perimeter around all major arteries leading into the state. And by dawn, with a synchronized signal streaming in from the sky, the doors would slam shut on Alabama.

"Well, that's it then," said Charlie, as he shut down the transmission. They sat together on the couch overlooking the street. Olivia leaned over, resting her head on his shoulder.

"Does that mean we're locked in?" she asked.

"No." Charlie patted her head affectionately. "It's one-directional. Anyone arriving from the interior will still be allowed passage out, after a certain amount of interrogation, but no one will be allowed in under any circumstances. Not without a destroyer escort and a few tanks, they won't."

"So, if we were to show up at the border we'd be safe?"

"Yes, I suppose we would. But getting us there would be anything but safe. For now we need to stay put right here, under our blanket of immunity, and hope someone either puts a bullet through the brain of our good general, or he has an epiphany and starts his own roadside lemonade stand."

"What the hell does that even mean?"

"I don't know." Charlie laughed, ruffling Olivia's hair with an outstretched hand. "It's late, I'm tired, and I wish I was drunk."

———◆———

Around noon of the next day the limousine returned. General Sedgewick exited alone, walked up the drive, and then ascended the stairs alongside the mortuary, where he politely knocked at the door. Charlie met him there.

"Colonel," said Charlie, opening the door with a slight smile playing at his lips.

Sedgewick returned the same degree of smile. "Don't push me, Chester. I like you. I really do. And I think we will be very useful to each other. Respect me in the manner I deserve, and I'll respect you back. Let's not put alternatives on the table."

Charlie bowed less than eloquently. "Well, then hell, *General*, come on in. Bless us with your presence and your wisdom." He

pointed to the couch. "That's Olivia," he said. "Briggs' daughter. She also gets some of that respect you're dishing out or we will definitely run into one of those alternatives."

"Of course." The general nodded. "Good to meet you, Miss." Samantha King walked in from the kitchen just then, followed by Briggs. "Ahh, Miss King, you're the reason I'm here."

Samantha nodded, sipping from a cup as nonchalantly as she could. "I'm flattered," she said. "You've been the main topic of conversation around here. If I can ever get through to CBN, I'm sure you'll make me quite famous."

Sedgewick laughed softly. "Sorry about that. We knocked down a few towers and cut a few wires on our way in. But only here in the south end of the state. I am told communications will be restored very shortly. Possibly within the hour. Your government has some very busy bees working just outside the lines."

"The lines?"

Charlie broke in. "Yeah, the lines. It's all part of the game the general is playing. You have to have lines, and you have to have rules. Otherwise it's not really a game, now is it, General? It's just chaos." Sedgewick, noting his title had been restored, nodded pleasantly at Charlie.

"Well said, Mister Benton. And yes, a game must have rules. We'll be going over them today, with everyone." Sedgewick's eyes turned again on Samantha King. "As I said before, you're the reason I'm here. When I learned of your presence, I knew there was a reason for it. You came for a story. A simple story about a tragedy and the events surrounding it. I offer you so much more than that. I want you to accompany me. Observe me. Chronicle me. When this is over, and the game, as Mister Benton so fondly calls it, has been played, someone needs to face the world with facts. Not rhetoric, not a crazy account of some lunatic who set loose a pack of wolves in the swamplands of Alabama, but a reckoning. And the truth of what went on. Twelve beautiful souls lost their lives. Think about it. Twelve wonderful young ladies in the bloom of youth. Who wanted only to frolic across the earth like lambs at play. And lambs they

became, only slaughtered ones. They needed an archangel to rise up in their defense. Well, I am here now. Late perhaps, but I am here." The general's face lowered, his eyes on the floor. "When they come to bury me, someone has to stand up and tell the truth. Tell the story. That's all I ask of you."

"Holy shit." Olivia jumped up from the couch. "I'm in." She looked first at her shocked father, then at Samantha, before her eyes came to rest on the general. "And I come with no bias. An innocent with a pen. I'll write the crap out of this." Moving across the room, she walked up very close to the general. "If you've come as a destroyer I'll expose you for it, but if you've come with a greater purpose, a noble one, then the world needs to know. As you say, the truth."

Sedgewick laughed aloud then, a thick smile spreading over his face. He looked at the girl, his lips betraying just a touch of warmth. "How old are you?"

"Sixteen. How old are you?"

"Sixty-one."

"Well then, if you were to step back, and I was to step forward, we would meet in just over twenty-two years. That's not even a single generation." Olivia spoke without taking the least breath to calculate. "And on Saturn that would amount to less than a year in real time. So, if you don't mind adding in a celestial component, we're a lot more closely connected than one might suppose."

The general's smile broadened as he turned back to Samantha King. "I want you both," he said. His eyes then sought out Shawn Briggs, who was standing with mouth open in the background. "Mister Briggs, if you don't mind? Your daughter would add a youthful perspective. As she said, an innocent one. I think that's where the greatest truth is always to be found, in innocence. She also has a quality of great... how do I say... exuberance. It's something I am especially attracted to. At my age one can never get enough of that."

Briggs spoke. "I'd prefer my daughter not be part of this, General. I mean no disrespect, but I'm fairly certain the wounds

she's already received from this whole affair are going to be with her for a long, long time."

While Olivia glared at her father, the general pouted for a moment. "I hear that," he said finally. "Well, let's think on it for a while. I am extremely grateful for the gift you've already given me. The opportunity. I hold you in the highest regard. White, as you may have suspected, is not my color of preference, but you wear it well."

"So where do we go from here, General?" Charlie cut in. "When do we get a look inside that head of yours?"

"Soon." The general's smile dampened. "I'm not hiding my intentions from any of you. In fact, that will become apparent this afternoon." The general waved a friendly hand. "I'd like to invite you all to accompany me now. We've got business to attend to in town." He looked around. "Where's Willie?"

A few minutes later they all climbed into the limo for the short drive into town. Willie sat with Olivia in the front-most guest seat, facing rearward, his hand tightly clutching hers. He leaned timidly against the girl, who sat there, upright but relaxed. The general smiled to himself at that. He sat in the rear seat, facing forward, and in the center, with Briggs and Samantha King surrounding him. Chester Benton sat up front with the driver.

As the car began the drive down the long main street into Harbor Springs, it became clear that whites still roamed about freely. Not in any great abundance, but enough so that it was noticeable. The general explained that a certain number of them had already been *freed*, having been adjudged by members of the black community to be positive, fair minded individuals with little perceived prejudice. A bus from the school had been brought out earlier in the day, its long rows of side windows curtained up with drapes of white, linen sheeting. Every yard or so, and adjacent to each seat, two large eyeholes were cut so one could sit comfortably aboard the bus, stare through the holes and not be observed by anyone from the outside. Black citizens were invited aboard, driven in close to the gymnasium, and all of the whites who had been gathered there were paraded in a grand circle around them, so the ones who had displayed an open

racial bias could be identified. When Charlie saw the bus in town a few minutes later parked next to the bank, he couldn't help but notice it would have made a perfect training vehicle for youngsters of the KKK.

"Nice bus," he chuckled, as the driver pulled up close to the front doors of the bank and stopped. "With eyehole curtains. They would have loved that back in the day."

The general leaned forward, laughing lightly. "Yes. It rather captures the mood of a bygone era, don't you think? An era that, with a few minor modifications, is coming home to roost." The six then climbed from the limo and entered the building. The bank was composed of one large room, which extended the full length of the place, with a row of teller cages and desks lined up against a side wall. Dozens of folding chairs, perhaps as many as a hundred, were laid uniformly throughout the room, each now holding a very anxious black member of the community, in an even mix of men and women. Some of the general's men were also present, but not many, and none were armed. Several of them brought out five additional chairs, setting them up to face the already seated audience. Sedgewick motioned his five guests to sit.

"I'm very glad to see all of you here," the general began. "It seems we have a full house, and since you attended voluntarily, that pleases me greatly. Each of you represents at least one family here in the township or its outlying areas. So I'm thinking we can reach just about everyone with this one meeting. This morning some of you participated with me in a cleansing of sorts. We hand-selected those less pigmented among you who were considered worthy, and those who were not." Sedgewick moved forward, until he was very close to those seated in the front. He smiled conspiratorially. "It will never be told who among you rode that bus. Not by me or anyone connected to me. If the information should seep from among yourselves, that will be your problem. But nothing will come from me or my men." The general turned, pointing directly at Briggs, who, of the five, sat nearest him. But his next comment clearly indicated them all. "I intentionally left my friends here off this morning's itinerary. They

knew nothing about it and are to be held completely blameless." The general walked over to Briggs, positioning himself behind the man, whom he then tapped lightly on the head. He moved past Olivia and Willie, Charlie and Samantha King, tapping each one in turn. "They are to be treated as my guests at all times. Harm even one of them and the consequences will be harsh. They will be roaming among you from time to time, and their business is to be considered my business." Moving back to the front, where he could directly address the crowd, he continued. "They are... the agents of my legacy."

The general then laid out some ground rules. "Those of you who wish may return with me to the school. You will be given the opportunity to select any white individuals who have acted especially egregious toward you. They will be put under your care. And your benevolence towards them, or lack thereof, will be entirely up to you. They are to be treated as your personal property, your *slaves*, if you will. They are to do your bidding exactly as you ask, or punishment will be meted out. One thing, however, that is especially important. Under no circumstances are you to punish arbitrarily on your own. Infractions are to be reported to my representatives for judgement and retribution. This is as much for your safety as anything else. When this ends, and it will, your hands need to be as free of white blood as possible. I will soon be making an announcement to the world of what is transpiring here, and I will emphasize that you have been ordered by me to participate. This should make any future adjustments by you back into the folds of society a bit easier to bear." Sedgewick nodded thoughtfully. "And that brings me to another important point. I want you to think long and hard before joining this enterprise of mine. If need be, my men and I can handle everything that needs to be done. We can operate the plantations, run the stores, and take care of the day-to-day operations of the town, while you go about your business as innocents. You can watch from the sidelines as a great theatre unfolds before you. Only those of you who burn inside to correct past wrongs, and are willing to potentially sacrifice yourselves should consider what I'm proposing. The rest of you can sit back with your families, watch... and enjoy."

A man from the audience raised his hand. "Yes," said the general, amicably pointing at him.

"As you said, most of us have family or friends that needs protectin'. But that don't mean we don't feel the hate. And not just our own hate, but the hate of our daddy's and our daddy's daddies. A hundred years of hate." The man looked at the faces around him. "We all feel it. It never goes away. Like a snake wrapped around your neck, just squeezin' and squeezin' till you can't breathe no more. That's why we're here, to see what this is all about." The man coughed uncomfortably. "But you ain't the Lord Jesus, and you ain't no messiah. You're just a man with a club. And when you leave, another man's gonna come along with a bigger club. And he's gonna call us nigger and beat the shit outta us. What we gonna do then?"

The general drew himself up, standing as tall and as straight as he could. "I am aware," he said, his voice loud and rich. He looked down at the man, then swept his eyes across the room. "That's why for most of you the game we're about to play is folly. You should go home, be with your loved ones and let me be the messenger here. My intention is merely to let you know what is about to happen, and give anyone who wishes it an opportunity to martyr themselves for a greater good." Sedgewick smiled. "I don't anticipate that will include many of you. Maybe none."

As they left the building the general's words turned prophetic, as not a single member of the audience followed them outside. Even Willie appeared confused, asking if maybe he should step back inside, into the fold of his people. "No." Olivia moved over close to the old man. "It'll be alright. Let's see this through together."

"Okay, Missy," said Willie as he rubbed a tired hand across his forehead. "Let's see it through."

Throughout the general's speech, the wheels inside Briggs' mind were racing. All he'd wanted was to do right, to set things right, as his job and moral compass dictated. There was no real bravery in the man. He knew that. In fact, most of what he had done was driven into him by his daughter, like a stake through the heart. His way would have been easier. Set something ferrous near that compass,

until the needle swung wildly in an alternate direction, allowing him to function less dangerously. He swore softly to himself. He should have kept his mouth shut and said nothing. Done nothing. The sheriff and the governor had been right. Sometimes when a person acts without thinking, things can go terribly wrong. Before entering the limo with the others, he grabbed Charlie, pulling him aside.

"Look, we need to talk. You told me if we came back down here with you things would be fine. My country needed me, you said. The president needed me." His face twisted as he spoke. "This is so screwed up. Olivia thinks this guy is some kind of ideologue. I can see it in her eyes. She has no idea how crazy this is, or what you're asking of us." Briggs' grip on Charlie's arm tightened. His voice was a hoarse whisper. "Get us out of here, Charlie. Please."

The general, stooping to enter the car, stopped, and swung in the direction of the two men. "Problem, gentlemen?" he asked.

"No, sir," responded Charlie. "Briggs here just wanted to borrow a dime for a candy bar." He stared at the general, as the general stared back.

"I remember those days. Ten-cent candy. Those days are gone, boys. Everything costs more now." Sedgewick pointed politely at the door, and stepped back to allow the two men to enter before him.

Chapter Twenty-Four

The scene at the gymnasium was not as calm as during their first visit, even though the crowd had been cut by almost half. Still, some four hundred frightened faces were huddled together at one end of the great room. For Olivia and Samantha, who were there for the first time, the realization that these people were prisoners, hostages, came as an awakening. The general gave the two a comforting glance as he ordered a row of chairs be assembled for his guests, directly upon the eagle in the center of the gym.

"We meet again," the general began, raising his arms to address the gathering. "I should say I am surprised, yet delighted, to see so many members of the community missing from your ranks today, having been pre-selected as worthy of our benevolence. That would indicate the level of depravity here in your little corner of the state is not as cancerous as once thought." Smacking his lips together, he continued, "It's still a sizeable tumor, however, which will need some attention." He laughed. "I again apologize for my own eloquence, as I realize most of you simply do not possess the intellectual acumen to draw upon a metaphor which compares you to a mass of degenerating tissue, but I'll leave that for you to deal with. I'm sure most of you feel like a hog does, just before slaughter. Only perhaps

the hog better understands what is about to befall it, which is why it screams so loudly, while you sit there sadly in a puddle of your own misery."

"What the fuck," whispered a man in the front row, not too distant from the general.

It was quiet enough that the words were almost discernable. "What was that?" General Sedgewick puffed himself up, stepping nearer to the source of the sound. As had happened on their last visit, an aide jumped out from the side.

"He said, 'What the fuck', General." The aide pointed at the transgressor.

"What the fuck, indeed." The general moved in close to the accused. He bent low, until their faces almost touched. Two other aides, large, muscular men with batons, stepped from their ranks. They moved swiftly to join the general near the bleacher. "Anything else you'd like to share with us? Anything at all?" Unsnapping the riding crop attached to his waist, Sedgewick fondled it in his hands like a treasure. Shifting slightly to his right, he reached out with the crop, running the smooth leather lash of the whip gently down the face of a woman seated next to the man. He rolled it down the woman's neck, and into her bosom, where the soft leather coils massaged at the tops of her breasts. "Ahh," said the general, moaning lightly. "What a lovely evening of entertainment you would provide for me and my men, my dear," he said, his voice purring. The man beside her stiffened, then trembled miserably, but his eyes looked down and stayed down. "Good," said the general, his face lighting up as the crop moved over to dance lightly across the man's shoulders. "You can learn." Stepping back from the crowd, he beamed. "I like this man. You should all take a lesson from him. He's just learned how to be a good nigger."

Olivia, sitting with Briggs on one side and Willie on the other, leaned close to her father. The two looked at each other. "Oh, my god. He's crazy." She mouthed the words. Briggs reached out to lock a hand onto her knee. He nodded without voicing anything in return, but their eyes spoke. At the other end of the row, seated next

to Charlie, Samantha King's eyes lit up. When arriving in Harbor
Springs her mission had been a simple one. Tell the story of a great
American tragedy. That would have been enough for her. Then she
had met Briggs, and was taken by the simplicity of the man. He
would be an even greater story, she told herself. An average man
with an average life in an average town, who had been graced with
greatness by uncovering the true nature of that same tragedy. But
now here, right here in this little gymnasium, in the middle of No
Place, Alabama, the real story unfolded. It was the general. She
watched him move about the gym like a puma watches its prey just
before pouncing. Her body language changed, her legs swinging
forward, her knees parting slightly. Her lips twitched in anticipation.
This was her story, and this glorious madman would help her write it.
Whatever it took, she would own this man.

General Sedgewick walked back to where his five guests sat. He
eyed them all one by one, reading them, evaluating their potential as
his allies. The girl, he thought, could perhaps be persuaded to idolize
him, telling his story fairly and without prejudice. Willie, her willing
accomplice, would follow any path she chose for them, so those
two were quite probably already in his camp. Briggs would present
more of an obstacle. The man possessed a certain moral fiber, a
confusing one, however, as he seemed timid, almost to the point of
cowardice, seldom speaking his mind or allowing his feelings to peek
out. In fact, he often hid behind his daughter's thoughts, allowing her
great leeway with their decisions. With a little work and manipulation,
he could dominate this man. Chester Benton was the one known
quantity. He was smart, strong and completely unbendable. As
close to a superhero as one could be, the general supposed. But
like all superheroes, Benton had a weakness. He cared. He would
never act outside the best interests of those around him. A simple
threat against the others would act as kryptonite, swiftly bringing
Mister Benton to his knees. That left Samantha King. The general's
appraisal of her was swift and certain. He looked down at her now,
watching her lips curl into a smile. This one was as cunning as she was
beautiful. But she needed him badly. Needed his story, just as she

needed air and sustenance. Her devotion to the story would be
indiscernible from her devotion to him. He could play with that, he
thought. A game within the game.

The general laughed aloud suddenly. He turned around to face
his audience. "For your pleasure I've prepared a bit of entertainment.
I want you all to relax, get to know me. I think that's been the
problem. You've seen me in much too severe a light. There's
really no reason we can't all be fond of one another." His laughter
intensified, until finally he motioned to one side of the gym, to
where a pair of brass handled doors stood. The doors swung open,
and in marched a group of young children, six in all, three girls and
three boys, each aged around four or five. All of them were white.
"Ahh," called out the general. "You're here." He clapped his hands
together, waving the children closer. "I'd like you all to observe the
new generation, and what they've been able to digest and put to
use in the space of less than a day. It offers new hope. And it will
most certainly close the debate many of my fellows have thrown at
me, that you people are simply not teachable." Moving to where the
children stood timidly looking out at the crowd, the general gently
grasped the hand of one little boy. He led the child in closer, until
they were but a few feet from the bleachers. Patting him on the head,
Sedgewick then nodded, smiling expectantly. The boy smiled back
shyly, but cleared his throat and chanted out,

> "Old Jim Crow spent a life aloof,
> Until one day he fell off the roof.
> And landing squarely on his head.
> Old Jim Crow was rightly dead."

"Yes, yes." The general was openly exuberant. "Let's kill the
raven bastard." He motioned for the other children to join the boy.
Soon they were all chanting loudly,

> "Old Jim Crow knew his way around,
> He could get you beat without a sound.
> Full of cunning and full of wit,

But mostly Crow was full of shit."

"Yes, yes," the general applauded vigorously. "Yes, little ones. You make me proud." Reaching out to a tiny girl, he pulled her away from the others, and led her right up against the lowest row of the bleacher, to where they could almost touch those gathered there. He kneeled down beside her, his arm curling around her waist. Pointing to a very pale skinned man who sat just inches away, he said, "And what's this, child?"

The girl smiled shyly. "It's a nigger man," she said, in a voice sweetly tuned.

"Ah," said the general, "No, little one, but you are so close." He turned the child so they were eye to eye. "It's just a nigger."

Not a single sound emanated from the crowd. General Sedgewick backed away, until he had gained sufficient distance to view everyone equally. He nodded to an aide and the children were ushered back through the doors. Drawing from his pocket a folded piece of paper, he unfolded it, holding it chest high where he could best read its contents. "I have here a set of rules," he began. "Not to worry, nothing out of the ordinary. Nothing written here should be offensive to anyone, as it draws its substance directly from our histories, yours and mine, and I can find no fault with it. Let's see," he said, as he scanned the document.

"Rule number one: From this day forward, and until the moment of your deliverance, you shall refer to yourselves only as niggers. You shall be called nigger, and whenever you address your fellows you will identify yourself as a nigger at all times."

"Rule number two: When addressing any citizen whose color indicates a racial superiority over your own, and that will include *any* color other than your own, you will preface every sentence with the words, 'yes sir' or 'no sir', or 'yes ma'am' or 'no ma'am', depending, of course, on the gender of that superior."

"Rule number three: Never... never are you to make direct eye contact with a person outside your race." The general looked up from the paper. "I can't emphasize this enough," he said stiffly. "If you're caught looking into the eyes of a black man there will be swift

punishment. And God help you…" He raised one hand high over his head. "If you are caught gawking at a black woman you will wish to hell you had never been born."

"Rule number four: You will at all times, and with good spirit, do the work set before you. It may be as simple as picking cotton or gathering vegetables from the garden. Or it may be as complex as shoveling shit from the bowels of an outhouse. You will appear always cheerful as you go about your daily tasks."

"Rule five." The general paused, a sly smile breaking out on his face. "My personal favorite, because it's filled with affection." He cleared his throat. "Rule five states that the women among you must always present themselves in as comely a manner as possible, and be ready to fulfill their master's requests at any time. And she will come willingly to him, submit to him, and be as a graceful flower unfolding."

"Oh, hell no, you sunovabitch!" a man screamed from high in the bleacher. He rose and crashed his way through a sea of faces, trying desperately to get to the general. Another man joined him, then another. The three almost made it, rolling out onto the court like a trio of angry bulls.

Charlie met the first of them, a small, muscular man, several paces onto the floor. He flew out of his chair, diving low into his target, swiping an arm at the knees. As the man crashed to the floor onto his stomach, Charlie leapt up, landed on the man, and pinned him down securely. "Stay down," he whispered harshly. "Just stay the hell down."

The other two attackers were treated less kindly. Two of the general's aides rushed forward, taking them down with batons. They were knocked to the floor, where they were beaten for several moments, until the general raised his hand and ordered the aides to desist. Sedgewick stepped forward then, a cruel smile tugging at his lips. His foot brushed roughly against the face of the nearest antagonist. "Another one of those failure to communicate moments," he said. His eyes caught Charlie's. "I live for this shit." Turning his attention to the crowd, he continued. "Every herd, whether it be

sheep or cows or slaves, has occasional outbreaks which need to be swiftly dealt with so as not to infect the entire herd. It can be anthrax, or mad cow, or even, as in this case, gross viral stupidity. It matters not, as long as those infected are removed and disposed of." The general shook his head as though shaking off a great trouble. "It's a sad duty, but a necessary one." Several more of the general's aides moved in from the side. Charlie released his grip on the man he'd been holding, as the three attackers were gathered up and dragged across the floor and out of the gym.

General Sedgewick held himself up stiffly, moving a pace or two closer to the gathering. "There are a few other rules I should probably go over with you, but we can do that another time. You niggers wear me down, I swear you do. For now, you will be separated and sent off to perform various work details. Many of you will be dispatched to work the local plantations, one of which I will be operating myself. Others will remain here in town. A few may even be claimed by citizens who feel some sort of special attachment towards you, some sort of history. That should make things interesting."

As the general spoke, Willie's fading eyes strained to focus on a specific area in the crowd. Suddenly he rose from his chair without a word, walking towards the general, and then past him until he drew himself up very close to a man seated in the left-most portion of the lowest row. He stood there, very still, as the man locked eyes with him. The general stepped up suddenly, swiping at the man's face with his whip. The lash cut deeply. "Look down, boy. Don't you dare look up."

Olivia arrived then, coming in swiftly from behind. "Willie, what are you doing?" she said, her voice shaking.

Willie's eyes remained riveted on the man. "This is Tom Clayton," he said. "We was friends once, a long time ago. Remember, Tom?" Reaching out, he tapped at Clayton with an outstretched finger. "Had a visit from some of your boys the other day. They beat me up pretty good."

Clayton started to raise his head, then stopped himself. "I'm

sorry, Willie," he said, his voice broken. "It was a mistake. I'm sorry."

The general said, "He had you beat?"

"Yes, sir. He owns the Cedar Creek Plantation, across the road from my place out on the highway. He don't take so well to havin' me for a neighbor."

"You want him? You want to own him?"

Willie's eyes flickered brightly. Just to Clayton's right sat a young teenage girl, about Olivia's age. He pointed at the girl. "This is Clayton's granddaughter," he said. "I want her."

Tom Clayton's head rose then, his eyes on fire. Rising from his seat, he grabbed at Willie's shirt. "You sunovabitch," he screamed. "I swear to God, Willie. I swear to God." That's as much as Clayton was able to say, as a baton crashed down on his head and he sank, barely conscious, to the floor.

"Take her," offered the general. He smiled knowingly at Willie. "A young wench like that. She'd make an old man forget all about being beaten."

As the limousine pulled up at the mortuary sometime later, the general spoke. "We've had quite an afternoon. And it'll only be more entertaining from here on out." Olivia and Briggs exited first, followed by Willie and his new possession, Tom Clayton's granddaughter, who wore a tether around her neck. It had been hanging freely, but now the general grabbed at the loose end, handing it to Willie. "Tight leash," he said, "and firm hand." The girl reacted numbly, but was very obedient. As Charlie exited the front passenger seat to join them, Sedgewick swung shut the rear door. The window rolled down and he leaned forward to speak. "I want to thank you, Chester. For coming to my aid today."

Charlie stood very tall. "I didn't do it for you. You must know that."

"No matter. The effect was the same. You can't help yourself, you know." The sly smile returned to the general's lips. "Oh, and Miss King won't be joining you tonight. If she is to chronicle me properly, I have much to discuss with her." Samantha King smiled coyly as she slid closer to the general. Then the limo swung around and drove away.

Chapter Twenty-Five

There are seven main highways entering into Alabama from the north, east and west, and as many as a dozen ancillary ones. As the state continued to combust from within, these passages were blocked at the border by federal troops. And every day, additional detachments would arrive, probing deeply into the Alabama countryside in an attempt to constrict conflict as they slowly inched their ways toward the main cities of Birmingham and Montgomery. The president ordered his field commanders to show the utmost restraint, using deadly force only as a last resort. Resistance, however, was light, as most dissenters had deserted the smaller outlying communities, choosing instead to swarm into the larger metropolitan areas where they could join the tens of thousands of others who already swarmed there.

As troops edged ever closer to Birmingham in the north, Manuel Ortiz drove south in his pickup, headed for Harbor Springs. The roadway was nearly devoid of traffic, as almost everyone was either participating in the unrest, or holed up somewhere in an attempt to wait it out. His heart was light as he drove along, his hands tapping jubilantly on the steering wheel. His *sniper* attack at the capital had been wildly successful. In his mind he had become the sole reason,

the antichrist, responsible for all of the hate which was now the south. "I came, I saw, I conquered," he chanted over and over. In his rear view mirror he noticed flashing lights approaching. "Shit," he said to himself. "The bastards are coming for me." He shook uncontrollably for a moment, then steadied himself and reasoned. "How the hell would they know anything about me? I'm just a man in a truck." Pulling to the side of the road he waited. Soon three state patrol cars swooshed past, their drivers not even giving him a passing glance. "Must be an emergency ahead," he said. "Maybe I can lend a hand."

A few minutes later, as he rounded a curve, he again saw the patrol cars, this time stopped and blockading the road ahead. Three white officers stood in the center of the highway, nodding at one another. Seeing him arrive, one stepped forward, raising his hand. Manuel's heart raced. He rolled down his window. "Yes, officer?"

The man tipped back the visor on his cap, then placed a hand on the pickup's door. "What's your business?" he asked.

Ortiz smiled courteously. "I'm headed down to Harbor Springs. To stay with family. Too much shit goin' on back there. Had to get out."

"I hear that," said the trooper. "Unfortunately, we can't let anybody in. Orders from the top. There's some kind of military crap goin' on down south. A lot of folks getting hurt. Wouldn't be safe to let you in."

"Oh," said Ortiz, genuinely surprised. "They have trouble in Harbor Springs?"

"Seems so." The trooper waved a hand. "At any rate you'll have to turn around. Maybe find yourself a safe place up the road. Dolan City is still pretty hospitable, I hear." As the man spoke another of the troopers moved up beside him. The new trooper nodded politely.

"Dolan's not bad," he said. "Blacks are all gone. Gone north for the show." The trooper leaned down to more closely inspect Ortiz. "You a Mex?" he asked, his voice not unfriendly.

"Yes, sir. But half-white," Ortiz smiled as he lied.

"You look all Mex." The man leaned closer. "But you ain't

black, so like we're sayin', you'll be okay in Dolan City. You just move along now."

"Yes, sir," said Manuel respectfully. Fond of his rasp as a killing tool, Ortiz was not limited by it. He believed strongly that whatever weapon worked under a particular set of circumstances was the weapon of choice. As he smiled at the two officers his hand slowly slipped beneath the seat, extracting a small .25 caliber automatic handgun, stolen from one of the Muslims back in California. His thumb flicked off the safety. "You all have a nice day," he said, as he raised the pistol and opened fire. The first round went directly into the face of the leaning trooper, with two more following closely. Then he turned the weapon on the second man, four rounds plucking away at the man's chest as he tumbled backwards onto the highway. Without a second's hesitation, Ortiz dropped the pistol, gunned the accelerator, and pointed his truck directly at the now frantic third officer who was attempting to draw his weapon. The trooper stood near one of the squad cars, and as Ortiz made impact, the man's body was crushed up against the rear passenger door, merging flesh with metal. The man screamed, but stayed erect, pinned there between the bumper of the truck and the car. Slumping forward onto the hood of the truck, he lay there moaning. Manuel smiled as he pulled from between the seat and the console one of his favorite rasps. "I didn't forget you, old friend," he said aloud, his voice rising in pitch.

———◆———

Manuel arrived in Harbor Springs sometime late in the day, as the sun leaned heavily to the west. The town seemed much too quiet. Too orderly. At every corner, groups of young black men gathered, a few armed with rifles, a few with sidearms, but mostly they were unarmed men clustered together in loose formation. The sidewalks contained even more blacks, but of all ages, ambling along from

one store to the next, or waiting curbside for transport. Several whites could also be seen from time to time, walking timidly along the narrow strips of pavement adjoining the street. They moved deliberately, as if a task was at hand, and they kept their eyes lowered to the ground. Ortiz wondered at this, but not too deeply. He had other things to think about. "Where is everyone?" he thought to himself. "There should be riotous mobs of people swarming everywhere. Was this not the town where the tragedy began? What the hell?"

Parking the truck on a side street, he exited, rounded a corner and headed for a drug store a half block ahead. Several men broke away from their group on that same corner, approached him and blocked his path. "Who are you?" one said crisply.

Manuel stopped and stiffened. "Manuel Ortiz," he said boldly, seeing no reason to lie. "I've just arrived from the north."

The men fanned out, partially surrounding him. "I don't know what you think you're doing here, but this is not an open town. It's secure."

Looking from one face to the next, Manuel spoke. "What does this mean? Secure? Are you military?"

"Yes," the man nearest him spoke. "We represent the people's government, under the command of General Sedgewick. And as I said, this town is secure." The man motioned toward a van parked at a nearby curb. "You'll have to come with us. You need to be designated."

"Designated?" Ortiz took a half-step backwards, calculating the odds of his making it back to the truck before these men could take him down. He also realized that he was weaponless, and helpless against such a numerically superior force. He forced a quiet smile. "Look, I didn't know. Why don't I just climb back into my pickup and head on out of town the way I came in. No harm, no foul."

"Bring him," someone hollered from the van, as two men reached out to grab Manuel's arms, escorting him to the waiting vehicle. Its rear doors swung open, exposing four very frightened white faces and one other man, who might have been a Mexican. Manuel began to struggle then, ripping one hand free, which he used

to smash the jaw of the man who had just released him. Several others jumped in, beating him down with batons, while the butt of at least one rifle impacted his head. The skirmish was over in a matter of seconds, as Ortiz found himself picked up from the pavement and flung head first into the van. As the doors slammed shut behind him it became instantly dark, to the point of pitch blackness. The van had no windows, and whatever light had once seeped from the driver's cab into the box had been completely blocked off. He lay there for several long minutes, feeling the vehicle's tires grind away on the asphalt. They were heading somewhere, fast. Finally, through the darkness, a voice spoke.

"You're about a dumb ass." Hoarse laughter followed.

Ortiz blurted out, "What's going on? Where the hell are they taking us?"

"What, are you stupid?" sang the same voice. "You can't fight these people. I suspect we're goin' to work out on one of the plantations, or maybe they're gonna beat the shit outta us for tryin' to escape."

Manuel attempted a laugh of his own. "I've already been beat," he said. "What do you mean work? I ain't workin' for nobody."

"Man," a new voice started in. "Where you been? Did you miss the little meetin' in the gym? The general made it pretty clear what he expects from us. We're to be worked like dogs."

"I don't know what you're talkin' about. I just drove into town. Just now."

Several voices sounded out soft laughter. One spoke. "You came here willingly? You are a dumb ass. How'd you get in here anyway? The roads in are supposed to be blocked by the state, or at least that's what we heard on the radio. They were supposed to set up a blockade sometime today. And the roads out are blocked by the general and his boys. He wants to keep us all here for his personal entertainment. They must have all been out dancin' when you came along."

"Lucky break," said a voice that was most likely the Mexican's. "You didn't see anybody? Nobody try to stop you?"

"Nope," lied Ortiz. "Saw a couple patrol cars, but they didn't pay much attention to me."

The van slowed then, the men inside swaying to the left as the driver swung to the right. The sound of the tires changed suddenly, from the smooth rumble of the open road to a more staccato grinding as the vehicle began to move over coarse earth or gravel. The men grew silent. Soon the van slowed even more, then braked harshly, flinging the men into each other. "Shit," one called out as the doors swung open.

"Bring them out here." General Sedgewick stood nearby, in the shade of a giant oak, his crop lashing in rhythm against his leg. Samantha King stood at his side, her eyes bright with anticipation. She had not yet observed the general's manner of greeting newcomers, especially deserters. The six men were soon assembled before them.

A young, soft spoken aide stepped forward, pointing to each man in turn. "These four," he said, pointing out the whites, "were caught out on the Dolan City highway, trying to make their way north. They were assigned sewage detail yesterday, out at the ponds. Apparently they decided to run for it."

The general stepped forward, out from the shade and into the light. The sun would be setting soon, but it was still summer in the south, and summer meant heat. Raising the crop, he brushed it across the chest of each of the four. Sweat beaded up on their faces. "So," said the general, "you chose to disobey our covenant. Rule four, I believe. To work willingly and in good spirits." He shook his head sadly. "Most of your fellows have chosen to cooperate. They've chosen to appreciate the opportunity given them, to fulfill their responsibilities and to prosper. And then there's you." Sedgewick turned to Samantha King. "This is your first chance to observe my methods out here in the real world. To see that a leader, properly educated in the ways of men, can mete out fair and judicious punishment. Get your pen ready, my dear."

The general signaled two aides to join him. He looked closely at the four men standing there. "Which of you is the eldest?" he

asked. The men briefly glanced at each other, and then one stepped slightly forward, nodding respectfully. "I see," said the general. He spoke aloud to anyone within listening range. "I choose the eldest out of compassion, and reason. On average, he has less time to live amongst us, and therefore will be surrendering something less in the way of a quality life if this should turn out badly." At another signal, the two aides dragged the man forward, wrestling him to the ground. Another aide walked over to a nearby wagon and, reaching into its bed, brought forth an old, rusty sledge, one with a ten-pound head. He moved over to the downed man, whose eyes grew large as the hammer drew near. "Crush a knee," commanded the general. Without a moment's hesitation the aide raised the sledge, the man screaming even before the blow descended. As the hammer crashed down, biting into flesh and bone, there was not as much sound as one might expect. No loud snapping or cracking or crunching. Rather, there emanated from the site of the blow a soft thud, with little resonance, as the knee fragmented in a massive, fleshy explosion. Samantha King's mouth flew open as her eyes widened in horror, and one of the three remaining men awaiting punishment sank to his knees, vomiting a great gusher of yellow liquid onto the ground. The man who had faced the hammer let out a single, short scream, and went limp. "That went well," said the general, his face unmoved. He turned his attention to the three remaining whites. "I take it you have each learned a lesson from this?"

The two still standing stammered out, "Yes, sir," and the one on the ground, trying to stifle his stomach, nodded in vigorous agreement.

"Good." The general nodded to an aide. "Take these three up to the slave quarters. See that they are fed and given comfortable lodging for the night. In the morning please return them to their duties at the sewer." Sedgewick smiled at the men. "You'll do just fine." The general then turned his attention to Ortiz and the other Mexican. "You two plan on giving me any problems?" he asked.

"No, sir." The two spoke up quickly and simultaneously.

Stepping up close to Ortiz, the general inspected him first. "And what's your story?" he asked.

One of the men who had captured Manuel spoke up. "We caught him sneaking into town, sir. He drove in this afternoon."

"Drove in?" Looking dumbfounded, the general glanced over at Samantha. Her face had recovered somewhat, and she tried to smile back at him. "Look at this one, my dear. Dumb bastard drove right in." He turned back to Ortiz. "What the hell were you thinking, boy? For the past three days everyone has been trying to get the hell out of here, not come cruising in."

Manuel's mind worked furiously. "I heard about you up in Montgomery," he lied. "From some folks who got out. I liked what I heard. I hate fuckin' whites, sir. I've hated them all my life. I was hopin' you'd give me a chance to work with you." Coughing, Ortiz quickly amended, "For you."

The general's eyes narrowed. The crop in his hand twitched excitedly. "You're not black enough to work for me, boy. I've got no place for a Mexican."

"Excuse me, sir." Ortiz decided to take a great gamble. "I faced three Alabama state troopers on the way in here. Just to be with you. White troopers."

"And just how did you manage to make it past them, these white troopers of yours?"

Ortiz drew in a deep breath, then exhaled. "I didn't go past them," he said. "I went through them. They're still layin' out there, I'm thinkin'. About ten miles north of town. As I said, I hate fuckin' whites, and I think I could be really handy for you... Sir."

The general whistled sharply, then called out to a man standing nearby. "Jesse. I want you to drive on up there. See if what this man says is true." He turned back to Ortiz. "If it's true, I'll give you your chance. We'll see just how black you are. If you're lying, however, you'll become my pet. And you won't like it much."

Chapter Twenty-Six

Some geneticists suspect that imbedded in the hominid genome base, there resides a gene that can trace its ancestry all the way back to the most primordial of times. It's a wicked little fellow, lying in wait, and not at all conscious of newly evolving human traits such as kindness or compassion. It is the rape gene, thought to be a human frailty, but which is more likely derived from a position of potency and power. The gene carries as a companion its own edict, and an astounding number of males possess it. The edict states that, under the blanket of official sanction, and void of consequences, many men will elect to gratify themselves sexually at the expense of any unfortunate female who happens to fall within their grasp. It is especially alluring to organized groups of men, who rape under the guise of a command structure that says it is both permissible and acceptable to do so. During World War II, as many as fifty thousand Chinese women in Nanking Province were assaulted by an invading Japanese army, a festival of evil that lasted for more than a year. And more recently, in places like Somalia and Bosnia and Syria, wild mobs of men have raped and tortured tens of thousands of women, with very few participants stepping forward to vilify the incidents.

Willie now possessed his very own female. He owned her.

What's more, she was white, and closely tied to a man who had devoted a good portion of his life to Willie's personal humiliation. As the general drove away in his limo, Willie tugged at the leash binding the girl's neck and Tom Clayton's granddaughter, eyes cast downward, followed him obediently to his truck.

"Willie?" Olivia stepped off the walkway leading from the mortuary to the residence. "What are you doing?"

Willie looked back at her. Across his face, like a mask, was a look she had never before seen in him. His eyes were hollow, empty cells, his face pale, and his mouth barely moved as he spoke. "Goin' out to my ranch, Missy. We're all safe now. The general said so. We can wander about without fear." He then shook his head almost imperceptibly. "I'm goin' home."

"What? Wait, I'll go with you." She turned to look for her father, but Briggs had already entered the residence.

"No," the old man said. "I've got things to do, and I don't want you around right now." As a feeling of hurt tugged Olivia's lips downward, Willie loaded the girl into the pickup, backed down the drive, and drove away. Olivia raced into the house.

"Dad, Dad," she cried. "Willie's gone. He just took the girl and he's gone."

Briggs moved over to the window overlooking the street. "Really?" Charlie came walking out from the bathroom, wiping his hands on a towel.

"What's up?" he asked.

"Willie just drove off with the girl. Said he was taking her out to his ranch."

Briggs looked at his daughter tenderly. "I wouldn't worry, honey. It's Willie."

"You didn't see his face. It's like he barely knew me. Like he felt nothing. Less than nothing." Olivia's eyes began to tear up.

Charlie spoke. "He's a man who's been carrying around a lot of pain. For a long, long time. And that girl represents everything bad about the world. He looks at her and sees Tom Clayton spitting on him." Charlie squirmed a bit, which was completely

alien to his character. He looked at Olivia. "Men sometimes lose themselves when they're confronted by hate. They can become very irrational."

"No," Olivia cried out defiantly, her mind fighting its way out from a dark place. "He would never hurt anyone. Never. No matter how bad he feels. He would die first." She moved over to the window to stand next to her father.

Briggs placed a warm arm around her. "It'll be okay," he reassured her. "And you're right, it's Willie."

"I'll go get him," said Charlie softly.

"Wait," said Olivia. "I trust him."

"I don't," answered Charlie as he headed for the door. "I can't."

As Willie and the girl drove out of town, tracing the highway back to his home, they passed by many young, black men. Most nodded respectfully, and a few waved a quiet greeting. As the general had promised, there was no interference. They also drove past occasional groups of whites, both men and women, collecting roadside litter or hacking away at foliage encroaching on sections of the highway. Neither spoke for a long time, the girl's eyes glancing longingly out the window, while Willie's concentrated on the roadway ahead, his hands tightly constricting the wheel.

Soon they began to pass the long, white stretches of fence marking the boundaries of Tom Clayton's plantation. The girl's face tightened. Willie glanced at her. "I knew your grandpa when I was a kid. Once, a long time ago, we was friends."

The girl turned, caught his eyes and quickly looked down. "I've seen you," she said.

"Your name's Molly, right?"

"Yes, sir." Tears began to show in the girl's eyes, forming first as a mist, but then rolling down her cheeks in tiny rivers. She sobbed openly. "I'm sorry, Mister. I don't know what my papa did to you, but he's not a bad man. We're not bad."

"What your papa did?" Willie's hand flew forward, impacting the dash of the truck. The slapping sound caused the girl to jump. "Well, let's see. The last time we was friendly he smashed my face

down in the mud, then sold me to his brother. That was a long time ago, when we was kids."

The girl looked up hopefully. "That's just kids," she said, her voice a tiny, broken thing. "Papa's changed. He would never do that now. Treat someone like that."

A laugh emanated from somewhere deep inside Willie's chest. "Yeah," he said, his voice dripping sarcasm. "Your papa's turned out to be a fine, neighborly man. Why just a few days ago he offered to make nigger pie outta me. He was gonna spread my ass all up and down the highway. Then he spit on me by way of sayin' goodbye. A fine man, your papa."

The girl looked up. "That doesn't sound like my papa, but I'm sorry if he did that."

The leash lay loosely coiled on the seat between them. Willie grabbed at it, yanking it savagely. "Get your goddam eyes off me," he said, his voice alive. "*If* he did it? If?" The girl quickly bowed her head, new tears starting to fall. As the leash bit into her neck, she whimpered. Willie watched her for a moment, until his anger abated. "You think maybe I'm lyin'? You think I got nuthin' better to do than make up nigger pie stories?"

"No, sir. I didn't mean anything by it. Please."

Willie's face softened somewhat. "Do you even know my name?"

The girl thought for a moment. "Mister Scarett?"

"Scarlett, goddammit. Willie Scarlett. You been livin' across the road from me your whole goddam life and you don't even know my name. Molly."

"I'm sorry."

Willie tugged at the leash again, but this time less savagely. "How many times you seen me passin' by? How many times you call me nigger?"

"I never said that."

"How many!" Willie exploded. "And if you goddam lie I'll rip your foul little head off."

"I don't know." Molly began to sob. "I've said it. I don't know how many times."

Willie glared at the girl. "You goddam right you said it. Your whole goddam family does, whenever they see me or anyone like me. It's true, isn't it?"

Molly continued to look down. "Yes," she said, in a whisper. A raging hate flowed out through Molly's tears. Inside she could hear a voice screaming *nigger*, over and over. She thought of her papa. She knew she had to be strong for him, as he would be for her. They were the Claytons, and a black man might lay claim to her, but there would come a time when her papa would rise up and make everything right. Clenching her teeth, she almost smiled, but then the hate closed in again.

When they arrived at the farm, Willie pulled up and parked close to the house. He stepped down from the pickup, moving around to the passenger side where he opened the door for Molly. "You won't be tied up, so you can get rid of the leash," he said. "You ain't no dog." Reaching out he grabbed the girl's chin, forcing it upward. "If you run there's a lot of men out there who would love to get their hands on you." He forced her eyes to look at him. "Better one of me than a bunch of them. But that's for you to decide." Releasing her, Willie walked up the porch steps and into the house. After a few moments the girl followed. She found him in the kitchen, pouring raw potatoes into the sink. "Scrub these and put 'em in a fry pan." He grabbed at one of her hands, inspecting it. "You ever do real work? You know how to cook?"

"I can cook." Molly began the process of washing the potatoes, running them under cold water and roughly scrubbing at their skins until ribbons of white appeared.

"Don't kill the damn things."

Looking up at him, her body began to shake uncontrollably. "I'm sorry." She thought maybe he would scream at her for making eye contact, but he didn't. Instead he just looked at her smugly, as if assessing her potential, and finding little of value. "I'm a virgin," she said finally, sobbing out the words.

"Is that why you're fuckin' up the potatoes?"

Just then a loud knocking sounded at the front door. Willie

moved from the kitchen to the great room, but before he arrived at the entryway the doors swung open and in walked Charlie. "Willie," he said.

"Charlie. What can I do for you?" Willie knew exactly why Charlie was there, and Charlie knew he knew.

"You need to come back with me. Or at least send the girl back. You know that." Charlie's eyes tried to reason with the old man.

"She's mine." Willie spoke defiantly, surprising even himself. "She was given to me by the general. She's mine."

"You know that's not true. Whatever your intentions, I can't allow it."

"*You* can't?" Willie's voice rose. "Who the hell are you to tell me what to do?" The old man's voice fell as quickly as it had risen. "I didn't choose for this to happen. But it has. You above all others should understand that, Charlie. For whatever reason, good or bad, this man has come into our lives and thrown out a few crumbs of hope." His eyes glistened. "For the first time I can remember, I don't feel like shit. I feel like I matter. Like I can walk down the street with my head up in the goddam air an' nobody better tell me to look down no more."

"Oh, Willie." Charlie smiled at the old man, and any gruffness he might have felt evaporated. "I know. I haven't really lived it, not since I was a boy anyway, but I've seen it. Seen it my whole life. I can't pretend to know what you feel, but I sure as hell know what I feel. Don't you see? You're going to become exactly what you despise most. The very thing you rail against." Charlie's smile hung there for a moment, then faded.

"Let me do this, Charlie. Please. I need this. To make me whole."

Chester Benton stood there, about as strong as a man can be. His mind wandered back to those times in his life when he'd wished to make a difference, stick a sword in the sand for something bigger than himself, but had either failed or turned his back. He tried to probe deep into the psyche of the man standing before him, begging him now to stand down. "I don't know, Willie," he said, his voice lowered to the point of sadness. "What I do know is there's a young

lady back down the road who cares about you a great deal. My take on it is she cares as much for you as anyone she's ever met. Christ, to hear her talk, I think she loves you. Letting her down would be the saddest thing you could ever do."

Willie's eyes lowered. "Did she ask you to come out here for me?"

"No," answered Charlie honestly. "She said not to, and that she trusts you. And that you would die before you would allow another person to come to harm, no matter the circumstance."

Willie coughed uncomfortably, and shuffled his feet. "Well then she don't know me as well as she thinks, maybe." For just a moment their eyes met, and Chester Benton had his answer, conclusively. For there, spread all across the face of the old man, was the unmistakable look of shame.

"I'm thinking she does."

As the two stood there, face to face, Molly Clayton walked in from the kitchen. She had a spoon in her hand which she waved stiffly in front of her. "The potatoes are ready to cook, Mister Scarlett," she said. Charlie noticed she had been crying, the bags beneath her eyes still swollen and puffy. But he also noticed the leash, once tied tightly around her throat, was gone.

"How about if Olivia and I come out to visit you tomorrow?" he said. "Would that be okay?"

"Yes." The old man's eyes lit up, not with fire, but with a warm light. "That would be fine. We'll be right here." Then he nodded, "Thank you, Charlie."

During their supper, neither the old man nor the girl spoke a single word. The meal was a simple one, of boiled chicken, potatoes and some greens Willie pulled from the garden just outside the back door. They sat across from each other as they ate, at a tired old wooden table, the girl's eyes on her plate, and Willie's eyes on the girl. Finally, he put down his fork, pushed himself up and said, "Come with me. There's sumthin' I wanna show you." He led the way into the great room, still in a state of disarray from the day of the beating. Moving over to a couch he motioned the girl to follow, and to sit. A large album lay on the floor there, mixed in with some other

books and magazines. Willie picked it up, opened it and laid it out on his lap. Molly, meanwhile, was as far at the other end of the couch as she could be. "Move over here. Next to me," he said gruffly. The girl complied, sliding closer, but still keeping a bit of distance between them. The old man smiled at that, sliding his own body toward the girl until their legs and arms pressed against one another. "Never touch a black man?" he asked. Molly, her eyes cast downward, said nothing.

"Look," said the old man, pointing at a page. "That's my mama, taken about sixty years ago. The little boy tuggin' at her dress? That's me." He tapped at an old black and white photo. "You recognize that porch?"

Molly looked down at the photo. Her eyes lit up slightly. "That's my papa's porch." She glanced up at Willie. "Isn't it?"

"Yup. Wasn't back then though. Belonged to your great-grandpa. My mama worked for him back then. She walked up there every day. Sometimes carryin' sacks of potatoes or berries that your great-grandma would buy from us. Sometimes carryin' me."

"You knew my great-grandma?" Molly's eyes lit up further.

"Not me," the old man laughed. "At least not that I remember. But my mama used to work for her. Sewin' stuff and cleanin' stuff. Worked there for a long time." Turning a page, Willie pointed to another photo. "There's your great-grandpa there. Ridin' a tractor. In fact, I still gots it."

"You have our tractor?"

"This one, the old blue one. Well, it ain't blue here, but it's blue. Got it out behind my chicken shed. They gave it to my pa. Didn't ask nuthin' for it neither. Jus' said it was broke down but still good enough for nigger use. My pa used to love to tell that story."

Molly's eyes dimmed. "I've got an old bike," she said. "I don't ride it much anymore."

Willie's eyes danced at the girl. "Same thing then." Pointing at another photo, he described it. "This one's from the pond out by the highway. See them boys? That's your papa Tom, your uncle Cole, and the little black boy is me." Willie chuckled. "Heck, we musta been

six or seven. All naked as hell and havin' fun. Like I said before, we was friends."

Molly reached out a hand, tracing a finger across the photo. "That's my papa?"

"Yup. He called me Willie then, and I called him Tom. I thought we would always be friends. But a boy don't know much. A couple years later everythin' changed. My pa said some other white men were laughin' at your great-grandpa for havin' a black boy rubbin' up against his own boys. I got banned after that. I had to stay on my own side of the highway. If I didn't, they'd beat the shit outta me."

"Oh," said Molly softly. "Oh."

"Well," said the old man, clapping shut the album. "Enough for tonight. We can look at some more tomorrow. I jus' wanted you to know I wasn't always the nigger across the road. One time, a long time ago, I was jus' Willie."

Rising from the couch, Willie motioned the girl to follow. They left the living area, entering into a long hallway. Pushing open the first door they came to, he pointed into the room, at a blue covered bed tucked up against a far wall. A feeling of dread washed over the girl and she trembled. "Get ready for bed," Willie said to her.

"What about the dishes?" she said almost desperately. "I should do the dishes."

"Never mind that. I'll tend to the dishes. You jus' get ready for bed." Willie left her then, walking further down the hall, where he disappeared through another doorway. Molly stood there for a long time, before moving finally to the bed. She sat down on it, her knees tightly clenched and her face to the door. There was no light on in the room, but indirect light from the hallway cast a soft glow on the floor and the walls. Very soon, she knew, he would come for her. She knew it as surely as she drew breath. All the women had spoken of it, gathered together in their tight little bunches in the gymnasium. The talk had been endless and frightening. Let these men isolate you, and rape would follow. It was inevitable and inescapable. All black men were like that, they said. It's all they wanted. For a moment she considered running. But where could she go? Bands of blacks roved

the countryside like hungry dogs. If they got ahold of her it would be torture beyond belief. She hadn't even kissed a boy yet. Not even touched one. And now she pictured naked black bodies writhing all over her. Acid rose in her throat, but she sat there, frozen. After what seemed like a long time, she could hear stirring in the room adjoining hers. She heard the old man cough, and then the sound of a door closing. Suddenly the lights went out and the room was cast into darkness. "Now," she thought, "It will happen now." The house grew still and quiet. Finally she heard a sound, one at first she couldn't identify. It was soft, almost purring. Then she realized what it was. The old man, in the next room, was snoring.

Chapter Twenty-Seven

The Cedar Creek plantation had stood as a symbol of the south for more than two hundred years. It wasn't always called Cedar Creek, however, having the current name attached around the turn of the twentieth century. Before that it was The Cotton Queen, six thousand acres of some of the finest cotton country in the world. The original mansion, on exactly the same site as the Claytons' present one, had been burned to the ground during the fourth year of the Great War, when General Sherman had implemented his infamous scorched earth policy as a way to drive the southern aristocracy from the land. Back then, and for many years before the war, over four-hundred blacks lived in long rows of shacks a half mile further down the road from the main house. Remnants of those shacks still lay out there along one side of the creek, where a few stacks of chimney stones and piles of rubble lay up close to a series of old sewage ponds. It was felt that because the blacks stunk anyway, tucking their hovels up near the ponds would keep all of the stink comfortably contained and comfortably distant. As a sort of happy coincidence —or intelligent design— the shacks stood at some distance to the west of the mansion, so afternoon winds coming in from the south and the east would act as a natural air

freshener, keeping any foul odors further at bay from the delicate palates of the white folk at the manor.

General Sedgewick, in charge of Cedar Creek, and in keeping with the spirit of the game and the olden times, now housed his own white plantation workers in tents along the banks of these same ponds. They had been unused, and flushed many times by nature over the past hundred years or so, but by rerouting all of the septic lines from the more modern migrant workers' quarters, it took only days for raw sewage to begin building up in shallow pools, creating a fecal slime which bathed the surrounding air with an odorous mist. Compounding conditions for the born-again slaves, stiff cotton quotas were handed out, requiring each male or female field-hand to pluck, bag and process more cotton than was practicable. The improbable task was made even more so by the fact that cotton had already been harvested just weeks prior to the general's takeover, so not all that much was left on the stalk. The remaining cotton was called a cull, or pickover, and filling bags with a product that did not even exist became a frustrating endeavor. The punishment for finishing the day with bags unfilled was a supper of bowls of a potato gruel instead of meat, and rancid water instead of milk or coffee. At some point, one of the general's own men complained.

"We're starving them, sir. There's nothing for them to pick, and nothing for them to eat. I don't think slaves were ever treated this badly."

The general shrugged and spoke, his reasoning impeccable. "We have a limited amount of time. I have to pour a lifetime of suffering into a few short weeks. Nobody's going to die here. But before we are done, I need them to want to. That's the whole point. This isn't intended to be a picnic or a campout. I want them to feel what the Dinkas felt in Sudan, what the Jews felt at Auschwitz, and what our own people felt right here on this goddam plantation. That their lives are worthless. And that they only draw breath because we allow them to do so." The general tapped at the aide's chest. "And remember, this isn't for them. They are the worst of their kind, and wouldn't be here now if it wasn't for their own suffocating cruelty.

This little experiment of ours is for more compassionate souls who will likely study us at some future date, and marvel at what transpired here."

Manuel Ortiz stood close by, listening to the general as he spoke. He was always close to the general now. Not as close as Samantha King, perhaps, but well within the boundary of Sedgewick's inner circle. The general liked him. Almost trusted him. Ever since it was confirmed that Ortiz had fought his way in to join them, the general had offered the Mexican close sanctuary, and a bond had formed between them. Of all the men who worked for the general, Manuel was the only one un-black. This might have been part of the reason for his quick acceptance, as often times when offered a choice among four black puppies or a spotted one, one will choose the spotted pup for its uniqueness, with no regard for its character. And Ortiz was well spotted, caught in between worlds, not light enough to be white, nor dark enough to be black. He snarled now at the aide who so brashly challenged the general. "They'll eat what the general says they'll eat." He spat the words out with a certain level of venom, then pointed at the aide. "And you'd do well to hold your tongue." An amused smile played at the general's lips as he nodded at the two men and walked away.

Later, as evening fell and the laborers returned to the tent village from the fields, Ortiz was there to greet them. This was his favorite time, the evening time, when all the whites, caked heavily with sweat and the clay soil of the delta, would stumble down the road, stopping off at the well to splash water on their backs and faces, the agony of the day clearly spelled out in their eyes. He patrolled the levee, a slight rise between the ponds and the tents, where he could holler down to the stragglers. "Hurry the hell up," he yelled out. "I just heard nobody made their quota. I guess that means shit for dinner again tonight." As he laughed aloud, two men approached, both slouched over from the burdens of the day. "Watch it, boys," he cautioned as they drew closer. His hand slid down the side of his jeans, to where a twelve inch pig-gutter was laced into its sheath.

"You come any closer and I'll slit your fuckin' throats." Both men stopped, their eyes raised to meet his. "You lookin' at me?"

One of the men looked quickly away, but the other, the larger of the two, continued to hold Manuel's gaze. "I'm sorry, sir," spoke the man. "We've been watchin' you for the past few days." Raising a hand weakly, he waved it at Ortiz. "You're not like the others, and you're new here. We've been watchin'." The man took a step closer and Manuel's hand closed on the handle of the knife. "Please," begged the man. "We don't mean any harm or disrespect. We just need your help. Please."

Ortiz himself now stepped closer, to the very edge of the levee. "Fuck you," he said.

The large man winced, then forced a smile. "Look. It won't be long before they come for us. You must know that. The lines of communication are back up now. Even in here we hear about it. The government is gathering an army that will smash their way in here like rollin' thunder. As soon as they finish up north they'll head down here for us. It could be any day now. You must know."

Ortiz dropped to one knee, plucking at a strand of wheat straw which grew in abundance on the untilled portions of the plantation. Sticking the straw between his teeth he chewed quietly for a moment. Then he spoke. "Everything ends. But I'll tell you one thing. A lot of mutherfuckers are gonna die before the soldier boys get here. And you two are gonna be high on the list. Bet on it."

The second man, the one who had averted his eyes, now turned and locked them onto Ortiz. "Listen, please," he began. "We're not just a couple of hicks. I'm Tom Clayton. I own this place and have a helluva lot of money in the bank. One helluva lot." The second man pointed at the first. "And this is John Parrish. He's the sheriff of the whole goddam county, for chrissake." The man's eyes grew wide and imploring. "We're not without influence here. We can be influential in what happens to you when this is over. You're not like the others, that's obvious. I have no idea how you got into this mess, but we can help get you out of it. And we will." Both men smiled hopefully. "Just help us."

Ortiz stood, spitting the straw from his mouth. His eyes worked their way from one man to the other, closely inspecting each. "I could have your balls cut off for this," he said finally. He whistled softly. "Shit, man, a sheriff and a land baron. You two idiots got yourself into one helluva fix. The general know who you are?"

"He knows me." Tom Clayton spoke. "The sunovabitch who lives across the road pointed me out to him. As a reward, the general gave him my granddaughter." The anguish in the man's voice was obvious.

"A black man's got her? A nigger?" asked Ortiz.

"Yes." A flood of relief washed over both men. Ortiz had just identified the word nigger as black, and not white. He wasn't one of them. "He's got her now. We need to get the hell out of here so we can organize somethin'. Help us. Help us and you can come out of this thing like a hero instead of in a body bag. Help us."

Manuel looked hard at the man who was not Tom Clayton. "You're a sheriff. Always nice to have law and order on one's side. How'd you come to be here?"

A fog formed in John Parrish's eyes. "They killed my son. We were out at his farm, just east of here, when a whole goddam platoon came blastin' their way in. Shot the hell out of the place. Toby tried to run for it. He didn't make it."

Manuel's eyes challenged the big man. "And that didn't piss you off enough to make you fight? Man shoots your son and you just put your hands in the air like a pussy?"

Parrish felt a quick rush of anger. "It wasn't like that. And it wasn't a man. There were fifty of the bastards, all with automatic weapons. It was like a goddam army."

"Still," Ortiz pressed. "It was your son. You think they did that at the Alamo? Five thousand screaming Mexicans storming the walls, and about ten fuck-scared Texans shitting their pants. And not one raises his pussy little hands?"

Parrish squirmed, his eyes lowered to the ground. "You weren't there," he stammered.

"You goddam right I wasn't there. If I'd been there, I'd be lying

dead in the dirt with my son, and not standing here like a pussy beggin' for a handout."

Just then, one of the general's aides, out sweeping the road for stragglers or deserters, rolled up in a jeep. He looked first at the two laborers, then at Ortiz. "Problem?"

"No," said Ortiz with a snarl. "These two fools just wanted to know if we'd be handing out any meat tonight. Seems they don't approve what's been on the menu." The man in the jeep laughed as he drove off, and Manuel stepped down from the levee, moving up very close to Parrish and Clayton. "Get the fuck out of my face," he said. "You both stink like hell." His eyes spoke to them for a moment, and then he walked away, heading for the mansion.

Chapter Twenty-Eight

When Charlie returned from Willie's farm to the mortuary, Olivia was waiting. She met him at the door. "Where are they?"

"He's keeping her tonight." He looked at her warmly. "You were right. They'll be fine. I told him we'll visit in the morning."

"And she's okay?"

"Yes."

"I told you."

"I know, and you were right." As they stood there in the doorway, a familiar scent drifted in on the evening air. "Your dad's doing some cooking tonight, I see."

Olivia crinkled her nose, taking in the scent. "I never notice anymore. But three more came in today. We've passed twenty, I think. He's not even doing certificates, just recording and cremating. The lockers are full and the bins upstairs are full. I don't ever remember a day without death, but this is worse, way worse. It's kind of sad, but I think I'm immune. I'm dead to it. I'm dead to it." She smiled. "Dead to death." As they moved into the room, Charlie placed his arm around Olivia's shoulder.

"I'm pretty dead to it myself," he said. Sitting down heavily on

the couch he brought out the Quasar and turned it on. "I think it's time we give the leader of the free world a bit of a head's up, and see if he's ready to get us the hell out of here."

"Oh, yay," Olivia squealed. "I'm in."

As the call was put through, an aide stuck his head into the oval office. "Chester Benton, sir. Coming in secure."

"Oh, god," muttered the president. "It's Charlie. Set it up here," he instructed the aide. For more than two weeks Errol Clarkson had been getting by on five hours of sleep each day. On a completely structured format. From midnight to four in the morning there was no disturbing the president. And again, at noon precisely, another hour was allotted for slumber. To ensure the rest time was not wasted, the White House medical staff would arrive promptly five minutes before each rest period to administer a sedative which would knock the president soundly out. "Another couple of weeks and I'll be an addict on the street," Clarkson told himself without the least amount of humor. It had only been three days since ISIS rebels had hit for the second time several major oil fields in southern Iraq, and now the Saudis were threatening to bomb both Yemen and Iran for distinctly different reasons for which there did not appear to be any diplomatic solution. The world was screaming at America to act, and the world was screaming at the president to act, and the whole while, just down the road, the sacred state of Alabama still found itself engulfed in flame. Federal troops had marched their way to within a few miles of Birmingham, but now militant bands of well-armed whites, ones who had refused to flee their homeland, were also pressing in toward the great city. Dixie flags waved across the land like misguided prophets, and banners proclaiming *White is Right* hung from any structure high enough to shout out their proclamation. And now Charlie was calling.

The president's screen flashed on as Charlie's screen flashed on, and the two men sat there staring at one another. Neither man spoke. Clarkson raised both his hands, running them stubbornly through his hair. Charlie brought both of his hands together at about chin level, touching finger to finger, squishing them back and forth.

Finally, after a silence that lasted more than a minute, Charlie said, "I hear you. I swear to god I do."

The president smiled then, shaking his head. "Say it for me, Charlie. Please."

Charlie laughed, just enough to show some sign of life. "Fuck," he said.

"Thanks, I needed that. It's great to have a friend who has a shrine full of profanity we can call on when we need it." Clarkson tapped at a cellphone on his desk. "All the towers are back up now, you know. You could use your damn cell."

"I know. But then I wouldn't get to see your pretty face in radiant Quasar color." Charlie's face grew serious. "What's the haps?"

"Same'ole, same'ole, baby. Whatever you're getting on the news is what I'm dealing with up here. You can't keep anything from the media. I think they even have cameras set up in my bathroom. I seriously want to kill myself right now, but I'm not sure I have the personal fortitude. Wish you were here."

"I'd do it. I'd get myself really good and drunk, and then I'd break your goddam neck. Problem solved."

"You hearing about what's going on in Birmingham? And we're just talking Birmingham. Wait till we head out for Montgomery."

"We're hearing it. Olivia, that's Miss Briggs if you remember, has the news on twenty-four-seven. We're getting it all."

Olivia, sitting on the couch at some distance from Charlie, leaned in, resting her head on his shoulder. "Hi, Mister President." She waved.

"Oh," said Clarkson. "I didn't know you were present. Hello, Miss Briggs." The president smiled sheepishly. "If I remember correctly, you aren't necessarily offended if our language moves a little off base?"

"Shit no, sir. You guys just talk away. All the tests seem to indicate I'm not a normal kid." All three of them laughed.

"So," said the president. "What's up down there?"

Charlie moved his face in closer to the screen. "You really don't know?"

"Well, I'm hearing you've got a madman on the loose. And he's making life pretty miserable for everyone. But no, we don't have many facts at this point. Our old friend at CBN, Samantha King, just released a five minute feed this morning. First time. Not very substantive, but it seems she's right on top of things, as usual."

"She is. She's living with our so-called madman this very instant. He's Anthony Sedgewick. Army man. I don't know if you'll remember, but we visited..."

"Military academy guy. A colonel." The president broke in with a wry laugh. "I remember, because my shoes were not on their best behavior when we visited his school. He frosted me pretty good. He thought it something of a travesty for a president to walk around publicly with unshined shoes. God, I think I threw them away."

"Well he's here now, and he's all dressed up as a general —four stars— and he's got at least a couple hundred young militants here with him. They've taken over the whole county. Colby. They're heavily armed and very organized. Our own military doesn't operate this well."

"What the hell does he want?"

"We're in the middle of a game." Charlie laughed softly. "I am not even kidding. He's gathered up all the whites and turned them into slaves. He's making a statement."

Clarkson shook his head. "What? That's crazy. Can he be reasoned with?"

"I'm thinking not. But he's got an ego the size of Kansas. I'd like to set the two of you up together. On the air. If anyone can talk him down it's you. And lovely Samantha will wet her pants at the chance to set this up."

Olivia leaned in. "She's a bitch."

"My dear Miss Briggs," said the president, "I'm liking you better and better."

"So," said Charlie, "are you up for it?"

Clarkson paused, then spoke. "You put us together and I'll see what I can do. I'm not going to bargain with the man though. You need to know that. We can't."

"I know. Just do the best you can." Charlie's brow tightened as he looked for a long moment at his friend. "There are always alternatives," he said quietly.

———————◆———————

Early the next morning, another feed from the plantation streamed into the New York studios of CBN. There was no warning given and no time to prepare. A pair of sequencing codes were dialed in, one from the White House, one from Samantha King, and the screen assigned directly to national emergency broadcasts crackled to life. The station director, seeing this, immediately called out, "Go live," and the morning news report was preempted.

"Mister President." Sedgewick sat on a bench out on the great porch of the mansion as he spoke. He bowed solemnly as the camera rolled. Samantha King sat closely but professionally beside him, her fingers tapping the buttons on a remote. "How gracious of you to speak with us. I know you have your hands full up north."

"General." Clarkson nodded as pleasantly as he could. "I see you've been promoted. Congratulations."

"Thank you, sir." The general's hand brushed across Samantha's knee. "It's nice to finally be in charge."

Clarkson winced slightly as he observed the hand, and the crew chief at CBN yelled out, "Close-up on the president's face. Now."

"Look, General," said the president, "I think I have a pretty good idea what you're trying to accomplish, and it seems to me you've made your point. Life isn't fair. And for some of us it's even worse than that. I get it, sir. If you're willing at this time to stand down, I'm sure we can reach some sort of agreement. The main thing is to make sure no one else gets hurt down there."

Sedgewick grinned wickedly. "Very kind of you, sir. But I'm not sure I've proven anything yet. We've a ways to go, so I'm afraid this won't be over for a while."

The CBN chief snarled, "The bastard's grinning. Close in on that goddam face."

"General. Eventually this has to end. You must know that. We know your strength, and you know ours. If we come rolling in, you and your men are in a very untenable position. It can only end one way. Let's not let that happen."

Sedgewick laughed aloud. "I'm aware of all the possibilities, sir. Queen to queen's bishop. It's not complicated. It's just that I've got a plantation to run right now, and I don't think I have the time to stand down, even if I wanted to. Besides, I have a lot of folks depending on me to put on a good show. When this is over everyone will know what the bonds of tyranny feel like. They're quite debilitating, you know?"

President Clarkson shook his head. "I'm not sure what to say to that, but I can sympathize with your position. I'm just trying to get through this with as much damage control as possible." Clarkson looked hopefully into the camera. "I give you my word I will stand beside you and help in any way I can. Let's just end this. Please."

"God," said the CBN chief. "The prez is begging. Pretty soon the poor bastard will be on his knees."

"No," said the general simply. "Ain't gonna happen, sir. We have too many plans. Too much fun stuff to accomplish here. The cotton won't harvest itself."

Clarkson drew himself up closer to the camera. "You're not a cotton farmer, General. And I'm informed the season is well over. There is no reason this can't be resolved peacefully. Especially by two men of honor."

General Sedgewick also leaned in closer to the camera. "Honor? I love that you said that. Love it. Honor is a gift for the soul." A playful smile tugged away at the general's mouth. "I expect you'll see what honor looks like when you come for me." Reaching out a hand he began to stroke at Samantha's hair, running his fingers through her long, sweeping curls. His other hand moved gently up from her knee, caressing her inner thigh. She pulled away slightly, forcing a smile as she tried to maintain some decorum as a journalist.

"Christ," called out the CBN chief, "He's hand-screwing her right on the air. What the hell? Get that camera off her crotch. This ain't fucking Penthouse." The general lifted his hand from Samantha's leg, picking up instead the riding crop that lay beside him on the bench. Without warning the crop whistled through the air, lashing loudly as it whipped into her face. As she screamed, blood oozed from a deep cut on her cheek. "Fuck," cried the chief. "He hit her. The sunovabitch hit her. Fuck!"

Sedgewick lashed out again, and again, reigning down blows on Samantha's head. He still had one hand wrapped tightly in her hair as she tried desperately to free herself. Finally, he released his grip and she was able to stumble from the screen. The general then sat there calmly, staring directly into the camera. He laid down the whip, using both hands to straighten his shirt. He shook his head slightly, as if clearing his mind of all things unpleasant. "You know," he said, "this morning I was banging her. She's not a bad kid. I just needed to demonstrate that it's not hard to provoke me." His face moved in until it filled the screen. "I don't give a damn about much. And if you come marching in here with your Johnny Boys, a most unpleasant circumstance will occur. I will unleash hell on earth on the good people of Colby County. They will have no chance for rebuke or rebuttal." Reaching down to pick up the remote which lay on the ground nearby, the general raised it to eye level, pointing it at the camera. "Good day, Mister President," he said curtly, and the screen went blank.

As the camera crew dismantled their equipment and left the Oval Office, the president turned to Daniel Rumstaadt, who had sat there on the leather couch, observing the conversation. "Wow. That's one crazy sunovabitch. I think I'm going to have Charlie kill him," he said matter-of-factly. "I don't know what other options we can pursue."

"What if there's a doomsday plan in place? Maybe he's already thought of that and has his men ready to take everybody out in the event of his death."

"It can't be any worse than it is. From what we've heard there

are a couple of dozen dead in there already. We can't just let the bastard continue."

Rumstaadt shook his head. "I don't know. He's probably watching Charlie closely, and we have to be very careful. There have been many hostage situations in our history. Maybe not this big, but there have been some substantial ones. And they haven't all ended well. You remember the Branch Davidians back in the nineties?"

Clarkson nodded. "Sort of. Waco, Texas, right? Crazy guy took over a ranch and locked himself away with a lot of women and children."

"That's right. We sat there for fifty-one days until reports filtered out that a lot of those children were being molested and tortured. That was on President Clinton's watch. Finally he ordered the Feds to end the standoff, so they crashed through the gates. Big mistake. Almost a hundred people died in a fiery hell when the madman blew the place up before the troops could pull off a rescue. I don't think anyone survived it."

"And your point is what? We wait forever? Until Sedgewick dies of old age?"

"That's not what I'm saying. We just need to be careful about whatever course we take."

The president stood, walked around the side of the great desk, and deposited himself on the couch beside Rumstaadt. "Well I'm not willing to wait fifty-one days while our beloved general toys with the lives of an entire county. That's not the way America works. Not on my watch, it isn't." Both men looked at each other while Clarkson pondered some possibilities. Finally he said, "See if Chris Cash is available this afternoon."

"You want the Secretary of the Navy?"

"Yeah. See if he's busy. And let's see if he happens to have any Seals layin' around who'd like to take a little vacation down south."

Chapter Twenty-Nine

Molly woke at first light. She had slept fitfully at best, and fully clothed, bunched up on a corner of the bed with a sheet wrapped tightly around her. A bit of sunlight crept onto the curtain of a nearby window, so she rose and went there. A sound, like metal against rock, came from somewhere outside. Pulling aside the curtain, she saw Willie a short distance away across a small yard, digging in the earth with a spade. As she looked outward, he looked up, and their eyes met. The old man nodded and Molly found herself lifting a hand in a quiet wave. He motioned to her then, to join him in the garden. When she arrived, Willie was on his knees, his gnarled old hands tugging away at a large thistle which stubbornly dug its roots deeply into the soil. "Damn things," he said. "Take over the whole garden if you let 'em."

"Should I help?" she asked.

Pulling a rag from a back pocket, Willie rose, wiping his hands, and pointed towards the barn. "No. I've got other stuff for you to do." They walked together to the barn, the girl keeping a pace or two of careful distance between them. "I want you to meet my ladies."

"Ladies?" Molly looked over at him, no longer afraid to make eye contact, but still wary. "I don't understand." The old man smiled,

and as he did so the sound of a motor roared out at them from the levee. They both turned to watch as a grey pickup with four armed men in its bed rolled down the incline and into the yard.

Willie moved instinctively in front of the girl, leaving her to watch from the barn as he walked to the middle of the yard, very close to where the truck rumbled to a halt. A large black man with a short, green military shirt that hung unbuttoned to his waist jumped out from the cab. And even though it was still early morning and cool, a slick mat of sweat glistened on the man's chest. "What can I do for you?" asked Willie cautiously. He addressed the man in front of him, but his eyes roamed to the back of the truck, to the four men who sat there.

"We're offering script," said the man, smiling slightly. From his pocket he pulled a stack of notes, which appeared much like old stock certificates or apple notes from the Great Depression. Willie thought right away that he recognized them. In the house, tucked away behind a brick wall in the kitchen, he had a basketful.

"What does that mean?" he asked.

"Script, old man, script." The man stepped closer to Willie. "It's the same as cash. The general has authorized us to issue it to the law abiding citizens of the valley as a way of saying thanks." The man took another step, shoving a fistful of the paper in Willie's direction. "You can buy shit in town. Anything you want. The regular currency has been devalued. It's worthless. This shit is like gold."

"I don't shop much," said the old man. "I got everythin' I need." The four in the truck began to laugh, leering in the direction of the barn, and the man addressing Willie looked past him, also at the barn.

"We figured we might work out a trade," he said, his voice growing bold. "We've got enough here for you to buy a new truck. Replace that piece of crap you're driving."

It was now Willie who stepped forward, his eyes piercing deeply into the eyes of the script-man. "What do you want here? I told you I don't need anythin'. And my truck's just fine. You need to go."

The man laughed. "Look, old man, you know what we want.

You've had the girl all to yourself for a day or two now. We were there when you took her. Sweet young thing. I'm sure she's given you all you can handle. Time to share the wealth." Again, he held out the notes. "You can get a new truck, for chrissakes. Drive into town right now and pick one out. We'll take care of things till you get back."

Willie's face, once fierce, now held fear. There was no possibility he could stand against these men. Even one of them. "The general said I'm not to be bothered. You all heard him."

The man's voice rose in pitch. "The general's the one who sent us here. To make the goddam trade. Are you stupid?"

"I'm not tradin' nuthin'. I told you, the general said she's mine, and I'm not to be bothered. If you want, we can go across the road right now and ask him. See if he's goin' back on his word. Or see if he even knows about this."

The man's eyes flickered almost imperceptibly. He lowered his hand, and a few of the notes slipped away, carried across the yard by the morning breeze. He watched them for a moment, trying to decide whether or not to chase them down. Then he looked back at Willie, his eyes black, even blacker than his skin. He seemed to be weighing the odds of a circumstance yet to be determined. "We could take her," he said.

"You could." Willie felt his legs begin to shake. "But you'd have to deal with me first. And maybe the general." The man nodded, his face unreadable. He glanced over at his companions, still sitting attentively in the truck. One of them had leveled a rifle, pointing it loosely at the old man.

"We're just trying to be peaceful. Be good neighbors. We didn't come to make trouble." He turned then, walked the few paces back to the truck and climbed into the cab.

During the entire confrontation Molly had been standing, frozen in place in front of the barn. She had plainly heard every syllable spoken, digesting each word as a separate little packet of fear. She knew nothing about the laws of genetics or the darkness men feel while succumbing to them, nor had the faintest idea of

the warped sense of passion conflict brings as its companion, but instinct told her she had just escaped a dreadful situation. The truck gone, and freed from the constraints of her fear, she slumped back heavily against the side-wall of the old building, her mouth yawning open with relief.

Willie approached her. "You okay?"

"Yes." Molly pushed herself up. She reached out to touch the old man's arm. It was the first time she had ever willingly touched a black person, and though she felt a rush of relief and gratitude, she still shuddered slightly. "I don't know what to say. Thank you."

"I didn't do nuthin'. Them boys was just off track a little."

"They wanted to hurt me."

Willie smiled at the girl. "Hell, they wanted to hurt me too."

Molly looked deeply into his eyes. "You could have had a new truck."

"Damn, girl. Them notes was worthless. Everybody in the county has a barrel of 'em tucked away from depression days. Could buy an apple with 'em back then, can't buy crap with 'em now. 'Specially not a new truck."

Molly nodded solemnly. "Still, you could have gone. Left me with them."

"You're nuts." Willie chuckled to himself and then to the girl. "Then who in the hell would peel up my potatoes?"

Swinging open one of the barn doors, the two moved inside. Instantly there was a flutter of wings, as a dozen or more impressively sized chickens descended on them from the rafters. One brushed against Molly's hair on its way to the ground, and the old man laughed heartily as the girl ran screaming for the door. "Get back in here," he sang. "These ladies don't bite."

Molly stepped back in. "They're chickens."

"What did you think they was?"

"I don't know. Owls or something."

"Owls? Well, damn, I guess that would make a body dance. Never been plucked up by no owl." Two of the chickens, both hens,

drifted over to inspect the girl. One began to pick away at her shoes, and she stepped back timidly.

"Are they all hens?" she asked

"Yup. No time for funny business. They're all equally in charge of egg production around here."

Molly frowned. "Eggs? Don't you need a rooster?"

"Nope," Willie laughed. "A lotta folks think that, but these ladies do just fine on their own. They used to lay an egg a day. Each. Now they're gettin' old and cranky, kinda like me. I'm lucky if I get three, maybe four eggs a week. But they keep tryin'."

"Why don't you just eat them and get new ones?"

The old man scowled. "Damn, girl, you be tough. I ain't no cannibal."

Molly looked at him with large, pouting lips. "We ate one last night."

Willie looked up from the hens, admonishing Molly with his eyes. "Not one of mine, we didn't. If I want an eatin' chicken, I'll trade for it or maybe pick one up at market. I know that other chicken don't deserve it neither, but you always choose friends over strangers. If you don't, you ain't alive. And you ain't kind."

Molly chewed on her lower lip. "We eat all our chickens."

"I figured." The old man leaned back against a bale of hay. "Didn't you ever take a likin' to an animal? I don't mean like a dog or nuthin'. I mean the kind who always winds up on the table. Didn't you ever care about one? You know, make it special?"

Molly nodded, her eyes bright with a memory. "I had a pig once. My papa gave it to me to raise. I used to sleep with it. I wasn't supposed to, but sometimes I'd sneak it into my bedroom late at night. His name was Wilbur, like in the story." She stumbled over the words, "He followed me everywhere, and I liked him a lot."

"How old were you?"

"Seven or eight, I think."

Willie reached down to pat the head of a fat, golden hen. "Then you loved him. You don't just like a pig when you're eight. Not if he's yours, you don't."

"Maybe."

"What happened?"

Molly chewed harder, her lip flushing white. "One day he was just gone. I went out to the barn and looked everywhere. And that night at dinner my papa laughed and told me to have another slice of Wilbur." Molly's eyes dimmed, and the old man's dimmed right along with hers. "Everyone laughed. A whole roomful of people who thought that was just the funniest thing. The next year I refused to take on a new pig. Papa said I was just being girly, but I still wouldn't do it."

Willie reached further down, picking up the hen. It nestled there in his arms for a moment, and then he handed it to the girl. "This is Harriet," he said softly. "You can love her if you want."

Chapter Thirty

Down the road a small way from Cedar Creek lay another plantation. Not one of the giants that proclaimed to be a king of cotton, but one with more of a farm like atmosphere, and comprised of only a few hundred acres. Watermelons were raised there, abundantly enough to supply a good portion of northern Florida, with a few tons left over that were shipped each spring to the east, to Atlanta. Parnell Grigsby owned the place, had in fact since he'd come home from the war in Iraq to find his mother, his last living relative, had died just a day or two before.

Parnell wasn't the sort of man who took to the land easily, nor one who loved working the earth, but instead one who kept clean hands and had more of a used car salesman approach to life. Townsfolk in Harbor Springs liked to tell the story that one time a few years back Grigsby sold a tractor to a neighbor, but considered that the deal had not gone in his favor. When the buyer tried to load it onto his hauler, he found he couldn't start it. "Where the hell are the keys?" he'd asked. Right there is when the story teller would smile and hold out a hand. "That'll be another fifty bucks," said Parnell.

Watermelons were a good business in the south, not a big

business, but a good one, and Parnell made a decent living at it. He employed some thirty or forty blacks year round, who lived in shacks out behind the main house, while another long shed further out, that once housed chickens, had been converted to house another dozen or so Mexicans who drove in each spring at harvest time to pick and stack the sweet fruit. The Mexicans were treated well as a common practice, for they could just as easily move along to one of the other farms if conditions were less than palatable, but the blacks, who had more limited prospects and were glued there to the land, received no such favor from Parnell. He would cajole them, yell at them, berate them, and occasionally, if they were young enough or timid enough to show weakness, he would drag them into the barn for a bit of a beating. He never hit them much, just a polite dusting if they needed it, but when the doors of the barn swung open, a meeker black man than walked in would walk out.

When the general arrived with his band of troops, Grigsby's was the first property they rolled into, being the one closest to the state line. And Grigsby himself became a part of the slave games. In fact, he became a game piece even before the general gathered up the other residents of Colby County and explained the rules. Right there in the yard of the manor house, on that very first day, as the general's whip brought him to his knees, the game began. One of the blacks who lived and worked there, a man named Lionel Conch —affectionately called "Konk" by his friends— stepped out from the group of laborers who had been gathered up, and hollered out, "Beat the shit out of him, suh." The general had turned and smiled at Konk, motioning him to step forward.

"You take issue with this man?" he asked.

"Yes, suh. He beat my boy." Konk turned slightly, pointing to a boy of about fourteen who stood timidly tucked into the crowd. "Look at him, suh." The boy's eyes were cast downward and he shuffled nervously. "He don't look up no mo'."

The general moved in closer to Grigsby, tapping at him aggressively with the crop. "You beat that boy?" he asked.

Grigsby looked up, his face defiant, even with the

helplessness of the situation, and the general knew this man might be contemptible, but he was no coward. "If I did, he deserved it," came the reply.

General Sedgewick turned back to the man known as Konk. "Gather up your boy and any other family you have here. You'll be coming with me. I am quite confident we'll find you a better circumstance down the road somewhere." The general smiled amusedly. "I'd leave you here, but I'm afraid you'd kill this bastard." Lashing out with the crop, he drove it into Grigsby's face, driving the meat of the whip, where it was still thickened, hard against the man's cheek. Grigsby cried out and rolled onto the ground.

"I've come as a savior," Sedgewick spoke out to the crowd. "You all know what's happening to the north. Birmingham is under siege, and the capital is a pile of rubble and ash. Our people have been beaten down for so long they are crying out. Up there they are being met with vengeance, but down here..." The general raised both hands to the sky. "Down here, you have me. A godsend, a protector. And I shall relish my role. I have a force behind me large enough and bold enough to manage any obstacle that may stand in our way. From this day forward, and until a higher power arrives to crucify me, no man, woman or child among you will walk in fear or humiliation." As the general spoke, the sound of engines gunning down the main highway could be heard. As the gathering looked on, a convoy of cars and trucks moved past, heading inland in the direction of the town.

"Hell yeah," cried out a voice.

The general smiled again. "Hell yeah, indeed." Moving over closer to the workers, he began to walk their ranks, inspecting the front row and as far into the crowd as he could. He had gone only a short distance when he stopped and poked his crop at the chest of a man. "You," he said, liking the way the man looked. "Who are you?"

A smallish, older black man, perhaps fifty, and of slight build, stepped forward as the general motioned him. "Thomas, sir. I'm Thomas." The general escorted the man away from the others, until they were well separated.

"I'm putting Thomas here in charge," Sedgewick declared. Some of the crowd nodded enthusiastically, but with puzzled faces as they still had no idea what was transpiring. "He will run this farm for me. It's mine now. You will each obey him and respect him, and his word shall be as law." The general pointed the crop at Parnell Grigsby, still moaning from his wound. "And this piece of shit over here is to be the property of the farm. He will no longer order you about, and he will no longer have any say whatsoever as to your conduct. In fact, it will be exactly the opposite. You may each treat him, with Thomas' permission, of course, in any manner you see fit."

A voice from the workers called out. "Thomas ain't no leader. He can't whup nobody." The general nodded politely. He beckoned the man who had spoken to come forward. The man was of average size, but well-muscled and quite sure of himself.

"You think you can beat Thomas?" Thomas, who stood but a few paces away, smiled meekly, and began to tremble.

"Hell yes, suh. Everyone can. You're choosin' yourself the wrong man." Without even a word spoken, two of the general's aides moved in from the side. Sedgewick stood there, studying this new man. He tapped the crop in his palm. Then one of the aides spun around suddenly, his leg swiping high and powerfully through the air. His foot contacted the face of the muscled man, and in less than a second the man lay writhing on the ground. Pointing at the aide who had delivered the blow, the general spoke.

"This is Thomas," he said. He pointed at the other aide. "And this is Thomas." Then he tapped at his own chest. "And I am Thomas. Please tell me you all understand what just happened here." Fifty faces nodded back with respectful enthusiasm.

"We hear you, suh," called out more than a few.

And that's how Parnell Grigsby came to be a common laborer on his own land. The general soon departed, leaving behind several of his troops as enforcers, as the convoy with more than two hundred of his followers headed into Harbor Springs to further spread the joys of the game.

Thomas' first order, issued meekly, was to assist the two fallen

men. The black one, the muscled one, was only briefly shaken up
and soon back on his feet. Thomas asked if he was okay, and the
man replied, "Yes, suh." Thomas marveled at this, but drew strength
from it. Attention was then turned on Parnell Grigsby, who was in
worse, but not broken shape. He was escorted to the manor house,
where Thomas had him laid out in his own bed, leaving him there
to recuperate under the watchful eye of one of the general's aides.
Then Thomas returned to the courtyard where dozens of hopeful
but still confused faces waited.

"I think I gets it," he began. "I ain't never been much, none
of us have. But that man there says we can all be whatever we want,
right here, right now. I'm also figurin' this ain't meant to last. It's
some kinda game he's playin'. An honest to god bible-thumpin' game,
where a servant of the Lord has walked into our midst and declared
us free."

"He ain't no servant of the Lord," a woman's voice called out.
"Might don't make right. Not in the new book, it don't." Several of
the general's aides, who stood nearby, searched the crowd for the
source of the words. They soon identified the lady who had spoken
them, but remained still.

Thomas smiled, and found for the first time in his life that the
smile was a benevolent one. "Lowly folks don't often get to feel like
this," he thought to himself as his smile broadened. Raising his arms
like a preacher, he spoke. "He might not be a man of God. He might
not even be a good man, but that don't mean spit. When a hand
opens a cage, the bird inside don't care if it's the hand of a good man
or bad. He's just gonna sing his ass off as he flies away." A woman
in the crowd, up front and very close to Thomas, grimaced. "Sorry,
Miss Jenkins," Thomas continued. "I mean sing his *butt* off." Smiles
broke out on the faces of the gathering, and chatter started.

"What does this mean?" asked one. "Are we jus' supposed to go
on like everythin's fine?" said another. "And how long is this gonna
last?" hollered out a third. "There's liable to be a major whuppin'
party when this is all over."

Thomas had lowered his arms, but now raised one in a request

for silence. "I don't know any more than you know. But I do know that I'm stayin'. Those of you who think it's a bad idea can go. That military man didn't say so, but he didn't say you had to stay here neither. So you go if you want, but I'm stayin'."

One of the men near the outer edges of the group looked over at one of the general's aides. "Is what he says true?" he asked the man. "Can we go?"

The aide looked across at another aide, who stepped forward. "The man you speak of is *the general*. He should always be addressed accordingly. And the rules only apply to whites, as far as we know. The rest of you are free to do whatever you want." The aide thought for a moment. "I would suggest, however, if you do decide to leave, you should head south, out of this state. You'll be safe there."

A man stepped out from the crowd. "What we really want to know is if we're gonna be safe here?" he asked.

"I don't know," answered the aide honestly. "For now you are."

For the next hour Thomas moved from group to group, family to family, and man to man. A few, mostly newcomers to the place, decided to pack up and head south. But most decided to stay on, held together by a fabric woven from curiosity and hope. Their worst fear, they decided, was if the government came rambling in to restore order, they could be beaten down and punished. But that only provoked grins and a certain amount of laughter from the crowd. They'd spent their whole lives being beaten down.

When those who had decided to leave had gone, Thomas walked up the drive to the main house. Two aides accompanied him, following respectfully a few paces behind. At one point Thomas turned to them. "Are you assigned to protect me, or watch me?" he asked. One of the men, the one who had spoken earlier to the crowd, answered.

"We're here for you. You have no restrictions. The general said we're to help, so we work entirely for you."

"Really?" said Thomas, somewhat incredulously. His voice became playful. "Well then drop and give me ten." Instantly the two men assumed the push-up position. "No, no, wait," called out

Thomas, smiling sheepishly. "I was jus' checkin', is all. Nobody ever did nuthin' I told 'em before." Both men rose, and both men smiled at him good-naturedly.

"We would have given you twenty," one of them said.

Once inside the house, Thomas went to check on Grigsby, still under guard. He was sitting up on the bed, and when Thomas entered the room he snarled. "You dumb shit, Thomas. I'm gonna have you beat so goddam bad you'll wish you was dead."

Thomas felt himself trembling, but just for a moment. Then the calm of great resolve washed over him. An hour earlier he would have cried out and run at the very sight of his angry boss. But an almost spiritual awakening had taken place out in the yard. Something he had never before felt. He'd heard about incidents like this. Where a great fear, like the fear of a tormenting bully, is always holding you down, suffocating you, and there's nothing you can do about it. Then, when you finally confront it, the fear sinks into the mud with the bully, and it's gone. "Shut up, Mister Grigsby," he said simply.

The aide who had been guarding Parnell Grigsby moved from his position near the door to the bedside. He pulled a baton from his waistband. "You want him beat, sir?" Grigsby looked up at the man, and for the first time a twinge of fear brushed across his face. He turned to Thomas.

"Don't you do it, Thomas," he said, both threatening and begging at the same time. "Don't you dare fuckin' do it."

An impulse of empowerment enveloped Thomas then. Another new and unexpected feeling. This had been such a rich day for him. Such a fine, rich day. He nearly glided over to the bed, sitting himself down closely beside the startled Parnell. Reaching out, he placed an arm around the man's shoulders almost affectionately. "Don't worry, Mister Grigsby," he said in a soft, warm voice. "I'm not gonna hurt you." Thomas rose then and walked back to the door where he turned. "I'd never hurt you," he said. "You see, I jus' found out somethin'. Jus' this minute. I'm better than you." The aide smiled quietly to himself, as Thomas walked out the door.

Chapter Thirty-One

Not everyone of color in the valley embraced the idea of re-gifting slavery. In fact, for most of the folks in and around Harbor Springs, the thought brought only visions of past demons and future injustice. And one day, just after noon, a car pulled up in front of the mortuary. Three women, two black, one white, and all very well dressed, stepped to the curb and ascended the steps to the house. Charlie met them at the door.

"Ladies," he said.

"We wonder if we might speak with Mister Briggs," one enquired. Before Charlie could even turn, Shawn Briggs came from the kitchen and stood beside him.

"Hi," he said. "What can I do for you?"

"Mister Briggs," the same lady continued. "We need your help. At the church. Would you come with us, please?"

A puzzled look crossed Briggs' face. "I guess." Charlie smiled, tapping at his own chest with a finger.

"No, Mister Benton," the lady said, her hand raised, her voice soft and apologetic. "It's nothing personal, but we just require Mister Briggs." As Briggs stepped through the doorway to accompany them, another of the women smiled back at Charlie.

"It's just that you're a government man. Everyone knows that. We need Mister Briggs because he isn't. If we add a political side to this it's going to shade everything. And that's just what we don't need. It's nothing personal."

The smile on Chester Benton's face never wavered. "Ladies," he said, "I have no idea why you're here, what you're talking about or why I'm beginning to feel somewhat discriminated against." He laughed weakly. "But you all play nice with my friend here and do whatever it is you plan to do. I'm gonna go make a pizza."

As the group walked away down the steps, Olivia came out from her bedroom. "Who was that?" she asked.

"Crazy people," said Charlie as he closed the door.

"Oh, that's nice," said Olivia as she headed into the kitchen. "I just heard the word pizza."

When Briggs walked into the Baptist church a few minutes later, he was surprised by what he saw. A hundred anxious faces, mostly black, but with a good sprinkling of white, turned from the pews to watch his arrival. At the pulpit, and aligned along a stage set up to address the room, was a group of men, eight or nine strong, standing at order and apparently waiting for him. The men's arms were interlocked, and it was interesting, and obviously intentional, that on each side of every black man stood a white man, and on each side of every white man stood a black man, in a black-white-black-white display of solidarity. The intent was so obvious it immediately tugged at Briggs' heart, and the room radiated a generous warmth. A man Briggs recognized as the pastor stepped forward to greet him, his hands outstretched.

"Welcome," he said. "We're excited you decided to join us."

One of the ladies who had escorted Briggs there spoke up. "He doesn't know why he's here, Pastor. We thought you should tell him."

"Oh," said the pastor. He offered Briggs a seat in the front-most pew, just a few feet away from the line of men. "It's amazing to me," he began, his voice almost wistful, "that people think we should all be jumping up and down at the prospect of turning back the clock on our history. And that we've learned nothing about the

past and the agonies it wrought." The pastor tapped lightly at Briggs' shoulder, then moved away to where he could more efficiently address the gathering. "Slavery isn't connected to color. It never was. The color of our skin is completely incidental, and the fact that the black community was the one enslaved is completely co-incidental." Many in the crowd nodded solemnly, though most had not yet the faintest idea the direction the pastor was heading. "Many men," the pastor smiled and pointed to a group of ladies sitting nearby, "and women. Those among us and around us who carry the burden of a heavy heart, and perhaps a tarnished soul, and seek to gain prosperity through the labors and agonies of others… they define the direction of slavery. They always have. And slavery abounds, not just targeting men, but also aimed at creatures who have been found useful in turning a profit or filling a belly. So oxen are yoked and whipped across the fields. Is that not slavery? And horses are made to bear masters as they cavort about, pigs are driven to slaughter and suffer the humiliation of having an apple shoved into their open, dead mouths as they look out upon the gluttons who feast on them. Man enslaves what he is able to enslave without regard. His only thoughts: is it useful to me? Can it profit me? Will it enrich my life? There are no boundaries where men roam in greed. And certainly not ones of color. If one man could enslave another man without retribution, he would do it, pure and simple. It is our weakness. It is our cross." The pastor smiled reverently. "Unless we rail against it as children, not of color, not even of God, but of right. If instead we buy into it, that it's acceptable to exact retribution, enslave the ancestors of the very people who once enslaved us, we become them. We are them. And there is no escape." He paused, letting his words sink in.

A plump, pleasant looking black woman a few rows back exclaimed, "It would'a been nice though, if my great granddaddy had'a thought of this first, and I'da grown up back in Africa with a white lady servin' me tea." Laughter broke out then, softening the pastor's speech. He seemed not in the least offended by it, smiling as he pointed at the lady and shook his fist.

Shawn Briggs drew himself up in the pew. "I wonder, Pastor, if you'd mind telling me why I'm here." He looked at those around him. "I like the fact that you're all standing together like this, but what exactly are you trying to accomplish?" His eyes dimmed. "You're not thinking of going up against the general?"

"No, Mister Briggs. Not directly. That would be a most foolhardy course." The men standing up on stage separated somewhat, moving forward, where they sat, legs dangling over the pulpit wall. "But we've all heard him. His heart seems to be in the right place, even if his mind has led him astray. He seems to want a better world for his people, or those he sees as his people. It's not a bad thing to want those who are downtrodden to feel the rush of power that comes to the uptrodden."

"Uptrodden?" Briggs smiled.

"You know what I mean. The general has told us specifically that he desires us to enjoy the fruits of his endeavors. There's no injustice in that, if his intentions are to lift our spirits. We think maybe he doesn't understand that's not at all what we want."

Feeling uncomfortable sitting there with the pastor looking down at him, Briggs rose, waving a careless hand. "With all due respect, I don't think you understand the general at all. He doesn't care if his actions benefit you, or anyone else. I can't see any sign of that. He wants to punish. That's it. That's his agenda. And anyone, black or white, standing in his way is going to be struck by a very harsh reality. Don't think this man is pliable, that he has a softness about him, just because he comes at you with a voice that seems to speak with reason. Believe me on this." Briggs turned impassioned eyes on the gathering. "The general's commandments are carved into the hardest of stone."

"As are ours," said the pastor, smiling back at him.

A woman just a few seats down from Briggs spoke up. "You don't think the general will change his position if we make it clear to him that we're opposed to it? There are more than a hundred of us here. That's a sizeable piece of the town. What if we all step forward?"

Briggs spent a thoughtful moment before answering. "I don't think the man cares what you think. You've only heard him speak, and I have to admit he comes across with great passion and eloquence. But I've seen him. I've seen his eyes blaze as he taunts people. I've watched him beat men down." Briggs' own eyes narrowed. "This man isn't out to correct past sins. He's out to gratify himself at the expense of anyone who dares to get in his way. Please, please don't rush into anything here. Nothing good will come of it."

The pastor moved a few steps, closer to where the elevated row of men sat, their dangling feet almost brushing the floor. He turned, his hands upraised and very preacher-like. "I don't wish to offend our guest, but I think perhaps Mister Briggs has seen a theatrical side of the general. A blustery side he puts on to exact obedience from his followers and penance from his detractors. In reality, the man who came before us at the bank the other day bore a certain humility. Something more like a servant of right than a master of injustice. I think he's misunderstood, and can be reasoned with."

"That's just nuts," said Briggs, speaking as much to himself as anyone else.

Outside the church, and not far away, the general sat comfortably back in his seat in the limo as it cruised through the town and in the direction of the meeting. Harbor Springs was especially quiet, with only one or two blacks out walking the sidewalks and a crew of white laborers busy in the street at one end of town, filling in potholes created when a summer storm had rumbled through the evening before. One well-muscled young worker stood and stretched, his blonde hair catching the afternoon sunlight, beads of sweat trickling down his chest. "A magnificent buck," thought the general. "What a splendid breeder he will make." The general smiled to himself. Subservience was perhaps the best tool ever invented to serve those standing at the top of the human heap. It was good to be at the top. And he could see now that slavery did, in fact, work. Splendidly. Tasks were completed in a timely manner. Goals were set and met, if not with enthusiasm, then with perseverance and fortitude, which was close enough. And punishment, at the right hand of the whole

slavery concept, could be meted out not just to invite correction, but as a means of merriment to those who meted it. His smile grew. It's good to be king, he thought. The limo slowed, the turn signal flashing diligently as Harry, the general's driver, turned into the lot adjoining the church.

The pastor continued. "I think if we send a letter out to the general, asking him to reassess his position. Perhaps when he sees how many of us there are. Perhaps he'll meet with us, and we'll let him know our feelings. He won't be unreasonable. Not with us."

"Oh, my," said Briggs, again mostly to himself.

A white woman, sitting on the center aisle a few rows back, spoke out. "I'm not sure how he'll react if he knows there are white folks here. He might not like that."

"You think?" A voice came from behind the gathering. A hundred faces turned. And there stood the general, in full uniform. He marched deliberately forward down the aisle, like a brigadier on parade. Pausing close to the white lady who had spoken, he leaned down, whispering, but audibly. "We're a little pale for this party, aren't we?"

The woman froze, as did everyone else in the room. The general straightened up then, turning in the direction from which he had come. A single unarmed aide stood calmly in the doorway. "As you can see," he continued, "I come unattended. Well..." he waved a hand, "almost. Maybe you'd be so kind as to tell me what's going on." Briggs, his face ashen, cleared his throat to speak. "Not you, Mister Briggs. I'm sure your being here is quite accidental. For you to betray me would be out of character. And a crushing disappointment. Have a seat, sir." Motioning with a hand at Briggs, he waited until the coroner had reseated himself, on the edge of the aisle in the front row. "Now," he said, "somebody, please."

The pastor took a small step forward, but it was a black woman, her eyes burning a bit too brightly at the general, who spoke. "I was never a slave," she said, her voice quivering but strong. "My mother was not a slave, sir, nor hers. The fact is, I'd have to go six, seven, eight generations just to find someone in my family who had any

recollection of slavery at all. And that's a long way back. The life my ancestors lived was theirs, just theirs." The woman straightened, and grew taller, taller even than her height suggested. "Life here hasn't always been easy for me," her arms swept the room. "Or any of us. My father once told me in America I could grow up to be anything I wanted, even president, if my stars all fell into place. Well I never saw that dream, nor had any idea how to step outside my circumstance to find it. When I was young I picked cotton. It's what was here and what was available for me to do. So I did it. I don't know what else I could have done. Today I have become educated and I teach, and I embrace my life. There were mountains for me to climb —we all climb them— every day. But that makes us stronger, not weaker, and I never felt like a slave. I never felt like I was owned." The woman reached out, brushing her hand against the hand of a white man who sat close beside her. "And I'm not serving that at my table. You've misread us. You've misread your own people, and you've made a mistake." She pointed at the general, much like a teacher might point while scolding a child. "You thought owning someone, bending them to your will, would make them less and you more. It doesn't. Quite the opposite. You're the one it lessens. You know, slavers at least had a purpose. They sought profit through cheap labor. You just seek vengeance, and the funny part is you're not even seeking it against the right people or in the right time. You're reaching a hundred and fifty years into the past. There's no one here to hold accountable for that."

"Well spoken, Madam." The general turned and scanned the gathering. His face tightened, showing a troubled look. "I can see from the sick sea of faces your point is well taken." Sedgewick's eyes lit up. "I would have thought you people would understand me by now. I'm not here for your pleasure. Your lives may not have been ruled by slavery itself, but certainly servitude, which is a close cousin. An unpleasant one. It's sad you can't see that. And vengeance isn't the bad thing you speak of. It's a cleaner, a scrubber. It removes stains, leaving in its stead a more fragrant place. And this is just a room, while out there is a whole world. A world that belongs

to me." He thumped hard against his chest. "You'd all do well to remember that."

"We just want you to stop," shouted out another woman, this one with much age crinkling away at her face. "There's nothing about this that speaks to God's will, or ours. Only your will, General."

"Well," said the general, as he turned and headed back down the aisle, "it's amusing you say that. That's really the point. It's the only one that matters."

As the general left the building, each of the hundred faces turned to look at the faces of their neighbors. No one smiled, and the looks given in return contained no real substance. Only a hollow emptiness. They finally understood the general.

Chapter Thirty-Two

Manuel Ortiz patrolled the rise between the ponds and the village. July had passed, but early August brought no real relief from the heat. A trickle of sweat chased down his neck, and Manuel swiped at it with a hand. It had been two weeks since his journey here to the southern lip of Alabama, two weeks since his last kill. Manuel was restless. The workers were beginning to straggle in now, and he watched each one, gauging them as individual targets, wondering what it would feel like to drive the rasp deeply into each of their necks. One man in particular awakened him. One whose eyes looked down hopelessly as he stumbled toward the cool waters of the well. "Dumb bastard," thought Ortiz. "I could slip up behind him right now and he wouldn't even know. And the others, each a soul lost in their own minds. They wouldn't even care." As he watched the line begin to form at the pump, movement off to the left caught his eye. Two men, apart from the rest, and choosing to trudge through the open field rather than use the roadway, moved slowly toward him. Both familiar faces, and not as downtrodden as the rest. He let them approach, their eyes on his, and his on theirs. "About close enough," he said finally. "Unless you've come to kiss my ass." The two stopped just short of the rise. "Well," he said, "you

bitches be crazy. Or maybe you haven't been properly taught that the only place you're allowed to look is down."

The bigger of the two, the sheriff John Parrish, spoke. "You didn't tell on us."

"And how would you know that?"

"If you had we'd be hangin' up somewhere like meat."

Ortiz grinned, reaching down as he often did to pluck a straw of wheat. He fingered the straw between his fingers, then tossed it spear-like in the direction of the two. "Maybe I'm savin' it," he said. "Barbeque comin' up this weekend. You two would roast up real nice. The general would love that."

Tom Clayton took a half-step forward. "Let's cut the crap," he said in a voice that sounded surprisingly like he was in charge. "If you were gonna tell, you'd have told. Just cut the crap and help us. Help us get the hell out of this place. I can make you a very rich man, and unlike your companions, you'll live to enjoy it. Get us the hell outta here."

"What makes you think I can do that? And if I did help, it would be me who's hangin' up on the rack."

"You're not one of them. We can see that. And you have the general's ear. We've seen him talkin' to you. With his own kind all around him, he chooses to speak to you."

Ortiz smiled, like a mischievous boy who has just been found out. "I have talents the general admires, that's all."

John Parrish forced a playful smile. "What, are you fuckin' gay?"

Manuel's eyes widened. His mouth opened slightly as his mind worked its way back in time. Back to a prison block in California where his body had been tossed around like trash. He remembered his first night in a cell there, with El Lobo pounding away at him. "My bitch," El lobo had called him, as he screamed out with passion. And later, others had as well. Lots of others. Ortiz found himself standing there now, atop the levee, with the man grinning up at him.

"You mutherfucker," he screamed. The pig-gutter appeared in his hand, its blade gleaming in the light of the fading afternoon sun.

Flying down the face of the levee he attacked the sheriff, ramming into him and knocking him to the ground.

Tom Clayton, also falling backwards as if he too had been attacked, yelled out, "Wait, wait. We was just funnin'. We didn't mean anythin' by it. We didn't mean anythin'."

John Parrish, much larger than Ortiz, landed on his back with the Mexican on top of him. Fear filled his eyes. Instead of reaching for Ortiz and attempting to fight back, his hands went limp and he began to cry. "God, no. Please. I didn't mean nuthin' by it. I swear to God."

As Manuel's eyes filled with darkness, the blade plunged downward, nicking into the big man's throat. The tip dug in, but just a short way, and as a trickle of blood began to gush out, Ortiz caught himself, leaning over until the faces of the two men were but inches apart. "You sunovabitch," he said, in between big gulps of air. He kicked himself upright, standing astride the sheriff. "I don't fuck men," he said, the venom dripping heavily from his voice. "I kill them. That's why the general likes me. And don't you ever goddam forget it."

Ortiz backed away then, not back up on the levee, but a few paces backward where he could once again regain control of himself. His body still trembled mightily, the knife now hanging loosely at his side. He looked at the two men lying on the ground in front of him. "Next time we talk," he said, "you be respectful. I wouldn't mind being rich, but I also wouldn't mind you being dead. Could go either way."

───◆───

Up at the manor house, Samantha King sat in isolation. The general had beaten her, slashed her with a whip. Her humiliation had been witnessed by much of the free world. The story she had so desperately sought, perhaps the greatest story ever told, had now

become a soap opera with her role that of just another woman victimized by a man. The real story, the one that belonged to her, the one of hate and war and national disembowelment now sat in the back of her mind, in a darkened place. She tuned in tirelessly to her home channel, CBN. Fifty minutes of every hour focused on the great crisis casting its shadow across the state of Alabama. The war machine assembled by the government was marching ever closer to Montgomery, the capital. There were reports of fire fights, and explosions, and mad marches of men cloaked in long white robes crying out for succession. And rushing out to meet them were the black robes, who called themselves simply *Justice*, thousands of angry blacks with maybe a handful of white sympathizers among them. Once the robes and hoods were affixed, one could never tell who lay beneath them. The news and the story were, of course, of greater significance than perhaps any single incident the country had ever before witnessed. But the north was robbing Samantha of her glory, bleeding the headlines away from the equally amazing tale of the slave games being played just down the road to the south. And now the general, with his whip, had further weakened her, humiliated her, destroying both her credibility and her story. A knock came at the door, and the general entered. Samantha sat at the farthest reaches of the room, on a bed of white linen and white lace.

"My dear," he said as softly as he could speak.

"Fuck off," Samantha replied.

General Sedgewick moved further into the room, to a chair by a window overlooking the courtyard. He sat, but first turned the chair to address the bed, and not the window. "You look lovely," he said. "You know why I had to do what I did. They weren't taking me seriously. I could see that. The president thought he could intimidate me with his talk of inevitabilities. He needed a demonstration. All of America did. So they'll know I'm not to be trifled with. Not by anyone."

She looked at the general contemptuously. "So you decided the best way to show that was to beat a woman? On fucking national television. You decide to beat a woman?"

Sedgewick leaned forward, his lips forming just the edges of a smile. "My intention was not to cause you harm. You must know that. I hold you in the highest regard. But I have a mission that transcends any form of emotional attachment. I needed to communicate that nothing will keep me from the task at hand. That if they were to come marching in here, I would not hesitate to do whatever is necessary to further my agenda." The general paused thoughtfully. "I have a favor to ask."

"A favor? Why don't you go fuck yourself as a favor?"

Sedgewick's face lit up with amusement, which he then tried to conceal. "I'm not quite sure how I'd go about that," he said, "but I do need something from you. Something important."

"I've got a two inch scar on the side of my face, you sunovabitch. And if we ever do get out of this, they're going to invite me on the Jerry Springer show." While the general's smile could no longer contain itself, she continued. "Do you know how many Pulitzers are awarded to journalists who go on Springer?"

"I'm guessing none."

"You're damn right it's none. I'm done. I'm finished. They'll turn me over to the janitorial staff. I'll be sweeping floors, for chrissake."

The general had an idea. "Or, or, you can come out of this as the most amazing of freedom fighters. A journalist who fought her way in here, was beaten down, but refused to stay down." He paused for a moment, sighing. "We both know the probability of my surviving this is not good. In fact, since I have already decided not to allow it, it's even worse than that. But you, my love, my chronicleer, you will go on. You will speak of your time with me as an agony. As a hostage, in bondage, and maybe there was a time or two when you could have escaped, run like a deer for the border. But you didn't. You chose instead to stay, to suffer abject abuse and humiliation at my hands, because you are, after all, a great journalist, and so you stayed." The general tapped at his temple. "Think. Could there be a more Pulitzer worthy story than the one you will tell?"

Samantha King's eyes lit up then, and burned brightly. She wondered if Sedgewick was conning her, or further using her, but

then realized it really didn't matter. Either way, with him gone it would be a great story. And the beating would appear not as a sign of weakness, but of strength, and determination.

"Maybe I could put a bullet in your brain as my rescuers arrive," she said, her voice not lacking in sincerity.

The general laughed. "Maybe we'll arrange that. It would be fitting."

"Then get me a fucking gun," she said. "I wanna keep it handy."

A few minutes later she walked with him outside, across and away from the courtyard, where they headed for the fields. A jeep pulled up, driven by one of the aides, but the general declined the offer of a ride, choosing instead to walk the land on foot, up close and personal. They walked for some distance as the sun started to dip below the horizon, the general reaching out at one point to grasp her hand, but Samantha pulled hers away. "Okay, so what do you want?" she asked.

"We've spoken a time or two to the country, and we've had a bit of a row with the president, but now it's time to get down and dirty. I want you to film life here on the plantation. I want us to walk among the whites, even interview them as they go about their daily labors. People need to see the life of a slave firsthand. It's not enough to just sit back in our chairs and talk about it. Let's get your cameras rolling out there in the fields and show them what it's like." The general chuckled. "And let's make sure to film me right smack in the middle of it, handling the plantation as a good master should. Let's make it all cozy and personal."

"Cozy? I thought you wanted the world to feel disgust at what's going on. To despise it to the point of nausea."

"I think you and I have a disparate opinion of the word *cozy*. In my world it means to cuddle up with someone who wishes you weren't there. Until they cry. And I'll be right there in the middle of their nightmare, telling them to stop." Samantha looked at Sedgewick, and thought she saw pain, which seemed strange. He continued, "You know, it's funny. When I was very young my mother used to beat me. Beat me for the darndest things. 'Why isn't your

bike put away'... Wop! 'Why are your pants dirty'... Wop! And I'd cry out in pain. And then an amazing thing would occur. She'd begin to beat me harder, screaming at me to stop with the tears." The general's eyes probed hers. "Do you know how hard it is to stop crying while you're being beaten? So," he said, turning away, "that's what I'd like to do. Get all cozy with my charges and let them know pain isn't always a necessary evil. It's simply necessary. It can be quite exhilarating, actually."

"You're a sick fuck," she said, the words tumbling out venomously.

The general nodded agreeably, and they walked on. Of the several thousand acres of open land at Cedar Creek, more than two thirds were devoted to cotton. The plantation was a large enough one that it contained its own ginning facility, a factory where the cotton could be processed before being shipped off to market. Only remnants of the current year's crop remained on the stalk by early August, but Sedgewick insisted the entire plantation operate as if the harvest was in full swing. As they moved among the fields and rows, they passed by dozens of white laborers, bent over or down on their knees, hands bleeding as the last of the crop, which hung mostly low to the ground, was plucked and bagged and made ready for transport. Haulers would arrive every few minutes, waiting at the ends of the rows, while pickers finished their bags and brought them up to the trucks. The problem was, each bag contained only token amounts of the white fluff, but the hauler would honk anyway, impatient for the cotton to be delivered. One of the general's aides stood closely by each truck as it arrived, shouting out to the slaves to hurry. Samantha and Sedgewick stopped nearby, watching the process for a time, and then the general stepped forward. "Wait a bit," he exclaimed, as a tired, elderly man stumbled up to one of the trucks. He pointed at the sack carried loosely in the man's hands. "This sack is hardly full." The aide in charge came running over.

"Sir?" he said.

The general pointed again. "This sack," he said, "It's nowhere near full enough. In fact, it's practically empty."

"Yes, sir," said the aide. "But as the general knows there is

very little to pick, and it's getting to be less and less every day. We're already re-picking rows we've hit before. I'm not sure what the general wants."

Sedgewick looked at the young man. He smiled. "You're one of my academy boys, yes? First tier. I recognize you."

"Yes, sir. It's an honor, sir."

"Well, son." The general tapped at the young man in a friendly fashion. "I'm not really caring how many times the damn place has been picked. I'm just caring that the bags are empty, and they need not be. My thought is, it's your job as my emissary to see that we get the most out of our niggers. That they do their very best for us. The very best they can. Do you see?"

"Yes, sir, I think so." The young man's face contorted into a frown. "But how do I make them pick cotton if there's none there to pick?"

"Well," said the general, delighted at this line of reasoning. "That's the rub. We have rules to follow. You know that. Why, back at the academy we were well structured, well disciplined. We can't let anything get in the way of that. Even here in the dirt we must maintain our decorum, our discipline. What I want you to do, what I need you to do, is make certain each bag coming up to the truck is brimming over with cotton. If anyone shows up at the truck with less than a full bag, he needs to be disciplined. In fact, he needs to be disciplined so well that he carries the lesson around with him wherever he goes." Pointing at the young man's waist he said, "You've been issued that baton for a reason. It's not there to make you look all tough and blustery. It's there as a tool, to assist you in your duties. Use it. Use it in the manner it was intended, and those bags will begin to fill up nicely."

Samantha King, standing closely by and studying every word the general spoke, now began to understand the general's line of reasoning, and the very insanity that guided it. She smiled. "I'm back," she said to herself. "I'm going to kill this crazy bastard, and make a million bucks on the story."

As they moved on, they had gone only a short distance when

the sound of a hard object was heard to impact a soft one. It's an easy sound to recognize, a *thwack* that arrives with authority, yet lacks the harshness one usually hears when both objects are based from a solid. The general, having heard it many times, turned. The elderly man with the near empty sack lay on the ground, his hands raised to both protect himself and implore his attacker to show mercy. The young aide stood over him, menacing with the baton. The general nodded approvingly, and the aide nodded back.

Soon they arrived at the gin, a block-long steel structure that housed the machinery of the plantation. As they walked inside the building the sounds of the presses and the gin itself purred efficiently. Cotton isn't just the white fur-ball most people recognize. It is much more. The seeds need to be separated by the ginning process, as do remnants of dirt, stems and leaves. And nothing is wasted. The cleaned seeds are either gathered into sacks or sent off to be pressed into oil or mash. The husks and the mash are turned into feed for cattle and poultry, while the fluff itself is baled into bundles of a quarter ton each, requiring four or five men to lift. Of course, forklifts, gurneys and conveyors moved most of the product along, but here at Cedar Creek the general had shut down that part of the plant, the highly mechanized part, so the farm relied more heavily on manual labor than rolling steel to push things about. "The slaves can lift it," he had declared, "or die beneath it. After all, that's what they're for."

It was hot in the building, far hotter that the air outside, for the metal absorbed the energy passed down by the sun, further passing it along to the laborers who worked in the heat and the dust inside. Only a few still toiled, as evening had arrived and most of the workers had been dismissed. Still, they were able to grasp the flavor of the place, and could imagine how wondrous it must be during the light of day with a hundred or more sweating bodies, bent and torn by the heat as they went about their tasks. "This is where we'll come tomorrow," he said to her. "I will dress for the occasion, and will offer encouragement to the slaves while you film my every word.

It will make great theatre, and will allow the world to see that under duress a white man sweats just as easily as a black one."

Samantha looked away, to the very end of the plant, where several bales of cotton stood, stacked against a wall. "That's it? There are only like three bales in here. It will be difficult to make you appear as a captain of industry with such a trifling amount of product."

"It's perfect," scoffed the general. "That will turn it into a beautiful thing. A hundred sweating pale-skinned bodies and three bales of cotton. The inefficiency one finds when one moves away from common sense and conventional labor and begins employing whites." Smiling to himself, Sedgewick moved to one of the machines, a press, and hoisted a leg up onto a ledge. Turning to face Samantha, he tucked one hand inside his shirt, at about chest high, posing there like Napoleon on a conquest. "You've given me a great idea," he said, smacking his lips together. From now on the name Cedar Creek shall not be spoken. We shall call ourselves, and affectionately so, *Three Bales*, the pride of the south. Those bales will represent us. I will present a forum that explains how, even with little or no cotton on the ground, a man and his niggers, when properly encouraged, can still endure. And you will film as I offer this encouragement."

"Tomorrow then," said Samantha, trying hard to hold back her disgust.

"Tomorrow then," said the general.

Chapter Thirty-Three

When Olivia and Charlie arrived at the farm, Willie and the girl, Molly, were just coming out from the barn. Olivia noticed the girl carried a hen, clutched tightly to her chest. The two came walking across the yard to greet them as they stepped down from the coroner's van. "She's got a chicken," Olivia whispered.

"Play nice," said Charlie.

The four stood there for a moment, face to face, the two men facing each other, as were the two girls. Olivia spoke, her eyes turned to Willie. "You missed spaghetti last night," she said in a tone that showed indifference.

Willie smiled apologetically. "We had chicken."

Olivia's eyes shifted to the girl, and the hen. "Well, not one of ours," the girl said defensively. "They're not for eating." The girl glanced up at Willie, seeking his approval, and Willie nodded.

"That's right," he said. "You don't eat your friends." As the old man spoke, Olivia's mind spun through a brief moment of anger. The girl had clearly said the word *ours* in reference to the bird, as if she and Willie were already well bonded. Olivia couldn't have known then that Molly still suffered from a certain degree of shock and fear, and would have said anything she thought would bring her into

favor with her owner. The truth is Molly still burned away inside, and was going through the motions of appeasement while feeling the emotions of a frightened deer.

"Mister Scarlett has been teaching me about farming," she said, attempting to sound proud of the fact.

"Good for you," said Olivia, still smarting. She pointed off to the west, to the land beyond the levee. "They didn't teach you that at your plantation? What do they teach over there? Knitting?" The girls stared at each other for a moment, each measuring the other, and not liking what they saw.

Charlie laughed, "Well," he said, "maybe we could knit a sweater for the chicken and combine all our talents."

Later, as the four sat inside, Charlie looked at Willie and nodded. "Everything okay then?"

Smiling back, a little irritated and a little amused, Willie said, "Everythin's fine. Everythin's under control, Charlie. Nuthin' goin' on here you wouldn't approve of."

Molly stared at Charlie then, understanding his question to the old man had been a sort of test. She blurted out, "Where's my papa?"

"I don't know, sweetie," said Charlie, his voice sincere.

Olivia, watching the girl intently, chewed down on her lip. "We could find out for you," she said, her voice equally sincere. The two girls again made eye contact, reassessing each other. It had been only a minute or two since their last assessment, but on whatever scale they were using, they'd both moved up a notch.

"Please," said Molly. "I'd really appreciate it."

"You girls go outside and play," said Charlie. "There's something I need to discuss with Mister Scarlett."

"Play?" said Olivia. "You want us to play? We're not kids."

"Sorry," Charlie apologized. "Of course. What I meant to say is, why don't you find a more suitable place where maybe you can teach Molly the inner workings of the solar system or something? Or maybe sing a little Bach."

"You don't sing Bach. You sit back and allow him to tantalize your senses."

"Olivia, please," Charlie begged.

"Yes, sir," she replied finally. The two girls rose, Olivia tapping at Willie's head before they left the room. "It was good spaghetti," she said.

When the two had gone, Charlie brought Willie up to speed on the current situation as he understood it. He was worried about the old man and the girl living in such close proximity to the general and his horde of worshippers. Willie described the earlier encounter with the squad of men who'd attempted to trade for Molly, and that only worsened Charlie's fears, as he said, "I don't care how devoted men are to their leader, you throw women into the mix and sooner or later bad things are going to happen." He spoke of his most recent talk with the president. The fires in Birmingham were all but out now, and siege had been laid around the perimeter of Montgomery, several hundred miles to the north. No one in, and no one out, unless those who wanted out were willing to crawl out under a banner of surrender. The texture of the black-white war had also changed somewhat, from raw hostility and the explosions of anger which grew from it, to a more sedate, fear-based conflict, where both sides began to feel real loss and real pain. Eventually, he said, all but the most radical would simply want to end the barbarity and go home. The president was banking on this, feeling patience and tolerance by federal troops would win out in the end. And the collateral damage caused by the war would hang more on the heads of the people than the army. Though no one would openly admit it, Charlie could see Thomas Banks, the secretary of state's stamp all over the current solution. Let the state destroy itself from within, and then the government could swoop in to offer aid and refreshments.

"The sunovabitch," Charlie said, speaking about the president. "My best friend, and his plan is to sit tight and let the flames burn themselves out before the dozers are sent in to mop up the mess."

"What should he do?" asked Willie, having a simpler mind and a limited knowledge of the nation's political landscape. "What would you do?"

"That's a tough one. But I don't think I could sleep at night knowing folks were being harmed while I sat outside the door with a coke and a bag of chips."

Willie smiled weakly, understanding this line of reasoning. "You let me keep the girl," he said. "You ate your chips while I kept her."

Charlie reached out a hand, placing it gently on the old man's knee. "I just needed to know you," he said. "Last night, there in the hallway, you showed me everything I needed."

"I didn't say nuthin'."

"You didn't have to. A man learns about other men in many ways. If he's observant, he does. I knew right then and there you would never hurt the girl. Besides, your other crazy girlfriend made it pretty clear she'd kill me if I doubted you. That was strong enough stuff for me."

The old man chuckled. "She's still mad at me?"

"Hell, Willie, she's jealous. She thought she had you all wrapped up, and then you run off with another woman." Charlie smiled. "That's a woman scorned if I ever saw one."

Willie squirmed delightedly. "I care a lot about her too, you know. I've never had many friends. Never wanted any. Always kept to myself. And then along comes this pretty little white girl —a white girl for chrissake— who about mauls me over as I lay bleedin' on the floor, and we been friends ever since."

"Well," Charlie laughed, "don't flatter yourself too much. That chick's crazy. I've never seen anything like her. I'm pretty sure you two were made for each other."

Willie, still beaming, leaned closer. "That Molly girl ain't a bad kid neither. She's got a lot of anger in her, but she didn't put it there."

Charlie grew serious. "I need to ask you something. Why'd you take her? I mean, Tom Clayton's sitting right there and the general offers him to you. Why'd you choose the girl? Revenge?"

"No," Willie looked down, as if studying the floor. "I do despise Tom Clayton, I swear to god I do. He's spent a good deal of his life makin' me miserable, so I'm thinkin' I got a right to my feelin's. But then I seen the girl sittin' there, fear all over her face. She looks up

at me, and mixed in with the fear there's a whole pitcher full of hate. A gift from her papa, I'm thinkin'. And then I looks off to the side and one of the general's boys is also lookin' at her. He's smilin', but it ain't a good smile. So I just sorta blurted out I wanted the girl."

Willie looked up and Charlie met his eyes. "Olivia's not just smart," Charlie said. "She's a helluva good judge of character."

Outside, the two girls headed for the barn. "Are you scared, being here?" Olivia asked.

Molly hesitated. She knew Olivia and the old man were friends. "A little. I don't know his plans for me."

"His plans? Willie doesn't make plans. He's not scheming some mad plot against you. He brought you here because it's where you need to be. It's taken me a while to figure that out."

"Need to be? I need to be with my papa. At home, my home."

"What you need to do is wake up. It will be a while before this situation resolves itself. And you need to be smart, which I'm thinking you're not very good at."

Molly looked sharply at Olivia. "I'm not stupid. And I don't see why I should have to act like I'm enjoying my stay here. I hate it. I hate everything about it."

"I get that," said Olivia. "By the way," she added, changing the subject, "where's your chicken?"

"On the back porch. Mister Scarlett gave her to me."

"Nice. Maybe later we can dissect it. Never been inside a chicken before."

Molly ignored the comment. "Why do you get to roam around free when everyone else is locked up?" she asked.

"You're not locked up."

"You know what I mean. Why are you free?"

"My dad, Shawn Briggs, is the coroner. He's the one who blew the lid off the whole church bus thing. He's the one who proved it wasn't an accident. The general gave us a free pass, I guess for opening up such a grand opportunity for him."

Molly looked at Olivia in amazement. "So you're the ones who started this whole mess. Just because of a bunch of dead black girls?"

Olivia's mouth fell open, then closed tightly before she spoke. "Black girls? That's the way you think? Not girls who were taken out and butchered, but black ones?" Olivia reached out to grab Molly by the arm. She spun her around. "And I suppose you think of Willie as some kind of inferior."

Molly cast her eyes downward, as Olivia released her grasp. "Well, no. I don't know. He's not like us, I know that. My papa says they're just different."

"Well, your papa apparently isn't all that smart."

Molly stepped back, putting a bit of distance between her and Olivia. "You don't know him," she said defiantly.

"What's the square root of eight-hundred-twelve?" Olivia asked suddenly, falling back on her strange sense of logic.

"What?"

"It's twenty-eight and change. How long does it take Neptune to orbit the Earth?"

"What? I don't know."

"It doesn't orbit the earth, you dumbass." Pointing a finger in Molly's face she continued, "I could ask you a thousand things and you wouldn't know the answer to even one. You know why? Because you're a stupid girl stuck in a gene pool that's left you completely disadvantaged. To prove it, along comes your beloved papa who tells you black folks are different. And not that they're just different, but their pigmentation makes them less worthy. Do you know how idiotic that sounds? You should start making your clothes out of that cris-crossy little flag your grandpa flies so proudly. I've seen it. You'd look really swell all dressed up in hate."

Tears began to pour down Molly's cheeks. "God, you're so mean," she cried out. "All I meant was he's different from us, and it's only common sense that I'd be afraid. I've never been around people like that. I'm just scared he might hurt me."

"Hurt you?" Olivia's irritation abated, and her voice now seemed amused. "He didn't take you to hurt you. He took you to save you."

Willie and Charlie stepped out onto the porch. They could see

the two girls talking together over by the barn. "Hey," Willie hollered out. "You two havin' fun?"

Molly, hearing him, looked up for a moment, then turned and ran for the back of the house. She disappeared there, and after a few seconds they heard a door slam. Olivia walked over to the two men. "We need to find her papa," she said. "She's stressing. I think she went off to be with her chicken."

"We can stop by and ask the general about him on the way home," said Charlie. "I don't imagine the man is enjoying a pleasant circumstance though, after Willie pointed out what he did."

"I shoulda kept my mouth shut."

"No, Willie, no. Then you wouldn't have the girl and someone else would."

As Charlie and Olivia climbed into the van, Willie approached the passenger side. Olivia rolled down the window. "What?" she challenged.

"I don't want you mad at me," he said. "I shoulda explained before I run off like that. I was a nervous wreck."

Olivia looked out at his gentle, sad face. "You worried me." The ice in her voice began to melt.

Reaching into the cab to touch her arm, a slight mist formed in the old man's eyes. "You're my best friend," he said, stabbing at a phrase he'd never before uttered.

Olivia said nothing. She bit down hard on her lip. Finally she nodded. "Okay then." As Charlie drove out of the yard a moment later, the two were still looking at one another.

When they reached the main highway, Charlie turned south, a direction that took them further away from town. He drove for a mile or so, until they came upon the entrance to Cedar Creek. As they approached, they noticed a group of white men working on the stanchions that held up the archway everyone had to pass under when visiting the plantation. Several of the general's aides, young, strong looking men with rifles, stood in the bed of a nearby truck, watching the laborers. "What's going on?" Charlie inquired of the guards as he turned in.

The men saluted respectfully, recognizing immediately the coroner's van and its importance. "Just the changing times, sir," a young man said. "Out with the old and in with the new. Cedar Creek has just been re-designated. We're Three Bales now." The aide smiled. "The general says we are the new pride of the new south."

"Catchy," said Olivia under her breath as the men moved aside to allow entry for the van. Rolling up the long drive, all seemed in order, and quite industrious. A line of several trucks ran along parallel to them on a side road, cotton haulers moving among the rows. White pickers were out in the fields in abundance, most bent over or on their knees as they scrambled about, trying to secure the last bits of fluff from the stalks. One man rose, taking a canteen from his waist, tipping it high as if it held but a few precious drops. A guard approached the man, lashing out with a baton, and sending the canteen flying. The man quickly bent back to his work.

When they arrived at the main house an aide came out to greet them. The general, they were told, was down at the gin with Miss King. He picked up a phone and spoke into it briefly, then waved them through.

General Sedgewick himself came out to meet them as they arrived. "My friends, this is such an unexpected pleasure. Come, come." He waved them forward, leading the way into the building. "Come and observe our prosperity."

The main entryway into the gin was almost exactly as wide as were the haulers that formed a continuous line as they drove through it. Elevated ramps inside the facility matched the height of the beds, so laborers could simply walk from the breezeway of the gin onto the approaching truck, unload it while it still moved slowly forward, and stack the parcels of cotton along the way. The truck would then wind its way in a half circle, exiting through another narrow corridor on its return trip to the fields. If a driver was proficient and the work was well timed and steady, a truck might never completely stop through several cycles. The general guided Charlie and Olivia in between two of the haulers and they walked up the ramp at a speed matching the one in front. Samantha King waited for them at the top.

"Good to see you," she said to Charlie, then to Olivia, "I've missed you, young lady."

Olivia's eyes danced delightedly. "Saw you on T.V.," she said. "With your boyfriend." Samantha's mouth twitched, but she said nothing in reply. The general motioned them over to a long processing area where several shirtless whites sweated as they poured the contents of the cotton sacks into the gin.

"Here is where the wonders of our enterprise begin," he said smugly. "Our product will be woven into fabrics the whole world will enjoy. Miss King is filming me today as I teach the new workers what we expect of them. It will be quite instructive, I believe."

"Where's the cotton?" asked Olivia, noticing the bins in front of them were almost empty and the bags waiting to be unpacked seemed unnecessarily light.

"Ahh," said the general, as he pulled from his chest pocket a cigar. He observed the cigar closely, holding it high for a visual inspection, then ran it lovingly beneath his nose. Satisfied, he clipped it then, with a tiny gold bladed knife, before slipping it between his lips and lighting it most elegantly. He puffed away for a moment or two, letting the smoke and the aroma fill his senses. "Ahh," he said again. "My dear Miss Briggs. We've been at it for more than a week now and you're the first aside from Miss King to ask the obvious question. Two brilliant women in my life, and both able to put the simplest of matters into perspective. Why does that not surprise me?" The general walked them along what would have been a long conveyer, had it been allowed to convey, until they arrived at the three bales stacked neatly up against a far wall, two on the bottom and the one atop, precisely between them. "Here you see firsthand the symbol of our very humanity. That which makes us so successful. The masses..." he kicked at the lower bales, "holding aloft the more prominent among us on their shoulders. We are being defined not by the sincerity of our labors, but by something that is eminently more reasonable. The color of our skin." The general had an idea. Signaling an aide, he called the man over. "Before the hour is out," he said curtly, "I want this top bale painted black. If it

is to symbolize us it should do so correctly. I don't care if you have to tar the damn thing, it will be black, and held aloft by its more subordinate companions."

Olivia looked slyly over at Charlie. "It must be good to be black," she whispered.

She then shifted her glance to Samantha King, who seemed just as perplexed as she. Samantha's shoulders lifted and she shrugged in sort of a "What can I say," motion, and then the general called on Charlie to walk with him. The two women were left standing alone. "That boyfriend thing hurt," said Samantha, not even looking at Olivia. "I'm not here by choice, you know?"

"I didn't see him force you to go. And I'm not stupid. I watch your face every time you're on the news. You revel in this shit. At least you did until he beat the crap out of you."

Samantha winced, still not looking at the girl. "Maybe I got caught up in the story a little too much." She had been talking quietly, but now her voice lowered even more. "Right now I hate his guts. I just want to kill the sunovabitch."

"Do us all a favor," said Olivia, as she walked away.

The general directed Charlie outside, walking him over to a fountain, where he dipped his mouth to drink. "Nigger water," he said. "I really shouldn't be drinking from here."

"What do you want, General?"

Sedgewick nodded, touching Charlie lightly on the arm. "I want to like you Chester. In fact, I already do. And I'm grateful for your past service to me. Even if it was, as you say, unintentional." Reaching down his hand, the general ran the remnants of the cigar through a small stream of water gushing up from the fountain. He flicked the stub carelessly to the ground. "When you leave here today I don't want you coming back."

"Here? You don't want me here?"

"I don't want you anywhere near where I am. You're becoming too dangerous. I suspect soon you may be asked to end my reign. And I have no doubt you will comply, even if you find the assignment distasteful."

Charlie smiled, his eyes like missiles, pointed straight at the general's. "I wouldn't find it distasteful," he said.

The general returned the smile. "I didn't think so, and I appreciate your honesty. We are men of honor, you and I. When called upon to act, we must. And so I need to take some necessary precautions to ensure my mission here doesn't end too abruptly."

"About that," said Charlie. "What exactly is your mission? You can't be trying to make a point. Your point died, General, the moment you decided to deal in death instead of mercy. A lot of folks have died around here because of you. At this point your impact can never be a positive one. Because of your cruelty, even your own people will find you hard to emulate." Charlie's look became an imploring one. "So what do you want? Tell me the truth."

The general began to laugh then, the pitch building as it enveloped him. And once he started he couldn't stop. His laughter echoed around them for a long time, until finally it lessened like a waning storm, then died down completely. "It's the damdest thing," he said. "You're the first one to ask. Imagine, I've been stomping around the countryside for some time now, and no one ever thought to ask why. It's for me, Chester. It's always been for me. It's my own antipathy I care about, and my absolution from it. That's what death brings. Absolution. How often does one get to plan one's death, and do so in such glorious fashion? I will never be forgotten, don't you see. Eventually the bastards will roll in here and take me down. And they'll be brash enough to think they've won." The general pointed back toward the gin. "Three bales, Chester, just three. Two white ones on the bottom and one black one on the top. That's the way a man should die. Carried about on the shoulders of those beneath him."

"You're a crazy fuck, General," said Charlie, echoing Samantha King's appraisal. "But there's more to you than that. This isn't about lionizing your death. I suspect you came down here to make a difference. A real difference. And maybe convince the world to somehow modify itself by your actions. What you failed to realize is you're just not that big a man." Charlie moved a step nearer the

general, until they were uncomfortably close. "There are a lot of black generals, General. Fine men who moved up the ladder as their abilities defined them. But not you. They held you back for a reason. Perhaps because of your own prejudice, and not because of theirs. It's never been because you are black. It's been because you are you… Sir."

Sedgewick chewed down hard on his lip. His mouth contorted somewhat as he spoke. "It's time for you to go. And as I said, I don't wish to see you here again."

Charlie stepped back, giving both men some space. He grinned. "What makes you think I won't kill you right here, right now?"

General Sedgwick swung his head to the side, pointing at a truck parked nearby. In its bed sat three men with rifles. Each man nodded obediently at the general. "I'll let you know when I'm ready." He turned then, his face expressionless, and walked up the ramp into the gin.

Chapter Thirty-Four

Every day for the next week, Samantha King offered live feeds, streamed through her video system to the mother station at CBN. Sometimes they would show laborers hard at work in the fields, sometimes the filthy, sweat-laced bodies of men and women who dragged themselves back to the camp each evening. But mostly they concentrated on the general and the kingdom he had created for himself right there at the gin. General Sedgewick was a natural, not so much at acting, for his actions were never scripted, but at tormenting and berating and punishing. That was where his mastery in front of the camera set him apart. He had a gift, a knack for adding the perfect level of humiliation to each of his commands. If a man was ordered to sweep the floors, the general might knock him down first, ordering the sweeping done while the man groveled on his knees. After one such incident, and live on the air, Samantha had asked him what he hoped to gain by subjecting the worker to torment. "Wouldn't the man get more done and be more efficient if he was allowed to stand?" she asked.

The general smiled benevolently. He reached to his collar, adjusting the microphone attached there. "First of all, my dear. It's not a man. And second, you know I am all about efficiency. But do

we strive for efficient sweeping, or an efficient learning tool that teaches one where he belongs, and where he does not? I'm thinking the latter."

As the general continued in his role as a great punisher, America watched, individually through a million sets of eyes, but collectively their hearts pounded in unison at the levels of depravity they witnessed. In Kansas, a father turned to his daughter, her cheeks streaming tears as the general beat down a boy who had come to ask for water.

"That's not us, baby," he said to her softly. "That will never be us."

And in a sports bar in Boston, a group of young men sat at the counter, their eyes transfixed on a giant screen on the wall. "He's gonna hit that boy," said one. "Five bucks says he don't," said another. All eyes flashed at the gambler. He looked back for a brief moment, and then lowered his eyes to the floor.

At first the conflict to the north had entranced the millions of followers who tuned in each day. When Birmingham was sacked, the country watched with mournful eyes. When Montgomery burned, and its capitol fell, mourning turned to despair. But the clashes there were only unusual by their size and dynamic, not their presence. It had been seen before, done before, on a lesser scale, perhaps, but dozens of incidents of rioting and unrest across America and the rest of the world had hardened people enough so that such events, however horrific, were accepted and even expected.

This slave playing was new, unlike anything that had ever been seen before, and the general played hard at it. There were scenes enacted each day that pushed up against the boundaries of understanding. They brought with them the complete and total stripping away of human decency. One time late in the day, a woman stumbled while delivering her cotton. The general stepped up to her, tearing away her filth encrusted blouse to expose her breasts. He grabbed at one, handling it almost savagely. "As a beast of burden this one is useless," he said, his voice filled with contempt. "Maybe we should milk her."

Samantha King always held the camera steady, but inside she

died a little at each of the general's acts. Finally, after days of filming, the general said, "Enough. Let's turn the damn thing off. I think they all understand now what a beautiful canvas pain provides. No paint required."

Chapter Thirty-Five

Article Five of the general's manifesto had yet to be put into play. That the white women of the valley should present themselves in a comely manner and be ready to serve their masters at all times. He'd been saving it, relishing it, letting his mind explore delicious possibilities. Many of the more attractive female members of the community had stayed on at the gymnasium, when the men and the women the general deemed too earthy had been sent off to labor. Bunks were set up for them there, in long rows across the court, barracks style, and they used the facilities just as would children attending the school. They were allowed to roam the grounds and the classrooms with little restriction, other than one rule that, should they step off campus for any reason, they would be gathered up and presented to the troops as a gift. So there was an incentive to stay close and stay put. A laundry room adjoined the girls' showers, and every couple of days a truck would pull up, depositing a great bundle of dirty clothing the troops had soiled which the women were expected to clean. It was their only task.

One day two huge trucks arrived and the women were gathered up for transfer. They were taken a short distance down the road, to the factory across from the Harbor Glen Lodge. Normally

the factory produced cab components for one of the big trucking companies, but the general had it shut down and emptied, so now it lay there as a long, metal warehouse, broken into two sections by a single thirty foot high wall.

Beds were brought over from the lodge —about forty in all— which were lined up neatly in the largest of the two sections, and assigned to the women as they arrived. The eldest of the ladies was about thirty-five, a long legged, pretty thing, and clasped tightly at her waist was her daughter, a cute young miss of fourteen. When the general first selected them from among the gathering he had noted aloud that the girl was surprisingly lovely, and about the same age as Elizabeth Courtier, the girl who had been brutalized in the woods. "My dear," the general had said to her, brushing his fingers gently across her cheek as she clung fast to her mother. "You symbolize all that is fresh in the world, and not yet tainted by corrosive influence. I shall endeavor to see you are treated well as you blossom." The mother had looked then at the general with pleading eyes.

For the smaller of the two sections, the one on the other side of the high wall, the general had a curious purpose. He gathered from among the laborers each of the boyfriends, husbands or fathers of the chosen women. They were chambered there, inches apart from their loved ones, separated only by a thin strip of steel. At first it seemed a merciful thing, that the two sides could press themselves up against the wall and coo out words of love and encouragement. But at the flick of a switch all could be taken away. At the top of the wall were mounted three huge ventilating fans, used to combat the summer's heat. Without them there, temperatures in the factory during the hottest of days would soar, making work intolerable. The one drawback was that once turned on, the turbines in the fans produced enough noise that sound between the walls would not carry. With the fans on, one could scream on one side, and someone on the other would never know it. One day, soon after the transfer, the general visited, first the women's side. He entered grandly, in full uniform, his chest adorned with ribbons, and the four pilfered stars atop each shoulder. The women, alerted to his arrival, were

already seated in a semi-circle of folding chairs set up opposite the main doorway. They were each dressed loosely, in baggy two-piece garments the general had ordered sewn for them in one of his other facilities. The bottoms were of a crisp white denim, and the tops made from a few bolts of camouflage material the troops had brought along on the journey. Every face that looked up at him appeared pale and guarded, much paler than their already white skins would indicate, and every face showed fear. The general smiled, pulling up his own chair as he sat there among them.

"I hope you are enjoying the clothing we have provided for you." He smiled broadly, making eye contact with as many as would return his gaze. "It wasn't easy putting this ensemble together. My desire was that you feel comfortable, yet easily identifiable in the event you chose to wander about. I'd like it very much if you could just relax for a moment and chat with me. I promise, nothing will befall you, not now. So let's just become acquainted." Adjusting his tie, the general squirmed a bit, as if even he found the situation uncomfortable. "It is not my intention to cause you torment," he continued, "but if we're honest, it's really you who have brought this upon yourselves. There are many fine ladies in your community who are out walking the streets right this minute, playing at whatever endeavor they choose. They have proven to be the best of you, and have earned through kindness and respect, the right to move about unopposed." The general brought a hand down and tapped away on his leg. "You, on the other hand, have each been identified as a transgressor. Instead of offering yourselves as friends to those around you, you have chosen a different path, a darker one. That's why you're here, to make up for past mistakes. To become better for it." Sedgewick rose then, moving up close to the gathering. One of the women noticed him fondling the crop which dangled from his side. She flinched as he drew near. Seeing this, the general removed the whip from its strap and tossed it to an aide standing at the back of the room. "Please," he said. "There will be no beatings here tonight. I suppose even I am guilty of transgression. I can see it in your eyes as you judge me." Returning to his chair, he again sat,

leaning forward, his chin in his hand. "I'd like to begin by telling you a story, one that has been passed down through generations of my family. Perhaps then we will better understand one another."

"A long time ago," he began, "when one of my great-grandfathers was a father, he had a daughter. She was lovely as a rose. They lived on a plantation not too far from here." The general smiled. "As you can see by my skin and my relationship to them, their life was not pleasant. But the child was an unusually happy one, finding joy in the simplest of things. She had a doll she loved, made of straw, with eyes of shiny pebbles gathered from the earth. The doll was her constant companion until, at the age of eight, she heard a baby crying and presented to the tiny thing her most coveted treasure. That's the kind of child she was. One day, a few weeks shy of her thirteenth birthday, she was discovered bathing in a pond by the plantation owner's son and several of his friends." The general's eyes sought out the young girl. She sat there clutching tightly to her mother, watching him, bewitched. "It's not hard to imagine what happened. They were young men, after all, and she was a sweet and pretty thing. When she returned home sometime later, she ran, battered and bleeding into the arms of her father, a man who loved her very much." The general's face darkened. "That night the man's soul died. He knew they would call again for her, many times, until she was all used up and only a shadow of herself, and there would be nothing he could do to stop it. His first thought was to rise up, destroy his daughter's destroyers, but that, he knew, would only rain down hellfire upon them all. Instead, he took his wonderful miss outside where they could gaze up at the stars and marvel in the Lord's glory. As the girl looked up, tears still streaming from her eyes, he brought forth a knife which he had hidden beneath his cloak. He released her then, released her from her torment, and made certain they could never hurt his little one again." The general rose, choosing to stand above the women instead of sit beside them. "I tell you this not to depress you, not to thrust further agony upon you, but to address the responsibility each of you has as you walk through life. Each of you played a part in the demise of that wonderful child.

Through your own ignorance and your own arrogance, you hand down generation after generation of disservice."

One woman, one of the older ones, and who sat farthest away from the general, called out, "How can we be responsible for something that happened before we were even born? How can you say that?" The general found the woman with his eyes, and smiled generously at her.

"If you don't understand, I haven't been a very competent teacher. Sometimes I get tangled up in my own intellect and forget what you people are. It's of no matter." Walking among the rows the general stopped before an attractive blonde. He leaned over, running his hand across her knee and caressing her inner thigh. She tried to pull away. "Stay," he commanded. The woman froze, her eyes open and frightened, staring up at his. "That's my darling," he said to her with great affection.

He walked again to the front of the room. "We are going to play a game," he said. "It will teach you what my words cannot. Most effectively." An aide rushed forward, delivering to the general a cap, which he held cupped in both hands. "Inside this cap are thirteen white marbles and one black one." Sedgewick reached into the cap, drawing forth a white marble. "For a fortnight, starting with tonight, I will pull from this cap one marble." Every woman in the room transfixed on the general. "If it is a white one, like this, your evening will be pleasant and unencumbered. If however..." Digging into the cap he produced the black marble, "it is the black one, the doors will open and in will march fifty of my men. They will stay for exactly two hours, and will take whatever pleasure they wish from you." The general chuckled. "My apologies, but they haven't been around women for a while, so you might find them a bit eager."

The young girl cried out, "They're going to rape us? You're going to let them rape us?" She looked at her mother, who frantically pulled her close.

"No, sweetheart," said the general as gently as he could. "I'm not a barbarian. They're going to enjoy you. And it's expected you will enjoy them back. If you're willing to set aside your inhibitions

the encounter could be a pleasant one. And remember, you'll be making up for past transgressions, so that's a good thing." Raising a hand, the general aligned a finger, pointing it straight at the heart of the young lady. "And I'm thinking the line forming for you will be an especially long one."

"You can't do this." The girl's mother shook defiantly.

"Please, please," the general raised both hands. "There's no reason to despair. Remember, there are thirteen white marbles standing in the way of the black. It may be a while before they come." Holding the cap over his head, Sedgewick called out, "Let's end the suspense and have our first draw, shall we?" He reached into the cap, mixing the marbles diligently before extracting one. It was white. The women gasped audibly, and the general smiled. He tossed the marble across the floor, where it rolled and rolled until it stopped finally against the leg of a chair. "Now there are but twelve white ones. Every evening the odds change a bit. That's what will make this so much fun."

As the general turned to leave the chamber, the mother of the young girl broke away, rushing at him. An aide stepped up, blocking her way. The woman's eyes were wide and desperate. "She's just a baby," she cried out. "She doesn't deserve this."

Sedgewick moved back into the room, and brushed the aide aside. "Of course, of course. I'm not without mercy. You may exempt your daughter if you like. Take on her burden as yours." The general reached to the aide's waist, pulling from its sheath a long, sharp knife. Flipping the blade in his hand he held the handle out to the desperate woman. "I understand completely," he said, his voice low and tender. "You have every right to save her." The woman took the knife as a reflex and stood there holding it loosely, her eyes blank, hollow orbs as the general and the aide turned and walked out the door.

On the men's side, husbands and fathers pressed frantic ears against the wall. "What is he saying?" one hollered out.

"Goddam, I can't hear," said another.

"They're too far away," shouted out a third. "Something about marbles. If the bastard hurts them I'll kill him."

It was only a moment later the men heard a latch thrown on their own door, on the outside wall of the chamber, and General Sedgewick walked into the room. He came alone at first, and had they thought it, or had time to plan it out, it would have been an easy thing to overpower and take the man down. Seconds later, however, a line of armed guards filed in, flanking the general, five on each side and five more at the door.

"Gentlemen," the general began. "My second meeting of the evening, but this one will be brief." One of the men, a large, strong-looking fellow, took a half step forward, his fists clenched, ready to do battle. Sedgewick smiled at him. "You need to stand down, my friend. Any move you make will not be a wise one. Stand down."

Surveying the gathering, the general spoke. "I need you all to sit. Now. That way there will be less chance for you to act in folly, and less chance you will do injury to yourself or your companions." All of the men sat then, some taking more time about it than others. "I've just had a meeting with your lovely ladies next door. And they've agreed, unanimously, I might add, to begin entertaining my troops starting tomorrow evening. I wanted to come here personally to assure each of you that the pressures on them will be light. No more than six or seven of my bucks to any one lady." Instantly, and at precisely the same moment, every one of the men in the chamber leapt to his feet. It was an amazing feat of instinctive coordination. And just as efficiently, the two ranks of men flanking the general jacked rounds into their receivers, leveling a long row of automatic weapons at the men.

Profanity flew through the air then, the men screaming all the filth their minds could summon, and some of them even advanced a step or two before reason brought them to a halt. The general raised a hand, but the men would not be stilled. They jumped about and ranted about, until time and the energy consumed by their anger wore them down. Throughout the tirade, the general stood by patiently. Finally, after a long period, the men quieted.

"I understand your frustrations," the general sighed. "I really do. And that's why I've decided to treat you with such leniency. Ordinarily I would have you pummeled for such insubordinations. But I understand." Pointing up to the highest reaches of the wall, he then said, "The fans will be going on now, as a sort of merciful gesture on my part. So you won't have to hear the laughter and frivolity that goes on next door as each of your women are taken with enthusiasm. The fans will stay on for the duration of your stay here. In addition, every evening, when my boys arrive to claim their rights, a red light will begin to flash." Sedgewick pointed to a lamp, elevated high over the door. "It will flash until the last of them is sated and has departed the building. At that time the light will be extinguished and the evening's entertainment will cease." The general backed away, towards the door. "So watch for the light, gentlemen, and enjoy." With these last words, the turbines could be heard warming up, spinning slowly at first with a low whine. By the time the door closed and the general departed, the noise was sufficiently loud enough to block any sounds coming from the other side.

As the general pulled away in the limousine, his driver, one of his top aides and a sort of subordinate friend, called out, "I'd appreciate being in the first wave, sir. If I may. There's some fine ladies in there."

The general laughed then. "Harry," he said. "I wouldn't make a very good rapist. I believe a woman should be willing. I'm a military man on a mission. That's all that went on here tonight. Those women aren't to be touched. But for the next fourteen days they will feel as though the gates of hell have opened for them. They'll lie there and wait, and wonder if perhaps tonight's the night the black marble calls for them. When it's over, they might just walk out of there a bit more humbled."

"But what about the men, sir? And the light?"

The general's laughter intensified. "That's my favorite part, the sorry bastards. Imagine, each evening when the red light flashes. They can hear nothing, do nothing, and so their minds will fill in all the torturous blanks. The writhing, screaming sounds inside their own heads will be haunting companions… every night."

Chapter Thirty-Six

While the general's foray into slavery was an efficient one, with methods of mental and physical abuse borne from a studied history, not everyone in the county was as proficient. Only a small handful of local blacks decided to participate. The majority were curious and interested, but chose to do their slave watching from afar. And so the few who decided to take on the burden of ownership faced uprisings, scuffles, and in more than one case, whites who just up and ran away. It seemed as though even the best intentioned were not always cut out to be slave masters.

Two neighbors who lived directly across the road from each other were Moss Daughtry and Juniper Jones, both middle-aged black men who had faced considerable humiliation at the hands of another neighbor, Johnny Pond. Pond, a white man who reveled in that very fact, owned a sizable chunk of land spanning both sides of the highway and often took issue with regards to the water rights of a small creek that fed all three properties. At his best, Johnny had one day shot all seven of Juniper's sheep for drinking water he considered his, and at his worst, there was the time he'd chained Moss to the back of a tractor and dragged him all the way into town to face Sheriff Parrish for what Pond claimed was out-and-out thievery.

It seemed Moss had come over to reclaim a stray pig that Pond was preparing to butcher for supper. Moss had grabbed the pig, and was attempting to carry it back home when Johnny Pond hit him over the head with a trace iron, and then dragged him off to the sheriff. When the sheriff asked Johnny how in hell it could be considered a crime for a man to collect his own pig, Pond had replied, "That's what I'd like to know about it." Sheriff Parrish scratched his head then, and sent both men home. But the abuse continued, year after year. So the general's coming had seemed a godsend, a chance for redemption. Both men jumped at the chance to own Pond, and Sedgewick, after hearing both their stories, had awarded Johnny and his eldest son to Moss, and Johnny's wife and other two sons to Juniper.

A few days later, old Moss wrote an editorial to the paper, which, in the hands of the general's men, was being used as a propaganda machine. General Sedgewick was so enamored with the piece that he had it blown up and posted all over the county. It read:

> *After careful observation it has come to my attention*
> *that being a slave is easy, and probably always has been.*
> *You just do your job, get beat a little, and do your job some more.*
> *It's owning a slave where all the hard work comes in. Knowing*
> *how to manage one and get the most out of him. It's no wonder*
> *folks think I walk around grumpy all the time. This slave owning*
> *stuff is damn hard work. And it makes me appreciate a lot more*
> *what white men musta gone through with all their niggers.*

The general was never quite sure whether Moss's attempt as a writer was pure sarcasm or a look into the mind of a crazy man, but in either event, he loved the piece. Moss had been given a whip by the general, not one of the puny riding crops like the general carried, but an honest-to-goodness cattle whip with a range of over fifteen feet. He practiced with it day and night, until he could flick Johnny Pond or his son ever so lightly, just enough to make them bleed or cry out a little.

Juniper Jones, on the other hand, on the other side of the road,

didn't have nearly as much mean in him. So Pond's wife and other
two sons, who had also shown disdain for black folks over the years,
were treated with a certain amount of respect, even kindness. Juniper
did want to teach them a lesson, so he still assigned them unpleasant
tasks, but as long as they tried and offered no trouble, he stayed
pretty much out of their way.

Soon after the article was released, General Sedgewick was
out visiting his constituents, as he liked to call the black folks of
Harbor Springs. They weren't aware of his revelation to Charlie, that
his motives were more of a self-glorification than a journey into
righteousness, so to them he was thought to be, if not a messiah,
at least a guardian of the people. As the limousine rolled down the
road, whatever black folks were up to, they would stop and run to
the roadside to wave and bow at his passing. On this particular day,
he turned into the driveway of Moss Daughtry, to thank him for his
most entertaining letter. The general reflected that Moss probably
felt just about the same as he, that the new slaves of the south could
be a most vexing breed. He chuckled to Harry that perhaps through
selective breeding they could cleanse some of the vexation out of
them, leaving the herd more suited and more subservient. "Hell,"
Harry had laughed, "they bred the shit outta us. Might as well return
the favor."

So, in good spirits, they turned up the drive. There was a large
oak situated just to the side of Daughtry's house, one of those
traditional southern oaks with massive branches reaching out in all
directions. The first thing they noticed was a white boy near the tree,
bent over on his knees, his face wrapped in his hands. He seemed to
be suffering over something. The boy looked up for a brief moment,
then plunged his head back into his hands. As they drew closer, they
saw what he saw, a sight that slammed into them. There, hanging
from one of the branches, his feet dangling just inches from the
ground, was a man. A white man. Daughtry, who had been sitting up
on his porch puffing at a pipe, rose then, one hand clasping the pipe,
and the other, the whip. He came down the steps to meet them. The
general stepped from the limo.

"What the hell happened here?" he demanded.

"Well, suh," began Moss, "I was tryin' to teach this dumb sunovabitch how I wanted my ditch dug. He and his boy there was diggin' it too crooked and too shallow. I told 'em, I musta told 'em fifty times, 'do the damn thing straight and dig the damn thing deep'. But they wouldn't listen to ole' Moss. Finally..." Moss pointed to the hanging man, "he just throws down his shovel and comes at me. I whipped the bastard as he came, but he got to me anyways. So I had to beat the sunovabitch down personal-like till he wasn't movin' no mo'. And I was so damn mad I went to the barn and got me a rope. I flung it up there and hung the bastard before he even come to." Moss spat at the ground. "I wish to hell I'd waited so he coulda seen what was gonna happen, but he never come to. So I jus' pulled him up, and he jus' swung there like a sack'a meat."

As Moss spoke they heard a cry, and across the road ran a woman and two boys. They ran up to the other boy and joined him, until the four, as one mass, crumbled screaming to the ground.

The general turned angry eyes on Moss Daughtry. "And by whose authority did you hang him? You know the rules. I made them very clear. Any punishments were to be handed down by me or my men. You've stepped way outside the lines here."

Daughtry tried to defend himself. "I jus' told you, suh. He was attackin' me. Hell, it's jus' lucky I'm not the one hangin' there."

Sedgewick raised his hands, running his fingers aggressively across his face. "Don't you see what you've done, you dumb bastard? You've become just like him. Like all of them. Hell man, I've got three hundred of them to contend with, while you've got two. I beat them, I berate them, I starve them just to get a bit of enjoyment from their misery. But I don't hang them." Menacing eyes stared hard at Moss Daughtry. "Hanging them ends the game."

A jeep had pulled in behind the limo. Several of the general's aides stepped down, moving up beside him. The general continued to stare at Daughtry, who now hung his head, afraid to look up. "String this bastard up," Sedgewick said to the man standing nearest him. "Right next to his buddy there. Let them go to hell

together." He turned to face his remaining aides. "Nobody ruins my fucking game."

As the limo backed away and moved down the road, a crowd began to gather. Whispers spread, and then loud lamentations. At first no one could believe that the general, their near-messiah, could order the death of one of their own. When it became clear he had, the waving and the bowing died down, until most of the faces they passed looked deliberately away. "Fuck them all," said the general.

As the limo moved toward town, the general ordered Harry to drive slowly past the mortuary. Smoke rose from the crematorium. It seldom stopped now, and the general reflected that two more bodies would soon be showing up. Briggs would be a busy man for some time to come.

Harry asked, "Do you want to stop here, sir?"

"No," replied the general. He smiled grimly. "I don't have enough of a guard with me, and Mister Benton would probably love to break my goddam neck."

"We still have a jeep behind us, sir. Four armed men, all with automatic weapons."

"No," repeated Sedgewick. "I'm not liking those odds. I've seen our friend there at work."

As they turned the corner for the drive into town, the general leaned forward to say something. That's when the rear window next to the general's face exploded. Harry screamed and hit the accelerator. He heard the general cry out. Glancing in his mirror he saw blood, lots of it, spread all over Sedgewick's face. He headed for the gymnasium, a place he knew would be well tended by troops. Many stayed there full time, at a location close enough to the main parts of town that they could respond almost immediately to any emergency. Bouncing his way over the curb, Harry slid his way onto the grass of an athletic field, tearing up great chunks of sod as the car raced for the building, finally sliding up so close they nearly crashed through a pair of giant glass doors.

"The general's been hit," cried out Harry, as several aides came rushing out from the gym. A stretcher was brought out, Sedgewick

lifted onto it and carried inside. There were two members of the medical staff on duty, one of whom ran for his instruments while the other tore at the general's shirt. Though most of the blood was spread thickly across the general's face, no wound could be found there. Stripping away the shirt, the source of the blood became apparent. A bullet had pierced his upper shoulder, tearing its way deeply into the muscled tissue there. The blood on Sedgewick's face was splatter, which had exploded its way along the top of the shoulder, riding the neck upward and sloshing out in a wave onto the general's left cheek. The wound was quite serious, with the only good news being the round had passed cleanly through the shoulder and required no complications to remove. The bad news was that there were two wounds to tend instead of one: entry and exit, both spewing out a lot of blood. The medic who had run for the instruments returned, and both medical personnel stood there, looking down as the blood seeped away. "Shit, we gotta stop the bleeding," said one.

"Right," said the other, his own blood rushing from his face. They continued to stare. General Sedgewick, who had been laying there in a state of pain and shock, now came roaring to life.

"Tourniquet the bastard and sew it up." He looked angrily around the room. "Where the hell is Harry? Harry!"

The driver rushed over. "Right here, sir. Right here."

"Get these sunsabitches motivated and sew me the hell up."

"Yes, sir." Harry drew from a side holster a military forty-five, lashing out at the closest of the medics. The pistol crashed into the side of the man's face, dropping him immediately to the floor. He stared hard at the remaining medic, cocking the hammer back and pointing the barrel straight into the man's face. "Sew, you sunovabitch, sew." Within seconds a needle flew into the general's shoulder, with one of the medic's hands addressing the front wound while the other hand compressed a bandage and pressed forward from the back.

The general grimaced from the pain, but refused to cry out. "That's how you motivate, Harry. God, I love ya." He grabbed the free hand of his subordinate friend, the hand not occupied by the

pistol, squeezing tightly. "If the bleeding doesn't stop in the next thirty seconds, you shoot this bastard."

———◆———

Seal Team Six, an elite squad out of Quantico, had been in and around Harbor Springs for the past three days. They'd set up camp at an abandoned farm on the outskirts of town, lying low during much of the day and venturing out for reconnaissance whenever darkness fell. Near the end of that third day, two members of the five man team had sneaked to the very edges of the community in an attempt to contact Chester Benton at the mortuary. They almost made it there. Winding their way among trees and brush at the end of a dead-end street, they saw smoke rising from the crematorium. At almost the same time, a limousine moved down the same street from the opposite end, coming right at them. It was later calculated they had less than twenty-two seconds to evaluate that the approaching car matched the description given to them by intelligence, jack a round into the receiver, fall into firing position, scope, identify, aim and fire the bullet intended to assassinate Colonel Anthony Sedgewick. And the shot had been a perfect one, a dead-on missile headed straight for the forehead of the target. Had not Sedgewick leaned forward at the last second, the mission would have been complete, and the slave games would now be just another anecdote of history gone awry.

———◆———

Sometime later a jeep pulled up at the mortuary. Along with the driver, it held four other heavily armed men. They waited there in the jeep until, after a few minutes, a transport truck pulled up behind them. A canvas flap at the rear of the truck was pulled back, and a

dozen additional armed troops piled out. They set up in formation along the sidewalk, forming a rank that extended the whole length of the block. Then the driver of the jeep picked up a microphone and flipped on a large speaker mounted on the dash.

"Chester Benton and Shawn Briggs." The sound of the amplified voice shocked the air. "Come out and be recognized, sirs. Come out now." There was no immediate response, so the driver continued. "Chester Benton and Shawn Briggs. Either come out or we will be forced to fire on the building." As the men waited, a girl appeared in one of the upper windows. She raised both hands, her middle fingers extended upwards. At the same time a door opened at the side of the building, and two men stepped out.

"What the hell is going on?" said Shawn Briggs. "We have immunity, granted by the general himself." Chester Benton said nothing.

"It's the general who has summoned you, sir," said the driver, still on the microphone. The sound screaming at the men seemed ridiculously loud with everyone standing right there, and realizing this, the driver flipped a switch and put the microphone down. "In case you haven't heard, the general's been shot."

"Is he dead?" Now they had Charlie's interest.

"No, sir. I just told you, he's summoning you. You're to come with us immediately."

"Who shot him?" Charlie smiled mischievously. "I'd like to offer my thanks."

The driver smiled back, less mischievously and more wickedly. "We're thinking it's you, sir. The general would like a private chat."

Charlie looked surprised, but not overly. "Why do you need Mister Briggs? He has work here burning up all the bodies you keep throwing on his doorstep, and he has a daughter to look after."

"The general is aware. But he's insisted Mister Briggs come along. The girl may stay. He gives his word she will not be harmed. Come along please."

Olivia now appeared at the door with the two men. Briggs hugged her, while Charlie said, "Call Willie. Have him come for you.

Stay there till you hear from us." The two men started down the steps, then Charlie turned. "And don't forget to feed Quasar before you go. A fish can't live without food."

Arriving at the jeep, Charlie spoke low and purposefully to the driver. "She gets hurt and you're a walking dead man." The man grinned at him. The kind of grin a man uses when he knows another man is helpless before him. Charlie saw the grin, and recognized it for what it was. "I've seen that look many times," he said, his voice low and smooth. "It's usually a fleeting thing."

As the convoy drove off, Olivia ran for the case she knew Charlie kept hidden beneath his bed. Within moments she had produced and prompted the Quasar, and was connected to the president. "They've taken my dad and Charlie."

Errol Clarkson looked at the girl on the screen, and tried not to appear worried. "It's okay, sweetheart. The general is not the kind of man who's going to hurt them, even if he could. He has too much honor. I promise you, he won't. They're like a prize to him, that's all."

"He's accusing Charlie of trying to kill him. Somebody tried, but not Charlie. He was right here with us."

"I know," said the president.

"What do you mean, you know? What? Was it you?"

The president drew in a deep breath. "Olivia look, there are things I can't talk about. Not just because it's you, I can't tell anyone." He tried to smile at her. "But things are happening now. Important things that will lead to a conclusion down there. Just be patient."

"Oh, my god. You sent someone in here to kill the goddam general and they totally fucked it up." Olivia yelled into the screen. "Why don't you just say it?"

The president's face hardened as he thought. "Look. You may be right." His eyes stared directly into hers, sending a silent message. "At some point something has to be done. People are dying and it needs to be stopped."

"Then let Charlie stop it. Sending a bunch of incompetents in here is just going to get people hurt. It already has. Leave us alone."

Clarkson looked at her sadly. "I can't. If they have Charlie now

they'll be watching him very closely. Charlie says you're the smartest person he's ever known. He used to say that about me, but recently you've taken over the top spot. Understand this. We have to stop this man. We have to. We'll do everything in our power to keep everyone safe, but we have to do this."

"He's got my dad."

"I know. But remember, he respects him very much. He just wants to watch the two of them, keep them out of the way. He would never hurt your father. Just be patient a bit longer. I have my best people on it, and they'll take care of this."

"Okay," said Olivia stubbornly. "Then just do it for chrissake."

Chapter Thirty-Seven

Manuel Ortiz waited on the levee. After days of deep thought, he had formulated a plan, and Manuel was not a stupid man. The laborers were coming in now, and he waited. Soon Tom Clayton and John Parish approached. Both men looked up at him hopefully. "I have decided to help you," he said. "But on certain conditions. I want a hundred thousand dollars the day this is over. I also want your word that you will speak highly of me, tell the authorities when they come that I was also a prisoner, and that I was most helpful in your escape."

"Done," both men said together. "Just get us the hell out of here."

"The general is not well. An assassination attempt was made on him yesterday. He feels the end is drawing near."

Tom Clayton spoke. "Then don't cross us. If this damn game of his is comin' to an end anyway, we don't really need you now do we?" As anger flushed across Manuel's face, Clayton raised a hand. "I don't mean anythin' by that. I'm just sayin' we need each other for the time bein'. Help us now, before our arrangement becomes unnecessary."

Manuel laughed wickedly. "You need me more than you know,

you stupid bastard. The general has in place a doomsday plan that goes into effect if anything should happen to him, or if the walls come crashing down. He calls it *Jonestown*, and everyone here is to be put to death immediately. There are to be no witnesses." Manuel was lying, but it was a good one. There had been no talk of killing anybody, but the two men had no way of knowing that.

Clayton's eyes widened. "Then get us out, now."

Manuel moved down from the levee, walking up quite close to the two. He pretended to lower his guard, to more easily form a bond of conspiracy. "Tonight we will meet, but separately, and I will lead you out of here."

"What do you mean separately?"

"We can't take a chance on two of you moving about together in the dark. It doubles the chance you'll be noticed. Leave separately…" He pointed to a grove of trees beyond the ponds, then tapped at John Parrish. "I will meet you there at ten-o'clock precisely. And you…" He looked at Clayton, nodded and glanced at another grove a few hundred yards distant. "We will come for you ten minutes later." He then looked at both men, scolding them with his eyes. "If either one of you is late the deal is off."

"What about the guards?" Several armed guards patrolled the camp every night, discouraging runaways. It was common knowledge they would shoot-to-kill any slave attempting escape, so in the three weeks since their capture, no one had dared to try.

"I am not without influence. I will deal with the guards. You just be where you're supposed to be when you're supposed to be there."

Later that night, sometime before ten, John Parrish rose from his bunk, stretched and yawned, and headed for the toilets. A guard standing nearby saw him rise, recognized his intention and paid him little mind. Another guard waited just outside. This one smacked his lips as he approached, whistling lightly. It was Manuel. Bending low, to keep his silhouette beneath the crest of the levee, Parrish broke into a run, jogging past the Mexican, and soon disappeared into the dark. A few minutes later he arrived at the grove. Leaning heavily against a tree, he breathed deeply from his exertion and waited for Ortiz to come for him.

Ortiz slipped through the night more like a cat than a man. Not a pebble moved at his passing, not a twig snapped. There was an ever so slight rustling in the grass as he drew near the trees, but it might have been the wind. John Parrish moved from the tree he first leaned on, choosing to sit on a weather-worn stump in an open glen where the Mexican could more easily find him. He heard the rustling. "Ortiz? Is that you? Ortiz?" he whispered hoarsely. Silence greeted him. He relaxed somewhat and continued his wait. Then he heard a short, distinct chirping, very close behind him. He swung his head around. Suddenly a blade flashed, slicing its way through the air and then deeply into the tissues of his throat. It was over so fast, Parrish had not even time to consider what happened. There was no pain, no anguish, no negative feeling of any kind. A warm, flushing numbness passed over him as he slid to the ground. Ortiz stood over him, then leaned down till their faces almost touched, but there was no recognition in the sheriff's eyes. Only warmth, and a cooing darkness which slowly closed in.

"Yeah, I'm gay, you bastard," hissed Ortiz. "And you're dead."

Carefully wiping the blade on the sheriff's shirt, Manuel moved quickly away, back to the duties of the camp.

The next morning, early, as the laborers returned to the fields, Manuel was again there on the rise. Tom Clayton approached him. "What the hell happened?" he asked. "Right after Parrish left a truck pulled up with a dozen fuckin' guards. I couldn't move. I thought you were in charge, for chrissake."

"I don't know," snarled Ortiz. "Maybe someone called for an extra detail. All I know is I waited out there in the brush for your goddam friend and he never showed up. The guards must have got him. Poor sunovabitch."

Clayton's voice lowered miserably. "What do we do now?"

"I'll take care of this, as I told you I would." Manuel pointed at the man. "I'll have you out of here as soon as I can. In the meantime I'll find out about your granddaughter. Make sure we can take her with us."

At the mention of Molly, Clayton's eyes turned bright. "And you'll get us both to the border? You swear it?"

"I told you I promised. Then you and I are gonna take a trip to the bank. Just the two of us."

Chapter Thirty-Eight

Molly's voice was smug. "So now they've got your daddy, too. I guess you're not so special after all."

Olivia contemplated whether or not to cross the room, take Molly by the hair and smash her face into a wall. Instead she said, "I'm sorry I gave you such a hard time the other day. I suppose everyone has to be what they're raised to be."

"I wasn't raised to be anything," said Molly defensively.

"I won't disagree with that."

Willie sat back in his rocker, thumbing through an almanac, but more intent on watching the girls than reading. "You know," he said after a long moment, "you two spend an awful lot of time bein' disagreeable. Did you ever consider there's no one right answer about anythin'? Molly there pretty much has to hate. I mean, here she is, locked up in a room with an ole black man and a crazy white girl. She can't go home, she can't visit with her friends. All she can do is sit here lookin' at us. We're askin' a lot of her to change the way she feels." He addressed Molly directly. "I wish you could see though, the two of us get along because Olivia don't see through colored glasses. I don't know why she don't, but she don't. Until I met her and her dad, I felt pretty much like you do. Only on the other side.

White folks scare me, the same way I scare you. That's 'cause we're tryin' so hard to grab onto all the differences between us. We thrive on the differences, not the similarities. And you don't know anythin' about me. Anythin' at all. For instance, do you know I like frogs? All the boys in town go out giggin' every chance they get. Spear the little buggers, pop 'em in a sack and take 'em home for fryin'. Now, I don't know why, but that upsets me sumpthin' awful. I eat chicken, you already know that, as long as I don't know 'em by name. And I've been known to chow down on a cow or a pig from time to time, or, hell yes, I'll eat the hell outta a gator. But I jus' don't hold with beatin' up on a frog."

Molly looked up from her seat on the floor. "I like frogs," she said.

"Well, there you go."

Olivia raised up slightly, "There you go? What does that even mean?"

Willie smiled, "Well, Miss Smarty Pants, you're the genius of the family. I'm surprised you haven't figured it out. What it means is, me and Molly both like frogs. It's kind of a first step." The old man had an idea. "Why, I bet if the three of us wrote down a whole buncha stuff we like, we'd find we're not as different as maybe we're thinkin'."

"Let's do it." Molly spoke out, almost eagerly.

"You two are crazy," said Olivia as she rose to go find paper and pencils. Soon the three were laboriously scribbling out words, and while there was no real comradery about it, neither was there any animosity.

Finally the pencils were put down and Willie said, "I'll go first." He studied his list intently. "Okay, who said they like cob corn? Who said that?" No one answered. "Okay, okay," said Willie, mildly dejected, "That's kinda weird, but I got lots more."

Molly went next. "Puppies," she said. "How 'bout puppies?"

"I've got dogs down here," smiled Olivia. "So we're close enough. Willie?"

"No, I didn't put down any dang dogs. The only animal I got is a mule. Oh, and a beaver. Anybody got one of those? Those are damn industrious animals."

Both girls grinned. "Sorry, Willie."

Then Olivia hollered out, "Solar flares. The kind that cause the aurora. They're gorgeous."

"The what?" Molly looked confused. "I've got rainbows. Is that close?"

Olivia shook her head, but Willie called out, "Hell yes, rainbows and soda flares are very close. That's a connection for sure." Olivia, catching on to her friend's simple deception and the reason for it, challenged the old man.

"Do you even know what a *soda* flare is?"

Willie looked stumped, and was. But his face perked up enthusiastically as he shouted out, "I jus' told ya. They're like rainbows. Ain't they?" He looked hopefully over at Olivia, who nodded her head sympathetically.

"Yes," she said finally, "they're just like rainbows."

By the end of the game the girls had agreed that at least half of their list contained a commonality, and somewhere earlier they'd begun to high-five each other when either they agreed, or Willie didn't. And Willie had yet to agree with anyone about anything. Finally he threw his hands up in exasperation, declaring, "Well, at least we both like frogs."

Later, after the girls dressed for bed, they ran into each other in the hall. "Goodnight, Molly," said Olivia.

"Goodnight, Olivia," said Molly. Both girls smiled as they passed, and the old man chuckled to himself as he turned down the lights.

"I ain't dumb," he said.

The next morning, after Olivia helped Molly feed the hens and tidy up around the house, she approached Willie, who was out in the garden. "We're going to go exploring. Check out the rest of the farm."

"Explorin'?" The old man looked up from his weeding, while Molly looked over at Olivia in surprise. "You girls stay right here. It's not safe out there. There are men roamin' all over the place."

"We know," said Olivia. "But that's out on the highway, not here on the farm. We're just going to look around a bit. Maybe take a walk into the woods." Molly looked as though she might protest, but quickly surrendered the idea when Olivia eyed her dangerously, and made a quick slashing motion with her hand. "There's nothing in the woods but woods, and we'll be extra careful."

"I don't like it," said the old man with a growl. "You can't go."

"Okay," said Olivia sweetly. "We'll be back in about an hour then."

"What?" Willie shook his head vigorously as Olivia grabbed at Molly's arm and began to drag her across the yard, in the direction of the levee. "I said no."

"I heard you." Olivia turned her head, smiling and waving at the same time. "We'll be very safe." As the girls disappeared behind a clump of cedar that grew up close to the drive, the old man rose and stood there, scratching at his ear.

Once the girls arrived at the top of the levee, there were two choices. The one to the left brought the roadway to an abrupt halt, before breaking into a winding path that led into the woods. The one to the right marked the road from the farm to the highway. Olivia glanced back to make certain they were no longer in sight of the house, then moved off to the right, down the road. Molly hesitated, looking first at the path, before turning, hands on hips, to stare at Olivia's back. "What are you doing?"

Olivia's head turned partway to the side. "I'm going for a walk." She kept walking. "You coming?"

Molly stood in place defiantly. "You're crazy. I'm not going out there. Didn't you hear what Willie said?"

Olivia stopped then, and turned. Her hands also found her hips, as the two girls stood some distance apart, staring at one another. "We're going to find your grandpa." She smiled smugly. "Anything else you need to know?" Olivia stood a moment longer, then turned once again and headed out towards the highway. Immediately she heard the sound of footsteps racing to catch up.

Before long they rounded a turn and the highway came into view. The two moved off to the side, concealing themselves behind one of the massive clumps of swamp sage which grew thickly along the edges of the road. The sound of a motor could be heard in the distance, and as they crouched there the sound grew nearer. Soon a truck appeared, followed by another, both brightly painted with green stripes which flashed out at them as the trucks drove past. "Those are our plantation trucks," whispered Molly. "You think my papa is there?"

"Yes. There's a good chance he is." Olivia chewed at her lip. "First of all, more than half the townsfolk were taken out there to work, and second, I think the general took a special interest in your papa after Willie pointed him out."

"Oh," said Molly. Her face twisted in pain. "You think he'll hurt him?"

"No," answered Olivia quickly. "That's not what I meant." She reached out and tapped gently at Molly's shoulder. "The general has been way too busy making a spectacle of himself to care much about hurting anyone. And now that he's been attacked, he has other things to worry about. Your papa will be just fine."

The girls moved further off the road then, fighting their way through more of the sage and climbing back down to the bottom of the levee where they encountered a marsh and a small creek which fed through a culvert passing beneath the highway. The creek was shallow, only a few inches deep, and as they approached the culvert they noticed an egret waited there at its entrance, at a point where the creek lost its channel and began to flow outward, away from the levee and into the marsh. The egret turned its attention on the girls for a moment, judging their intent. Its head cocked to one side,

eyes probing them until, after a very short time, it decided they were more of a nuisance than a danger and returned its eyes to focus on the thin layer of water and mud at its feet. The girls paused to watch. After a few seconds the bird's neck swung downward violently, its beak lancing down, forcefully poking its way into the mud. When the beak came back up, it held fast a small frog that wriggled futilely, its tiny legs kicking away at the air. The egret flipped its beak upward and released the frog for a brief last moment of freedom, before catching it headfirst on the way down and gulping it in. As the frog disappeared down the bird's throat, both girls, without any communication between them thought of the old man. "Willie would beat that bitch with a stick," said Olivia.

"A big damn stick," said Molly.

Thirty minutes later they had worked their way, first through the narrow tunnel carved beneath the highway, and then along several hundred yards of creekbed until they were deep into the heart of the plantation. The banks of the creek were fairly high here, and quite steep, as torrential southern rains caused rushing water to swipe away at them during much of the year. For some distance there was simply nowhere they could climb out to see what waited above. Finally they came to a place where the east bank had broken. Time had tumbled it away and left large chunks of earth and rock exposed, which cascaded down at them like huge stepping stones. Olivia began to scramble up the first of the rocks, stretching out and using her hands to climb the larger ones, and hopping across the smaller ones until, in less than a minute she had achieved the top. She lay there quite still, sprawled out and completely hidden by a mass of wheat grass that grew all along the border of the bank. Molly, startled by her friend's sudden departure, stood silently at the bottom and waited, watching with a certain admiration as the girl scrambled upwards. Finally Olivia turned her head to the side and hissed. "Get up here. This is it."

"I'm not a damn monkey," Molly hissed back, as she began, much more laboriously, to climb. Soon both girls were lying atop the bank, their faces just poking out through the last layers of tall grass.

In front of them, and pushing out into the distance, was one of the plantation's many cotton fields. Laborers were everywhere. Dozens of them, on their knees, or walking along on heavy legs among the rows. The day was not yet half over, but was already very hot. The few faces that were close enough to be seen all wore a kind of slick, sweaty, lifeless expression. An older woman, not too distant, paused in her trek across the field. She carried in one hand a sack, one that seemed not heavily laden, but still enough of a burden that it caused her to seek a moment of rest. A guard approached the woman. Her head raised slightly, her eyes just grazing his, and she quickly readjusted the sack and scurried on her way with renewed energy. Both girls wondered at that.

Molly's eyes scanned the field intently, finally working their way across a dirt road to the gin, which stood in the distance. "I don't see him," she whispered. Her voice lowered until the words became almost indecipherable. A visible sadness crept over her face. "He's too old to be working out here. And it's so hot."

"He'll be fine." Olivia nudged at her almost affectionately. "Your grandfather is tough. If he can handle you, I'm thinking he can handle just about anything." Molly glanced at her and tried to smile.

As both girls focused again on the area around the gin, Olivia's eyes flashed. "Look, by that hauler just coming in. The man standing there. That could be him." Molly turned intently to study the man as Olivia pointed. "I think it's him." The hauler drove between the girls and the man just then, blocking their view. Molly held her breath as she waited for it to pass. A bit of dust from the truck's wheels formed a sort of screen as it drove away, but as it cleared Molly squealed out delightedly.

"Papa. It's him. It's my papa." She reached out to grab Olivia by the arm, squeezing tightly. "He's okay." Molly began to cry then, and though she tried hard not to, Olivia felt tears flood into her own eyes as well.

They watched Tom Clayton for several more minutes, trying to judge his condition and his circumstance. As each new hauler

approached Clayton would step out into the roadway, look in both directions as he studied the one just arriving and the one having just departed, then either hold his hand up to pause the arriving truck, or wave it briskly through. His job, it seemed, was to maintain a proper distance between the trucks so the unloading at the gin would go smoothly.

"It's a good job," said Molly between her tears. "I was afraid it would be too hard for him."

"It's a great job." Olivia carefully contemplated what she said next. "And it's not necessarily a bad thing for him to see what it's like."

Molly turned. "What's that supposed to mean?"

Olivia looked back at her, not unfriendly. "Don't take it wrong, but your grandfather has always been in charge, always been the boss. And maybe he hasn't always been as kind about it as he could be." As Molly's eyes began to mount a defense, Olivia continued. "He had Willie beat, you know. They beat the hell out of him. Because your grandfather ordered it. I'm thinking that's not the kindest way to resolve a situation."

Molly's eyes tried to hold onto Olivia's, tried to force them into submission, but after only a few short seconds they looked down in defeat. "I didn't know they beat him. But I do know he wrecked one of my papa's wagons. And he did it out of meanness."

"Is that what you really think?" Olivia's face softened, though Molly couldn't see it. "You think Willie could do anything out of meanness? Seriously? He can't even eat a chicken with a name, for chrissakes. He did it because he was tired. Sometimes when a person has taken all that they can take, they just get tired."

Molly's eyes looked up again, but any fire they might have held was gone from them. Her face warmed as she turned to once again study her grandfather. "Still, he's not bad. He takes care of a lot of people."

Olivia smiled then, and reached out to brush away the grass in front of Molly's face, allowing her a better view. "I know. Maybe

when this is over we'll have a chance to reassess what's important. That would be a good thing for all of us."

They lay in silence then, for a good piece of time. Olivia scanned the gin and the fields, studying and soaking in as much information as she could about the general's master plan, while Molly's eyes looked soulfully at her grandfather and never left him. The two became so deeply engrossed in their personal endeavors they failed to notice a shadow that cast over them without warning. It was a sudden movement, and the sound that accompanied it that finally brought their faces up. And there, just feet away, stood a guard. His face was very dark, and void of emotion as he stared down at them. The barrel of the rifle held in his hands swung slightly in their direction, not in a particularly menacing way, but with a simple statement that seemed to say, "I have a gun, and anything you might try to do would not be wise." The girls froze in place, their heads slightly twisted in the man's direction, their eyes locked onto his. And they waited. After what seemed an eternity the guard edged closer. The two girls clasped hands and pressed tightly against one another. The man dropped to his knees, placing the rifle on the ground beside him. A hand came up, fumbling briefly through a chest pocket, where he extracted a pack of gum. He removed a piece, the hand then extending outward in an offering. He held it there for a long time. Finally, Olivia, who was closest to him, reached out and accepted the gum, her fingers trembling so badly they almost dropped it. The guard then withdrew another piece, which he also offered up. Olivia took that one also, this time more quickly and more surely. The whole time their eyes never left the man's, and his never left theirs. Suddenly, a whistle blew from somewhere in the distance. The guard turned his head, seeming to study the sound as he grabbed his rifle and rose. He turned back to the girls briefly, and Molly thought perhaps he nodded at them. Olivia was not as sure. Then he simply walked away, across a small clearing and into the long rows of cotton. The girls stared after him for a long time, not breathing, not moving, but staring. Finally and simultaneously they exhaled, and drew in another deep breath.

"Oh, my god," Molly gasped out. "Did you just see that?" Olivia

looked back at her, somewhat amazed.

"Yeah, I was there."

Molly shook her head, trying to clear her senses. "I've never been so scared. Ever. I thought he was going to... you know... hurt us."

Olivia reached out to touch her, brushing several loose curls of hair back from Molly's face. It was an almost motherly gesture. "I'm guessing we have to do a little more reassessing than we thought."

The girls waited a while longer, Molly having one last moment with her grandfather, before they started the long trek back to the farm.

Chapter Thirty-Nine

General Sedgewick was laid out in the master suite of the Clayton manor house. His wound seemed to be healing, but where the screaming piece of metal had ripped a large, jagged hole in his shoulder during its exit, there had been a massive amount of blood loss. So the general lay there, weak and worried. He doubted Chester Benton had anything to do with the assassination attempt. If the president's friend came for him, it would be up close and personal. It was more likely that insurgents had slunk their way into the county, with orders to take out the general at any cost. They had come very close. And in case his assumption was an incorrect one, it was comforting to know that Benton, along with Briggs, was safely tucked away in a nearby warehouse under heavy guard.

The war to the north was winding down. Birmingham was secure, Montgomery finally contained, and the president now had the extra time and resources available to begin a play against the general's regime in the south. Sedgewick was under no illusion that his dream of conquest could become a permanent one. It had been nearly a month since the invasion, about the time frame he had allotted himself. He called on Harry, his most trusted aide, to start pulling the troops away from Harbor Springs and its outlying areas,

condensing them into camps and outposts bordering the plantation. The town could convert itself into whatever sort of barbarism it wanted, but the plantation, where the general decided his last stand would take place, had to be preserved.

"I want all the men called in. All of them," he told Harry. "We'll turn this place into a fortress. One of men instead of walls. And the slaves are to be gathered together and placed in the gin. Bolt them in and let no one escape. That will be our bargaining chip when they come for us."

"You think they will come?" asked Harry, concern spreading across his face.

"I know they will come. We've known it for a long time." The general let out a humorless laugh. "Since the day we arrived we have been on deathwatch, dead men walking, with very limited prospects."

"We could run."

"To where, Harry? To where? Maybe we should flit from state to state setting up new games wherever we go. That would be something to see. A rolling wave of dying conquerors, losing men and momentum as we roll on." Sedgewick grabbed Harry's arm, trying to be affectionate about it. "Eventually it would be just the two of us standing under an old oak somewhere, as they place the noose around our necks. I've got to admit, that would be living."

As Harry departed, the general forced himself up from the bed, grimacing in pain with every movement. He staggered to the window, where he looked out over the valley. Laborers still toiled in the fields, gathering up some last bits of imaginary cotton. He watched as one of his aides approached a woman carrying a near-empty sack. She stumbled, catching herself by one knee as the sun beat down on her. The aide lashed out, cracking the woman across the shoulders with a baton. It wasn't a hard blow, just enough to get her attention and remind her of the task. The woman rose without complaint, continuing her trek down a long row. "That's good stuff," thought the general. "My aides learn from me, my slaves learn from them. Perfect pitch and perfect harmony." A sudden chill swept over him. Somewhere out there was a man with a rifle, drooling over

the prospects of another opportunity. The general pulled shut the curtains and moved away from the window. Samantha King entered the room just then.

"My dear," said the general.

"Enjoying the view?" she said, as Sedgewick moved across the room, sitting back down on the bed. "Men in windows make wonderful targets."

The general nodded. "We think alike. In fact, we're very much alike."

"If I thought that were true I'd shoot myself."

The general patted a hand on the bedspread. "Sit with me. Tell me about your day."

Samantha walked to the window, redrawing the curtains as light flooded in. She turned to face him. "I hear you've got Charlie and Briggs locked up. They steal your stars or something?"

"Ah, yes, it's Charlie, isn't it? I've never been privy to that name. It's always been the more formal Chester for me, whenever we speak."

"Well," Samantha looked unkindly at the general, "whenever someone wants you dead it's usually best to keep things on a more formal level. Removes the chance for any sentimentality."

"Ouch, the lady bites today. Perhaps it's you who've come to kill the master."

"You never gave me my gun or I'd be blowing smoke off the barrel right now."

"Look." The general turned to her with as much sincerity as he possessed. "I'm sorry for what happened between us. I've said it a hundred times. It was simply necessary to show the world that I would do anything to achieve my goals. Even beat a woman. That was intended to shock, which I'm certain it did. The residuals to you were unintentional. Please…" Sedgewick extended a hand, "how can I make it up to you?"

"I'm your chronicler, remember? When this is over you'll get the truth you so desperately wanted. Every word I write will be exactly as you intended. And I'll get all the riches and fame I need,

thanks to you. So there's really nothing to make up for." Samantha King stood in the middle of the room looking almost pitifully at the general. "Which is a good thing, because unfortunately for you, you don't have much time." Bowing her head, she walked out the door.

Chapter Forty

As the general's men began to withdraw to the plantation, one thing became quickly obvious. Not all were present. Not even close to all. It seems as long as a messiah is spreading broad wings across the land, followers will stand fast and glorify themselves in fulfilling his mission. Retreat inward, however, and chaos abounds, the instinct to continue outward momentum too compelling to ignore. And there had been incidents between them. When the troops had asked for the women of the county to be awarded as plunder, the general had refused. "We're here for a greater glory than to satisfy your basest urges," he had reminded them. Still, many of the men, given the choice of a woman or glory, would have chosen the woman. And there was the hanging of Moss Daughtry, the old man awarded slaves and then lynched for causing the death of one. It seemed unnecessarily white to many of the young black patriots guarding the vaults of the general's ideals, who began to secretly question Sedgewick's motives. "No game is perfect," the general had said. "If we have to sacrifice some of our own to teach the lessons of slavery, and the hardships that accompany it, we will do so." But many thought the hanging of a black man by another black man went well beyond the scope of anything instructional.

So the count, as Harry presented it, was alarming. "We have about half left. Maybe a hundred, hundred and twenty-five."

"Still," said the general, sitting up in bed as he fondly brushed his fingers across the stars adorning his jacket, "if there are that many willing to martyr themselves for our cause, we have achieved something momentous. Something astounding. Remember, Jesus commanded but twelve. And several of those had second thoughts." Sedgewick smiled smugly. "If that's the competition, I'd say we're standing up nicely."

Harry, who had been the general's aide for many long and loyal years, couldn't quite strike down the thought of the general in a match against the savior. "I guess that's one way to look at it, sir," he said, as he took his leave.

———◆———

At dawn of the next day an Apache attack helicopter, flying close to treetop level, swooped in over the highway leading into Harbor Springs. As it approached Cedar Creek —now Three Bales— the pilot dipped the rotor, swinging the copter to the left, and guiding it right over the manor house. A gunner, hanging from one of its doorways, swung his machine gun in a slow arc, sweeping it deliberately in the direction of dozens of the general's men who guarded the gates and perimeter. No shots were fired, but troops scattered madly about, trying to dodge the imaginary fire. It was a message sent, and a message received.

Manuel Ortiz, standing out in the rising sun, watched as the copter completed its fly-by. He had been one of only three members of Sedgewick's staff to receive personal instructions to lock away the workers. He shouted out orders now, hurrying the slaves along to the gin, but many were defiant, turning their faces to the sky and shouting out as the helicopter flew past. "Get your asses inside," he yelled at them. He caught Tom Clayton's eye, shrugging at the man as

he moved the laborers into the building. When everyone was safely locked away, a large group of aides gathered outside by the fountain.

"That's it then," said one. "They're coming."

"Let them come," said another. "We've trained for this. The general says as long as we hold the high ground here at the plantation, and control the prisoners, no one will dare fire on us." Several of the men turned to Ortiz, who was considered wise among them because of his usual disinclination to enter into petty talk, and because he was the only man among them upon whom the general occasionally called into private counsel.

"What do you think, Ortiz?"

Manuel appeared hesitant to speak. He nodded at the men, the ever-present straw jutting from his lips. "I think my opinion and your opinions are of little matter. But the fact is, they will come, and they will win. We all know there's no beating them. The general carried us here and bound us to him. And now he's locked himself away for his own preservation. So we are left, standing in a goddam field, alone and vulnerable. It's time for us to run." A grand plan began to form in Manuel's mind. An idea that could allow him to emerge unscathed, perhaps even as a hero if things worked out perfectly. But his plan would not be an easy one.

"Run? That's the path a coward takes." The speaker bristled at Ortiz. "We owe the general our loyalty. And you?" The man pointed at the Mexican. "The general could have kicked your ass the day they dragged you in here. Instead, just because you spin a good story, he allows you into his inner circle. How can you be so disloyal?"

Manuel laughed. "My loyalty to the general is not as strong as it once was. I'd rather stand with you, my brothers." For the first time ever, Ortiz spoke as though he, too, was black, forming a bond with these men. "I still respect the general, but he's denied us every pleasure, insisting we walk about as much like slaves as the workers. He's even begun to hang those of our own kind. When a black man hangs another black man it becomes a desecration. And the truth is, if we stay, we die. And if we die, where is the dream we came here with? The general can't resurrect it for us because he'll be dead. Better

if we run now, preserve ourselves while we still can." He pointed out toward the gates, and then up toward the sky. "That helicopter. It could have fired on us. We could be dead right now, probably should be. We still have a chance, if we run."

One or two still argued their sworn loyalty to the general. They were quickly shouted down. "Ortiz is right," called out several of the men. "Let's get the hell out of here while we still can."

Word of the conversation spread quickly among the troops, with many deciding to abandon the plantation and try to slink their ways back into the folds of society. Ortiz also shrewdly pointed out that few of them were identifiable. They had trained covertly, worshipped their oracle secretly, and had arrived in Colby County as a mass of blackened brotherhood, one face as indistinguishable as the next. As many deserted their posts, and many more prepared to, Manuel worked his way over to a building not far from the gin. Of the four guards assigned there, only one remained, and Ortiz relieved him. He looked around, making certain no one watched, then slipped the latch and moved inside.

Chester Benton and Shawn Briggs sat at a table, facing the doorway. As Ortiz entered, both men stiffened. "Shhh," the Mexican put a finger to his lips, motioning for silence as he moved closer. "I'm a friend," he said softly.

"You don't look like one." Charlie assessed the Mexican's armament, consisting of a pistol, knife and the customary baton. "You look like one of the guards."

Ortiz drew the pistol from its holster, flipping it in his hand. He placed the gun on the table, within easy reach of the two men. As a precaution, the clip, still intact, had been emptied, but they had no way of knowing that. "I'm not one of them," he assured them. "I came here a few days ago. Just stumbled in on my way through. The general was going to have me executed, I think, so I told him I'd come to serve."

"And he believed you?" Charlie sensed a lie.

"No," said Ortiz, sensing Charlie's doubt. Then he told a story, knowing part of a truth can become the truth, if wielded correctly.

"But on my way into Harbor Springs I came across a state trooper crawling in the highway. He was hurt bad, said he'd been fired on by some of the general's men, but had gotten away. I tried to help him, but he died in my arms." Manuel paused, looking as sadly as he could. "When the general threatened me I said it was me who'd killed the trooper, had left him dead up the road. And that I'd fought my way in here to join his army. He sent men to check it out, and when they returned to report the dead man, I was accepted into the fold. I have even become one of his favorites."

Charlie reached over and picked up the pistol. He fondled the gun, hefting it for weight. Ortiz watched him carefully. "It's empty."

Manuel smiled. "I'm a careful man. That doesn't make me a dishonest one."

"What do you want?" It was Briggs who asked.

"I want to help you. Escape."

Charlie leaned over, handing the weapon back to the Mexican. He knew he could take this man, but there would be heavily armed guards waiting just outside the door. "We heard the copter. We're not stupid. All hell is about to rain down here, and you're trying to save your sorry ass."

Manuel holstered the pistol. He looked at the two with serious eyes. "There has been an order given to execute all of the workers and the two of you," he lied. "I wanted you to know I won't let that happen. I am not one of them, and I will be back to free you."

"In that case," Charlie spoke, doubt still in his voice, "you have our thanks." As the Mexican left, he turned to Briggs. "We're getting out of here at first light."

"How?" asked Briggs, his voice showing not the slightest doubt, but simple curiosity.

"Probably by stepping over a lot of guards. One way or another, we're leaving."

Chapter Forty-One

As darkness fell, sounds could be heard echoing through the valley. The sounds of big trucks and big machinery to the east, in the direction of the Georgia border. Ortiz moved along the road toward the main gate. "Tomorrow will be a very eventful day," he told himself. Most of the general's troops had deserted the plantation, many because of his impassioned plea, and many more because of the disciplinary lapse caused by the general's absence. Sedgewick chose to stay holed up in the residence, mending his wounds and awaiting the inevitable. Enough loyalists remained, however, that the gates were still well guarded by the time Manuel arrived. As he stood in the dark some distance away, the guttural sounds of men in conversation drifted towards him. There was no laughter among the guards as was usual, no frivolous joke telling one might imagine takes places on a lonely outpost in the middle of the night. Just serious talk about the events to come.

Ortiz moved away from the road, drifting to his left through a field of cotton stubble. After a few minutes he had gone a sufficient enough distance that the sounds of voices died out. Climbing a fence, he waded a shallow creek, then moved across the highway and into the trees on the other side. Soon he came to another roadway,

this one much smaller, carved from the soil of a levee. It stayed straight for a few hundred yards, then dipped down an embankment and swung into an open yard where he could see lights and a house. This was his favorite kind of work, moving about in the darkness like a shadow, but one with deadly intent. He had learned Clayton's granddaughter lived here, right across the road from the plantation. She had been given by the general to one of the town's residents, and further study indicated it was an old black man who should offer little resistance.

His plan, thought out carefully during his nights patrolling the work camp, was to kidnap the girl. Tuck her away somewhere safe and secure until Tom Clayton fulfilled his promise of payment as reward. He knew if he simply took Clayton to the girl, helping them both escape to the border, he would never see that payment. El Lobo had once said to him, "Control the cards and you control the game. Let someone else control them and they'll deal you shit off the bottom every time."

Manuel slid in close to the house, climbing a railing onto the porch where he stood for a long moment, listening. He heard laughter coming from inside, and pleasant chatter, not the kind of sounds one would expect from behind a master's door. Gliding over to a window, he glanced into the residence. Soft lights played on the walls, and there, at the end of a long room, sat a man, comfortably slouched back in an old stuffed rocker while two girls curled up on the floor beside him. Two girls? Manuel's head spun. It had been made clear to him that Clayton had one granddaughter, although a description of her had never been handed out, so seeing his objective before him now in multiples presented a fresh challenge. Standing there in the shadows, a new plan began to emerge. Holding onto even one child could be difficult and complicated. Would it not be more practical to dispose of them both, together with the old man, and simply inform Clayton he had her hidden away at a location to be disclosed after payment? It seemed less honorable this way, but eminently more efficient. And Ortiz was all about efficiency.

As he continued to watch it became obvious the relationships

in the room were not adversarial ones. The two girls laughed openly, seeming to be completely at ease in the old man's presence. And the old man glowed in the aura of their youth. This too was puzzling. Masters were seldom known to consort with their concubines, and when they did it was hardly in a way that encouraged frivolity. Yet frivolity prevailed in this house. Manuel felt an anger rise from deep within, not one he could control, because it came at him like an altered state, with bile rising in his throat. His life had contained few moments of warmth, tantalizing bits of time when he was very young and his mother had slipped away to bring him treats. She had been beaten for it, beaten for loving him, and now as he watched the glow emanating from the room, his anger could no longer be contained. Drawing his pistol, Manuel smashed it against the glass of the window. As the glass shattered, he leapt over the sill, tumbling into the room. Before the three who sat there could even react, Ortiz stood over them, threatening with his gun. "Good evening," he said, his tone cold and sardonic. He smiled at them. "I knocked but no one answered."

The girls froze. And Willie, at first also frozen, rose out of his chair. "What do you want here?" The old man's voice shook badly, but he managed to move slightly, putting his body between the gunman and the girls.

"Which of you is Molly?" Ortiz asked, knowing it really didn't make a difference. They were all going to die.

"I asked what you wanted." Willie, the fear nearly overwhelming him, forced himself to step closer to the intruder.

"I just told you. I want Molly. She's to be my whore now." Ortiz laughed aloud as he stepped to the side, trying to better see the girls who cowered on the floor. As he did so Molly screamed and flung the photo album she'd been viewing. The throw was not a good one, missing Ortiz by a wide margin, but it offered a moment of distraction. Willie flung himself at the Mexican, and as he made contact, immediately realized he was in the arms of a power much greater than his own. The struggle was a brief one, with the old man being tossed easily to the floor. As Ortiz leveled the pistol at Willie's

face, Olivia jumped up, striking out with a glass she held in her hand. Manuel sensed her coming, turning his head to face the girl as her hand, and the glass in it, crashed into his forehead. He staggered backwards, dropping the gun. In an instant, Ortiz drew his knife. Lashing out at Oliva, he felt the blade strike flesh, and watched as the girl fell to the floor. He stood there for a brief instant, the look of a madman masking his face. "Sunovabitch!" he screamed. Then he leapt at Olivia, to finish her, and as he did so the room erupted in a blast of heat and light. A roar so loud it almost knocked Manuel off his feet. He felt a shock wave pound at his back. Spinning around he saw the old man, on his knees, the pistol in his hand. Fire streaked out through the barrel and a second blast reverberated through the room. Ortiz screamed again, not from fear, but from futility. He dove for the window, rolling out onto the porch, his head and body racked by pulsating pain. And then he ran. Stumbling from the porch, blood-soaked and disoriented, his back on fire and his mind engulfed in blind rage, he ran.

Willie and Molly both crawled the few feet to Olivia. They arrived at exactly the same time. She sat up slowly. "The bastard almost got me," she said, trying to work a smile across her lips. Molly fumbled with Olivia's blouse, tearing the buttons free at her waist. Blood oozed out, soaking the blouse and seeping its way down into her jeans. "Oh, shit," Olivia moaned. Willie patted her on the head, then rose and ran to the kitchen. He returned almost instantly with bandages and salve.

"Just nicked you," he said. "Bloody little bastard though. Hell, I've had spankin's worse than this." His face grew warm and kind. "You girls were so damn brave."

Molly reached out, placing her hand on Willie's arm. Then her head moved over next to the hand, her face burying itself into his shoulder. "*We* were?" Tears formed in her eyes. "You were willing to die for me," she said, her voice shaking. "Both of you were."

"Well," said Olivia, wincing in pain as the old man smeared some salve into the wound. "I think we make a splendid team."

Chapter Forty-Two

As expected, dawn brought with it an awakening. A convoy of armored vehicles rolled down the highway, headed straight for the plantation. Leading the procession were two rows of tanks, their plated steel tracks tearing up great chunks of asphalt as they rumbled forward. Behind them came the mine sweeps, even though no mines were thought to be in play, and separated by a short distance further back were more than forty light artillery and personnel carriers. Then came the buses, filled with platoons of soldiers from Fort Ord, and some three hundred marines sent over from Camp Lejeune in North Carolina. In all, the president sent in more than one hundred tanks and vehicles in support of two-thousand troops. Most of his advisors considered that to be over-kill, but a conference among the generals at the Pentagon had urged him to arrive with a component of shock and awe. They couldn't have known that by the time they arrived all that would remain of Colonel Sedgewick's loyalists were a few dozen very disoriented and very frightened young men.

About a mile before reaching the gates of Three Bales, tanks and infantry began to deploy, leaving the highway and smashing their way through creeks, bogs and fences as they began to wrap

serpent-like around the perimeter of the great estate. It was not the president's plan to attack, but merely to apply a stranglehold on the entire area. A system known as siege, a method used by field commanders worldwide for thousands of years. If an opponent had limited resources, and time was not of the essence, it was foolproof and much more merciful than blasting down the walls on the way to victory. One simply sat in siege, negotiated if possible, and waited. While a large sector of the arriving force crashed and splashed its way about, carving out a huge circular path, about one third of the force remained on the highway, moving steadily in the direction of the gate. Once there, several of the tanks turned in, one of them smashing down the newly erected sign denoting the general's *New South*. A command post was set up then, just inside the boundaries, using two of the tanks as walls, and stringing a large canvas between them.

"This is Emancipator One, Emancipator One," called out the tank commander over his radio. "Do you read me?"

"Niner-Niner-Five, checking in, loud and clear, sir," came a quick response.

"Niner-Six," another voice called out. "All settled in, sir."

"Niner-Seven reporting in. Just got home. Someone stole my T.V. Anyone got beer?" said a third.

"Don't be a wiseass, Nowitzsky," said the commander. He looked out, down the long road leading into the plantation. It was eerily quiet. In the distance, chugging across one of the fields and coming at them about as slowly as a vehicle could move was an old cotton hauler. All eyes watched as it approached.

"Major?" asked a sergeant standing a few feet from the commander.

The major studied the hauler, trying to calculate its speed and intent. There was still time. "Target, but hold fire," he said. "Let's see what the bastard's up to."

"Target," hollered out the sergeant. "Target only." Instantly the sounds of metal grating on metal could be heard, as the turrets on several of the great tanks began to rotate in a low arc, tracking the

hauler. On a group of armored carriers farther down the highway, gunners jacked back on their receivers, machine guns swinging into play. Finally, when the truck had approached to within a hundred yards, it stopped. For a long moment there was no movement, but then a metal gate swung open, and a dozen or so of General Sedgewick's remaining soldiers scrambled out and set up in formation right there in the middle of the field.

"What the hell is that?" said the major, standing suddenly so he could peer over the side of the tank closest him. "What are those idiots doing?" The troops began to fan out, until they made a broad line. There were fourteen men standing close enough that the major could see the looks of blank determination on each of their faces. "Do they wanna fight?" The commander spoke as much to himself as anyone else, shaking his head incredulously. "Do they seriously wanna fight? I've got twenty fucking tanks here. And a thousand fucking men." He glanced over at the sergeant. "This is insane." As he spoke they could hear a voice, rising and coming at them through the morning air.

"Steady," it rang out. "Front rank, prepare." Seven of the general's men broke off, advancing forward a few paces, where they then dropped to one knee, and took aim at the tanks. The rear rank, also composed of seven, stood in place, but raised their weapons until they, too, were ready to fire. Both ranks froze in position.

"It's a bluff," called out the commander. He smiled smugly. "Nobody's that stupid." Even before the words escaped his lips, the fourteen young, beautifully brave and wonderfully insane men in the field opened fire. A round struck the turret nearest the major, ricocheting madly away as it made contact with the impenetrable steel. The bullet twisted its way towards the command table, smashing into a laptop set up there. The computer spun off the table. "Shit," hollered out the major, as he dove for cover. Reaching up, the major snatched a mic from the table before crouching down, low to the ground, behind one of the steel tracks of the giant war machine. "Parelli," he screamed into the mic. "You getting this shit?" Instantly a response crackled back.

"Yes, sir. I'm right here with you, Chief." The voice coughed as it spoke, filled with nervous tension, and the major could hear more rounds striking metal up and down the highway. "You want me to take them out?"

"I don't know," the major shouted back. "We're not supposed to engage."

"Well they're sure as hell engaging us, sir. What are we supposed to do, sit here on our asses until one of us gets tagged?" Lifting his head slightly the commander raised his eyes just enough to see the open field. The men there were still in precise formation, apparently randomly firing at targets of their own choosing.

"Sunovabitch," said the major. He studied the troops for the briefest of moments, then spoke again into the mic. "You see that big bastard in the middle of the rear rank? With a white scarf around his neck?"

"Yes, sir," came the immediate reply.

"Put him down." The major paused, shaking his head almost sadly. "Put him down now."

"Yes, sir."

The commander's aide crawled up alongside. He was a sergeant with many years of service, and had seen much conflict. Still, his face showed the pain of a man involved in a most unpleasant task. "They can't have much ammo, sir," he said matter-of-factly. "And they're Americans."

The major looked at his sergeant, stared at the man, and an equal amount of pain spread across his face as well. "I'm aware, sergeant," he said. "I just can't take the chance." They both studied the field then, and the giant soldier standing in the middle of it. Suddenly, off to their left a single shot rang out, and simultaneous to the sound, a tiny puff of dust plucked away at the big man's chest. He stepped back a half-step, but the resolve on his face remained unchanged. All firing stopped then, with even the men in the field pausing to look over at their comrade. Both of his arms lowered, but slowly and methodically, until the rifle hung there in one of his hands, suspended by a single finger still locked into the trigger guard.

A blackened stain began to appear at the man's chest, spreading quickly. Still the man stood there. The radio crackled to life.

"Again, sir?"

"No," the major replied, his voice quivering. "He's done."

The big man began to move then, the rifle still dangling from the lone finger. He marched forward, past the rank of kneeling men, and out into the open. He stumbled once, but caught himself, and continued onward. Without seeking a thought or needing one, the major rose, moving out from the shelter of the tank where he began to walk toward the big man. No one else on either side dared a breath. The stain of black spread further, spreading outward and downward, until it reached the big man's waist. There the blood appeared, and the black turned red, trickling out onto the man's belt, and dripping onto his shoes and onto the ground. But still he moved on. Finally, they met, the major and the young soldier, standing alone but together in the middle of the field. The young man reached his free hand down, grasping the barrel of the rifle. Using the last of his strength he raised it, by the barrel, and presented it to the major. The major took it. He looked deeply into the young man's eyes, and he nodded. "You did well, son," he said simply. "You were very brave." The soldier smiled back, stood there for another long moment, and then collapsed to the ground. He was dead before impact. The major turned slightly, a fog moving in over his eyes. He addressed the remaining men, standing a few yards away. "Is that enough war for you?" he asked.

Chapter Forty-Three

Before first light had even struck, Charlie climbed up onto one of the steel beams supporting the building they were housed in, pried open an old vent and crawled out onto the roof. In the distance he heard the sounds of the convoy revving up for the march, identifying immediately what was about to happen. Edging his way along the roofline, he peered into the semi-darkness below. The drop to the ground was about fifteen feet, just far enough to sprain or break an ankle, so his intention was to locate a guard he could use for a landing zone, breaking both a neck and his fall with the same movement. "Conservation of energy," he said to himself with a sick grin. A law of physics. He thought of how proud Olivia would be that he had come up with this, but dismissed the idea of telling her as he considered she would then make him explain it. He leaned out over the edge, ready to jump. There were no guards below. Whistling sharply, he called down to Briggs. "There ain't shit out here."

"No guards?" answered Briggs, his voice filled with hope.

"No. And nothing soft and cushy for me to land on."

"Well, just jump and get me the heck out of here."

Charlie grinned. "You're a very caring man, Briggs. I wish you were out here right now so I could land on your face." Feeling his

way to the lowest edge of the building, Charlie lay flat on the roof. He swung his legs, and then body, slowly over the side, trying to hold on to the sharp metal roof edge as he lowered himself downward. The metal, cheaply corrugated, bent inward, causing him to lose grip, and he fell. There was a solid thump as he impacted the ground outside the door.

Briggs said nothing, and there was a long silence. Finally Charlie spoke. "So you're not gonna ask me if I'm okay?"

An audible sigh of relief came from inside the building. "I was afraid to."

Charlie rose stiffly, unlatched the door, and the two worked their way over to the gin. It was light enough now that visibility was good, and there were still no guards in sight. "The bastards deserted. The poor general must be commiserating all by himself."

As they swung open the doorway to the factory, a mob of anxious white faces looked out at them. A woman fainted, and then the man standing next to her also collapsed. Another man stepped up. "Are they gone? We heard machinery comin'. Thought they were gonna bulldoze the gin."

"With us in it," someone from the back hollered.

"It's alright. It's the government. They've come to rescue us." Cries and sighs of relief flooded through the building. Charlie placed a hand on Briggs' shoulder. "This is Shawn Briggs, the coroner. Most of you probably already know him." Nodding at Briggs, he continued. "He's going to lead you out of here now. Not out the front. If there is resistance, and a fight, that's where it will take place. We don't want anyone to get hurt. I want you all to head north from here, toward the city. It should be easy going, just cotton fields. When you reach the fence-line you can turn east and pick up the highway. There will be help there, and you will be safe."

Briggs looked with concern at his friend. "What about you?"

"I'll be okay. Someone has to deal with the general. He's not the sort of man to go down easily. And Miss King is in there with him. God knows what that man is capable of. I've got to get her out."

Briggs nodded, then turned to the gathering. "Let's do what the man says. Let's get the hell out of here."

Chapter Forty-Four

Manuel Ortiz staggered back across the highway and onto the plantation just minutes before the light of day would have given his position away. Weakened from loss of blood, his rage had died down, but not his hate. Stumbling along through a field, he found bits of cotton here and there which he stuffed into the gaping hole in his back, somewhat stemming the flow. Even through the pain he found it amusing that cotton, the very thing a doctor would have plugged him up with, was available in this time of need as a gift from the earth. He headed for the mansion, the manor house where the general languished, nursing wounds of his own. There was still a chance, he thought. By the time he neared the manor, the same sounds the others heard began to reach his ears. "They come now," he said aloud, as the coughing of diesel engines echoed down the valley. "I've got big work to do." He slid up onto the steps leading to the main entrance, stopping to rest by leaning himself against one of the pillars that held aloft the upper balconies. The pain begged him to linger there, but stronger urges, tearing away at his insides, caused him to stagger to the doorway, and then into the house. The first thing to confront one when entering the Clayton mansion was a grand staircase, leading in a sweeping curve to the

upper master suite, where the general rested. Ortiz moved to the stairs, gaining the first one with great effort, and then the second. As he climbed, his mind began to swirl, his senses washed over in a soft haze. He wasn't even aware when he'd reached the landing just above the last step. He leaned heavily on the bannister there, the pain in his back all but gone now. Somehow, through great resolve or ordinary stubbornness, he crossed a hallway and pushed open the door to Sedgewick's suite. The general's driver, Harry, stood there in the room, just behind the general, who sat in a stiff arm chair drawn up close to the window. The general looked out through the glass, at the tanks and troops amassing on the road.

"How many do we have left?" he asked, a touch of sadness attached to his words.

"Just a few, sir. Perhaps twenty or so."

Sedgewick smiled then, the smile of a man not yet broken, or at least not yet aware he was. "Well," he said softly, "still better than Jesus, aye Harry?"

"Yes, sir," said the driver.

"It was just a game, you know?"

"Yes, sir. I thought you played splendidly."

The general chuckled, mostly to himself. "Thirty years I gave to the bastards, Harry. Thirty years of them telling me what a wonderful job I was doing. And every time they handed a star to one of my peers, they would tell me again. One time I actually had a brigadier sit me down and say how he wished he could be a colonel again. 'Less responsibility,' he said. 'You're so lucky, Sedgwick,' he said. I wanted to shake his fucking head and rip the goddam star off his coat and pin it to his ass."

Harry cleared his throat. "That's all in the past, sir. You've done well here."

The general nodded and smiled, still looking out the window. "You're right, Harry, I have. Hell, man, I'm like a king here, a god. If I say hang the man, they hang him. If I say cut off his balls, out comes the knife. The goddam president doesn't wield that kind of power."

Ortiz leaned down, drawing a knife from his boot. He swayed

there in the doorway, trying to summon the strength for an attack. He could still be a hero, still receive the accolades of a grateful nation. All he had to do was take the general down. Slit the general's throat, and Harry's. Hell, he thought, the president would probably give him a medal. He just needed to find the strength. He stumbled a step into the room, but froze suddenly as Harry drew a pistol from his waistband. Slowly Harry's hand rose, until the barrel of the gun moved to within inches of the general's head.

"No one wields that kind of power, sir. Only you," said Harry. "They'll be coming for us soon. I just wanted you to know how proud I've been to serve under you." With that last honor bestowed, Harry squeezed the trigger and the general's head exploded in a spray of blood and brain matter. Manuel's eyes, even through their haze, widened in disbelief.

"You sunovabitch," he yelled, thinking the driver was out to steal his prize. "The bastard's mine."

Harry turned, surprised. Recognizing Manuel he nodded respectfully. "Ortiz," he said, his voice choking with emotion. "You can have us both." He then raised the gun to his own head and pulled the trigger once more.

Even as the sound of the blast echoed through the mansion, Manuel moved as quickly as he could to the two bodies. The shock of the incident had partially cleared his senses. Still, he stood there swaying as he fought with his mind about what to do next. A sound hammered away at him. It was a scream. He turned to see Samantha King standing in the doorway, her hands flying to her mouth. "I tried to stop them," he called out to her. "They wouldn't listen to me."

Samantha looked at Ortiz. She knew him to be one of the general's aides. One of his favorites. She also recognized him as dangerous. He was the one who had bragged so brashly about smashing through a wall of troopers to gain entry into Harbor Springs. An inner voice cried out for caution. Then she noticed the blood dripping down his side, a pool beginning to form around his feet. She saw him stumble as he took a step towards her, one hand raised in an appeal for help. Without further thought she ran to him. "You're hurt," she stammered.

"Yes," he said, trying to find reason within himself. His mind raced. This woman possessed the key to a door that needed to stay tightly locked. "I told you. I tried to stop them. I think I've been shot."

Samantha moved swiftly. Grabbing Ortiz by his outstretched arm she caught him as he fell into her. "They were fools," she said, her voice shaking. "This was never intended to end well." She noticed Manuel's other arm hung loosely at his side. He raised it slightly, displaying a bloodied hand. There was a knife in it. She looked at the knife, her mouth contorting as her mind worked furiously to interpret the meaning in what she saw. "Oh, god," she mumbled then, as a force slammed into her stomach. She felt herself sliding downward as the strangest thought fluttered its way into her brain, one of sliding through warm pudding, as her blood mixed with his and she sloshed to the floor. There was no pain involved, just a gentle warming sensation, and then a feeling of leaving herself.

A cry came from downstairs. "Samantha? Samantha King?" Quickly Ortiz, mustering the last of his senses, grabbed at the general's body, still slumped in the chair. Using all his strength he pulled it to the floor, next to the others. He grappled with the three, churning them into a loose pile of limbs and torsos. Then he burrowed in among them, lifting Harry's legs and placing them on top of his own. Footsteps approached, racing up the stairs, and he began to call out.

"Help me," he cried. "I tried to stop them from hurting her. As God is my witness, I tried." Manuel started sobbing then, as Chester Benton leaned down to gently pull him from the pile.

"It's okay," said Charlie, recognizing the Mexican as the man who had offered assistance the night before. He looked at the three bodies, still tangled together inches away. There must have been a hell of a fight in this room, he thought.

"I tried, I tried," moaned Ortiz.

"I know," said Charlie, placing a cushion from the chair beneath the man's head. "The colonel was one sick bastard. I'm sure you did all you could." Within minutes, army paramedics arrived, rushing

in to render aid. The Mexican was badly injured, but expected to pull through. They worked on him for a long time, mopping up and stitching, stemming the flow of blood from the wound in his back. And while they worked, Charlie sat on the floor nearby, holding Samantha King's head in his lap. "I'm sorry," he said to her over and over. "I'm so sorry."

Chapter Forty-Five

Errol Clarkson sat in his leather chair behind the great desk in the Oval Office. He'd been sitting there a lot lately. Partly because it's where the citizens of America expected him to be during a time of crisis, and partly because Chester Benton wasn't in close enough proximity to kick him out of it. He smiled wryly as he thought of Charlie, the smile staying only a brief moment before it flitted away in concern over the whereabouts of his best friend. Communication between the two had been abruptly cut off two days earlier, and he had no idea of Charlie's condition or circumstance. Olivia Briggs had contacted him with word that he had been arrested by the general's men, and that led the president to imagine a number of scenarios, none of them pleasant.

Daniel Rumstaadt tapped twice at the door and entered. "Any word?" he asked, his voice filled with a concern the president appreciated.

"Not yet," said Clarkson. Reaching into the desk he pulled out Charlie's Superman toy, standing it upright on the desktop. "No news since they took him away. He might have made a move to kill the colonel. I put it on the table the last time we spoke. I'm not sure I should have."

Although it would have been quite permissible to sit, Rumstaadt continued to stand, preferring to assume a position of near attention. "We both know he's more than capable. And he's not dumb. Whatever path he takes, it will be a wise one."

"If there's a path presented to him," said the president, his head lowering. "Sometimes there's no path offered, or the one you're on ends abruptly. We don't always have a choice."

Rumstaadt removed a folded paper from his jacket pocket, unfolded it and laid it out flat on the desk. "We're in now," he said blandly. "Completely. Our boys have the plantation where the colonel is staying surrounded. It seems his vast army of worshippers have jumped ship. As we suspected, resistance was not just light, it was nonexistent."

The president lifted his face then, his eyes resting on the homeland chief. "Damn, it was too easy. I wish we'd have kept Charlie out of it. Placing him in there might have been completely unnecessary."

"Or not, sir. I suspect Charlie had a certain influence on what's happened. He's certainly taken good care of the coroner and his family. And there's no reason to think he's not standing in there now, with the colonel dead at his feet. Let's give it some time."

"Is anyone negotiating? Do we even know if anyone's alive in there?"

"Not yet, but it's just a matter of time. The one thing we do know is the colonel is not going anywhere. And he damn well knows it. It's not likely he'll harm anyone at this stage. If he did, he'd have nothing to bargain with."

Clarkson smiled, a sad, broken smile. "If a man intends to martyr himself, it seldom matters what sort of collateral damage takes place around him. He might even encourage it."

Rumstaadt leaned forward, placing both hands on the edge of the desk. "Either way, sir, your decisions have been firm and sound. And very presidential. No one could ever fault you for them."

"Well that's just great then. It's nice to know if you send your best friend to his death, at least the decision to do so was... presidential. That should be fun to live with."

Rumstaadt leaned even further forward, swinging his face downward until it was on the same level as the president's. "You know, sir. There's no rationale in the world that could blame this on your watch. This was all set up a long time ago, by the damn Wall Builder. I know we had plenty of racial impropriety before that, but he certainly intensified it. We've never been the same."

The president's face, still grave, took on a childlike, inquisitive look. "How in the hell can we hold a past administration and its war on Muslims and Mexicans, responsible for what is clearly a black-white issue?"

"It's not just black-white. It's every color other than white-white. I'm the Homeland Chief, remember? It's my job to get stuff. And I get this. The stupid bastard builds a wall, and everything on the Mexican side of the border that could float started streaming across the gulf. Someone forgot to tell him he couldn't fence off a thousand miles of coastline, together with a dozen port cities and a hundred secluded beaches along the way." Rumstaadt laughed aloud. "So instead of crossing desert and tunneling through hardened ground, everyone with a few hundred bucks to spare just boarded a sea-bucket and floated across. We had the Coast Guard going nuts. Twenty of our vessels against thousands of any damn floating objects that would hold an outboard motor. And all coming at once, in a wave, every couple of weeks. Those were fun times. We were like gulls trying to gulp down baby turtles as they headed for the sea. Just too many turtles and not enough gulls."

Clarkson's mouth pinched inward. "Still not seeing it. How does illegal immigration translate into African Americans burning down a state?"

Runstaadt stood upright. He now stood well above the president. His look became benevolent. "Because it was perceived as racist. It wasn't just a wall. It was an anti-Mexican wall. Not just America saying our southern border is now closed. But America saying no to Mexicans. The same way it had earlier to Muslims. There was certainly no border wall up against Canada, or officials turning back Europeans at the airports."

"I know, I know, I get all that. But what about the black-white part?"

Rumstaadt's face softened. "No pun intended, but blacks could read the writing on the wall. America had just jumped up and slapped hard at two major ethnicities. And now, riding along in the tailwind are the murders of twelve little black girls. It doesn't take a mastermind to figure out who blacks think they're coming for next."

President Clarkson's face twisted. "Then when is it over? When in the hell does it end?"

"It won't be over until there's only one color left standing, or, dare I say it… God moves in with a mighty hand and removes all the goddam walls."

With that last comment from the chief, Clarkson rose from behind his desk. He tapped the Superman figure fondly on its head, before heading for the door. "Well, I suppose it's our job to deal with it. So let's go face the press, Daniel. Tell them their little war down south is grinding to a halt and break all their hearts."

Chapter Forty-Six

As Briggs led the townsfolk of Harbor Springs toward their homes, using a trail that would keep them out of harm's way, one man struck out on his own. It was Tom Clayton. He raced after Charlie, down the long road leading from the gin in the direction of the main gate. As Charlie turned left to head for the mansion, Clayton continued in a line straight as an arrow for the highway. "Molly," he called out over and over, "Molly."

<hr>

Willie awoke early that morning, early even by his standards. Distant sounds picked away at his ears. He rose, threw on a housecoat, and headed for the door. Out on the porch he could hear much clearer the sounds of massive machinery moving down the highway. He went back inside, heading for the hallway and the bedrooms where the girls slept. "Girls," he called out, knocking loudly at each door. "Girls, wake up. Somethin' big is goin' on. I think they're comin'." He returned to the porch, walking over to the steps, where

he sat and waited. Soon both girls emerged, tired and ruffled, Molly wearing an old pink robe and Olivia in her jeans, with one of Willie's too-big shirts flowing all around her. She grimaced as she walked, the knife wound in her side still fresh enough to cause pain.

"What is it?" asked Molly. The girls sat on either side of the old man as they snuggled together and listened.

"I dunno," said Willie. "I think the government has come. I think it's over." There was a sadness in his voice. The last days had been happy ones for him.

Olivia reached out to touch Willie's hand. "It's okay," she said. "Charlie and my dad will be coming soon."

Molly jumped up, excited. "My papa will be coming for me." She looked down at the other two, her eyes glistening.

Willie caught her eyes with his. "I'm happy for you," he said. "Then everythin' can go back the way it was."

Up on the levee, they could hear a four-wheeler, possibly a jeep, churning down the roadway, coming fast. Then they saw bits of it, flitting between the trees as it raced towards them. It slashed down finally, nearly missing the driveway, and spun its way into the yard, a shower of dust and pebbles flying as it slid to a halt just a few feet from the porch. The driver was a young soldier, crisply erect at the wheel. Alongside him appeared to be an officer, tiny silver bars flashing out from his shoulders. As the officer stepped down from the passenger side, they saw the shape of another man emerge from the back of the jeep, scrambling his way out until the officer and this new man stood side by side. It was Tom Clayton.

Molly's face lit up. "Papa," she cried out joyously. Clayton looked back at her, tears streaming from his eyes. There stood his beloved granddaughter, worn, disheveled, and having gone through an ordeal he could only imagine. Willie stood then, placing an arm around the girl's shoulder. He pushed her gently forward, his eyes also beginning to mist.

"Go girl," he whispered. "Go to your papa." Clayton heard none of that. All he knew was that Willie, a man he'd known as trash his whole life, stood there now, filthy hands all over his little girl.

Before Molly could take a step, Clayton reached out, grabbing at the holstered pistol of the military man standing beside him. He ripped the gun free, drawing back the hammer as he raised the weapon, centering the sights on Willie. The valley exploded in three rapid blasts then, three shots fired, the first nicking away at the old man's ear, the second finding the softened flesh of a shoulder, and the third, burrowing its way deep into the old man's chest. Willie's hand had been extended, as he was about to say, "I took good care of her for you, Mister Clayton." But no words ever escaped his lips. He staggered the few steps to the ground, collapsing to his knees there, his eyes locked on Tom Clayton's.

Olivia rose from her seat on the step, the horror of the incident slowly working its way into her mind. She screamed then, and Molly screamed beside her. Molly's hands spread wide, her arms reaching out in the direction of her grandfather as her face twisted in agony.

"No, Papa, no," she cried out in a voice so broken it would haunt Tom Clayton for the rest of his life. "He protected me." Her eyes left her grandfather's then, and both girls rushed down the steps, crumbling to the earth beside the old man. Clayton stood there, the gun in his hand lowered to his side, where it hung as a lifeless thing. The rage left him, his face tilting downward in confusion. He stayed that way for a long time, or what seemed a long time, and when he finally looked up again, he knew. A lifetime of hating the black man across the road who never hated back. Tom Clayton knew.

Willie lay there now, face up, and Olivia raised his head, placing it gently in her lap. He looked at Molly first, smiling up at her as just a touch of blood worked its way across his lips. "You're a good girl, Molly," he said. Turning his head he found Olivia. His mouth started to move, started to speak, but he could find nothing to say to her. Nothing she didn't already know. "Hell," he thought to himself as the smile began to wane, "The girl knows everything." He noticed she was crying, great rivers of tears flowing down the sides of her face. It was her gift to him. What a wonderful friend she had turned out to be. A young white girl and an old black man. What a pair. He tried to move his hand, but found he couldn't, so he tried again. This

time he was able to lift it, brushing gnarled old fingers against her cheek. She clutched at them, and pressed them to her lips. As he closed his eyes, the smile returned, and he had a last thought... Of all the moments of his life, this one was the best.

EPILOGUE

ONE MONTH LATER

"Alabama taught us a great lesson." Errol Clarkson stood before a gathering on a lawn just off to the side of the rose garden. It was a perfect day, with the sun and the breeze mingling together in precisely the right proportions. The president was just concluding his speech. "I can only hope we've learned from it. There might not always be a great love between us, perhaps, but there has to be an understanding of our differences. That's where our strength lies. In understanding, and in tolerance. And we must —must— support one another in our endeavors. The very reason our ancestors bled themselves to journey to this wondrous land was for its acceptance of all peaceful peoples, no matter what their beliefs, colors, or chosen paths. My wish for all of you here today, and for everyone across this great country, is that we can now, finally, enter into a tranquil union amongst ourselves. God blesses us here. And may God sweep over our heads, and over our flag, a blessed blanket of peace, so we may never again face the fires of hate, but instead feel the warm hand of friendship. We are brothers. We are sisters. We are America."

On the same day, in a quiet valley near Shenandoah, in the Virginia heartland, a group of Muslim worshippers gathered in prayer. Since an annual pilgrimage to the land of Mecca was impractical for

them, they had chosen this gentle place upon the American land-scape to gather and to pray. They, too, had witnessed the recent fires which raged across the south, and a portion of prayer time was set aside to ask Allah to heal the hearts of those afflicted by hate in this new land they had grown to love. Laying out their blankets to face the setting sun, the gathering sank to their knees, heads bowed as they began their period of worship.

On a hill just above, another group looked down upon them. A group of hardened, angry men. Several Muslim children, not involved in the worship, began to ascend the hill, laughing and picking at wildflowers as they climbed. They saw the men standing a short distance away, and they paused. One little girl waved, and smiled shyly. She stooped to pluck at a poppy, which she held out in her hand. "Fuckin' Muslims," one of the men snarled. They attacked then, a single force with a single mind, sweeping down off the hill. The children met them first, the meeting brief and final. "If it moves, kill it," someone roared, as the men headed for the gathering.

We are America.